ROYAL HIGHNESS

Thomas Mann was born in 1875 in Lübeck of a line of prosperous and influential merchants. His father was head of the ancestral firm and was twice mayor of the free city. Brought up in the company of five brothers and sisters, he completed his education under the drastic discipline of North German schoolmasters, and entered an insurance office in Munich at the age of nineteen.

Secretly he wrote his first tale, *Fallen*, and shortly afterwards left the insurance office to study art and literature at the University in Munich. After spending a year in Rome, he devoted himself exclusively to writing. His major works include *Buddenbrooks*, *Death in Venice*, *The Magic Mountain*, and the tetralogy *Joseph and His Brothers*, the first volume of which was published in 1923. He was awarded the Nobel Prize for Literature in 1929.

In 1933 Mann left Germany to live in Switzerland and then, after several previous visits, he settled in the United States, living first in Princeton, New Jersey, and later in California, where he wrote *Doctor Faustus* and *The Holy Sinner*. He revisited his native country in 1949, and in 1952 he returned to Switzerland, where *The Black Swan* and *The Confessions of Felix Krull* were written, and where he died in 1955.

D0940785

THOMAS MANN

Royal Highness

Translated from the German
by A. Cecil Curtis

Fully revised by Constance McNab

PENGUIN BOOKS

Penguin Books Ltd, Harmondsworth, Middlesex, England
Penguin Books Australia Ltd, Ringwood, Victoria, Australia
Penguin Books (N.Z.) Ltd, 182-190 Wairau Road, Auckland 10, New Zealand

—

Königliche Hoheit first published 1909
This translation first published by Sidgwick & Jackson 1916
Published by Secker & Warburg 1940
Revised version published by The New English Library 1962
Published in Penguin Books 1975
All rights reserved

—

Made and printed in Great Britain by
Hazell Watson & Viney Ltd
Aylesbury, Bucks
Set in Linotype Granjon

This book is sold subject to the condition
that it shall not, by way of trade or otherwise,
be lent, re-sold, hired out, or otherwise circulated
without the publisher's prior consent in any form of
binding or cover other than that in which it is
published and without a similar condition
including this condition being imposed
on the subsequent purchaser

CONTENTS

PRELUDE

THE scene is the Albrechtsstrasse, the main artery of the capital which runs from the Albrechtsplatz and the Old Castle to the barracks of the Fusiliers of the Guards; it is noon, on an ordinary weekday; the season is immaterial. The weather is indifferent, on the fair side. It is not raining but the sky is overcast; it is a uniform light grey, ordinary-looking and undramatic, and the street is steeped in a dull and sober atmosphere which robs it of every suggestion of mystery or strangeness. There is a moderate amount of traffic, without too big a crowd or excessive noise, corresponding to the leisurely character of the town. Tram-cars glide past and a few horse cabs pass, the inhabitants move along the pavement; a colourless crowd, passers-by, the public, 'the people'.

Two officers, their hands in the slanting pockets of their grey military greatcoats, approach each other; one is a General and the other a Lieutenant. The General is coming from the Castle, the Lieutenant from the direction of the barracks. The Lieutenant is very young, almost a child. He has narrow shoulders, dark hair, and the wide cheekbones common in this part of the world, blue, faintly tired-looking eyes and a boyish face with a friendly but reserved expression. The General has snow-white hair; he is tall and burly, an altogether imposing figure. His eyebrows seem made of cotton wool, and his moustache droops over his mouth and chin. He moves slowly and powerfully, his sword clatters against the pavement, his plume flutters in the wind, and at every step he takes the big red lapel of his coat flaps slowly up and down. And thus the two men come face to face. Can this encounter lead to complications? Surely not. Every observer can foresee its natural course. We have age on one side and on the other, youth; authority faces obedience; venerable distinction, tender beginnings. A mighty hieratic distance and a host of regulations separate the two. Things must take their natural course! Instead of which, what do we see? Instead, the following surprising, awkward, enchanting, topsy-turvy scene takes place. The General, when he becomes aware of the young Lieutenant, alters his bearing in a surprising manner. He draws himself up, yet at the same time seems to efface himself. He, as it were, tones down the splendour of his appearance, he stops his sabre from clattering, and while his face assumes a fierce and awkward expression he is obviously undecided which way to look, and tries to conceal the fact by staring sideways from beneath his bushy eyebrows at the pavement ahead of him. To a close observer the young Lieutenant too betrays some slight embarrassment; strange to say, he appears to succeed better than the grey-haired General in hiding it with a certain grace and discipline. The tension of his mouth relaxes into a smile at once modest and genial, his eyes look past the General and into the distance, assuming an expression that is both quiet and effortlessly self-possessed. By now they have come within three paces of each other. And instead of the prescribed salute the young Lieutenant slightly raises his head, and at the same time draws his right hand – only his right, mind you – out of his coat pocket and makes with this same white-gloved right hand a little encouraging and condescending gesture, barely opening the fingers with the palm upturned, no more, but the General, who has awaited this sign with his arms to his sides, abruptly touches his helmet, steps down from the pavement with a half bow and deferentially salutes the Lieutenant, looking at him from below with devoted, watery eyes in a crimson face. His hand raised to his cap the Lieutenant returns the respectful salute of his superior officer, returns it with a look of childlike friendliness – and passes on.

A miracle! A fantastic scene! He walks on. People look at him but he looks at no one; he looks straight ahead and through the crowd, with something of the manner of a woman who knows herself to be observed. The people greet him and he returns their greetings, cordially and yet distantly. He appears to be walking with some difficulty; it is as though he were not used to walking, or as though the general attention bothered him, so irregular and faltering is his gait, indeed, at times he seems to be limping. A policeman springs to attention, an elegantly dressed woman, on emerging from a shop, smilingly makes a deep curtsy. People's heads turn and beckon, brows are raised, his name is mentioned in a discreet whisper.

It is Klaus Heinrich, the younger brother of Albrecht II, and heir presumptive to the throne. There he goes, he is still within view. Known by all and yet a stranger, he moves among the crowd, surrounded by it and yet as though isolated in a void. He walks alone and on his narrow shoulders carries the burden of his royal station.

ONE

THE CONSTRICTION

ARTILLERY salvoes were fired when the various new-fangled means of communication in the capital spread the news that the Grand Duchess Dorothea had given birth to a prince for the second time at Grimmburg. Seventy-two rounds resounded through the town and surrounding country, fired by the soldiers from the bastions of the citadel. Directly afterwards the fire brigade also, not to be outdone, fired with the town salute-guns; but in their firing there were long pauses between each round, which caused much merriment among the populace.

From the top of a wooded hill the Grimmburg dominated the picturesque little town of the same name, whose grey sloping roofs were mirrored in a tributary stream and which could be reached from the capital within half an hour by a local railway which ran at a loss. The castle towered up there, sturdily built by the founder of the Grand Ducal dynasty, Margrave Klaus Grimmbart, in the dim beginnings of German history, since then repeatedly rejuvenated and repaired, fitted with the conveniences of the changing times, always kept in a habitable state, and especially honoured as the ancestral seat of the ruling house and the cradle of the dynasty. For it was a rule and tradition of the house that all direct descendants of the Margrave, every child of the reigning couple, must be born there. Nor was this tradition to be ignored. The country had had free-thinking and sceptical sovereigns who had made fun of it, and yet had complied with a shrug. It was now much too late to break away from it. Whether reasonable and enlightened or not, why, without any particular need, break with a time-honoured custom which so to speak had proved itself? The people were convinced that there was something in it. Twice in the course of fifteen generations children of the reigning sovereign, owing to some chance occurrence, had been born in other castles; twice they had come to an unnatural and ignoble end. But from Heinrich the

Penitent and Johann the Headstrong and their proud and lovely sisters, all the sovereign Dukes, down to Albrecht, the father of the present Duke, and the Grand Duke himself, Johann Albrecht III, had been born in the castle, and there, six years ago, Dorothea had given birth to her first-born, the Heir Apparent.

The castle was a retreat as dignified as it was peaceful. The coolness of the rooms and the green shade of the surroundings made it preferable as a summer residence to the formal, gracious beauty of Hollerbrunn. The ascent from the town, up a badly paved lane between shabby cottages and a tumbling wall, through massive gates to an old inn close to the entrance of the courtyard with a stone statue of the founder, Klaus Grimmbart, in the centre, was picturesque without being comfortable. Extensive grounds, however, covered the rear part of the castle hill, and easy paths led down the wooded gently sloping park, offering ideal opportunities for carriages, drives and leisurely promenades.

As for the interior of the castle, it had last been cleaned and redecorated at the beginning of the reign of Johann Albrecht III, at a cost which had evoked much comment. The décor of the ducal apartments had been renewed and added to in a style at once baronial and comfortable; the escutcheons in the Hall of Justice had been carefully restored to their original patterns. The gilding of the intricate patterns on the vaulted ceilings looked fresh and cheerful, all the rooms had been fitted with parquet, and both the larger and the smaller banqueting-halls had been adorned with huge wall-paintings from the brush of Professor von Lindemann, a distinguished Academician, representing scenes from the history of the reigning house executed in the bright and polished manner which was far removed from and quite unaffected by the restless tendencies of modern schools. Nothing was wanting. As the old chimneys of the castle and its many-coloured stoves, reaching tier upon tier right up to the ceiling, were no longer fit to use, anthracite stoves had been installed in view of the possibility of the place being used as a winter residence.

But the day of the seventy-two salvoes fell at the best time of the year, late spring, early summer, the beginning of June, the day after Whitsuntide. Johann Albrecht, who had been informed early in the morning by telegram that the labour had begun at dawn, reached Grimmburg station at eight o'clock, travelling by the local railway (which ran at a loss), to be greeted with congratulations by three or four officials: the mayor, the judge, the rector, and the local doctor. He drove immediately to the castle. The Grand Duke was accompanied by the Minister of State, Doctor Baron von Knobelsdorff, and his aide-de-camp, General Count Schmettern. Shortly afterwards two or three more ministers arrived at the castle: Court Chaplain and President of the Church Council Dom Wislezenus, one or two court officials, and a younger aide-de-camp, Captain von Lichterloh. Although the Grand Duke's physician-in-ordinary, Major-General Doctor Eschrich, was attending the mother, Johann Albrecht had been seized with the whim of summoning the young local doctor, a certain Doctor Sammet, who moreover was of Jewish origin. This unassuming, industrious and sober man, who was overwhelmed with work of his own and not in the least expecting such an honour, kept repeating with a stammer: 'With pleasure ... with pleasure,' which provoked much amusement.

The Bridal Chamber served as bedroom to the Grand Duchess; an octagonal, gaily painted room on the first floor whose tall windows disclosed a splendid view over the trees, the hills and the winding river. It was decorated with a frieze of medallion-shaped portraits, the likenesses of ducal brides who had awaited their lords and masters here in the old days. Dorothea was lying in bed. A broad, strong ribbon was tied round the foot of her bed to which she clung like a child playing at horses, and her fine, well-made body heaved with effort. The midwife, Frau Doctor Gnadebusch, a gentle and learned woman with small, fineboned hands and brown eyes which took on a mysterious expression behind the thick, round lenses, supported the Duchess, saying:

'Steady, steady now, Your Royal Highness ... it won't be long ... It's quite easy ... now once more ... that was nothing ... permit me: open your knees ... keep your chin down ...'

A nurse, dressed like her in white linen, assisted her and during the pauses moved lightly about the room carrying basins and bandages. The physician-in-ordinary, a morose man with a greying beard, whose left eyelid seemed to droop, superintended the birth. He wore his operating coat over his major-general's uniform. From time to time Dorothea's trusted Mistress of the Robes, Baroness von Schulenburg-Tressen, peeped into the room to ascertain the progress of the labour. She was a portly and asthmatic lady of markedly middle-class appearance, who nonetheless liked to expose a vast expanse of bosom at Court Balls. She kissed her mistress's hand and returned to a distant room in which a couple of emaciated ladies-in-waiting chatted with the Duchess's gentleman of the bedchamber on duty, Count Windisch; Doctor Sammet, who wore his linen coat like a domino flung over his frock-coat, stood modestly and attentively by the washstand.

Johann Albrecht remained in a study which was divided from the Bridal Chamber by the so-called Powder Closet and a connecting passage. It was called the Library, in view of several manuscript folios propped up slantwise on top of the heavy bookcase, and which contained the history of the castle. The room was furnished as a writing-room. Globes adorned the walls. The strong wind from the hills blew through the open bow-window. The Grand Duke had ordered tea, and his personal valet Prahl had brought the tray himself; but it stood forgotten on the leaf of the writing desk, and Johann Albrecht paced from wall to wall, prone to a tense and restless state of mind. His patent leather boots creaked ceaselessly. Aide-de-camp Lichterloh listened to that noise while he waited listlessly in the almost bare passage.

The Minister, the chief commanding aide-de-camp, the court chaplain, and the court officials, nine or ten in all, were waiting in the State Rooms on the ground floor. They sauntered through the large and the small Banqueting Halls, where banners and weapons were suspended between Professor Lindemann's paintings, they leaned against the slender pillars, which spread into brightly coloured vaulting above their heads. They stood before the tall, narrow windows which almost touched the ceiling and gazed through the leaded panes across the river and the town. They loitered on stone benches, which skirted the walls, or in the armchairs in front of the fireplace whose gothic cornices were supported by ludicrously small, stooping and flying stone monsters. The gold braid on the uniforms of these dignitaries, their decorations pinned to padded chests, and the broad stripes of gold on their trousers shone brightly in the light of day.

The conversation flagged. Three-cornered hats and white-gloved hands were constantly being raised to screen convulsive yawns. Nearly all the gentlemen present had watery eyes. Several among them had not had time for breakfast. Some sought entertainment by timidly examining the operating tools and the spherical jar of chloroform in its leather casing deposited by Doctor Eschrich in case of emergency. After the Lord Marshal von Bühl zu Bühl, a big man with strutting movements, a brown wig, gold-rimmed pince-nez, and long, discoloured fingernails had told several anecdotes in his abrupt, jerky manner, he settled in an armchair and profited by his gift of going to sleep with his eyes open; of losing consciousness of time and place while retaining a correct attitude and without infringing the dignity of the place.

Doctor von Schröder, Minister of Finance and Agriculture, had had a conversation with the Minister of State, Doctor Baron von Knobelsdorff, Minister of Home Affairs, of Foreign Affairs and of the Grand Ducal Household. It was a disconnected chat, beginning with reflections on art, which went on to questions of economics and finance, alluded, somewhat disparagingly, to a high court official, and even concerned itself with the most exalted personages. It began with the two gentlemen standing, with their hats behind their backs, in front of one of the paintings in the large Banqueting Hall, each of them saying less than he thought. The Minister of Finance said: 'And this one? What does it represent? Your Excellency is so knowledgeable.'

'Not really. It is the investiture of two young princes of the blood by their uncle, the Emperor. As your Excellency can see, the two young men are kneeling and taking the oath with great solemnity on the Emperor's sword.'

'Very good, unusually good! What colouring! Brilliant. What lovely golden locks the princes have! And the Emperor –

he is a real Emperor! Yes, Lindemann deserves the distinctions conferred on him.'

'Indeed he does, indeed he does.'

Doctor von Schröder, a tall man with a white beard, a pair of thick gold-rimmed spectacles perched on his blanched nose, a small tummy protruding abruptly from beneath his belt, and a stout neck bursting from the stiff, embroidered collar of his frock-coat, assumed a somewhat doubtful air while continuing to regard the picture in front of him. He was seized with a slight malaise which sometimes gripped him during his conversations with the baron. This man Knobelsdorff, this favourite and high official was an ambiguous fellow. At times his comments and replies had an undefinable tinge of irony. He was a widely travelled man; he had been all over the world; he had much general knowledge and interests of a strange and unconventional kind. And yet he was a model of correctness. Herr von Schröder could not make him out. However much one agreed with him it was impossible to feel that he was one's own sort. His views were full of unspoken reserve; his judgements so tolerant that one was left guessing whether they implied approval or contempt. But the most suspicious thing about him was his smile, of the eyes only, and which did not spread to his lips but seemed to originate in the fine wrinkles radiating from the corners of his eyes, or else to have in time caused these to appear. Baron Knobelsdorff was younger than the Minister of Finance, a man in the prime of life although his clipped moustache and smooth hair with a centre parting were about to turn grey; for the rest a squat, short-necked man and visibly constricted by his braided Court dress. For an instant he left Herr von Schröder to his perplexity and then went on: 'Only it might perhaps have been in the interests of our worthy administration of the Privy Purse if the famed maestro had rested content with a few more titles and decorations – to put it bluntly, what do you think they paid for this pleasing masterpiece?'

Herr von Schröder regained his animation. The hope, the desire to come to an understanding with the Baron, to, after all, achieve intimate and confidential terms with him excited him.

'Just what I was thinking,' he said, turning round to resume his stroll through the galleries. 'Your Excellency has taken the question out of my mouth. How much was spent on this "Investiture"? How much on the rest of these paintings? The restoration of the castle six years ago amounted to, *in summa*, one million marks.'

'At least that.'

'A tidy sum! Audited and approved by the Lord Marshal Bühl zu Bühl who is abandoning himself over there to a state of pleasant catalepsy; audited, approved and disbursed by the Keeper of the Privy Purse, Count Trümmerhauff.'

'Disbursed, or owing?'

'One of the two. This total, I repeat, debited to a fund, a fund . . .'

'Briefly, the fund of the Grand Ducal Financial Administration.'

'Your Excellency knows as well as I do what this means. Truly, it makes me shudder. I swear I am neither a miser nor a hypochondriac but I shudder when I think that under the present circumstances we go and calmly waste a million marks – on what? On a pretty whim, on the splendid restoration of a family seat needed to put children into the world.'

Herr von Knobelsdorff laughed. 'Yes, heaven knows romanticism is a luxury, and an expensive one too! Your Excellency, I entirely agree with you. But consider, after all the whole trouble in the Grand Ducal finances is due to this same romantic luxury. The root of the evil lies in the fact that the ruling dynasty are farmers; their capital consists in arable land, their income in agricultural profits. To this day they have not made up their minds to switch to industry and business. With regrettable obstinacy they allow themselves to be guided by certain obsolete ideological principles, such as, for instance, ideas of trust and dignity. The Ducal property is in fact an entailed Trust. Profitable sales are out of the question. Mortgages, the raising of capital or credit for commercial improvements they deem improper. The administration is seriously handicapped in the free exploitation of business opportunities by its ideas of dignity. You'll forgive me, won't you? I'm telling you the absolute truth. People who pay so much attention to propriety as they do of

course cannot and will not keep pace with the liberal and unbridled initiative of less ideologically hampered business men.
Now then, what, in comparison with this negative luxury, does
the positive million signify, which has been sacrificed to a pretty
whim, to borrow your Excellency's expression? If it only
stopped there! But we have the regular expenses of a fairly
dignified Court to meet. There is the upkeep of the various
castles and their grounds, Hollerbrunn, Monbrillant, Jägerpreis,
am I right? Eremitage, Delphinenort, Fasanerie and the rest. I
had forgotten Segenhaus and the Haderstein ruins, not to mention the Old Castle. They are not well kept but they all cost
money. And the Court Theatre, the Picture Gallery, the Library
have to be subsidized. Hundreds of pensions have to be paid,
even without legal obligations, purely from motives of trust and
dignity. And look at the princely way in which the Grand Duke
behaved during the last floods ... but I'm making a regular
speech!'

'A speech,' said the Minister of Finance, 'which your Excellency thought would shock me, while you really only confirmed
my own view. Dear Baron' – here Herr von Schröder laid his
hand on his heart – 'I'm convinced that there is no longer room
for any misunderstanding as to my opinion, my loyal opinion,
between you and me. The king can do no wrong ... The
sovereign is beyond reproach. But here we have to do with a
default ... in both senses of the word! ... a default which I have
no hesitation in laying at the door of Count Trümmerhauff. His
predecessors may be pardoned for having concealed from their
sovereigns the true state of the court finances in those days,
nothing else was expected of them. But Count Trümmerhauff's
attitude now is not pardonable. In his position as Keeper of the
Privy Purse he ought to have felt it incumbent on him to put a
brake on the prevailing insouciance, to open His Royal Highness's eyes relentlessly to the facts ...'

Herr von Knobelsdorff smiled with raised eyebrows.

'Really?' said he. 'So your Excellency is of the opinion that
that is what the Count was appointed for! I can picture to myself
the justifiable astonishment of his lordship, if you lay before
him your view of the position. No, no ... your Excellency need

be under no delusion; that appointment was a quite deliberate
expression of his wishes on the part of His Royal Highness,
which the Count must be the first to respect. It expressed not
only an attitude of "I don't know", but also of "I do not wish
to know". A man may be an exclusively decorative personality
and yet be acute enough to grasp this. Besides ... honestly ...
we've all of us grasped it. And the only grain of comfort for all
of us is this: that there isn't a prince alive to whom it would be
more fatal to mention his debts than to His Royal Highness.
Our Prince has a something about him which would stop any
tactless remarks of that sort before they were spoken.'

'Quite true, quite true,' said Herr von Schröder. He sighed
and pensively stroked the swansdown trimming of his hat. The
two men were sitting, half facing each other, on a raised window
seat inside a large embrasure outside which ran a narrow stone
corridor, a sort of gallery whose pointed arches disclosed a view
of the town. Herr von Schröder resumed:

'You answer me, Baron, you pretend to contradict me, and
yet your words show more disillusionment and bitterness than
my own.'

Herr von Knobelsdorff said nothing, but made a vague gesture of assent.

'It may be so,' said the Finance Minister, and nodded gloomily
at his hat. 'Your Excellency may be quite right, perhaps we are
all to blame, we and our predecessors. The things that ought to
have been prevented! For consider, Baron; ten years ago an
opportunity offered itself of putting the finances of the Court
on a sound footing, on a better footing anyhow, if you like.
It was lost. We understand each other. The Grand Duke, attrac-
tive man that he is, had it then in his power to clear things up
by a marriage which from a sound point of view might have
been called dazzling. Instead of that ... speaking not for myself,
of course, but I shall never forget the dejection on the people's
faces when the amount of the dowry became known.'

'The Grand Duchess,' said Herr von Knobelsdorff, and the
wrinkles at the corners of his eyes disappeared almost entirely,
'is one of the most beautiful women I have ever seen.'

'That is an answer one would expect of your Excellency. It

is the answer of an aesthete, an answer which would have held quite as good if His Royal Highness's choice, like his brother Lambert's, had fallen on a member of the royal ballet.'

'Oh, there was no danger of that. The Prince's taste is a fastidious one, as he has shown. His requirements have always been a direct antithesis to the lack of taste which Prince Lambert has shown all his life. It was a long time before he decided to marry. We had almost given up hope of a direct heir to the throne. They were resigned for better or worse to Prince Lambert, whose . . . unsuitability to be heir to the throne we need not discuss. Then a few weeks after his succession to the throne Johann Albrecht meets Princess Dorothea and exclaims: 'I'll marry her or no one!' And the Grand Duchy has a new sovereign lady. Your Excellency mentions the doubtful faces when the figures of the dowry were published; you did not mention the joy which prevailed in spite of it. A penniless princess, to be sure. But does such beauty count for nothing? I shall never forget her entry. Her first smile captured every heart. Your Excellency must allow me once more to profess my belief in the idealism of the people. The people want to see their ideal, their highest aspirations, their dream, something akin to their own souls embodied in their rulers; that, and not their bank accounts; there are others to represent those.'

'That is precisely it; those others are absent.'

'A regrettable absence. The main point is, Dorothea has presented us with an heir apparent.'

'To whom Heaven may grant some financial sense.'

'I entirely agree.'

Here ended the conversation of the two ministers. It stopped short, it was interrupted by aide-de-camp von Lichterloh who announced the happy issue of the confinement. The smaller banqueting-hall was soon filled with officials. One of the great carved doors was quickly thrown open, and the aide-de-camp appeared in the hall. He had a red face, blue soldier's eyes, a bristling flaxen moustache and the silver braid of the Guards on his collar. He looked somewhat excited, like a man who had been released from deadly boredom and was primed with good news. Conscious of the unusualness of the occasion, he boldly ignored the rules of decorum and etiquette. He saluted the company gaily, and, spreading his elbows, raised the hilt of his sword almost to his breast crying: 'Beg leave to announce: a prince!'

'*À la bonne heure*,' said aide-de-camp Count Schmettern.

'Delightful, that's delightful, I call that perfectly delightful,' said the Lord Marshal Bühl zu Bühl in his babbling voice; he had recovered consciousness at once.

The president of the Church Council Dom Wislizenus, a clean-shaven handsome man who, as the son of a general and thanks to his personal distinction, had attained to his high office at a comparatively early age, and on whose black silk gown shone the star of an order, folded his white hands below his breast and uttered in a melodious voice: 'God bless His Grand Ducal Highness!'

'You forget, Captain,' said Herr von Knobelsdorff, smiling, 'that in making your announcement you are encroaching on my privileges and province. Until I have made a thorough investigation the question whether it is a prince or a princess remains undecided.'

This remark was greeted with general laughter, and Herr von Lichterloh replied: 'At your orders, Excellency! Indeed, I have the honour to beg Your Excellency in Their Highnesses' name.'

This banter referred to the Minister of State's charge as registrar of the Grand Ducal House, in which capacity he was called to determine the sex of the princely offspring with his own eyes and to make an official declaration. Herr von Knobelsdorff complied with this formality in the so-called Powder Closet, where the new-born baby had been bathed, but he remained there longer than he had anticipated, as he was puzzled and detained by a painful discovery, which he did not, at first, mention to anyone, save the midwife.

Doctor Gnadebusch uncovered the child, and her mysteriously glittering eyes behind the thick lenses travelled between the Minister of State and the little copper-coloured creature, as it groped with one small hand – only one – as if to say: 'Is it all right?' It was all right, Herr von Knobelsdorff was satisfied and the midwife wrapped the child up again. But even then she continued to look down at the baby and up at the Baron, until she had drawn his eyes to the point to which she wished to attract them. The wrinkles at the corners of his eyes disappeared, he examined, compared, tested, scrutinized the child for two or three minutes, and at last asked: 'Has the Grand Duke seen this yet?'

'No, Your Excellency.'

'When the Grand Duke sees this,' said Herr von Knobelsdorff, 'tell him it will adjust itself in time.'

And to the gentlemen on the ground floor he announced: 'A splendid prince!'

But ten or fifteen minutes after him the Grand Duke also made the disagreeable discovery – that was unavoidable, and resulted for Surgeon-General Eschrich in a short, extremely unpleasant scene, but for Doctor Sammet of Grimmburg it led to an interview with the Grand Duke which raised him considerably in the latter's estimation and was useful to him in his subsequent career. What happened was briefly as follows:

After the birth Johann Albrecht had again retired to the library, and then returned to sit for some time at the bedside with his wife's hand in his. Thereupon he went into the powdercloset where the infant now lay in his high, richly gilded cradle, half covered with a blue silk curtain, and sat down in an armchair by the side of his little son. But while he sat and watched the sleeping infant it happened that he noticed what it was hoped that he would not notice yet. He drew back the coverlet, his face clouded over, and then he did exactly what Herr von Knobelsdorff had done before him, looked from Doctor Gnadebusch to the nurse and back again, both of whom said nothing, cast one glance at the half-open door into the bridal chamber, and returned to the library in a state of agitation.

Here he at once pressed the silver bell topped with an eagle on his writing desk, and very curtly and coldly addressed Herr von Lichterloh who entered with rattling spurs: 'I wish to see Herr Eschrich.'

When the Grand Duke was angry with any member of his suite, he was wont to strip the culprit for the moment of all his titles and dignities, and to leave him nothing but his bare name.

The aide-de-camp clicked his heels once more and withdrew. Johann Albrecht paced up and down with angrily creaking boots and then, upon hearing Herr von Lichterloh introduce the doctor into the ante-room, he stood behind his desk, in the attitude he adopted when granting audience.

As he stood there, his head turned imperiously in half-profile, his left hand planted on his hip, drawing back his satin-fronted frock-coat from his white waistcoat, he exactly resembled his portrait by Professor von Lindemann, which hung beside the big looking-glass over the mantelpiece in the Hall of Twelve Months in his residential castle, opposite the portrait of Dorothea, and of which countless engravings, photographs, and picture postcards had been published. The only difference was that Johann Albrecht in the portrait seemed to be of heroic stature, while he really was scarcely of medium height. His forehead was high and bald, and his blue eyes with deep shadows looked out from beneath grey brows with a distant expression of weary pride. He had the broad, rather too prominent cheek-bones which were characteristic of his people. His side-whiskers and the tiny *mouche* below his lower lip were grey, his twirled moustache almost white. From the distended nostrils of his short but proudly arched nose two unusually deep lines ran down into his beard. The lemon coloured ribbon of the Order of the ducal house showed in the opening of his piqué waistcoat. The Grand Duke wore a carnation buttonhole.

Major-General Eschrich entered with a deep bow. He had discarded his operating coat. His eyelids drooped more heavily than usual over his eyes. He looked morose and wretched.

The Grand Duke, his left hand on his hip, stretched out his right hand and with upturned palm, waved it several times abruptly and impatiently back and forward.

'I am awaiting an explanation, a justification, Major-General,' he said, his voice shaking with irritation. 'Will you be kind enough to account for what has happened? What is the matter with the child's arm?'

The physician-in-ordinary raised his hands a little, in a faint gesture of helplessness and innocence. He said:

'May it please Your Royal Highness ... an unfortunate accident. Unfavourable circumstances during the pregnancy of Her Royal Highness ...'

'Stuff and nonsense!' The Grand Duke was so agitated that he did not wish for a justification, in fact he would not allow one. 'I would remind you, sir, that I am beside myself. Unfortunate occurrence! It was your business to take precautions against unfortunate occurrences ...'

The Major-General stood in a servile position and addressed the floor at his feet in a low, submissive tone of voice.

'I humbly beg to be allowed to remind you that I, at least, am not alone responsible. Privy Councillor Grasanger – an authority on gynaecology – examined her Royal Highness. But nobody can be held responsible in this case ...'

'Nobody ... Really! I shall take the liberty of holding you responsible ... You are answerable to me ... You were in charge during the pregnancy, you superintended the confinement. I have relied on the knowledge to be expected from your rank, Major-General, I have trusted to your experience. I am bitterly disappointed, bitterly disappointed. All that your skill can boast of is ... that a crippled child has been born. ...'

'Would your Royal Highness graciously consider ...'

'I have considered. I have weighed and found wanting. Thank you!'

Major-General Eschrich retired backwards, bowing all the while. In the ante-room he shrugged his shoulders. His face had grown very red. The Grand Duke fell to pacing up and down the Library once more in princely wrath, with creaking boots, incensed, ignorant and foolish in his isolation. However, whether it was that he wished to humiliate the physician-in-ordinary still further, or that he regretted having robbed himself of any explanation – ten minutes later the unexpected happened, in that the Grand Duke sent Herr von Lichterloh to summon the young Doctor Sammet to the Library.

The doctor, when he received the message, said again: 'With pleasure ... with pleasure,' and even changed colour a little, but then composed himself admirably. It is true that he was not complete master of the prescribed etiquette, and bowed too soon, while he was still in the door, so that the aide-de-camp could not close it behind him, and had to ask him in a whisper to move forward; but afterwards he stood in an easy and unconstrained attitude, and gave reassuring answers, although he showed that he was naturally rather slow of speech, beginning his sentences with hesitating noises and frequently interspersing them with a 'Yes', as if to confirm what he was saying. He wore his dark blond hair cut *en brosse* and his moustache untrimmed. His chin and cheeks were clean-shaved, and rather sore from it. He carried his head a little on one side, and the gaze of his grey eyes told of shrewdness and active kindness. His nose betrayed his origin by a sudden downward curve above the moustache. With his dress-coat he wore a black stock, and his shiny boots were of provincial cut. With one hand on his silver watch-chain he kept his elbow close to his side. His whole appearance suggested honesty and professional skill; he inspired confidence.

The Grand Duke addressed him unusually graciously, rather in the manner of a teacher who has been scolding a naughty boy, and turns to another with a sudden assumption of mildness.

'I have sent for you, doctor . . . I want information from you about this peculiarity in the body of the new-born prince. ... I assume that it has not escaped your notice ... I am confronted with a riddle ... an extremely painful riddle. ... In a word, I desire your opinion.' And the Grand Duke, changing his position, ended with a gracious motion of his hand, which encouraged the doctor to speak.

Doctor Sammet looked at him silently and attentively, as if waiting for the Grand Duke to terminate his princely lines. Then he said: 'Yes. We have here to do with a case which is not of very common occurrence, but is nonetheless well known and familar to us. It is actually a case of atrophy.'

'I beg your pardon. Atrophy?'

'Forgive me, Royal Highness. I mean stunted growth. Yes.'

'Quite right. Stunted growth. That is correct. The left hand is stunted. But this is unheard of. I cannot understand it. Such a thing has never happened in my family. People talk nowadays about heredity.'

Again the doctor looked silently and attentively at the lonely

and domineering man, to whom the news had only just penetrated that people were talking lately about heredity. He
answered simply: 'Pardon me, Royal Highness, but in this case
there can be no question of heredity.'

'Really! You're quite sure!' said the Grand Duke with faint
mockery. 'That is at least one consolation. But will you be so
kind as to tell me what there can be a question of, then?'

'With pleasure, Royal Highness. The cause of the malformation is entirely mechanical, yes. It has been caused by a mechanical constriction during the development of the embryo. We
call such malformations constriction-formations, yes.'

The Grand Duke listened with anxious disgust: he obviously
feared the effect of each succeeding word on his sensitiveness.
He kept his brows knit and his mouth open: the two furrows
running down to his beard seemed deeper than ever. He said:
'Constriction-formations ... but how in the world ... I am quite
sure every precaution must have been taken ...'

'Constriction-formations,' answered Dr Sammet, 'can occur
in various ways. But we can say with comparative certainty that
in our case . . . in this case it is the amnion which is to
blame.'

'I beg your pardon ... the amnion?'

'That is one of the fœtal membranes, Royal Highness. Yes.
And in certain circumstances the removal of this membrane
from the embryo may be retarded and proceed so slowly that
threads and cords are left stretching from one to the other ...
amniotic threads as we call them, yes. These threads may be dangerous, for they can bind and knot themselves round the whole
of a child's limb; they can entirely intercept, for instance, the life-
ducts of a hand and even amputate it. Yes.'

'Great heavens ... amputate it. So we must be thankful
that it has not come to an amputation of the hand?'

'That might have happened. Yes. But all that has happened
is an unfastening, resulting in an atrophy.'

'And that could not be discovered, foreseen, prevented?'

'No, Royal Highness. Absolutely not. It is quite certain that
no blame whatever attaches to anybody. Such constrictions do
their work in secret. We are powerless against them. Yes.'

'And the malformation is incurable? The hand will remain stunted?'

Dr Sammet hesitated; he looked kindly at the Grand Duke.

'It will never be quite normal, certainly not,' he said cautiously. 'But the stunted hand will grow a little larger than it is at present, oh yes, it assuredly will. ...'

'Will he be able to use it? For instance ... to hold his reins or to make gestures, like anyone else ... ?'

'Use it ... a little ... perhaps not much. And he's got his right hand, that's all right.'

'Will it be very obvious?' asked the Grand Duke, and scanned Dr Sammet's face earnestly. 'Very noticeable? Will it detract much from his general appearance do you think?'

'Many people,' answered Dr Sammet evasively, 'live and work under greater disadvantages. Yes.'

The Grand Duke turned away and paced once more up and down the room. Doctor Sammet deferentially made way for him and withdrew towards the door. At last the Grand Duke resumed his position at the writing table and said: 'I have now heard what I wanted to know, doctor; I thank you for your report. You understand your business, no doubt about that. Why do you live in Grimmburg? Why do you not practise in the capital?'

'I am still young, Royal Highness, and before I devote myself to practising as a specialist in the capital I should like a few years of really varied practice, of general experience and research. A country town like Grimmburg affords the best opportunity of that. Yes.'

'Very sound, very admirable of you. In what do you propose to specialize later on?'

'In children's diseases, Royal Highness. I intend to be a children's specialist, yes.'

'You are a Jew?' asked the Grand Duke, throwing back his head and narrowing his eyes.

'Yes, Royal Highness.'

'Ah – will you answer me one more question? Have you ever found your origin to stand in your way, a drawback in your professional career? I ask as a ruler, who is especially concerned

that the principle of "Equal chances for all" shall hold good un-
conditionally and privately, not only officially.'

'Everybody in the Grand Duchy,' answered Dr Sammet, 'has
the right to work.' But he did not stop there: moving his
elbows like a pair of short wings, in an awkward, impassioned
way, he made a few hesitating noises, and then added in a
restrained but eager voice: 'No principle of equalization, if I
may be allowed to remark, will ever prevent the incidence in the
life of the community of exceptional and abnormal men who are
distinguished from the bourgeois by their nobleness or infamy.
It is the duty of the individual not to concern himself as to the
precise nature of the distinction between him and the common
herd, but to see what is the essential in that distinction and to
recognize that it imposes on him an exceptional obligation towards society. A man is at an advantage, not at a disadvantage,
compared with the regular and therefore complacent majority,
if he has one motive more than they to extraordinary exertions.
Yes, yes,' repeated Dr Sammet. The double affirmative was
meant to confirm his answer.

'Good . . . not bad; very remarkable, anyhow,' said the Grand
Duke judicially. The doctor's words sounded familiar, yet
somehow implied an infringement of his royalty. He dismissed
the young man, saying: 'Well, Doctor, my time is not my own.
Thank you. This conversation – apart from its painful occasion
– has pleased me very much. I have the pleasure of bestowing
on you the Albrecht Cross of the Third Class with the Crown.
I shall remember you. Thank you.'

This is what passed between the doctor from Grimmburg
and the Grand Duke. Shortly after Johann Albrecht left the
castle and returned to the capital by special train, chiefly to show
himself to the rejoicing populace, but also to grant several audiences in the palace. It was arranged that he should return to the
ancestral seat the same evening, and take up his residence there
for the next few weeks.

All those present at the confinement at Grimmburg who did
not belong to the Grand Duchess's suite were also accommodated
in the special train of the bankrupt local railway, some of them
travelling in the Sovereign's own saloon. But the Grand Duke

drove from the castle to the station alone with von Knobelsdorff, the Minister of State, in an open landau, one of the brown Court carriages with the little golden crown on the door. The white feathers in the hats of the chasseurs in front fluttered in the summer breeze. Johann Albrecht was grave and silent on the journey; he seemed to be worried and morose. And although Herr von Knobelsdorff knew that the Grand Duke, even in private, disliked anybody addressing him unasked and un-invited, yet at last he made up his mind to break the silence.

'Your Royal Highness,' he said entreatingly, 'seems to take the small anomaly which was discovered on the body of the Prince very much to heart, and yet one would think that on a day like this the reasons for joy and proud gratitude would far outweigh ...'

'My dear Knobelsdorff,' replied Johann Albrecht, with some irritation and almost in tears, 'you will forgive my ill-humour. Surely you don't expect me to break out in song. I see no reason for it at all. True enough, the Grand Duchess is doing fine, and the child is a boy, that is a blessing too. But he has to be born with an atrophy, a constriction caused by amniotic threads. No-body is to blame, it is a misfortune; but misfortunes for which nobody is to blame are the most terrible of all misfortunes, and the sight of their Sovereign ought to awaken in his people other feelings than those of sympathy. The Heir Apparent is delicate, needs constant care. It was a miracle that he survived that attack of pleurisy two years ago, and it will be nothing less than a miracle if he lives to attain his majority. Now Heaven grants me a second son – he seems strong, but he comes into the world with only one hand. The other is stunted, useless, a deformity, he will have to hide it. What a drawback! What an impedi-ment! He will have to brave it out all his life. It will have to be made known gradually, so as not to cause too much of a shock on his first public appearance. No, I cannot get over it. A prince with one hand.'

'With one hand,' said Herr von Knobelsdorff. 'Did your Royal Highness use that expression deliberately?'

'Deliberately?'

'You did not, then? ... For the Prince has two hands, yet as one is stunted, one might if one liked also describe him as a prince with one hand.'

'And so what?'

'And one must almost wish, not that your Royal Highness's second son, but that the heir to the throne were the victim of this small misfortune.'

'What do you mean by that?'

'Why, Your Royal Highness will laugh at me; but I am thinking of the gypsy woman.'

'The gypsy woman? I am listening, dear Baron!'

'Of the gypsy woman – forgive me – who a hundred years ago prophesied the birth of a prince to Your Royal Highness's house – a prince "with one hand" – that is how tradition puts it – and attached to the birth of that prince a certain, strangely formulated prophecy.'

The Grand Duke turned on his seat and stared silently at Herr von Knobelsdorff whose radiating wrinkles had appeared at the corner of his eyes.

'Very entertaining,' he said and resumed his former attitude.

'Prophecies,' continued Herr von Knobelsdorff, 'generally come true to this extent, that circumstances arise which one can interpret, if one has a mind to, in their sense. And the broadness of the terms in which every proper prophecy is couched makes this all the more easy. "With one hand" – that is real oracular style. What has actually happened is a moderate case of atrophy. But that much counts for a good deal, for what is there to prevent me, what is there to prevent the people, from assuming the whole by this partial fulfilment, and declaring that the conditional part of the prophecy has been fulfilled? The people will do so; if not at once, at any rate if the rest of the prophecy, the actual promise, is in any way realized, it will put two and two together, as it always has done, in its wish to see what is written turn out true. I don't see how it is going to come about – the Prince is a younger son, he will not come to the throne, the intentions of fate are obscure. But the one-handed prince is there – and so may he bestow on us as much as he can.'

The Grand Duke did not answer, secretly thrilled by dreams of the future of his dynasty.

'Well, Knobelsdorff, I won't chide you. You want to comfort me and you haven't done too badly. But we must do our duty.'

The air resounded with the distant cheer of many voices. The people of Grimmburg surged behind a cordon at the station. Officials were standing spaced out in front of it, waiting for the carriages. The spectators spotted the mayor, raising his top hat, wiping his brow with a printed handkerchief and peering closely at a slip of paper whose contents he was memorizing. Johann Albrecht assumed the expression appropriate for listening to the simple address, and to answering briefly and graciously: 'Most excellent, Mr Mayor.' The small town was beflagged; its bells were ringing.

In the capital all the bells pealed. At night there were illuminations; not by formal request of the authorities but spontaneously – the whole city was a blaze of light.

TWO

THE COUNTRY

THE country measured eight thousand square kilometres, and numbered one million inhabitants.

A handsome, quiet, unhurried country. Its forests rustled dreamily; its broad acres stretched far and wide, showing signs of honest care; its industries were undeveloped to the point of indigence.

It possessed brick kilns, a few salt and silver mines, that was about all. One might mention the tourist traffic, but to call it flourishing would be an exaggeration. The alkaline springs in the immediate neighbourhood of the capital, which formed the centre of a pleasant thermal establishment, had turned the capital into a spa. But whereas at the end of the Middle Ages this health resort was famous and frequented by visitors from afar, it had later lost its repute, eclipsed by other spa's, and had been forgotten. The most valuable of its springs, called the Ditlinde spring, which was exceptionally rich in lithium salts, had been opened up quite recently, during the reign of Johann Albrecht III, and since emphatic and sufficiently loud methods of publicizing it were not employed, its waters had not yet succeeded in capturing the attention of world markets. One hundred thousand bottles were exported yearly; if anything rather less than that. And but few foreigners came to take the waters on the spot.

Every year the Diet was the scene of speeches concerning the unsatisfactory financial returns of public means of locomotion, which referred to the total loss at which the local railways functioned, and to the fact that the main lines paid no dividends whatsoever; distressing but unalterable and inveterate facts, which the Minister of Trade tried to explain away, in lucid but repetitive expositions, by the peaceful commercial and industrial circumstances of the country, as well as by the inadequacy of the local coal industry. Critics would add a few words on the defective organization of municipal communications. But the spirit of contradiction and opposition was never very strong in the Diet, the prevailing frame of mind among the deputies being one of ponderous and simple-minded loyalty.

Therefore the railway revenues did not by any means rank first in the income from government shares of private investors; in this country of woods and pasture the revenues derived from forestry had always occupied first place. That these, too, had decreased in an alarming manner was much more difficult to justify, although the reasons for it were only too plentiful.

The people loved their woods. They were a fair and sturdy type, with blue, introspective eyes and broad, rather too prominent cheekbones, an honest and reflective, wholesome and backward race. They clung to their forest with all the tenacity of their nature, it lived in their songs, to the artists whom it nurtured it was the source and origin of their inspiration, and the object of popular gratitude, not only in regard to the effect on their minds and spirits. The poor gathered their firewood in the wood; it gave it them freely, they had it for nothing. They stooped as they went, they gathered all sorts of berries and mushrooms among its trunks and these brought them a small profit. That was not all. The people recognized that their forest had a definitely favourable influence on the climate and on public health in the country; they were well aware that without the splendid forests which surrounded the capital the Thermal Gardens would never have filled with lucrative strangers; in short, this not over-industrious and up-to-date people should have acknowledged that the forest represented the most important asset, the most profitable heritage of the country.

And yet this forest had been sinned against, outraged for ages and ages. The Grand Ducal Forestry Department of Woods and Forests deserved all the reproaches that were laid against it. That Department had not political insight enough to see that the wood must be maintained and kept as inalienable common property, if it was to be useful not only to the present generation, but also to those to come; and that it would surely avenge itself if it were exploited recklessly and short-sightedly, without regard to the future, for the benefit of the present.

That was what happened in the past and was happening now. In the first place vast stretches of soil had been impoverished by the reckless and excessive spoliation of its natural manure. Matters had repeatedly gone so far that not only the most recent carpet of needles and leaves, but the greatest part of the fall of years past had been removed and used in the fields partly as litter, partly as humus. There were many forests which had been completely stripped of mould; some had been crippled by raking; and that was true of the communal woodlands as well as those belonging to the State.

Had the forest been put to these uses merely in order to supply a momentary need of agriculture it would have been excusable. But although those who declared an agricultural system based on the use of forest manure to be unsound, even dangerous, were not wanting, the trade in woodlitter went on without any particular justification, on purely fiscal grounds, so it was said, that is to say for reasons which on close examination boiled down to one only, that of making money. For it was money which was needed. But in order to raise it ceaseless inroads were made on the capital, until one fine day it was realized with dismay that an unsuspected depreciation in that capital had ensued.

The people were a peasant race, and in their misguided, artificial and inappropriate zeal they now felt compelled to be contemporary and adopt ruthless business methods. One instance of this was dairy-farming; it should be mentioned here. Loud complaints were heard, especially in the annual medical reports, that a deterioration was noticeable in the nourishment, and consequently in the development of the rural population. What was the reason? The owners of livestock were bent on turning all the full milk at their disposal into ready money. The spreading of the dairy industry, the development and lucrative nature of the dairy trade tempted them to disregard the claims of their own establishments. The nourishing milk diet became a rarity in the country, and in its stead recourse was had to unsubstantial skimmed milk, inferior substitutes, vegetable fats and, unfortunately, alcoholic drinks. Critics talked of undernourishment, of a downright physical and moral debilitation of the rural population; they laid their facts before the Diet, and the Government promised to give the matter its earnest consideration.

But it was only too obvious that the Government was basically motivated by the same spirit as the misguided farmers. The State forests were successively robbed of their timber; once cut it was gone and this meant a continual deterioration of public property. This might have been necessary from time to time, when insect pests invaded the forests, but often enough it was due simply to the fiscal reasons referred to; and instead of using the proceeds of the clearings for the purchase of new tracts of land, instead of replanting the fallow land as quickly as possible, in brief, instead of balancing the damage to the public fortune by an increase of its capital value the available currency had been devoted to the payment of current expenses and the redemption of bonds. Of course it was certain that a reduction of the national debt was highly desirable, but the critics were of the opinion that it was not the moment to devote special revenues to replenish the funds set aside for this purpose.

Those who had no interest in glossing over facts would only describe the national finances as a hopeless muddle. The country carried a debt of six hundred million marks – it laboured under the burden with patience and devotion, but also with secret groans. For the burden, much too heavy in itself, was tripled through the rise in the rate of interest and through conditions of repayment imposed on a country whose credit was already shaken, whose exchange was low, and which had come to be regarded with special interest by the tycoons of the financial world.

The succession of financial crises appeared to be never-ending. The list of failures seemed without beginning or end. And a maladministration, which was made no better by frequent changes in its personnel, regarded borrowing as the only cure for the creeping sickness in the State finances. Even the Chancellor of the Exchequer, von Schröder, whose probity and singleness of purpose were beyond all doubt, had been given a peerage by the Grand Duke because he had succeeded in placing a loan at a high rate of interest in the most difficult circumstances. His heart was set on an improvement in the credit of the State: but as his resource was to contract new debts while he paid off the old, his policy proved to be no better than a well-meant but costly blind. For the simultaneous sale and purchase of bonds meant a higher purchase than selling price, involving the loss of thousands of pounds.

It seemed as though the country were incapable of producing a man of adequate financial calibre. Improper practices and a policy of 'hushing-up' were the fashion. The budget was drawn up in such a manner that it had become impossible to distinguish between ordinary and extraordinary State requirements. Ordinary and extraordinary items were jumbled up together, and those responsible for the budgets deceived themselves, and everybody else, as to the real state of affairs, by appropriating loans, which were supposed to be raised for extraordinary purposes, to cover a deficit in the ordinary exchequer ... The holder of the finance portfolio at one time was actually an ex-court marshal.

Doctor Krippenreuther, who assumed office towards the end of Johann Albrecht's reign, was the minister who, convinced like Herr von Schröder of the necessity for a radical reduction in the national debt, induced the members of Parliament to impose a final and extreme increase in taxation. But the country, which was already impoverished, stood on the verge of insolvency, and Krippenreuther merely made himself thoroughly unpopular. His policy in fact meant nothing but a transfer of funds from one hand to another, and which moreover entailed a loss; for the increase in taxation laid a burden on the national economy which weighed more heavily and more directly on the people than that removed by the reduction of the national debt.

What was the answer to these problems? Where, then, were help and a remedy to be found? A miracle, so it seemed, was needed – and meanwhile the sternest economy. The people were pious and loyal, they loved their princes as themselves, they were permeated with the sublimity of the monarchical idea, they saw in it a reflection of the Deity. But the economic depression was too painful, too general. Even to the most ignorant the crippled and deforested woods told a tale of woe. Thus it could happen that repeated appeals were made in the Diet for a curtailment of the Civil List, and a reduction of allowances and Crown endowments.

The Civil List amounted to half a million, the revenues of the Crown demesnes to seven hundred and fifty thousand marks. That was all. And the Crown was in debt – to what extent was perhaps known to Count Trümmerhauff, the keeper of the Grand Ducal Purse, a correct gentleman without an inkling of financial talent. This Johann Albrecht ignored; at any rate he gave the impression of ignoring it, and therein followed the example of his forebears who had rarely deigned to give more than a passing thought to their debts.

The people's attitude of veneration was reflected in their princes' extraordinary sense of their own dignity, which had sometimes assumed fanciful and even extravagant forms, and that at all times had found its most obvious, and indeed alarming, expression in a tendency to extravagance and a reckless ostentation as exaggerated as the dignity it represented. One Grimmburger had been nicknamed 'the Luxurious' – wellnigh every one of them deserved this epithet. The state of indebtedness of the dynasty was therefore a historical and hereditary condition, reaching back to the times when all loans were a private concern of the sovereign, and when Johann the Headstrong, wishing to raise a loan, had pledged the freedom of some of his most prominent subjects.

Those days were gone forever; and Johann Albrecht, by instinct a typical Grimmburger, was unfortunately no longer in a position to give free rein to his instincts. His father had squandered the family fortunes, which, reduced to little more than nothing, had been spent on the building of pleasaunces with French names and marble colonnades, on parks with complicated fountains, on a spectacular Opera House and all sorts of gilded spectacles. Figures were figures, and, much against the inclination of the Grand Duke, in fact without his consent, the Court was gradually cut down.

The household of Princess Katherina, the Grand Duke's sister, was spoken of with sympathy in the capital. She had been married to a member of a neighbouring ruling House, and been left a widow, and had come back to her brother's house, where she lived with her red-headed children in what used to be the Heir Apparent's palace on the Albrechtsstrasse, before whose gates a gigantic doorkeeper stood all day long in a pompous attitude with staff and shoulder-belt complete, within whose walls life went on in such exemplary, parsimonious fashion.

Prince Lambert, the Grand Duke's brother, did not come in for much attention. There was a coolness between him and his brothers and sisters, who could not forgive him his *mésalliance*, and he hardly ever came to Court. He lived in a villa over-looking the Municipal Gardens with his wife, an ex-ballerina from the Court Theatre, who bore the title of Baroness von Rohrdorf after one of the Prince's estates, and his debts fitted his appearance, that of an emaciated sportsman, an inveterate theatregoer and balletomane. He had dropped his title, behaved entirely as a private citizen, and if his household had the reputation of slovenly indigence it did not rouse much public interest.

But changes had taken place in the Old Castle itself, reductions in expenditure which were discussed in the capital and in the countryside, usually in a pained and affectionate manner, for at heart the people wished to see themselves represented with due splendour and munificence. Several of the highest charges at Court had been amalgamated for economy's sake, and for years past Herr von Bühl zu Bühl had been Lord Marshal, Chief Master of Ceremonies, and Marshal of the Household all in one. There had been many discharges in the Board of Green Cloth and the servants' hall, among the pike-staffs, yeomen of the guard, and grooms, the master cooks and chief confectioners, the court and chamber lackeys. The establishment of the royal stable had been reduced to the barest minimum ... And what was the good of it all? The Grand Duke's contempt for money showed itself in sudden outbursts against the squeeze; and while the catering at the Court functions reached the extreme limits of permissible simplicity, while supper after the Thursday concert in the Marble Banqueting Hall invariably consisted of roast beef with Sauce Remoulade and ice-cream, served on gilt-legged tables covered with crimson velvet tablecloths; while the daily fare at the Grand Duke's own candle-decked table was that of an ordinary middle-class civil servant's family, he defiantly

spent a whole year's income on the restoration of the Grimmburg.

Meanwhile his other castles fell into ruin. Herr von Bühl
simply had not the means at his disposal for their upkeep,
which was a pity in many cases. Those which lay at some little
distance from the capital or right out in the country, those
elegant and luxurious retreats cradled in natural beauty, and
whose coquettish names spoke of rest, solitude, pleasure, diver-
sions and freedom from care, or else recalled a flower or a jewel,
served as a goal to holiday-makers, both from the capital and
foreigners, and brought in a certain amount of entrance fees
which sometimes, but not always, were devoted to their upkeep.
This was not the case, however, with those in the immediate
neighbourhood. There was the small Empire château, the Eremitage, situated on the northern periphery of the suburbs;
secretive and of a classical grace, but long abandoned and neglected in the midst of luxuriant, únkept grounds adjoining the
Municipal Gardens, and overlooking a small, muddy pond.
There was Delphinenort at only fifteen minutes' walking distance, on the north side of the Public Gardens, all of which had
formerly belonged to the Crown, its neglected façade mirrored
in the immense quadrangular basin of a fountain. Both were in
a lamentable condition. That Delphinenort in particular, that
illustrious building in the early Baroque style, with its noble
portico of superimposed columns, its tall windows divided
into small panes, carved with leafy garlands, with Roman busts
in niches, with its splendid staircase and general air of restrained
magnificence should be abandoned for good, or so it seemed, was
the regret of all lovers of architectural beauty; and when one
day, as the result of unforeseen and truly adventurous circumstances, it was restored to its former glory, among them at any
rate the satisfaction was general. For the rest, Delphinenort
could be reached in fifteen or twenty minutes from the Thermal
Gardens which lay a little to the north-west of the city, and were
connected with the centre by a direct tramline.

Kept up for the use of the Grand Ducal household were the
castle of Hollerbrunn, a summer seat consisting of an expanse
of white buildings with Chinese roofs, on the farther side of a

chain of hills which surrounded the capital, coolly and pleasantly situated by the river and famed for the lilac hedges of its grounds; also Jägerpreis, a hunting lodge totally overgrown with ivy lying in the midst of the forests to the west; and lastly, the castle in the capital called the Old Castle, although none of more recent date existed.

It was named thus, with no idea of comparison, simply because of its age, and the critics declared that its redecoration was more urgent than that of the Grimmburg. Even the rooms which served for official occasions, and those inhabited by the Grand Ducal family, were faded and shabby, not to speak of the many uninhabited and disused tracts in the oldest parts of the intricate building, with their blind mirrors and flyblown chandeliers and window panes. For some time past the public had been refused admission to them – a measure obviously due to the shocking state of the castle. But those who happened to see the rooms, tradesmen and the members of the household staff, gave out that sea grass stuffing burst from more than one proud and pompous piece of furniture.

The castle and the church attached to it formed one grey, irregular and tortuous complex of towers, galleries and gateways, half fortress and half palace. Various periods had contributed to its completion, and large parts of it were decaying, weatherbeaten, damaged, and ready to fall to pieces. Its walls descended steeply to the western region of the city whence it was accessible by tumble-down steps fastened together with rusty iron bars. But the huge main gate, guarded by lion protomes, and surrounded by the proud and pious motto: *Turris fortissima nomen Domini*, in almost illegible carving, faced the Albrechtsplatz. This was the scene of sentry and sentry box, changing of the guards, drums, parades, and gangs of street urchins.

The Old Castle had three courtyards whose corners were flanked by handsome towers with winding stairs, and between whose flagstones of basalt grew an unnecessary amount of weeds. But in the centre of one of these courtyards stood a rosebush. It had been standing there for ages in a bed, although no other attempt at gardening was to be seen. It was a rosebush like any other; the castellan tended it, it slept beneath the snow, received rain and sunshine, and in due season it bore roses. These were exceptionally fine blooms, perfectly shaped, with deep red, velvety petals, a pleasure to behold and a real masterpiece of nature. But these roses had one odd and gruesome peculiarity; they had no scent: or rather, they had a scent, but for some unknown reason it was not the scent of roses, but of *decay* – a slight but unmistakable smell of decay. Everybody knew this; it was mentioned in the guide-books, and visitors came to the courtyard to convince themselves of it with their own noses. According to popular fancy it was written somewhere that at some time or other, on a day of general rejoicing, the blossoms of the rosebush would begin to exhale a sweet natural perfume.

After all, it was only to be expected that the popular imagination would be exercised by the wonderful rosebush. It was exercised in precisely the same way by the 'owl-chamber' in the Old Castle, which was used as a lumber-room. It was situated in an innocuous position, not far from the Gala Rooms and the Hall of Knights, where the Court officials used to assemble for the Grand Levee, and thus in a comparatively modern part of the building. But it was reputed to be haunted, in so far as from time to time movements and noises originated there which could not be heard outside the place and whose origin was unascertainable. People swore that they were of supernatural origin, and many would have it that they became especially noticeable when important and decisive events in the Grand Ducal family were impending — a more or less gratuitous rumour which deserved no more serious attention than other popular expressions of a historical and dynastic frame of mind, as for instance a certain dark prophecy which had been handed down for hundreds of years and may be mentioned in this connection. It came from an old gypsy woman, and was to the effect that a prince 'with one hand' would bring the greatest good fortune to the country. The old hag had said: 'He will give to the country with one hand more than all the rest could give it with two.' That is how the prophecy was recorded, and how it was quoted from time to time.

The capital was built round the Old Castle, consisting of an old and a new town, with their public buildings, monuments, fountains and gardens, streets and squares, named after princes, artists, deserving statesmen, and distinguished citizens, divided into two very unequal halves by the river spanned by several bridges, and which flowed in a great loop round the southern end of the Municipal Gardens, and was lost in the surrounding hills. It was a University town with its own Academy. These institutions were not very well frequented and were the haunt of contemplative and a trifle old-fashioned dons; the Professor of Mathematics, Privy Councillor Klinghammer, was the only one who had a distinguished name in the academic world. The Court Theatre, though poorly subsidized, maintained a decent level of performance. There was a little musical, literary and artistic life; a certain number of foreigners came to the capital, wishing to share in its well-regulated life and such intellectual attractions as it offered, among them wealthy invalids, who settled down in the villas round the spa-gardens and were held in honour by the State and the community as doughty payers of taxes.

Such was the capital, and such was the country; this was the general situation.

THREE

HINNERKE THE SHOEMAKER

THE Grand Duke's second son made his first public appearance on the occasion of his christening. This festivity aroused the same interest in the country as always attached to happenings within the Royal Family circle. It took place after weeks of discussion and research as to the manner of its arrangement; it was held in the Court Church by the President of the Church Council, Dom Wislezenus, with all the due ceremonial, and in public, to the extent that the Lord Marshal's office, by the Prince's orders, had issued invitations to it to every class of society.

Herr von Bühl zu Bühl, a courtly ritualist of the greatest circumspection and accuracy, in his full-dress uniform superintended, with the help of two masters of ceremonies, the whole of the intricate proceedings; the gathering of the princely guests in the Gala Rooms, the solemn procession in which they, attended by pages and chamberlains, walked up the staircase of Heinrich the Luxurious and through a covered passage into the church, the entry of the spectators from the highest to the lowest, the distribution of the seats, the observance of due decorum during the religious service itself, the order of precedence at the congratulations which took place directly after the service was ended. He panted and puffed, squirmed, brandished his staff, smiled dramatically, and bowed while retreating backwards.

The Court Church was decorated with plants and tapestries. In addition to the representatives of the nobility attached to the Court and the landed aristocracy, and to the greater and lesser ranks of the Civil Service, merchants, countryfolk and simple workmen filled the pews, their hearts full of exalted feelings. In a half-circle of crimson velvet armchairs in front of the altar sat the relations of the infant, foreign royalty acting as godfathers and godmothers or the representatives of others who had been unable to attend in person. The assemblage at the christening of the Heir Apparent six years before had not been more distinguished. For in view of Albrecht's delicacy, the advanced age of the Grand Duke, and the death of Grimmburg relations, the person of the second-born prince was at once recognized as an important guarantee for the future of the dynasty. Little Albrecht took no part in the ceremony; he was kept to his bed with an indisposition which Surgeon-General Eschrich declared to be of a nervous character.

Dom Wislezenus preached from a text of the Grand Duke's own choosing. The *Courier,* a local paper with a chatty gossip column, had given a full account of how the Grand Duke had one day personally fetched the huge family Bible with the metal clasp from the rarely visited Library, had shut himself up with it in his study, searched in it for a whole hour, at last copied the text he had chosen on to a piece of paper with his pocket-pencil, signed it 'Johann Albrecht', and sent it to the Court Chaplain. Dom Wislezenus treated it like a musical score, a *Leitmotiv* so to speak. He turned it inside out, pointed out its various meanings and left no aspect of it unmentioned; he announced it in a whisper, then with the whole power of his lungs, and whereas, at the beginning of his performance, delivered gently and reflectively, it had seemed a thin, almost ethereal theme, it appeared at the end, when he impressed it on the congregation for the last time, to be richly orchestrated, fully interpreted and deeply pregnant with meaning. He then passed on to the actual baptism, and performed it thoroughly so that all could see, and with due stress on every detail.

This, then, was the day of the prince's first public appearance, and that he was the chief actor in the drama was clearly shown by the fact that he was the last to come on the stage, and that his entry was distinct from that of the rest of the company. Preceded by Herr von Bühl, he entered slowly, in the arms of the Mistress of the Robes, Baroness von Schulenburg-Tressen, and all eyes were fixed on him. He lay asleep, wrapped in lace and white silk tied with ribbons. His appearance moved and gladdened the congregation and caused general delight. The centre and object of general attention, he kept perfectly quiet, undemanding, and by the nature of things as yet quiescent.

It was to his credit that he did not cause disturbances, did not act or resist but, doubtless from an inborn trustfulness, quietly resigned himself to the state which surrounded him, upheld him, and as yet dispensed him from all personal effect ...

The arms in which he reposed were frequently changed at fixed points in the ceremony. Baroness Schulenburg handed him with a curtsey to his aunt, Katharina, who, with a severe look on her face, wore her newly altered and dyed lilac silk dress and crown jewels in her hair. She laid him, when the moment came, solemnly in his mother Dorothea's arms, who, in all her stately beauty, with a smile on her proud and lovely mouth, held him out a while to be blessed, and then passed him on. A cousin held him for a minute or two, a child of eleven or twelve years with fair curls, skinny legs, bare, shivering arms and a wide sash of red silk tied in a huge bow at the back of her childish white dress. Her peaked face was anxiously turned towards the Master of Ceremonies.

Once the Prince woke up; but the flickering altar candles and a many-hued shaft of sunlight dust blinded him so that he closed his eyes again. And as his head was void of thoughts and filled merely with gentle, unsubstantial dreams, and as he was at the moment free of pain he promptly fell asleep again.

While sleeping he received a number of names, but his first names were: Klaus Heinrich.

And he slept on in his cot with its gilded cornice and blue silk curtains, while the Grand Ducal family feasted in his honour in the Marble Hall, and the other guests lunched in the Hall of Knights.

The newspapers commented on his first appearance; they described his looks and his apparel, they emphasized his truly princely behaviour, and expressed the moving and uplifting impression he had made. After that the public heard little of him for some time, and he heard nothing of them.

He knew nothing as yet, understood nothing as yet, guessed nothing of the difficulty, danger, and sternness of the life prescribed for him; nothing in his conduct suggested that he felt any contrast between himself and the great public. His small existence was an irresponsible, carefully supervised dream, played on a stage remote from the public gaze; and this stage was peopled with numerous and colourful shapes, some static and others moving, some transient and others enduring.

Of the permanent ones, the parents were far in the background, and not altogether distinguishable. They were his parents, that was certain, and they were exalted and benign. When they approached it was as though everything else receded on both sides, forming a corridor of reverence along which they advanced towards him, to show him a momentary tenderness ... The nearest and clearest objects were two women with white caps and aprons, apparently two wholly kind, clean and loving creatures who tended his small body in every way and heeded his cries ... another intimate part of his life was his brother Albrecht; but he was grave, distant and far advanced.

When Klaus Heinrich was two years old, another birth took place in the Grimmburg, and a princess came into the world. Thirty-six guns were allotted to her because she was a girl, and at the font she received the name Ditlinde. She was Klaus Heinrich's sister, and it was a good thing for him that she arrived. At first she was surprisingly small and easily hurt, but she soon grew like him, caught up with him, and the two became inseparable. He lived in her company, together with her he learnt to see, experience and understand the world which they shared.

It was a world and these were experiences bound to render them reflective. In winter they lived in the Old Castle. In summer they lived at Hollerbrunn, the summer residence, by the banks of a cool river, surrounded by the scent of lilac hedges adorned with white statues. On the way there, or if at any other time papa or mamma took them out in one of the brown lacquered carriages with the small golden crown on the carriage door, the passers-by stopped and cheered; for papa was the Prince and ruler of the country, therefore they themselves were a Prince and a Princess – evidently in precisely the same sense as the princes and princesses in the French fairy tales which their Swiss governess read to them. That was worth consideration and without doubt a special case. When other children heard these stories, they necessarily regarded the princes who figured in

them from a great distance, and as exceptional beings whose
rank was an idealization of reality, of whom to think obviously
meant to be lifted above the humdrum of everyday existence.
But Klaus Heinrich and Ditlinde regarded these beings with
calm composure as their equals, for they breathed the same air;
they, too, lived in a castle, they stood on a fraternal footing
with them and did not feel transported from reality when they
identified themselves with them. Did they, therefore, live always
and perpetually on those heights to which others rose only while
listening to a fairy story? The Swiss governess, judging from
their behaviour, would certainly not have been able to deny it
if this question could have been put to her in so many words.

The Swiss governess was the widow of a Calvinist minister
and was in charge of both children while each of them had two
separate nursery maids. Madame was black and white throughout; her bonnet was white and her dress black. Her face was
white, with a white wart on one cheek, and her smooth, gun-
metal hair was pepper and salt. She was very precise and easily
shocked. Over quite small matters which she would find inexcus-
able she wrung her hands and raised her eyes to heaven. But her
most effective, though silent punishment for serious offences
was 'the sad look', implying that one had forgotten oneself.
As from a certain day, and following her instructions, she began
to address Klaus Heinrich and Ditlinde as 'Your Grand Ducal
Highness', and from that day she became more easily shocked
than ever.

Albrecht, however, was addressed as 'Your Royal Highness'.
Aunt Katharina's children, it appeared, were members of the
family only on the distaff side, and therefore were of less importance. But Albrecht was Crown Prince and Heir Apparent,
and it was quite befitting that he should look so pale and distant
and spend a lot of time in bed. He wore Austrian jerkins with
flap pockets and a Dragoner. His head bulged at the back, he
had narrow temples and a long, intelligent face. While still quite
small he had endured a serious illness during which, in Major-
General Eschrich's words, his heart had temporarily 'shifted to
the right'. In any case he had seen death face to face, and that
may well have intensified his innate shy dignity. He seemed to

be extremely reserved, cold from embarrassment and haughty from a lack of natural grace. He lisped a little and then blushed for doing so, for he was accustomed to keep a strict watch on himself. His shoulder-blades were slightly uneven. One of his eyes was weaker than the other, so that he used glasses for his homework, which helped to make him look old and wise. Albrecht's tutor, Doctor Veit, a man with a drooping, mud-coloured moustache, sunken cheeks and pale, unnaturally distended eyes, kept invariably to his left side. Doctor Veit was always dressed in black, and carried a book dangling down his thigh, with his index-finger thrust between its leaves.

Klaus Heinrich felt that Albrecht scorned him, and he understood that it was not only because of his youth. He himself was tender-hearted and prone to tears, that was his nature. He cried when anybody 'looked sadly' at him, and when he knocked his forehead against a corner of the nursery table, so that it bled, he howled from sympathy with his forehead. But Albrecht had faced Death, yet never cried on any condition. He stuck his short, rounded underlip a little forward, and sucked it lightly against the upper one – that was all. He was most superior. He was so well bred. In all questions as to what was *comme il faut* the Swiss governess upheld him most emphatically as a model. He would never have allowed himself to converse with the gorgeously attired puppets who belonged to the Castle and were not men or human beings, but simple lackeys – as Klaus Heinrich had sometimes done in unguarded moments. For Albrecht was not curious. The look in his eyes was that of a lonely boy who had no wish to let the world intrude upon him. Klaus Heinrich, on the contrary, chatted with the lackeys from that very wish, and from an urgent, though perhaps dangerous and unseemly desire to feel some contact with what lay outside the charmed circle. But the lackeys, young and old, at the doors, in the corridors and the passage-rooms, with their sand-coloured gaiters and brown coats, on the red-gold lace of which the same little crown as on the carriage doors was repeated again and again – they straightened their great hands on the seams of their thick velvet breeches, bent a little forward towards him, so that the aiguillettes dangled from their shoulders, and gave vapid and befitting answers, whose most important part was the address 'Grand Ducal Highness', and smiled as they did so with an expression of discreet sympathy as if to say 'You Lilywhite boy!' Sometimes when he got the chance, Klaus Heinrich went on voyages of discovery in uninhabited parts of the Castle, with Ditlinde, his sister, when she was old enough.

At that time he was having lessons from Schulrat – School Councillor – Dröge, Rector of the Municipal State Schools, who had been appointed as his first tutor. Schulrat Dröge was of a precise turn of mind. His index-finger with its dry and wrinkled skin and gold signet ring without a gem followed the line of print when Klaus Heinrich read, stopping until the word before him had been spelt out. He arrived in a frock-coat and white waistcoat, with the ribbon of some lesser order in his buttonhole, wearing square and shiny boots with tops of natural leather. He sported a greying beard shaped like a skittle, and from his large, flat ears protruded tufts of bushy grey hair. His brown hair was cut *en brosse* round the temples, with a precise parting which revealed the dry, yellow scalp, porous like embroidery canvas. But at the back of his head and at the sides wisps of grey showed beneath the coarse brown hair. He nodded briefly to the lackeys who opened the door leading to the large panelled schoolroom where Klaus Heinrich waited for him. He bowed to Klaus Heinrich, not only on entering and casually, but with slow deliberation, coming up to him and waiting for the proffered hand of his exalted pupil. Klaus Heinrich tendered it, and the fact that he did so twice, on arrival and departure, and that he did so in a gracious, smooth and winning manner, as he had seen his father shake hands with the gentlemen of his suite, seemed to him more important and essential to him than all the lessons between the two rites.

After Schulrat Dröge had come and gone innumerable times, Klaus Heinrich had imperceptibly gained a knowledge of all sorts of practical matters; and against all expectations and intent found himself proficient in the subjects of reading, writing and arithmetic, and could reel off to order the names of towns in the Grand Duchy pretty well without an omission. But, as has been said, this was not what in his opinion was really necessary and essential for him. From time to time, when he was inattentive at his lessons, the School Councillor rebuked him with a reference to his exalted calling. 'Your exalted calling requires you ...' he would say, or: 'You owe it to your exalted calling ...' What was his calling, and how was it exalted? Why did the lackeys smile as if to say: 'You Lilywhite boy!' and why was his governess so deeply shocked when he slipped up even a little in speech or manner? He took stock of his surroundings, and sometimes, when he looked steadily and long, and forced himself to probe the meaning of what surrounded him, he felt an inkling of that essential something which specially concerned him.

He stood in a room, one of the Gala Rooms called the Silver Room where, as he knew, his father the Grand Duke held formal receptions – he found himself in this room alone, and took a good look round.

It was winter-time and very cold. His little shoes were reflected in the tawny parquet floor, transparent like glass and divided into squares, which spread at his feet like a skating rink. The ceiling, covered with silver arabesques, was so high that a long staff of metal was needed to allow the many-armed silver chandelier containing innumerable tall, white candles to swing in the middle of the vast expanse. Coats of arms in faded colours and framed in silver filled the space below the ceiling. The walls were covered with white damask mounted on silver which in places had worn thin and turned yellow with age. A sort of monumental baldachin, resting on two strong silver columns and decorated in front with a silver garland gathered in two places, and with the portrait of a powdered female ancestor draped in imitation ermine, looking down, formed the chimneypiece. Ponderous armchairs covered in threadbare white damask, the woodwork worked in silver leaf, surrounded the cold hearth. On the side walls opposite each other towered huge silver-framed mirrors, whose glass was mottled with blind spots, whose broad white marble sideboards supported two candlesticks each, the lower placed before the taller, filled with long white candles, like the wall brackets, like the four great candelabra in the corners of the room. Framing the tall windows to the right which overlooked the Albrechtsplatz and whose outer ledges were cushioned with snow, were curtains of heavy white silk, spotted with yellow, gathered by silver cords, and with under-curtains of faded lace. In the centre of the room, beneath the chandelier, stood a table of moderate size, its silver pedestal fashioned in imitation of a rugged treetrunk, with an octagonal top of milky mother-of-pearl – it stood there without chairs, apparently useless and at best meant to serve as a support when the lackeys flung open the door to admit the solemn figures in Court dress who had come to present their respects.

Klaus Heinrich looked at this room, and clearly saw that there was nothing here to remind him of the matter-of-factness which Schulrat Dröge, for all his bows, usually impressed upon him. Here all was Sunday and solemnity, just as in church where the School Councillor's demands would have been equally out of place. A severe and empty pomp reigned here, a formal sym-metry which, being devoid of usefulness and comfort, was con-tent to represent nothing but itself – some lofty and exacting service no doubt, which seemed anything but easy and com-fortable, which set high standards of conduct and discipline and controlled self-abnegation, but whose object was an undefined concept. And it was cold in the Silver Hall, cold as in the palace of the Snow Queen where the children's hearts turn to ice.

Klaus Heinrich walked over the glassy floor and stood at the table in the middle. He laid his right hand lightly on the mother-of-pearl table, and placed the left on his hip, so far behind that it rested almost in the small of his back, and was not visible from in front, for it was an ugly sight, brown and wrinkled, and had not kept pace with the right in its growth. He stood resting on one leg, with the other a little advanced, and kept his eyes fixed on the silver ornaments of the door. It was not the place nor the attitude for dreaming, and yet he dreamed.

He saw his father and looked at him, as he did at this room, trying to understand him. He saw the weary pride of his blue eyes, the lines which ran proudly and morosely from his nostrils to his beard, and which were sometimes deepened and accen-tuated by boredom. Nobody dared address him, or approach him and speak to him unasked – not even the children; it was forbidden, it was dangerous. True, he would answer, but distantly and coldly, and a look of helpless embarrassment would pass over his face, and sudden confusion which Klaus Heinrich understood only too well.

Papa addressed his subjects and dismissed them; this is what he was expected to do. He held Cercle at the beginning of the Court Ball and after the dinner which inaugurated the winter season. He passed with mamma through the rooms and halls in which the members of the Court were gathered, went through the Marble Hall and the Gala Rooms, through the Picture Gallery, the Hall of Knights, the Hall of the Twelve Months, the Audience Chamber, and the Ballroom – went not only in a fixed direction, but along a fixed path which bustling Herr von Bühl kept free for him, and addressed a few words here and there to the ladies and gentlemen of his suite. Whoever he addressed made a sweeping bow or curtsey, left a space of gleaming parquet between him or herself and papa, and answered soberly and deeply moved. Thereupon papa greeted them over the intervening space, from the stronghold of precise regulations which prescribed the others' movements and warranted his own attitude, greeted them smilingly and lightly and passed on. Smilingly and lightly . . . Of course, of course, Klaus Heinrich quite understood the look of helpless embarrassment which suddenly invaded papa's face when anybody was impetuous enough to address him unasked – understood it and shared it anxiously. It wounded some soft and vulnerable part of their innermost being, leaving them helpless as though exposed to a brutal incursion. And yet it was this very part which dimmed their eyes and carved deep lines of boredom.

Klaus Heinrich stood and saw – he saw his mother and her beauty, which was famed and extolled far and wide. He saw her stand erect in ceremonial dress in front of her large mirror lit by candles; for sometimes, on solemn occasions, he was allowed to be present when the Court hairdresser and her lady's maids put the last touches to her toilette. Herr von Knobelsdorff too was present when mamma was adorned with jewels from the Crown regalia, surveyed, and noted down which gems were being worn. The wrinkles at the corners of his eyes radiated as he made mamma laugh with his funny jokes, which brought out the lovely dimples in her soft cheeks. But it was laughter full of artifice and condescension, and she glanced at the mirror as she laughed as though she were practising it.

People said that Slav blood flowed in her veins, and that was what gave her deep blue eyes a sweet radiance, and made her fragrant hair dark as night. Klaus Heinrich was like her, so he heard people say, in that he too had steel-blue eyes with dark hair, while Albrecht and Ditlinde were fair, just as papa had been before his hair turned grey. But he was far from handsome, owing to the breadth of his cheekbones, and especially to his left hand, which mamma was always reminding him to hide adroitly, in the side-pocket of his coat, behind his back, or under the breast of his jacket, especially when an affectionate impulse prompted him to throw both arms round her. Her look was cold as she bade him mind his hand.

He saw her as she was in the portrait in the Marble Hall; wearing a dress of shot silk with lace flounces and long gloves which showed a mere fraction of her ivory coloured arm under the puffed sleeve, a tiara in the night of her dark hair, her magnificent figure erect, a smile of cool perfection on her wonderful severe lips – and in the background a peacock with metallic blue feathers opening his vainglorious fan-shaped tail. Her face was soft, but beauty had hardened its expression, and it was easy to see that her heart, too, was hardened and absorbed in her beauty. On days preceding a ball or Cercle she slept late and ate nothing but the yolks of eggs, so as not to overload herself. Then in the evening she moved on papa's arm along the prescribed orbit through the ballrooms – grey haired dignitaries blushed when she deigned address them, and the *Courier* wrote that it was not only because of her exalted rank that Her Royal Highness had been queen of the ball. Yes, people felt happier for the sight of her, whether it was at Court or outside in the streets, or in the afternoon, driving or riding in the park, and the people's hearts beat faster. Flowers and cheers met her, all hearts went out to her, and it was clear that in cheering her the people cheered themselves, and at the moment felt elevated and believed in great things. But Klaus Heinrich knew well that mamma had spent

long, painstaking hours on her beauty, that her smiles and greetings were the result of practice and calculation, and that her
heart never missed a beat for anyone.

Did she love anyone – himself, Klaus Heinrich, for instance,
for all his likeness to her? Why, of course she did, when she had
time to, even when she coldly reminded him of his hand. But it
seemed as if she reserved any expression or sign of her tender
feelings for occasions when lookers-on were present who were
likely to be edified by them. Klaus Heinrich and Ditlinde did
not often come into contact with their mother, chiefly because
they, unlike Albrecht, the Heir Apparent, for some time past,
did not have their meals at their parents' table, but apart with
the Swiss governess; and when they were summoned to mamma's boudoir, which happened once a week, the interview consisted of a few casual questions and polite answers – giving no
scope for displays of feeling – while its whole drift seemed to be
the proper way to sit in an armchair balancing a teacup full of
milk.

But at the concerts which took place in the Marble Hall every
other Thursday, under the name of 'The Grand Duchess's
Thursdays', and were so arranged that the Court sat at small
tables with gilt legs covered with red velvet tablecloths, while
the leading tenor Schramm, accompanied by an orchestra, sang
so lustily that the veins stood out on his bald temples – at the concerts Klaus Heinrich and Ditlinde, in their best clothes, were
sometimes allowed in the Hall for one song and the succeeding
pause, when mamma showed how fond she was of them, showed
it to them and to everybody else in so heartfelt and expressive a
way that nobody could have any doubt about it. She summoned
them to the table at which she sat, and told them with a happy
smile to stay beside her, laid their cheeks on her shoulders or
bosom, looked at them with a soft, soulful look in her eyes and
kissed them both on forehead and mouth. Then the ladies bent
their heads with an enraptured mien and their eyelids quivered,
while the gentlemen nodded slowly and bit their moustaches, in
order to manfully control their emotion. Yes, it was beautiful,
and the children felt they had their share in the effect, which
was greater than anything the court tenor Schramm could pro-

duce with his most enraptured notes, and they nestled close to
mamma. Because Klaus Heinrich for one realized that by the
nature of things it was not their business to have simple feelings
and be made happy by them, but rather that it was a question
of displaying their affection, and thereby to gladden the hearts
of the assembled guests.

Occasionally the people in the town and park were also allowed to see that mamma loved them. For while Albrecht drove
or rode with the Grand Duke early in the morning – and that
although he was not a good horseman – Klaus Heinrich and
Ditlinde had to take turns from time to time at accompanying
mamma on her drives, which took place in the spring and
autumn at the time of the afternoon promenade, with Baroness
Schulenburg-Tressen in attendance. Klaus Heinrich was a little
excited and feverish before these drives, to which unfortunately
no enjoyment, but on the contrary a great deal of trouble and
effort attached. For directly the open carriage drove through the
Lion Gate on the Albrechtsplatz, past the Grenadier Guards
standing to attention, crowds of people awaited them, men and
women and children who cheered and eyed them avidly; and this
meant pulling oneself together, smiling, hiding the left hand
and saluting in such a way as to make the people happy. And
so it went on during the whole drive through the city and out
into the countryside. Other vehicles were obliged to keep a distance, the police saw to that. But the pedestrians stood on the
kerb, the ladies curtseyed, the gentlemen pressed their hats against
the seams of their trousers and lifted their gaze full of devotion
and urgent curiosity – and this was Klaus Heinrich's impression :
that all these people existed merely in order to be present and to
stare, while he existed in order to be seen and stared at; and that
was far more difficult. He kept his left hand in the pocket of his
overcoat and smiled as mamma wished him to, while he felt that
his cheeks were burning. But the *Courier* reported that the
cheeks of the little Prince had been ruddy with health.

Klaus Heinrich was thirteen years old when he stood at the
solitary table of mother-of-pearl in the midst of the chilly Silver
Hall, trying to understand the nature of the essential something
which was expected of him. And as he entered deeply into

what he saw: the empty, threadbare pride of these rooms loftily oblivious of usefulness and comfort, the symmetry of white candles which seemed to express an exalted and exacting service and a controlled self-abnegation, the brief distress on his father's face when he was addressed unasked, the cool and carefully tended beauty of his mother which offered itself smilingly to public enthusiasm, and the devoted and urgently curious gaze of the people – he was seized with an intimation, an approximate and wordless understanding of what was expected of him. But at the same time he was filled with horror, a terror of such a destiny as his, a dread of his 'exalted calling', so strong that he spun round and covered his eyes with his hands, both hands, the small wrinkled left hand too, and sank down at the lonely table and cried, cried with pity for himself and his heart, until Mademoiselle came and wrung her hands and raised her eyes to heaven and questioned him and led him away. He made out that he had been frightened, and that was the truth.

He had known nothing, understood nothing, suspected nothing of the difficulty and sternness of the life ahead of him. He had been gay and carefree and had given much cause for being shocked. But soon impressions multiplied which made it impossible for him to disregard his true position. In the northern suburbs, not far from the Thermal Gardens, a new road had been built; he was informed that the City Council had decided to call it Klaus Heinrich-Strasse. During a carriage drive his mother stopped at an antique dealer; she wished to make a purchase. The footman waited at the carriage door, the public gathered round, the dealer busied himself round them, there was nothing new in that. But Klaus Heinrich for the first time noticed his photograph in the shop window. It was hanging next to those of artists and distinguished men, men with lofty brows, whose eyes bespake the loneliness of fame.

On the whole he managed to gain approval. His bearing increased in dignity, and mindful of his calling he acquired a decorous composure. But the strange thing was that his longing increased at the same time; that roving inquisitiveness which Schulrat Dröge was not the man to satisfy, and which had led him to chat with the lackeys. He had given up doing that; it did not lead to anything. They smiled: 'Lilywhite boy', and they confirmed by their smile that his world of the symmetrically marshalled candles presented an unconscious antithesis to the world outside, but they were no manner of help to him. He looked about him during the carriage drives, during the walks with Ditlinde and the Swiss governess in the Municipal Gardens, followed by a groom. He felt that if they were all of one mind to stare at him, while he was all alone and made conspicuous just to be stared at, he was thereby excluded from their being and existence. He half guessed that they were not always as he saw them, when they stopped and greeted him with deferential looks; and that it was with them as with the children when they heard about fairy princes, and were thereby refined and elevated above their workaday selves. But he did not know what they looked like and were when they were not refined and elevated above their workaday selves – his 'exalted calling' concealed this from him, and it was a dangerous and improper wish to allow his heart to be moved by things which his exaltedness concealed from him. And yet he wished it, he wished it from a jealousy and that roving inquisitiveness which sometimes drove him to undertake voyages of exploration into unknown regions of the Old Castle, with Ditlinde his sister, when the opportunity arose.

They called it 'rummaging', and great was the charm of 'rummaging'; for it was difficult to acquire familiarity with the ground-plan and structure of the Old Castle, and every time they penetrated far enough into the remoter parts they found rooms, closets, and empty halls which they had never seen before, or strange roundabout ways to rooms they already knew. But once during their wanderings they had an encounter; an adventure befell them which, though apparently unimportant, made a great impression on Klaus Heinrich and opened his eyes.

The opportunity came. While the Swiss governess was absent on leave to attend the evening service, they had drunk their milk from teacups with the Grand Duchess attended by two ladies-in-waiting, had been dismissed and directed to go back hand-in-hand to their ordinary occupations in the nursery, which lay not far off. It was thought that they needed nobody to go with them; Klaus Heinrich was old enough to take care of Dit-linde, of course. He was; and in the corridor he said : 'Yes, Dit-linde, we will certainly return to the nursery, but you know, we needn't go the shortest and most boring way. Let's rummage a bit first. If one climbs the stairs to the next floor and follows the corridor to where the vault begins, one gets to a hall with pil-lars. And if one ascends the winding staircase behind the Hall of Pillars one comes to a room with wooden beams; lots of strange objects are lying about there. But I don't know what lies behind that room, and that's what we've got to find out. Come on, let's go.'

'Yes, let's,' said Ditlinde, 'but not too far, Klaus Heinrich, and not where it's too dusty, for this dress shows everything.'

She was wearing a dress of dark-red velvet, trimmed with satin of the same colour. She had at that time dimples in her elbows, and light golden hair that curled round her ears like ram's horns. In later years she turned ash blonde and skinny. She had too the broad, rather too prominent cheekbones of her father and race, but they were delicately fashioned and did not impair the fairness of her small heartshaped face. But with Klaus Hein-rich they were strong and accentuated, so that they seemed some-what to press on his steel-blue eyes and to narrow and elongate their shape. His dark hair was smoothly parted, cut in a careful rectangle above the temples and brushed to one side and away from his forehead. He wore an open jacket with a waistcoat but-toning at the throat and a white turn-down collar. In his right hand he held Ditlinde's little hand, but his left arm hung down with its brown, wrinkled and undeveloped hand, thin and short from the shoulder. He was glad that he could let it hang without bothering to conceal it, and he himself could look round and investigate things to his heart's content.

So off they went and had a good rummaging session. Quiet reigned in the corridors and they hardly saw a footman in the distance. They climbed a flight of stairs and followed the cor-ridor to where the vaulting began, showing that they were in the part of the castle which dated from Johann the Headstrong and Heinrich the Confessor, as Klaus Heinrich knew and explained. They reached the Hall of Pillars and Klaus Heinrich whistled

several notes in quick succession, for the first still sounded when
the last was uttered, and a clear echo rang out beneath the vaulted
ceiling. They scrambled groping and often on hands and knees
up the stone winding staircase which opened behind one of the
heavy doors, and reached the room with the wooden ceiling, in
which there were several strange objects. There were some large
and clumsy muskets, broken and with thickly rusted locks which
maybe had been too derelict for the museum, and a disused
throne seat with torn crimson velvet cushions, short, wide-splayed
lion legs, and cupids hovering over the chairback, bearing a
crown. Then there was a twisted and dusty horrid looking cage-
like object which intrigued them greatly. If they were not mistaken it was a rat trap, for they could see the iron spike to fix the
bacon on, and it was dreadful to think how the door had
snapped shut behind the large and vicious beast. It all took time,
and when they stood up after examining the trap their faces
were hot, and their clothes filthy with rust and dust. Klaus Heinrich brushed them both, but it was not much good, for his hands
were grey as well. And suddenly they realized that dusk had
fallen. They must return at once, Ditlinde insisted anxiously, it
had become too late to go any farther.

'It's an awful shame,' said Klaus Heinrich. 'Who knows what
else we mightn't have found, and when we shall get another
chance of rummaging, Ditlinde.' But he followed his sister all
the same and they hurried back down the winding staircase,
crossed the Hall of Pillars and came out into the arcade, intend-
ing to hurry home hand-in-hand.

They wandered for a while, but Klaus Heinrich shook his
head, for it seemed to him that this was not the way he had
come. They went still farther; but several signs told them that
they had mistaken their direction. This stone seat with the
gryphon heads had not been standing here before. That pointed
window looked to the west over the low-lying quarter of the
town and not over the inner courtyard with the rosebush. They
had taken the wrong turning, there was no denying it; perhaps
they had left the Hall of Pillars by the wrong exit, anyhow they
had completely lost their way.

They retraced their steps for a bit but were too nervous to go on for long and turned right back again, deciding to push on the way they had come so far. They advanced in an airless, musty atmosphere, and large untouched cobwebs spread in the corners. They were worried now and Ditlinde especially felt guilty and on the brink of tears. Their absence would be noted, Mademoiselle would receive them with her 'sad look', perhaps she would even tell the Grand Duke, they would never find the way, would be forgotten and die of hunger. And where there are rat traps, Klaus Heinrich, there are also rats ... Klaus Heinrich reassured her. It was merely a question of finding the place where the armour and crossed standards hung; from that point he was quite sure of his direction. And suddenly – they had just passed a bend in the winding passage – suddenly something happened. It startled them dreadfully.

What they had heard was more than the echo of their own steps, they were other, strange steps, heavier than theirs, they came towards them now quickly, now hesitatingly, and were accompanied by a snorting and grumbling which made their blood run cold. Ditlinde made as if to run away from fright: but Klaus Heinrich would not let go her hand, and they stood with starting eyes waiting for what was coming.

It was a man who was just visible in the half-darkness, and, calmly considered, his appearance was not horrifying. He was squat in figure, and dressed like a veteran soldier on Remembrance Day. He wore a frock-coat of old-fashioned cut, a woollen comforter round his neck and a medal on his breast. In one hand he held a curly top-hat and in the other the bone handle of his clumsily rolled umbrella, which he tapped on the flagstones in time with his steps. His thin grey hair was brushed in matted wisps from one ear upward and across his skull. He had arched black eyebrows and a yellowish-white beard like the Grand Duke, and heavy lids over watery blue eyes with pouches of withered skin; he had the usual high cheekbones, and the lines in his red face were like crevasses. When he came up against the children he seemed to recognize them, for he flattened himself against the wall of the corridor as if to stand to attention, and began to execute a series of bows by jerking his whole body forward from the balls of his feet, and assuming a deferential expression while holding his top-hat upside down in front of him. Klaus Heinrich meant to pass him by with a nod, but was surprised into halting, for the veteran began to speak.

'I beg pardon!' he grunted suddenly; then went on in a more natural voice: 'I earnestly beg your young Highnesses' pardon! But would your young Highnesses mind showing me the way to the nearest exit? It needn't be the Albrecht Gate – not in the least, any gate leading out of the castle will do, if I may take the liberty of asking your young Highnesses.'

Klaus Heinrich had laid his left hand on his hip, right behind, so that it lay almost in his back, and he looked at the floor in front of him. He had been addressed unasked, he had been engaged directly and unavoidably in conversation; he thought of his father and knitted his brows. He pondered feverishly over the question as to how he ought to behave in this false and incorrect situation. Albrecht would have pursed his mouth, drawn at his upper lip with his short, rounded lower lip, and passed on in silence – that much was certain. But what was the point of rummaging if at the first serious adventure one was to pass on in stiff and offended silence? And the man was honest and meant no evil; Klaus Heinrich could see that when he forced himself to raise his eyes. He said simply: 'You come with us, that will be the best way. I'll gladly show you where you have to turn to get to an exit.' And so they went on together.

'Thanks,' said the man. 'Ever so many thanks for your kindness. Heaven knows I should never have thought that I should live to walk about the Old Castle one day with your young Highnesses. But there it is, and after all my vexations, and I have been vexed, terribly vexed, that much is certain – after all my vexations I now have this honour and this pleasure.'

Klaus Heinrich longed to ask what might have been the cause of so much vexation; but the veteran went straight on (and tapped his umbrella in time on the flagstones as he walked). 'And I recognized your young Highnesses straight away, although it's a bit dim in here in the corridors, for I've seen you many times driving out in a carriage and have always been glad, because I myself have just such a couple of brats at home, I mean to say, mine are brats, mine are, and the boy is called Klaus Heinrich too.'

'Just like me?' asked Klaus Heinrich, suddenly pleased. 'What a coincidence!'

'Coincidence? Nay, after *you*!' said the man. 'That's no coincidence when he's called expressly after you, for he's only a couple of months younger, and there are lots more in the town and country who are called that, and all of them after you. Nay, one can hardly call that a coincidence.'

Klaus Heinrich concealed his hand and remained silent.

'Yes, recognized you at once,' said the man. 'And I thought, thank Heaven, thought I, that's what I call fortune and misfortune, and they'll help you out of the trap in which you've landed yourself, you old blockhead, and you've good reason to laugh, thought I, for there's many a one who has tottered about here, fooled by those scoundrels, and who hasn't been so lucky.'

'Scoundrels?' thought Klaus Heinrich, 'and they fooled them?' He looked straight in front of him, he did not dare to ask. A fear, a hope struck him … He said quite quietly: 'They, they fooled you?'

'Not half!' said the man. 'I should think they did, the rascals did, and no mistake! I can tell your young Highnesses that much, young though you are it'll do you good to know that these people are a perfect pest. A man arrives and delivers his work with all due respect. But bless my soul!' he exclaimed suddenly and tapped his forehead with his hat. 'I haven't yet introduced myself to your young Highnesses and told you who I am, have I? Hinnerke. Master-cobbler Hinnerke, Court Purveyor, pensioner and medallist.' And with the index finger of his large, rough and mottled hand he pointed at the medal on his breast. 'The fact is, that His Royal Highness, your father, has been graciously pleased to order a pair of boots from me, top-boots, riding boots, with spurs, and made of the best quality patent leather. They're my speciality, and I made them myself and took a lot of trouble about them, and they were ready today and ever so smart. "You must go yourself," says I to myself… I have a boy who delivers, but I says to myself: "You must go yourself, they are for the Grand Duke," so I rig myself out and take my boots and go to the castle. "Right," say the lackeys down at the gate and want to take them from me. "No," says I, for I don't trust them. It's my reputation and my warrant gets me my orders, I want to tell them, and not the tips I give to the lackeys. But the fellows are spoilt by the purveyors and all they want is to rook me for their trouble. "No," say I, for I'm not a one for bribing and underhand dealings. "I'll deliver them myself, and if I can't give them to the Grand Duke himself, I'll give them to Valet Prahl." They are hopping mad but they say : "In that case you must go upstairs." So I go. Upstairs are others and they say : "Right!" and want to take charge of the boots, but I ask for Valet Prahl and won't be put off. They say "He's having his tea," but I'm determined and say, "Then I'll wait till he's finished." And just as I say it, who comes by in his buckled shoes but Valet Prahl. And he sees me, and I give him the boots with a few modest words, and he says "All right!" and actually adds: "They're fine," and nods and takes them off. Now I'm satisfied, for Prahl, he's safe, so off I go. "Hi!" cries somebody, "Mr Hinnerke! You're going the wrong way!" "Damn!" says I, and turn round and walk the other way. But that was the silliest thing I could do, for they had fooled me and I was going where I didn't mean to go. I walk on a bit and meet another of them fellows and ask him for the Albrecht Gate. But he spots at once what's up and says : "Go up the stairs and keep to the left and down again, that way you'll take a short cut!" And I believe he means it kindly and do what he says, and get more and more muddled and altogether lose my bearings. Then I see that it's not my fault, but the rogues', and it strikes me that I have heard that they often play that trick on Court tradesmen who don't tip them, and let them wander about till they sweat. And my fury makes me blind and stupid, and I get to places where there's not a living soul, and don't know where I am and get properly put about. And at last I meet your young Highnesses. Yes, that's how it is with me and my boots!' ended Shoemaker Hinnerke, and wiped his forehead with the back of his hand.

Klaus Heinrich squeezed Ditlinde's hand.

His heart beat so loudly that he quite forgot to hide his left hand. So that was it. Here was a glimpse of those things which were hidden from him by his 'exalted calling', the behaviour of people when they were in their workaday frame of mind. Those lackeys – he was silent, words failed him.

'I see your young Highnesses don't answer,' said the cobbler and his honest voice betrayed emotion. 'Perhaps I oughtn't to have told you because it isn't your business to know all this wickedness. And yet I think it can do no harm,' he said, and cocked his head to one side and snapped his fingers, 'no harm at all, in view of the future that is, of later on.'

'Those lackeys,' said Klaus Heinrich, taking the plunge, 'are they very wicked? I can well imagine . . .'

'Wicked?' said the cobbler, 'they're good-for-nothings. That's the name for them. Do you know what they're good for? They keep the goods back when no tip's forthcoming, keep them back when the tradesman delivers them punctually at the time ordered, and only hand them over days late, so that the tradesman gets blamed, and is considered by the Grand Duke to have failed in his duty and he loses his orders. That's what they do without scruple, and the whole town knows it . . .'

'Yes, that is bad!' said Klaus Heinrich. He was all ears. He hardly realized as yet how deeply shocked he was. 'Do they do anything else?' he said. 'I'm quite sure they must do other things of the same kind.'

'You bet!' said the man, and laughed. 'No, they don't miss a chance, let me tell your Highnesses, they have all sorts of tricks. As for instance that business of opening the doors. This is what they do. Your father, our gracious Grand Duke, grants an audience to somebody, let's suppose he's a new hand and it's his first time at Court, and he arrives in his dress-suit, all hot and bothered for it's no small matter to stand before His Royal Highness for the first time. The lackeys laugh at him because they are at home in here, and tow him into the ante-room and he doesn't know whether he's coming or going and of course forgets to tip them. Then his big moment arrives, the aide-de-camp calls out his name, the lackeys fling open the door and direct him into the room where His Grand Ducal Highness is waiting. He stands in there and bows and makes his replies, and the Grand Duke in his kindness shakes him by the hand, and now he is

dismissed and marches backward, and thinks the folding doors
are going to open behind him as he has been told they would.
But they don't open, I'm telling your young Highnesses, for the
lackeys are mad because they haven't been tipped, and they don't
move a finger out there. He of course isn't allowed to turn round,
on no account is he to show his back to the Grand Duke, that
would be a terrible blunder and an insult to your illustrious Sire.
He feels behind his back for the door knob and can't find it, and
gets the jitters and fumbles at the door, and when at last by the
mercy of Providence he finds the knob it's an old-fashioned lock,
and he doesn't understand it and fiddles and dislocates his arm
and tires himself out and keeps bowing all the time in his agitation until at last His Highness graciously lets him out with his
own hand. Yes, that's the pranks they play with the folding-
doors! But all that's nothing to what I'm going to tell your
young Highnesses ...'

They had been so deep in conversation that they had scarcely
noticed where they were going, had gone down the stairs and
reached the ground floor close to the Albrecht Gate. Eiermann,
one of the Grand Duchess's personal grooms, came towards
them. He wore a lilac dress-coat and side-whiskers. He had been
sent out to search for their Grand Ducal Highnesses. He shook
his head while still at a distance, in lively concern, and pursed his
lips like a funnel. But when he noticed shoemaker Hinnerke
walking beside the children and tapping the floor with his umbrella all the muscles of his face gave way and his jaw dropped.

There was scarcely time for thanks and farewells, Eiermann
was in such a hurry to part the children from the shoemaker.
And with many a gloomy prophecy he led their Grand Ducal
Highnesses up to their room to the Swiss governess.

She did raise her eyes to heaven and wring her hands over
their absence and the state of their clothes. Worst of all: she
looked at them 'sadly'. But Klaus Heinrich confined his con-
trition to a bare minimum. He thought: 'Those lackeys', they
smiled at him as if to say: 'Lilywhite boy', because they took
some money from the tradesmen and left them to stray about
the corridors if they did not get any, kept the goods back so that
the tradespeople might get blamed, and did not open the folding-

doors and the petitioners had to squirm. That's what happened inside the castle, and what might it not be like outside? Outside among the people who stared at him so devotedly from a distance when he drove past and saluted them? But how had the man dared tell him? Not once had he addressed him as Grand Ducal Highness; he had forced himself on them and had violated his reserve. And yet, why was it so gratifying to hear all that about the lackeys? Why did his heart beat with wild pleasure, touched by the bold, unruly things in which his royal station had no part?

FOUR

DOCTOR ÜBERBEIN

KLAUS HEINRICH spent three years of his boyhood with other boys of his age, the sons of landowners and titled Court officials, in a kind of aristocratic seminary, a boarding school which von Knobelsdorff had set up for his sake at a hunting lodge called the Fasanerie.

A property of the Crown for centuries past, the Fasanerie gave its name to the first stopping place of the State railway running north-west from the capital, and in turn derived it from a pheasant preserve situated not far off among meadows and woods, which had been the hobby of a former ruler. The castle, a one-storied, box-shaped country house with a shingle roof topped by lightning conductors, with stables and coach-houses, stood close to the edge of extensive fir plantations. With a row of old lime trees in front, it looked out over a broad expanse of meadowland fringed by a circle of blue, wooded hills, and intersected by paths, with the smooth playgrounds and hurdles for horse jumping in the foreground. Facing a corner of the lodge was an inn, a beer- and coffee-garden with tall trees, which a discreet man called Stavenüter had rented, and which on summer Sundays was thronged with holidaymakers, especially cyclists from the city. The pupils of the Fasanerie were not allowed to visit the beer-garden except with a master.

They were five boys, not counting Klaus Heinrich; Trümmerhauff, Gumplach, Platow, Prenzlau, and Wehrzahn. They were called the 'Pheasants' in the countryside. They had a landau from the Court stables which had seen better days, a dog-cart, a sledge, and a few hacks. And when in winter some of the meadows were flooded and frozen over, they had the opportunity to skate. There were one cook, two chambermaids, one coachman, and two lackeys at the 'Pheasantry', one of whom could drive at a pinch.

Professor Kürtchen, a small, suspicious and irritable bachelor with the airs of an actor and manners of an old-fashioned Franconian cavalier, was their head-master. He wore a stubby grey moustache, a pair of gold spectacles in front of his restless brown eyes, and always out-of-doors a top hat on the back of his head. He stuck his belly out as he walked and held his little fists on each side of his stomach like a long-distance runner. He treated Klaus Heinrich with self-satisfied tact, but was full of suspicion of the noble arrogance of his other pupils and hissed like a tom-cat when he sensed any signs of contempt for himself as a commoner. When out for a walk, and if there were people close by, he loved to stop and gather his pupils in a knot around him and explain something to them, drawing diagrams in the sand with his stick. He addressed Frau Amelung, the house-keeper, a captain's widow who smelt strongly of valerian, as 'my lady', and was proud of his knowledge of what was good form.

Professor Kürtchen was assisted by a younger master with a doctor's degree and a cheerful, active, pompously eloquent manner and an emotional disposition who influenced Klaus Heinrich's views and his ideas on himself perhaps more than was good for him. A games master called Zotte had also been appointed. The assistant teacher, be it mentioned in passing, was called Überbein, Raoul Überbein. The rest of the staff came every day by railway from the capital.

Klaus Heinrich noticed with gratification that the demands made on him from the point of view of learning diminished with each passing day. Schulrat Dröge's wrinkled forefinger no longer paused on the lines, when he had done his work; and during the lessons as well as while correcting his written work, Professor Kürtchen seized every opportunity of showing his tact. Quite soon after the beginning of the first term – it was after elevenses in the dining-room with the tall windows on the ground floor – he summoned Klaus Heinrich to his study up-stairs and said in so many words: 'It is against the interest of all concerned that during our common periods of study your Grand Ducal Highness should be called upon to answer questions which at the time may be unwelcome to you. On the other hand it is desirable that your Grand Ducal Highness should always indi-

cate your readiness to reply to questions by raising your hand.
I therefore beg your Grand Ducal Highness, for my own orienta-
tion, to stretch out your arm full length in the case of an unwelcome question, but if you are willing to answer raise it only
halfway and at right angles.' As for Doctor Überbein, he filled
the classroom with a resounding loquacity; his cheerful tenor disguised his teaching purpose without his losing sight of it. He
had made no special arrangements with Klaus Heinrich but
questioned him when it occurred to him to do so, in a free and
easy manner without causing him any embarrassment. And
Klaus Heinrich's impractical replies seemed to enchant Doctor
Überbein, and to inspire him with merry enthusiasm. 'Ohoho!'
he would exclaim and throw back his head, roaring with laughter. 'Come, Klaus Heinrich! Oh princely blue blood! Such
innocence! The rude problems of life have caught you unawares! Well then, it is for me, experienced man of the world
that I am, to unravel matters for you.' And he would supply
the right answer; and not question another boy after Klaus
Heinrich had failed. The method of instruction of the other
masters was that of an unassuming lecture. The games master
Zotte had received instructions from high quarters to conduct
the physical exercises with every regard for Klaus Heinrich's left
hand – so strictly that the attention of the Prince himself or of
his companions should never be drawn unnecessarily to his little
failing. So the exercises were limited to running games, and during the riding lessons, which Herr Zotte also gave, all feats of
daring were rigorously excluded.

Klaus Heinrich's relations with his five companions were not
what one might call intimate, nor did they lead to familiarity.
He remained separate, he never became one of them and was not
absorbed in their number. They were five, and he was one; the
Prince, the five, and the masters, that was the establishment.
Several factors stood in the way of a free and easy friendship.
The five had been summoned to be his companions, they were
not asked to supply the right answer when during lessons he
had replied wrongly, they had to adapt themselves to his con-
stitution when riding or playing games. They found themselves
reminded *ad nauseam* of the advantages they gained by being

allowed to share his life and studies. A few of them, the young von Gumplach, von Platow and von Wehrzahn, the sons of country squires of moderate means, remained under the impact of the gratified pride showed by their parents when the invitation from the Ministry had arrived, and of the felicitations proffered from all sides. Count Prenzlau, called Bogumil, on the other hand, was a fat, red-haired boy with freckles and a breathless way of speaking, the son of the richest and most ancient land-owning family in the country, spoilt and full of self-assurance. He was well aware that his parents could not very well refuse Baron von Knobelsdorff's invitation, but that it had not seemed to them by any means an unmixed blessing and that he, Count Bogumil, could have lived much better and more in keeping with his position on his father's estates. He found the hacks bad, the landau shabby, and the dog-cart old-fashioned; he grumbled privately over the fare. Dagobert Count Trümmerhauff, a delicate boy who looked like a greyhound and spoke with a lisp, was his inseparable companion.

They constantly used an expression which perfectly described their fault-finding aristocratic attitude, and which they kept repeating in a biting guttural tone of voice: 'A hellish bore.' It was a 'hellish bore' to wear detachable collars. It was a 'hellish bore' to play tennis in one's ordinary clothes. But Klaus Heinrich felt himself unequal to using this expression. He had not hitherto known that one could wear shirts with attached collars and possess as many suits as Bogumil Prenzlau did. He would have liked to say 'a hellish bore', but it occurred to him that he himself was wearing darned socks. He found himself inelegant beside Prenzlau and clumsy compared with Trümmerhauff. Trümmerhauff was thoroughbred like an animal. He had a long, pointed nose with a ridge as sharp as a blade, and wide, quivering, almost transparent nostrils; blue veins showed on his delicate temples and his minute ears had no lobes. His wide, coloured cuffs fastened with gold links disclosed feminine hands with pointed nails, and he wore a gold bracelet. He lisped with half-closed lids. No, it was obvious that Klaus Heinrich could not compete with Trümmerhauff in elegance. His right hand was rather broad, he had cheekbones like the man in the street, and he looked downright robust next to Dagobert. Quite possibly Albrecht would have known how to say 'a hellish bore' with the 'pheasants'. He on the other hand was no aristocrat, decidedly not, the facts clearly spoke against it. His name for instance, Klaus Heinrich; the cobblers' sons all over the country were called that, and the children of Herr Stavenüter across the road, who used their fingers instead of a handkerchief, were called after him, his parents, and his brother. But the children of the nobility were called Bogumil and Dagobert. Klaus Heinrich stood alone and isolated among the five.

He made one friend, however, at the Fasanerie, and that was Doctor Überbein the assistant master. Raoul Überbein was no Adonis. He had a red beard and exceedingly ugly, protruding, pointed ears. But his hands were small and delicate. He always wore a white tie, which lent a festive note to his appearance, although his wardrobe was scanty. Out of doors he wore a waterproof Loden cloak of coarse wool, and when out riding – and Doctor Überbein was an accomplished horseman – an old frockcoat whose tails he fastened with safety pins, light-buttoned breeches, and a new hat.

In what consisted the fascination he had for Klaus Heinrich? That fascination was extremely complex. The 'pheasants' had not been together for long before a rumour began to circulate that the assistant master had saved a child some years ago by rescuing it from a bog or swamp, and that he was the proud owner of a life-saving medal. That was one impression he gave. Later other details of Doctor Überbein's life came to light, and Klaus Heinrich too heard of them. It was said that his origin was obscure, that he had no father. His mother had been an actress who had arranged for his adoption by impecunious people in return for a sum of money, and formerly he had known hunger, which accounted for the greenish tinge of his complexion. These were things which did not bear thinking about; wild, remote things to which Doctor Überbein himself sometimes alluded, when for example the lordlings, conscious of his obscure origin, behaved impudently towards him. 'Spoilt brats, mother's darlings,' he would say with sharp displeasure. 'I've seen enough of life to deserve some respect from you young gentlemen!' And this fact, that Doctor Überbein had 'seen life and been tried by circumstance', did not fail to impress Klaus Heinrich. But the main attraction of the Doctor, which distinguished him clearly from everybody else, lay in the directness of his approach to Klaus Heinrich, in the tone in which he addressed him from the beginning. There was none of the stiff reticence of the palace servants, of the governess's shocked horror, of Schulrat Dröge's matter-of-fact reverence, nor of Professor Kürtchen's self-complacent deference; and none of the shy and loyal, yet prying manner with which the people in the street stared at Klaus Heinrich. During the first few days after the seminary assembled he kept silent and confined himself to observation. But then he approached the prince with a jovial and cheerful frankness, a fresh paternal camaraderie such as Klaus Heinrich had never met with before. It startled him at first, and he looked in alarm at the doctor's greenish face; but his confusion found no echo in the doctor and in no way discouraged him; it merely confirmed him in his hearty insouciance, and it was not long before Klaus Heinrich warmed to him. For there was nothing vulgar or familiar in Doctor Überbein's manner, not even anything intentional and pedagogic. It expressed the superiority of a man who had seen life and been tried by circumstances, and at the same time was a proud and delicate homage for Klaus Heinrich's different birth and personality. It showed affection and appreciation besides being a gay offer of a pact between their essentially different personalities. He addressed him as 'Your Highness' once or twice, then simply as 'Prince', and then simply 'Klaus Heinrich'. And he stuck to the last.

When the 'pheasants' went out for a ride, these two rode at the head, the doctor on his stout piebald to the left of Klaus Heinrich on his docile chestnut. They rode at a trot across the snow or fallen leaves, through the slush of the first thaw, or in the brooding summer heat, on woodland paths, across country and through the villages, and Doctor Überbein told stories from his past life. Überbein had been the name of his foster parents, a poor ageing couple, the husband a small bank-clerk, and he bore this name by law of adoption. That he should be called Raoul had been the decision and mandate of his mother when she handed over the agreed sum with his ill-fated little person to these good people – obviously a sentimental wish dictated by piety. At least it was quite possible that his real father had been called Raoul, and it was to be hoped that his surname had harmonized with it. For the rest it had been rather irresponsible on the part of his foster parents to adopt a child as there hadn't been enough to eat in the Überbein household, and probably it was want which had made them jump at the money offer. As a boy he had received only the scantiest education, but he had taken the liberty of showing his mettle, had distinguished himself, and as he was keen to become a teacher, a public grant provided him with the means for a University education. Well, he had finished his course at the seminary, not without distinction, for he had set his heart on doing so, and then had been given a post as a teacher at a primary school, with a colossal salary, out of which he occasionally managed to assist his honest adoptive parents and prove his gratitude, until they died almost simultaneously. And a happy release it had been for them. And so he had been left alone in the world, his very birth a misfortune, poor as a fieldmouse and endowed by fate with a greenish face and dog's ears with which to ingratiate himself. A favourable start, was it not? But such a start was the right start – quite definitely, that was so. A miserable boyhood, loneliness and exclusion from happiness, from the happy-go-lucky times of youth, and a strict and exclusive concentration of achievement – this way one did not turn soft, one's moral fibre was braced, one did not sit back and relax, and therefore overtook others who did. What could be better for the development of one's faculties than to be dependent on them alone. What an advantage over those who were not obliged to work. People who began the day with a cigar. At one time, by the bedside of one of his snotty small charges, in a room which did not exactly smell of spring flowers, Raoul Überbein had made friends with a young man, a few years his senior, but in a similar position and like him ill-fated by birth in so far as he was a Jew. Klaus Heinrich knew him – indeed he might be said to have got to know him on a very intimate occasion. Sammet was his name, a doctor of medicine; he happened by chance to have been in the Grimmburg when

Klaus Heinrich was born, and had set up a couple of years later in the capital as a children's specialist. Well, he had been like Überbein and still was, and in those days they had had many a good talk about destiny and courage. Damn it all, they had both been tried by circumstances and no mistake.

Überbein, for his part, looked back with sincere pleasure to the time when he had been an elementary schoolteacher. His activities had not been entirely confined to the classroom, he had amused himself by showing also some personal and human concern for the welfare of his small charges, by visiting them at home where family life was not always altogether ideal, and in doing so he had not failed to bring away impressions of the most varied kind. Indeed, if he had not already been familiar with life's stern countenance he would have found plenty of opportunity to discover it then. For the rest, he had not ceased to study by himself, had given private lessons to the podgy sons of rich businessmen, and had tightened his belt in order to be able to buy books – had spent the long, silent nights and the leisure time they afforded in study. And one day had passed the Civil Service examination by special permission, and had been promoted, and transferred to a grammar school. As a matter of fact, he had been sorry to leave his small charges, but that's how things had worked out. And then it happened that he was chosen as assistant master at the Fasanerie, his unfortunate origins notwithstanding.

That was Doctor Überbein's story, and listening to it Klaus Heinrich was filled with feelings of friendship. He shared his contempt for those who had no need to work, and who began the day with a cigar; he experienced joy and fear when Überbein talked in his jolly, blustering way of 'seeing life' and being 'tried' and of 'life's stern countenance', and he followed his luckless and courageous career from his adoption to his appointment as a teacher at the grammar school with genuine sympathy. It seemed to him as though he were in some way qualified to take part in a conversation about destiny and courage. He felt himself unbend, the experience of his own fifteen years of life came to life, an urge to return the confidences and abandon his reserve overcame him and he made an attempt to tell Überbein

all about himself. But the strange thing was that Doctor Überbein checked him, that he was decidedly opposed to such things.
'No, no, Klaus Heinrich,' he said, 'you must not go on. No
confidences if you please. It isn't as if I didn't know that you
have all sorts of things to tell me. I knew that after I'd watched
you for half a day. But you quite misunderstand me if you think
that I'm likely to encourage you to weep on my shoulder. In
the first place, sooner or later you'd regret it. And in the second,
the pleasures of a confidential intimacy are not for you. You see,
I can talk like that. Who am I? An assistant master. Not an
entirely ordinary one, if you like, but nothing more than that. A
classifiable individual unit. But you? What are you? That is much
harder to define. Shall we say : A concept, a sort of ideal, a vessel, a symbolic existence, Klaus Heinrich, and therefore a formal
existence. But formality and intimacy – haven't you learnt yet that
they are mutually exclusive? They are, you know. You have no
right to confidential intimacy, and if you tried you would see
for yourself that it is not for you, and would find it unsatisfactory and in bad taste. I must remind you to keep your distance, Klaus Heinrich.' Klaus Heinrich raised his crop with a
smile and they rode on.

On another occasion Doctor Überbein said casually : 'Popularity is a kind of intimacy that is not very profound, but grand
and comprehensive.' And that was all he said on the subject.

Sometimes in the summer, during the long morning break
they sat together in the deserted beer-garden, or walked across
the lawn where the 'pheasants' were playing games and talked,
or stopped for a lemon squash at Stavenüter's farm. Herr Stavenüter beamed as he wiped the rough table and brought the fizzy
lemon drink with his own hands. The glass ball in the bottle-
neck had to be pushed in. 'Good stuff!' said Herr Stavenüter.
'The best that money can buy. No substitute, Grand Ducal Highness, and you, Herr Doctor, but real sweetened fruit juice. I can
honestly recommend it!' Then he made the children sing in
honour of the visitors. They were three, two girls and one boy,
and they could sing trios. They stood some way off under the
green canopy of chestnut leaves and sang folk-songs, and used
their fingers instead of handkerchiefs. Once they sang a song

beginning: 'We are all but mortal men', and Doctor Überbein showed his displeasure over this number of the programme by making disparaging remarks. 'A poor song,' he said and leant sideways towards Klaus Heinrich. 'A truly vulgar song. A cheap song, Klaus Heinrich, it should not appeal to you.' Later, when the children had stopped singing he returned to the topic of this song and called it downright wet. 'We are all men, all of us,' he repeated, 'God have mercy on us, yes, without a doubt we are. But on the other hand one might perhaps remember that it is the more exceptional among us who enable us to emphasize this truth. You see,' he said, leaning back, crossing his legs and stroking his beard upward from underneath his chin, 'You see, Klaus Heinrich, a man who has spiritual needs will not be able to refrain from searching for the exceptional in this commonplace world of ours, and will love it wherever and whenever he finds it. He must be annoyed at such a cheap song, such a sheepish denial of the exceptional, be it in a high or a low place, or in both at once. Am I talking of myself? Nonsense! I am only an assistant master. But God knows what makes me say it – I find I derive no pleasure from emphasizing the fact that we are all assistant masters at heart. I love the exceptional in every form and in every sense. I love those who carry the dignity of their exceptional nature in their hearts; the men of mark who can be spotted as strangers, all those at whom the masses gape and stare; I wish for them that they may embrace their destiny, and what I do not wish for them is to accept the cheap and lukewarm half-truth which we have just heard set to music. Why had I to become your tutor, Klaus Heinrich? I am a gypsy, an industrious one if you wish, but still born a gypsy. My suitability to be a servant of princes is not particularly convincing. Why did I gladly obey the summons when it reached me, in spite of my industry and although my birth was an unfortunate accident? Because, Klaus Heinrich, I see in your existence the clearest, most emphatic and best-preserved form of the exceptional. I have become your tutor because I would like to keep your destiny alive in you. Isolation, etiquette, obligation, courage, bearing, manners – whoever lives with these things, has he no right to despise others? Ought he to be guided by mere humanitarianism and familiarity? No, come on, let us go, Klaus Heinrich, if that is agreeable to you. They're tactless brats, these little Stavenüters.' Klaus Heinrich laughed; he gave the children a tip from his pocket-money and they left.

'Yes, yes,' resumed Doctor Überbein during one of their forest promenades – a gap had formed between them and the five 'pheasants' – 'the mind's urge to venerate needs to restrain itself these days. Where do we find greatness? I ask you! But all real greatness and vocation apart, there is always something which I call Highness, chosen and isolated, melancholy forms of existence which must be approached with tender sympathy. Greatness is strong, it wears jack-boots; it has no need of the chivalrous services of the mind. But Highness is appealing. Damn me if it isn't the most appealing thing on earth.'

Once or twice a year the whole Fasanerie repaired to the capital to attend the Opera or a play at the Grand Ducal Court Theatre: Klaus Heinrich's birthday in particular was the signal for such a visit to the theatre. He would then sit quietly in his carved armchair, leaning against the red plush ledge of the Court box, whose roof rested on the heads of two female figures with crossed hands and empty stern faces, and watched his colleagues, the princes, whose destinies were played out on the stage, while he stood the fire of the opera glasses which from time to time, even during the play, were directed at him from the audience. Professor Kürtchen sat on his left hand and Doctor Überbein with the 'pheasants' in an adjoining box.

Once they attended a performance of the *Magic Flute*, and on the return journey to Fasanerie station, in a first class compartment, Doctor Überbein made the whole class laugh by imitating the way the singers talked when their roles obliged them to switch over to prose dialogue. 'He is a Prince!' he said unctuously, and replied in a sing-song sanctimonious drawl: 'He is more than a prince, he is a man!' Even Professor Kürtchen thought it so funny that he bleated like a goat. But the following day, in the course of a private lesson in Klaus Heinrich's study with the round mahogany table, the whitewashed ceiling and the Greek torso on top of the tiled stove, Doctor Überbein repeated the parody and added: 'Good God, that

was news in his day; it was a message, an astonishing truth!
There are paradoxes which have been reversed for so long that
one has to put them back on their feet in order to drive home
their impact; "He is a man; he is more than a man!" that,
after all, is bolder, more beautiful, even more true. The reverse
is mere humanitarianism, but I am no great believer in humanitarianism. I take pleasure in debunking it. One has, in a certain
sense, to belong to those of whom the masses say: "They, after
all, are human too", or one is merely a bore, an assistant master.
I cannot honestly wish for a general levelling of all conflict and
distance, God help me, I am made that way, and the idea of the
principe uomo is to me to speak plainly, an abomination. I hope
that it does not particularly attract you, Klaus Heinrich? You
see, there have always been princes and outstanding individuals
who lived their exceptional lives frivolously, stupidly, oblivious
of their dignity or grossly denying it and quite ready to play
skittles with the citizens in shirt sleeves without feeling a painful violation of their inner selves. But these are negligible, as in
ultimate analysis all that lacks mind is negligible. For mind,
Klaus Heinrich, is the inexorable Master of Ceremonies who
insists on dignity, who in a sense creates dignity and is the arch
enemy and noble opponent of all humane "Gemütlichkeit".
"More than that?" No! To do one's representational duty; to
stand for the many by being oneself; to be the exalted and disciplined expression of the masses, that means naturally to be
more than merely human, Klaus Heinrich – that is why you are
addressed as Your Highness.'

Thus argued Doctor Überbein in his booming, hearty and
eloquent manner, and what he said possibly influenced Klaus
Heinrich's mind and susceptibilities more than was good for
him. The Prince was in his sixteenth year and quite able, if not
to understand, at least to absorb the essence of ideas of the sort.
The decisive factor was that Doctor Überbein's teachings and
exhortations were strongly supported by the force of his personality. When Schulrat Dröge, who had bowed before the ducal
lackeys, reminded Klaus Heinrich of his 'exalted calling' it had
been no more than an accepted formula, used to lend emphasis
to his practical demands and devoid of inner meaning. But when

Doctor Überbein, whose very birth had been an unfortunate accident, as he himself was wont to say, and whose face had a greenish tinge because he had suffered hunger as a child – when this man who had rescued a child from a bog swamp, had seen life and been tried in every way by circumstances, who not only did not bow before the lackeys but occasionally bawled at them loudly, and who had addressed Klaus Heinrich by his Christian names on the third day of their acquaintance without asking leave to do so – when that man declared with a paternal smile that Klaus Heinrich's path was 'on lonely peaks above the masses of humanity' (he rather fancied this expression), it came as something fresh and liberating and called for a response in his inmost being. When Klaus Heinrich listened to the doctor's loud and high-spirited account of his past and 'life's stern countenance', it made him feel as he used to when rummaging with his sister Ditlinde. And that the man who could talk thus, this 'experienced man of the world' as he called himself, did not treat him with deferential reserve like all the others, but in spite of a free and ready homage regarded him as a kindred soul with a like destiny and courage, was something that warmed Klaus Heinrich's heart and filled him with gratitude, and it accounted for the magic and lasting bond between him and the assistant master.

Soon after his sixteenth birthday (Albrecht, the Heir Apparent, was already living in the South on account of his poor health) the Prince and the five 'pheasants' were confirmed in the Court Church. The *Courier* reported it without sensational comment. Dom Wislezenus, the President of the Church Council, preached on a Bible text chosen, as usual, by the Grand Duke, and on this occasion Klaus Heinrich was gazetted Lieutenant, although he had not the foggiest notion of military matters. Practical matters disappeared more and more from his existence. And in accordance with this trend the confirmation ceremony, too, lacked incisive significance, and the Prince returned immediately to the Fasanerie, to resume his life with his tutors and companions without any change.

It was not till a year later that he left his old-fashioned, homely schoolroom with the torso on the stove; the college was dissolved, and while his five aristocratic companions were transferred to the Cadet Corps, Klaus Heinrich took up his residence once more at the Old Castle, in order to attend the top form of the local grammar school, in accordance with an arrangement made by Herr von Knobelsdorff and the Grand Duke. This was a well thought out and popular measure, but one which meant little from the point of view of practical studies. Professor Kürtchen returned to his post at the State School; he taught Klaus Heinrich as before in several subjects, and was more anxious than ever to exercise his tact during the classes. It also transpired that he had informed the rest of the staff of the agreement with Klaus Heinrich concerning his willingness or otherwise to answer questions. As to Doctor Überbein, who had also returned to the Grammar School, he had not yet advanced far enough in his unusual career to be able to teach the top form. But at Klaus Heinrich's lively, even insistent request, conveyed to the Grand Duke indirectly, and so to speak through the official channels by the benevolent Herr von Knobelsdorff, the assistant master was appointed private tutor and superintendent of home studies, came daily to the castle, bawled at the lackeys, and had every opportunity of influencing the Prince with his boisterous and fanciful talk.

Perhaps it was due partly to this influence that Klaus Heinrich's relations with the boys with whom he shared the worn school benches remained even looser and more distant than his connection with the five at the Fasanerie, and that therefore the main object of this year of study was not achieved. The breaks, which during the winter and the summer term united all the pupils in the large paved courtyard, offered much opportunity for camaraderie. But these periods intended for the boys' relaxation brought for Klaus Heinrich the first taste of an effort with which his life was to be so full. Naturally he was, at least during the first term, the cynosure of all eyes in the playground; no easy matter for him in view of the fact that here the surroundings deprived him of every external support and attribute of dignity, and he was obliged to play on the same pavement with those whose sole idea was to stare at him. The smaller boys, full of childish irresponsibility, hung about close to him and gaped, while the bigger ones hovered around wide-eyed, or glanced at him surreptitiously from under the eyelids. After a while the excitement subsided, but whether the fault was Klaus Heinrich's or the other boys', the camaraderie made no real progress. One saw the Prince on the right of the Principal or the teacher in charge, followed and surrounded by the curious, stroll up and down the courtyard. One could observe him chatting with his schoolfellows outside his classroom. What a pleasing scene it was! He half sat, half leant against the slope of the glazed brick wall, one foot placed over the other, and his left hand pressed against the small of his back, with the fifteen inmates of the top class grouped round in a semicircle. There were only fifteen boys this year, for the last promotions had been made with an eye on the social suitability of the pupils for the Selects who for a whole year were to be on terms of *per Du* with Klaus Heinrich.* Such was the custom at the school. Klaus Heinrich would address one of them, who would then advance a little from the semicircle and reply with brief, small bows. Both of them would smile; one always smiled when one spoke to Klaus Heinrich. He might for instance ask:

'Have you finished your German essay for next Tuesday?'

'No, Prince Klaus Heinrich, not yet; I haven't done the last part.'

'It's a difficult subject. I haven't an idea yet what to say.'

'Oh, your Highness, you'll soon think of something!'

'No, it's difficult. You got an alpha in arithmetic, didn't you?'

'Yes, Prince Klaus Heinrich, I was lucky.'

'No, you deserve it. I shall never understand it!'

Murmurs of amusement and gratification in the semicircle. Klaus Heinrich would turn to another schoolfellow, and the first stepped back at once. Everybody felt that the really important point was not the essay nor the arithmetic, but the conversation as an event and an undertaking, one's bearing and manner, the way one advanced and retreated, the successful handling of a gentle, cool and superior situation. Perhaps it was the consciousness of this which brought smiles to everybody's face.

* In German there are two nouns: 'Sie' and 'Du', the formal and the intimate address, corresponding to the French 'vous' and 'tu'. – Translator's note.

Sometimes, when the loose semicircle was grouped before him, Klaus Heinrich would say something like: 'Professor Nicolovius looks like an owl.' This caused great hilarity among his comrades. It was the sign for a general unbending; they kicked over the traces, they let fly, they shouted 'Ho, ho, ho!' in chorus with their breaking voices, and one of them declared on such an occasion that Klaus Heinrich was a 'ripping chap'. But Klaus Heinrich did not often say such things, and only said them when he saw the smile on their faces freeze and grow wan, and signs of boredom, or even impatience, show themselves; said them by way of cheering them, and watched the brief tumult which followed with curiosity and dismay.

It was not Anselm Schickedanz who had called him a 'ripping chap', and yet it was directly for his benefit that Klaus Heinrich had compared Professor Nicolovius to an owl. Anselm Schickedanz had laughed like the others at his joke, but not in quite the same approving way, rather as if to say: 'Good Lord!' He was a dark-haired boy with narrow hips, who had the reputation in the whole school of being a devil of a chap. The tone in the top form that year was exemplary. The obligations which membership of Klaus Heinrich's form entailed had been impressed on every boy from various quarters, and Klaus Heinrich was not going to tempt them to forget this obligation. But that Anselm Schickedanz was a devil of a chap had repeatedly reached Klaus Heinrich's ears, and when he looked at him he felt a kind of satisfaction in believing these hearsay rumours, although it was a riddle how the other had come by this reputation. He made several private inquiries, broaching the subject as if by chance, and tried here and there to learn something of Schickedanz's devilry. He discovered nothing definite. But the replies, malicious and laudatory ones, filled him with intimations of a crazy charm, which was apparent to everyone save him – and this intimation was almost a pain. One of them when talking of Anselm Schickedanz said outright, falling unawares into the forbidden form of address: 'Yes, Highness, you should see him when you aren't around!'

Klaus Heinrich would never see him when he wasn't around, would never get close to him, nor get to know him. He scrutinized him covertly as he stood among the others in the semi-circle, smiling and self-controlled like all the rest. They were on their best behaviour in Klaus Heinrich's presence, his very being was the cause of that, he knew it well, and he would never know what Schickedanz was like, how he behaved when he let himself go. At the thought he felt something like jealousy, a small, burning twinge of regret.

At this juncture a painful and shocking occurrence took place which did not reach the ears of the Grand Ducal couple because Doctor Überbein kept his mouth shut, and about which almost nothing transpired in the capital because all those who had a part in it felt guilty and kept silent, obviously from a feeling of shame. I refer to the improprieties which happened in connection with Klaus Heinrich's presence at the annual Citizens' Ball, and in which Fräulein Unschlitt, the daughter of a wealthy soap manufacturer, played a certain part.

The Citizens' Ball was a standing institution in the social life of the capital, an official and at the same time informal dance, held every winter by the City Councillors at the Bürgergarten Hotel, a large and recently rebuilt and redecorated establishment in the southern suburbs, which afforded the bourgeoisie an occasion to keep in touch with Court circles. It was known that Johann Albrecht III had never cared for this civil and rather informal dance, at which he appeared in a black frock-coat, to lead the polonaise with the Lady Mayoress, and that he was wont to retire at the earliest possible moment. All the more favourably was it noted when his second son, although not obliged to do so, made his appearance at the ball that year; indeed, it became known, at his own urgent request. It was said that the Prince had prevailed on Herr von Knobelsdorff to transmit his earnest wish to the Grand Duchess, who in turn contrived to obtain her husband's consent.

Outwardly the dance pursued its usual course. The illustrious persons, Princess Katharina in a dyed silk dress and a stiff, small hat, accompanied by her children, Prince Lambert and his dainty wife, and lastly Johann Albrecht and Dorothea with Klaus Heinrich descended at the Bürgergarten Hotel, and were received in the hall by the City Councillors, whose frock-coats were decorated with beribboned rosettes. Several ministers, aides-de-camp, in mufti, numerous ladies and gentlemen of the Court, the leading members of society and the landed aristocracy were among those present. In the big, white ballroom the Grand Ducal pair received a string of presentations, and then, to the strains of a band playing in the round gallery up above, Johann Albrecht with the Mayoress and Dorothea with the Mayor opened the ball by leading a procession round the room.

Then, while the polonaise gave way to a waltz, contentment spread, cheeks began to glow, and sentimental or erotic feelings with their concomitant of pain began to kindle here, there, and everywhere in the warm human throng. The royal guests stood as royal guests are bound to stand on similar occasions; graciously smiling and apart, along the upper narrow length of the ballroom, underneath the gallery. From time to time Johann Albrecht engaged a person of distinction in conversation, while Dorothea spoke to a lady. Those who were thus addressed stepped briskly forward and back again; they kept their distance with a small bow or a curtsey, they bent their heads to one side, nodded and smiled in this position in replying to the questions and remarks addressed to them – replied eagerly and smartly, wholly given to the moment, with a sudden and deferential transition from intense gaiety to deep earnestness, and this they did with a passionate intensity obviously absent from their everyday existence, and evidently in a state of exaltation. The curious, out of breath from dancing, watched these purposefully pointless conversations with a strangely tense expression achieved by raising their eyebrows with a smile.

Klaus Heinrich was the object of much attention. With his red-haired cousins, who were already in the army but wore mufti on that evening, he kept a little behind his parents, resting on one leg, his left hand pressed against the small of his back, showing the public his right half-profile. A reporter of the *Courier*, who had been sent to cover the dance, made notes on him in a corner. The Prince could be seen to hail his Doctor Überbein with his white-gloved right hand when the latter, with his flaming beard and greenish face, came past the cordon of onlookers, and how he advanced some way in towards the middle of the ballroom to meet him. The doctor, with big enamel studs in his shirt front, bowed as Klaus Heinrich proffered him his hand, but then began to talk at once in his easy and paternal manner. The Prince seemed to be rejecting a proposal and to laugh uneasily as he did so, but then a number of people distinctly heard Doctor Überbein say: 'No, nonsense Klaus Heinrich, what was the good of learning. What did the Swiss governess teach you your steps for, when you were a small boy? I don't understand why you go to a ball if you won't dance! One, two, three, we'll soon find you a partner!' And with a continual shower of witty sallies he presented to the Prince four or five young girls whom he picked at random and led towards him. They ducked and straightened themselves one after the other, in the sweeping, undulatory movement of the *plongeon*, bit their lower lips and did their best. Klaus Heinrich stood with his heels together and murmured: 'How do you do ... delighted...'

To one of them he went so far as to say: 'It's a good party, isn't it, Fräulein?'

'Yes, Grand Ducal Highness, we are having great fun,' she replied in a high twittering voice. She was a tall girl of the bourgeoisie, on the bony side, dressed in white organdie, her fair hair wavy and fluffed out above her handsome face, with a gold chain round her bare neck where the prominent collarbones could be seen, and large white hands in mittens. She added: 'The *Quadrille* comes next. Won't your Grand Ducal Highness dance?'

'I don't know,' he said. 'I really don't know.'

He looked round. The throng in the ballroom fell into a geometrical pattern. Lines and squares formed; the dancers took up their positions and called out to their partners opposite. The music had not yet started.

Klaus Heinrich inquired from his cousins. Yes, they were taking part in the Lancers, they already held their lucky partners by their hands.

Klaus Heinrich was seen to step behind his mother's red damask chair and address her in a lively whisper, and she to turn her neck with a regal gesture and convey his request to her husband, and the Grand Duke to nod his assent. And then it caused some amusement when the Prince bounded away with youthful impetuosity, so as not to miss the beginning of the dance.

The reporter of the *Courier*, notebook in one hand, pencil in the other, peered from his corner into the ballroom in order to see whom the Prince was going to engage. It was the tall, blonde girl with the collarbones and the large white hands, Fräulein Unschlitt, the daughter of the soap manufacturer. She was standing where Klaus Heinrich had left her.

'Are you still here?' he said breathlessly. 'May I have this dance? Come!'

The sets were made up. They wandered about for a bit without finding a place. A gentleman with a rosette with streamers hurried towards them, seized a young pair by the shoulders and induced them to leave their stand under the chandelier so that his Grand Ducal Highness and Fräulein Unschlitt might join in the dance. The band had been hesitating, but now it struck up, the figure of the dance began, and Klaus Heinrich revolved with the others.

The doors into the next rooms stood open. In one of them one could discern a buffet with a flower arrangement, punchbowls and serving dishes full of sandwiches. The dance extended right into that room, two sets of couples were dancing in it. In the other room stood tables with white cloths which were still empty.

Klaus Heinrich advanced and receded, smiled at strange faces, extended his hand and grasped others, and time and again seized the large white hand of his partner, put his right arm round the soft waist swathed in white organdie, and revolved with her on the spot, while he kept his left hand, which also wore a small white glove, on the small of his back. The dancers laughed and talked while they revolved and advanced. He made mistakes, forgot his figures, confused the others, and stood lost, not knowing which way to turn. 'You must put me right!' he said in the general confusion. 'I'm upsetting everything! Dig me in the ribs!' And the others gradually plucked up courage and set him right; laughingly ordered him from place to place, even touched his hand and shoved him a little when it was necessary.

Especially the handsome girl with the collarbones took it upon herself to shove him.

Spirits rose with every figure. The movements became freer, the exclamations bolder. The dancers began to stamp their feet, and swing their arms backwards and forward, holding each other by the hand. Klaus Heinrich too stamped, tentatively at first, and then more boldly. As for swinging his arms, the handsome girl saw to that when they advanced together. Also every time she danced facing him she made an exaggerated curtsey, which increased the general merriment.

The refreshment room was full of giggles which attracted everybody's envious glances. Someone had escaped from his place in there, and with one leap had grabbed a sandwich from the buffet table which he chewed triumphantly while stamping and swinging, amidst general laughter.

'What cheek!' said the handsome girl. 'They don't stand on ceremony!' But the idea gave her no peace. Before one could say knife she had broken away, had dashed off lightly and nimbly between the lines, had seized a sandwich from the buffet and was back in her place.

Klaus Heinrich was the one who applauded her most heartily. His left hand was a difficulty, but he managed without it, slapping his right hand against his thigh and doubling up with laughter. Then he became quiet and rather pale. He was struggling with himself ... the dance was nearing its end. What he meant to do he must do quickly. They had already got to the Grand Chain. And when it was almost too late he did what he had been struggling with himself to do. He broke away, ran swiftly through the chain of dancers, muttering apologies when he collided with anyone, reached the buffet, grabbed a sandwich, rushed back and slid into his place; and that was not all. He thrust the sandwich – one with egg and anchovy – between the lips of his partner, the girl with the large white hands – she curtseyed a little and took a bite without using her hands, bit off almost the half of it and with his head thrust back he swallowed the other half! The high spirits of their set found vent in the Grand Chain which was just beginning. Throughout the ball-room a crosswise and intricate movement and changing of hands began. It stopped, the movement changed direction, then began once more, amidst chatter and laughter, with mistakes, entanglements and hastily rectified muddles.

Klaus Heinrich pressed the hands he clasped without knowing to whom they belonged. He smiled happily, his smoothly parted hair was ruffled, a strand fell forward across his forehead; his shirt front bulged a little out of his waistcoat, and in his hot eyes was that look of tender emotion which sometimes is the expression of happiness. He repeated several times while he revolved and changed hands: 'What fun! What glorious fun!' He came face to face with his cousins, and to them too he said: 'We've had such fun – our crowd over there!'

Then came the clapping and reunion. The dance was over. Klaus Heinrich once more faced the handsome girl with the collarbones, and when the music changed tune he again put his arm round her slender waist and they danced in the throng.

Klaus Heinrich did not dance well and frequently collided with other couples, because he kept his left hand pressed against his back; but he brought his partner somehow or other to the entrance of the refreshment room where they stopped and had a pineapple cup proffered by the waiter. They sat on two velvet stools close to the entrance and chatted about the Lancers, the Citizens' Ball, and other social functions in which the handsome girl had taken part that winter.

It was then that a gentleman of the suite, Major von Platow, the Grand Duke's aide-de-camp, came up to Klaus Heinrich, bowed and begged leave to announce that Their Royal Highnesses were about to leave. He had been charged ... but Klaus Heinrich gave him to understand so eagerly that he wished to stay on that the aide-de-camp did not like to insist upon his errand. The Prince uttered exclamations of almost outraged regret and was obviously painfully upset at the idea of going home at once. 'We are having such fun!' he said, stood up, and even gripped the Major's arm gently. 'Dear Major von Platow, please intercede for me; talk to His Excellency, do anything you like, but to leave now when are we having such fun – I'm quite sure my cousins are going to stay on.' The Major looked at the handsome girl with the big white hands, and she smiled back

at him; he, too, smiled, and promised to do his best. This little
scene happened while the Grand Duke and the Grand Duchess
were taking leave of the City Councillors at the entrance of the
Bürgergarten. Immediately afterwards dancing was resumed on
the first floor.

The ball was at its height. The official part was over, and in-
formality came into its own. The tables with white cloths in the
adjoining room were occupied by families drinking pineapple
cup and eating supper. The young went to and fro, sat down
restless and out of breath on the edge of chairs, to eat a mouth-
ful and gulp down a drink, and plunge back into the merry
throng. On the ground floor was a medieval 'Bierstube' eagerly
sought out by the older men. The large ballroom and the buffet
room were entirely monopolized by the dancers. The buffet
room was occupied by fifteen to eighteen young people, the sons
and daughters of the City, Klaus Heinrich among them. A sort
of private party went on in there; they danced to the strains of
music floating in from the main ballroom.

Doctor Überbein, the Prince's tutor, was seen there for a
minute or two, having a brief conversation with his pupil. He
was heard, watch in hand, to mention Herr von Knobelsdorff,
and say that he would be downstairs in the *Bierstube* and would
return to fetch the Prince. Then he left. The time was half past
ten.

And while he sat below, conversing with acquaintances
over a tankard of beer for an hour or so, maybe an hour and a
half, not more, those scandalous occurrences took place in the
buffet room, those truly inexplicable excesses to which he eventually put a stop though unfortunately too late.

The punch provided was weak; it contained more soda water
than champagne, and if the young people lost their heads it was
due more to the intoxication of the dance than to alcohol. But in
view of the Prince's character and the solid bourgeois origin of
the rest of the company, that was not enough to explain what
happened. Another and peculiar intoxication acted on both sides.
The strange thing was that Klaus Heinrich was fully aware of
each separate stage of this intoxication, and yet had not the will
power to shake it off.

He was happy. On his cheeks he felt the same warmth he saw burning in the faces of the others, and his gaze, obscured by a gentle confusion, roamed happily, embraced this or that figure and said: 'We!' His lips, too, shaped the syllable, shaped it for the pure joy of repeating it, forming sentences in which 'We' occurred; 'Shall we sit down? Shall we have another turn? Shall we have a drink? Let's make up two sets.' Especially to the girl with the collarbones Klaus Heinrich addressed remarks with 'We' in them. He had quite forgotten his left hand, it hung by his side, he felt so happy that it did not worry him and he never thought of hiding it. Many now saw for the first time what was the matter with it, and looked curiously or with an unconscious grimace at the short, emaciated arm inside the sleeve of his dress suit, at the minute and slightly soiled white glove which covered the hand. But as Klaus Heinrich did not worry about it they plucked up courage, and it so happened that during the round dance someone unconcernedly grasped the malformed hand.

He did not withdraw it. He felt himself borne along, nay, carried away by a current of sympathy, a strong, unbridled sympathy which grew, increased, gathered momentum from itself, possessed itself of him ever more recklessly, took hold of him ever more rudely and insistently, and seemed to lift him triumphantly from the floor. What was happening? It was difficult to define, difficult to pin down. Words floated in the air, brief exclamations, unsaid things, expressed nonetheless with looks and gestures, and in all that was said and done. 'Let him just once ...!' 'Down, down, down with him ...!' 'Get him, get going ...!' A stumpy girl with a snub nose who asked him for a galop when the ladies' choice was announced, suddenly said without apparent reason, just as she was about to take off with him: 'Shucks!'

He saw a kind of lust kindled in every eye, and saw that it was their pleasure to bring him down to their own level, to have him there among themselves. His happy dream of being with them, among them, one of them, was pricked from time to time by a cold piercing feeling that he was deluding himself, that the warm and glorious word 'We' deceived him, that he was not, after all, absorbed in their midst, that he remained the centre and object of their attention but differently now, and in a worse sense than before. They were his enemies so to speak: he saw it in the destructiveness of their gaze. He heard as from a distance, and with hot dismay, how the handsome girl with the large white hands called him simply by his Christian name, and he was well aware that she did so with quite a different inflection from that of Doctor Überbein when he did the same thing. She had the right and the permission to do so, in a certain sense, but was there no one here to shield his dignity, if he did not do so himself? It was as though they tore at his clothes, and sometimes a wild and sneering note crept into their exuberance. A fair and lanky young man with pince-nez, with whom he collided while dancing, said quite loudly so that everyone could hear it: 'Now then, must you?' And there was malice in the way in which the handsome girl whirled him round, for a long while and with bared teeth, until he was ready to drop with giddiness. While they spun round he gazed with swimming eyes at the collarbones near her neck, under the white and rather coarse-grained skin.

They crashed. They had carried it too far and fell headlong as they tried to stop revolving, and on top of them tumbled another couple, not quite by chance, as it was, but pushed by the lanky young man with pince-nez. There was a scrimmage on the floor, and Klaus Heinrich heard above him in the room the chorus which he remembered from the school playground, when he ventured a daring joke in order to amuse his companions: 'Ho, ho, ho!' But here it sounded more malicious, evil.

When shortly after midnight, and unfortunately with some brief delay, Doctor Überbein appeared on the threshold of the buffet room the following sight confronted him: his young pupil sat all alone on a green plush sofa by the left hand wall, his dress-suit disarranged and oddly decorated. The flowers which had adorned the buffet in two Chinese vases were stuck into the opening of his waistcoat, between the studs of his shirt-front, even inside his collar. Round his neck lay the gold chain which belonged to the girl with the collarbones, and on his head the flat metal cover of a punch bowl was balanced like a hat. He murmured: 'What are you doing ... What are you doing?' while the dancers hand-in-hand in a semicircle, with giggles, laughter and cries of 'Ho, ho, ho!' moved back and forth, now to the right and then to the left.

An unnatural flush suffused Doctor Überbein's greenish countenance, especially beneath the eyes. 'Stop! Stop it!' he cried in his resonant voice, and he advanced with long strides into the sudden silence, consternation and dismay, faced the Prince and with two, three gestures removed the flowers, flung away the chain, the dish cover, bowed, and said gravely: 'May I beg Your Grand Ducal Highness ...'

'I've been an ass, an ass!' he repeated when they got outside. Klaus Heinrich left the Citizens' Ball in his company.

This was the painful incident which happened during Klaus Heinrich's year at school. As I have said, no one among the witnesses talked about it – even to the Prince, Doctor Überbein did not mention the event for many years to come – and as no one clothed it in words, it remained incorporeal, and promptly faded away, at least apparently, into oblivion.

The Citizens' Ball had taken place in January. Shrove Tuesday, with the Court Ball and the Big Levee in the Old Castle, which wound up the winter season – annual festivities which Klaus Heinrich did not yet attend – were over. Then came Easter, and with it the close of the school year; Klaus Heinrich's final examination, that edifying formality, in the course of which the question: 'You agree, do you not, Grand Ducal Highness?' constantly recurred on the lips of the examiners, and at which the Prince acquitted himself admirably in his very conspicuous position. It was not a very important juncture in his life; Klaus Heinrich remained in the capital. But after Whitsuntide his eighteenth birthday drew near, and with it a complex of festive ceremonies, which marked a serious turning-point in his life, and which for days on end imposed upon him an exalted and lofty service.

He had attained his majority, had been pronounced to be of age. For the first time again since his baptism, he was the centre of attention and chief actor in a great ceremony, but while he had then quietly, irresponsibly, and patiently resigned himself to the formalities which surrounded and protected him, it was incumbent on him on this day, in the midst of binding prescriptions and stern regulations, hemmed in by the drapery of weighty precedent, to inspire the spectators and to please them by maintaining an attitude of dignity and good-breeding, and at the same time to appear perfectly at ease.

It may be added that I use the word 'drapery' not only as a figure of speech. The Prince wore a crimson robe on this occasion, a faded and theatrical garment, which his father and grandfather before him had worn at their coming-of-age, and which, notwithstanding days of airing, still smelt of camphor. The crimson robe had originally belonged to the robes of the Knights of the Grimmburg Gryphon, but was now nothing more than a ceremonial garb for the use of princes attaining their majority. Albrecht, the Heir Apparent, had never worn the family one. As his birthday fell in the winter, he always spent it in the south, in a place with a warm and dry climate, whither he was thinking of returning this autumn too, and as at the time of his eighteenth birthday his health had not permitted him to travel home, it had been decided to declare him officially of age by proxy, and to dispense with the court ceremony.

As to Klaus Heinrich, there was only one opinion, especially among the representatives of the public: the robe suited him admirably, and he himself, notwithstanding the way in which it hampered his movements, found it a blessing, as it made it easy for him to hide his left hand. Between the canopied bed and the bellying chest of drawers in his bedroom, that was situated on the second floor looking out on the yard with the rosebush, he made himself ready for the show, carefully and precisely, with the help of his valet, Neumann, a quiet and accurate man who had been recently attached to him as keeper of his wardrobe and personal servant.

Neumann was an ex-barber, and was filled, especially in the direction of his original calling, with that passionate conscientiousness, that insatiable knowledge of the ideal, which gives rise to the highest skill. He did not shave like any ordinary barber, he was not content to leave no stubble behind, he shaved in such a way that every shadow of a beard, every recollection of one, was removed, and without hurting the skin he managed to restore to it all its softness and smoothness. He cut Klaus

Heinrich's hair exactly square above the ears, and arranged it with all the assiduity required, in his opinion, by this preparation for the Prince's ceremonial appearance. He managed that the parting should come over the left eye and run slanting back over the crown of the head so that no tufts or wisps should stick up on it; he brushed the hair on the right side up from the forehead into a prim crest on which no hat or helmet could make an impression. Then Klaus Heinrich, with his help, squeezed himself carefully into his uniform of lieutenant in the Grenadier Guards, whose high-braided collar and tight fit favoured a dignified bearing, put on the lemon-coloured silk band and the flat gold chain of the Family Order, and went down to the picture gallery where the members of the family and the foreign relations of the Grand Ducal pair were waiting. The Court was waiting in the adjoining Hall of the Knights, and it was there that Johann Albrecht himself invested his son with the crimson robe.

Herr von Bühl zu Bühl had marshalled a procession, the ceremonial procession from the Hall of the Knights to the Throne-room. It had cost him no little worry. The composition of the Court made it difficult to contrive an impressive arrangement, and Herr von Bühl zu Bühl especially lamented the lack of upper Court officials, which on such occasions made itself most severely felt. The Royal Mews had recently been put under Herr von Bühl, and he felt himself quite up to his various functions, but he asked everybody how he could be expected to make a good impression, when the most important posts were filled simply by the Master of the Royal Hunt, von Stieglitz, and the director of the Grand Ducal Court Theatre, a general with a limp.

While he, in his capacity as Lord Marshal, Chief Master of the Ceremonies, and House Marshal, in his embroidered robes and brown toupee, covered with decorations, his gold pince-nez on his nose, walked behind the cadets with strutting steps and planted his staff in front of him, he pondered mournfully over what came behind him. The cadets, dressed as pages, their hair parted over the left eye, opened the procession ahead of him. A few chamberlains – not many, for some were wanted for the end of the procession – in silk stockings, their plumed hats under their arms and the key on their coat-tails, followed close at his heels. Next came Herr von Stieglitz and His Excellency the limping Director of the Court Theatre in front of Klaus Heinrich who, in his robe and walking between his illustrious parents, followed by his brother and sister, formed the actual nucleus of the procession. Behind their Ducal Highnesses came von Knobelsdorff, the Minister of Home Affairs and President of the Council, with wrinkles radiating from his eyes. A small group of aides-de-camp and palace ladies followed: General Count Schmettern and Major von Platow, a Count Trümmerhauff, cousin of the Keeper of the Privy Purse, as military aide-de-camp of the Heir Apparent, and the Grand Duchess's women led by the short-winded Baroness von Schulenburg-Tressen. Then, attended by the aides-de-camp, chamberlains and ladies-in-waiting, came Princess Katharina with her red-haired children, Prince Lambert with his dainty wife, and the foreign relations or their representatives. More pages ended the procession.

Thus they went at a measured pace from the Hall of the Knights through the Gala Halls, the Hall of the Twelve Months, and the Marble Hall into the Throne-room. Lackeys, with red-gold aiguillettes on their brown coats, dramatically guarded the open double doors in pairs. Through the wide windows the early sun of June streamed in gaily without let or hindrance.

During this solemn march, walking between his parents, Klaus Heinrich took a good look at the elaborate dreariness, the worn pomp of the State Rooms, deprived of the kindness of artificial light. The bright daylight cheerfully and soberly revealed their decay. From the big chandeliers with their chains swathed in silk, stripped of dustcovers in honour of the day, rose dense rows of unlit candles; but crystal drops were missing everywhere, festoons dangled from their crowns, which gave them a decayed and toothless appearance. The silk damask upholstery of the State furniture, which was arranged stiffly and monotonously round the walls, was threadbare, the gilt of the frames chipped off, big blind patches marred the surfaces of the tall candle-decked mirrors, and daylight shone through the moth-holes in the faded and discoloured curtains. The gold and silver borders of the tapestry hangings had come unstuck in several places, and were hanging disconsolately from the walls. Even in the Silver Hall of the Gala Rooms, where the Grand Duke was wont to hold solemn receptions, and in the centre of which stood a mother-of-pearl table with a silver tree trunk for base, a piece of silver stucco had fallen from the ceiling, leaving a gaping patch of white plaster.

But why was it that these rooms somehow seemed to defy the sober, mocking daylight, and proudly dismissed its challenge? Klaus Heinrich looked sideways at his father... The condition of the rooms seemed not to worry him. Never of more than medium height, the Grand Duke had become almost small in the course of years, but he advanced imperiously with his head thrown back, the lemon-coloured ribbon of the Order over his General's uniform, which he had donned today, though he had no military leanings. From under his high and bald forehead and grey eyebrows his bistred blue eyes looked into the distance with an expression of weary pride, and from his pointed white moustache two deep lines carved by age in the yellow skin descended towards his whiskers, imparting to his face a look of contempt. No, the bright daylight could not impair these rooms; the dilapidation not only did not lessen their dignity; in a curious way it intensified it. They confronted the warm and sunny world outside with their lofty discomfort, their stage décor symmetry, their strange and musty play-house or church atmosphere, the severe background of a cult and ritual at which Klaus Heinrich now officiated for the first time.

The cortège passed a pair of lackeys who pressed their lips together and closed their eyes with a relentless expression, and entered the white and gold expanse of the Throne-room. A wave of devotion, of dipping and rising, scraping, bowing and saluting swept through the room as it passed the lines of the assembled guests. They were the diplomats with their wives, the Court nobility and the landed aristocracy, the regimental corps of the capital, the ministers, among whom could be seen the falsely optimistic countenance of the new Minister of Finance, Dr Krippenreuther, the Knights of the Grand Order of the Grimmburg Gryphon, the President of the Diet, dignitaries of all kinds. High up in the little box above the big looking-glass by the entrance door could be descried the press representatives peering over each other's shoulders and busily writing in their notebooks ... In front of the throne baldachin, a symmetrical arrangement of velvet folds, crowned with ostrich feathers, and bordered with gold braid which ought to have been renewed, the procession divided as in a polonaise, and went through the carefully prescribed evolutions.

The pages and chamberlains fell aside to right and left. Herr von Bühl, his face turned to the throne and his staff uplifted, stepped backwards and stood still in the middle of the hall. The Grand Ducal pair and their children walked up the rounded, red-carpeted steps to the capacious gilded chairs which stood at the top. The remaining members of the House, with the foreign princes, ranged themselves on both sides of the throne; behind them stood the suite, the maids-of-honour and the gentlemen in attendance, and the pages occupied the steps. At a gesture from Johann Albrecht, Herr von Knobelsdorff, who had previously taken up his stand over against the throne, advanced briskly in a half circle towards the velvet covered table which stood by the side of the steps, and began at once to read from various documents, initiating the official formalities.

Klaus Heinrich was declared to be of age and fit and entitled to wear the crown, should necessity require it – every eye was turned on him at this place, and on his Royal Highness Prince Albrecht, his elder brother, who stood close to him. The Heir Apparent was wearing the uniform of a captain in the Hussar regiment to which he nominally belonged. Above his silver-braided collar showed an unmilitary width of stiff white collar, and on it rested his delicate, intelligent and sickly head, with its long skull and narrow temples, the straw-coloured down on his upper lip, and the blue, lonely-looking eyes which had seen death. He looked not in the least like a cavalry officer, yet so slender and unapproachably aristocratic that Klaus Heinrich, with his typical cheekbones, seemed almost plebeian beside him. The Heir Apparent pursed up his lips when everybody looked at him, protruded his short rounded underlip, and sucked it lightly against the upper one.

Several of the country's orders were bestowed on the Prince who had just come of age, including the Albrecht Cross and the Grand Order of the Grimmburg Gryphon, not to mention that he was confirmed in the Family Order whose insignia he had possessed since his tenth birthday. Afterwards came the congratulations in the form of a Grand Défilé of the whole Court, led by the fawning Herr von Bühl, and the Gala luncheon in the Marble Hall and the Hall of the Twelve Months followed.

During the next few days the foreign royalty was entertained. A garden party was given in Hollerbrunn, with fireworks and dancing for the young people of the Court in the park. Festive excursions with pages in attendance were made through the sunny countryside to Monbrillant, Jägerpreis, and Haderstein Ruins, and the people, that stocky race with the introspective eyes and high cheekbones, stood by the wayside and cheered themselves and their representatives. In the capital Klaus Heinrich's photographs hung in the windows of the art-dealers, and the *Courier* actually published a printed likeness of him, a popular and strangely idealized representation, showing the Prince in the purple robe. But then came yet another great day – Klaus Heinrich's formal entry into the Army, into the regiment of the Grenadier Guards.

This is what happened. The regiment to which fell the honour of having Klaus Heinrich as one of its officers was drawn up on the Albrechtsplatz in open formation. Plumed helmets bobbed in the centre. The Princes of the House and the generals were all present. The public, a black mass against the gay background, crowded behind the barriers. Cameras were levelled in several places at the scene of the action. The Grand Duchess with the princesses and their ladies, watched the show from the windows of the Old Castle.

First of all, Klaus Heinrich, dressed as a lieutenant, reported himself formally to the Grand Duke. He advanced sternly, without the shadow of a smile, towards his father, clapped his heels together and humbly acquainted him with his presence. The Grand Duke thanked him briefly also without a smile, and then in his turn, followed by his aides-de-camp, advanced in his full dress uniform and plumed helmet into the square. Klaus Heinrich stood before the lowered colours, an embroidered, faded and half tattered piece of gold cloth, and took the oath. The Grand Duke made a speech in abrupt sentences and the sharp voice of command which he reserved for such occasions, in which he called his son 'Your Grand Ducal Highness' and publicly clasped the Prince's hand. The Colonel of the Grenadier Guards, with crimson cheeks, led a cheer for the Grand Duke in which the guests, the regiment, and the public joined. A march past followed, and the parade ended with a military luncheon in the castle.

This picturesque ceremony in the Albrechtsplatz was without practical significance; its effect began and ended there. Klaus Heinrich did not join the garrison but the same day departed to Hollerbrunn with his parents and his brother and sister, to spend the summer in the cool, Franconian rooms by the river, between the towering hedges of the park, and then, for so it was ordained in the prescribed plan of his existence, to go up to the University in the autumn; not that of the capital, but the second one of the country, accompanied by Doctor Überbein, his tutor.

The appointment of this young scholar as mentor was once more attributable to an express, ardent wish of the Prince, and indeed, in selecting a tutor and the older companions whom Klaus Heinrich was to have at his side during this year of student freedom, it was considered necessary to give a reasonable amount of consideration to his expressed wishes. Yet there was much to be said against this choice; it was unpopular, or at least criticized aloud or in whispers in many quarters.

Raoul Überbein was not popular in the capital. Due respect was paid to his life-saving medal and his alarming ambition, but the man was not a genial fellow-citizen, not a good mixer, nor an ideal official. The more charitable saw in him an eccentric with an embittered and unhappy, restless disposition, who observed no Sunday, knew no holiday, no relaxation, and did not know how to unbend among friends after the day's work was done. This illegitimate son of an adventuress, by sheer strength of will, had worked his way up from the bottom, from an obscure and prospectless youth, to being first a primary teacher, then an academic dignitary and University lecturer, and had lived to see his appointment – had 'wangled it' as some people put it – to the Fasanerie as teacher of the Grand Ducal Prince; in spite of which he knew no rest, no contentment, no comfortable enjoyment of his life and leisure. But life, as some bright spark justly pointed out in relation to Doctor Überbein, life did not consist solely of one's professional achievements; it had its purely human claims and duties, to neglect which was a more grievous sin than a certain laxity towards oneself or others in the domain of work, and only that personality could be considered integrated which succeeded in giving its due to each side, to the professional and the human side. Überbein's lack of professional camaraderie inevitably prejudiced people against him. He avoided all social intercourse with his colleagues, and his circle of friends was confined to the person of one man of another scientific sphere, a surgeon and children's specialist with the unpleasant name of Sammet, a very popular surgeon to boot, who shared certain characteristics with Überbein. But it was only very rarely – and then only as a sort of favour – that he turned up at the club where the teachers gathered after the day's toil, for a glass of beer, a game of cards, or a free exchange of views on public and personal questions – but he passed his evenings, and, as his landlady reported, also a great part of the night, working at science in his study, while his complexion grew more livid, and his eyes showed distinct signs of strain. The authorities had felt compelled, shortly after his return from the Fasanerie, to promote him to the post of a senior master. What more was he aiming at? A headmaster's post? A High School professor's chair? Minister of Education? One thing was certain: that his insatiable and restless ambition concealed arrogance and conceit – or rather, failed to conceal it. His manner, his loud and blustering way of speaking annoyed, irritated and exasperated people. His manner towards the members of the teaching profession who were his seniors and in higher positions than himself was not all that could be desired. He treated everybody, from the Principal down to the humblest assistant master, with a paternal condescension, and his habit of talking of himself as of a man who had 'knocked about', of gassing about 'Fate and Duty', and thereby displaying his benevolent contempt for all those who 'weren't obliged to' and 'smoked cigars in the morning', showed conceit pure and simple. His pupils adored him; he achieved remarkable results with them, that was agreed. But on the whole the Doctor had many enemies in the town, more than he ever guessed, and the misgiving that his influence on the Prince might be an undesirable one was even mentioned in a section of the daily press.

Anyhow Überbein obtained leave from the Latin school, and went first of all alone, in the capacity of billeting officer, on a visit to the famous University town, within whose walls Klaus Heinrich was destined to pass his year as a student, and on his return he was received in audience by Excellency von Knobelsdorff, the Minister of the Grand Ducal House, to receive the usual instructions. Their tenor was that almost the most important object of this year was to establish traditions of comradeship on the common ground of academic freedom between the Prince and the student corps, especially in the interests of the dynasty – the regulation phrases, which Herr von Knobelsdorff rattled off almost casually, and which Doctor Überbein listened to with a silent bow, while he drew his mouth, and with it his red beard, a little to one side. Then followed Klaus Heinrich's departure with his mentor, a dog-cart and a servant or two, for the university.

A pleasant year, full of the charm of intellectual freedom, lived under the public eye and in the mirror of publicity, yet without real significance of any sort. Misgivings which had been felt in some quarters lest Doctor Überbein, through misjudging and misunderstanding the position, might worry the Prince unduly with demands in the direction of actual studies, proved unfounded. On the contrary, it was obvious that the doctor quite realized the difference between his own earnest, and his pupil's exalted, sphere of existence. On the other hand (whether it was the mentor's or the Prince's own fault does not matter) the freedom and the unconstrained camaraderie, like the instruction, were interpreted in a very relative and symbolical sense so that neither the one nor the other, neither the knowledge nor the freedom, could be said to be the essence and peculiarity of the year. Its essence and peculiarity were rather, as it appeared, the

year in itself, as the embodiment of custom and impressive cere-
moniousness to which Klaus Heinrich deferred in the mimetic
rites on his last birthday – the only difference being that now he
wore a student's cap, a so-called 'Stürmer', in lieu of the crimson
robe in which he was portrayed on a photograph promptly issued
by the *Courier* to its readers.

As to his studies, his matriculation was not marked by any
particular festivities, though some reference was made to the
honour which Klaus Heinrich's admission bestowed on the university, and the lectures which he attended began with the
address: 'Grand Ducal Highness!' He drove in his dog-cart
with a groom from a pretty villa overgrown with creepers which
the Lord Marshal's office had leased for him in a distinguished
and not too expensive street of the garden city, noticed and
cheered by passers-by, to the lectures, and there he sat with the
consciousness that the whole thing was unessential and unnecessary for his exalted calling, yet with a show of courteous attention. Charming anecdotes circulated and gladdened all hearts:
as to how the Prince showed his interest during the lectures.
Towards the end of a course of natural history (for Klaus
Heinrich attended these courses too, for the sake of general
knowledge), the professor, by way of illustration, had filled a
metal globe with water and had declared that the water, when
frozen, would burst the globe by expansion, and he promised to
show the class the fragments. Now he had not kept his word; at
the following lecture the broken globe was not forthcoming,
probably because he had forgotten. But then Klaus Heinrich had
inquired after the result of the experiment. Just like any ordinary
student he had joined the others who gathered round the professor with questions after the lecture, and had addressed him
simply with 'Has the bomb exploded?' whereupon the professor, at first quite mystified, expressed his thanks with glad surprise and, indeed, emotion, for the kind interest shown him.

Klaus Heinrich became an honorary member of the students'
association – honorary only because he was not allowed to fence
– and now and then, clad in his 'Stürmer' cap, he would join
their ritual drinking bouts. But as his guardians were well aware
that the relaxed and stupefied condition induced by the con-

sumption of alcoholic drinks was not at all compatible with his exalted calling, he was not allowed to take part in the drinking contests, and the students were compelled, here and elsewhere, to bear his dignity in mind. Their own rude customs were reduced to a symbolic approximation; the general tone became exemplary, as it had been in the Selecta; old folk-songs were sung and these sessions were, on the whole, gala and parade nights, refined editions of the usual thing. '*Du*' as a form of address had been agreed upon between Klaus Heinrich and his fellow students as expression and base of a free-and-easy relationship. But the general consensus was that it sounded utterly false and artificial, however great the efforts to make it otherwise, and that one always fell back unconsciously into the form of address which took due notice of his station.

This was the effect of his presence, his friendly and self-contained bearing which remained untouched by any actual involvement, which sometimes produced strange, even comical phenomena in the demeanour of the persons with whom the Prince came into contact. One evening, at a soirée which one of his professors gave, he engaged a guest in conversation – a fat man of some age, a King's Counsel by his title, who, despite his social importance, enjoyed the reputation of a great roué and a regular old sinner. The conversation, the subject of which is a matter of no consequence and indeed would be difficult to specify, lasted for a considerable time because no opportunity of breaking it off presented itself. And suddenly, in the middle of his talk with the Prince, the barrister whistled – whistled with his thick lips one of those pointless sequences of notes which one utters when one is embarrassed and wants to appear at one's ease, and then tried to cover his comic breach of manners by clearing his throat and coughing. Klaus Heinrich was accustomed to experiences of that kind, and tactfully passed on.

If at any time he wanted to make a purchase and went to a shop his entry caused a minor panic. He would ask for what he wanted, a button perhaps, but the salesgirl would not understand him, would look dazed and, unable to fix her attention on the button, but obviously absorbed in something else – something outside and above her duties as a shop-assistant – would drop a few things, turn the boxes upside down in obvious helplessness, and it was all Klaus Heinrich could do to restore her composure by his friendly manner.

Such, as I have said, was the effect of his attitude, and in the city it was often described as arrogance and blameworthy contempt for fellow-creatures – others roundly denied the arrogance, and Doctor Überbein when the subject was broached to him at a social gathering, would put the question, whether 'every inducement to contempt for his fellow-creatures being readily conceded', any such contempt really was possible in a case like the present of complete detachment from all the activities of ordinary men. Indeed, any remark of that kind he met in his unanswerable blustering way by the assertion that the Prince not only did not despise his fellow-creatures but respected them all, even the most worthless among them; respected them so deeply and took them so seriously at their face value and believed in the good in them that a wretched, overestimated and over-taxed ordinary fellow felt quite overcome.

The society of the University town had not time to reach definite verdicts on the question. Before one could turn round the University year was over and Klaus Heinrich departed, and in accordance with the programme set for him, he returned to the capital and his father's residence, where in spite of his arm he was to spend a whole year in military service. He was attached to the Dragoons of the Guard for six months, and directed the taking up of intervals of eight paces for lance-exercises as well as the forming of squares, as though he were a regular soldier; then changed his weapon and transferred to the Grenadier Guards, so as to get an insight into infantry work also. It even fell to him to march to the Castle and command the changing of the Guard – a spectacle which attracted large crowds. He emerged briskly from the guardroom and, with his star on his breast, placed himself with drawn sword on the flank of the company and gave not quite correct orders which, however, did not much matter as the stalwart soldiers executed the right movements just the same. On guest nights, too, at the officers' mess, he sat on the Colonel's right, and by his presence prevented the officers from unbuttoning their uniform collars and gambling after dinner. After this, being now twenty years old, he started on an 'educational tour' - no longer in the company of Doctor Überbein, but in that of a military attendant and courier, Captain von Braunbart-Schellendorf of the Guards, a fair-haired officer who was destined to be Klaus Heinrich's aide-de-camp, and to whom the tour gave an opportunity of establishing himself on a footing of intimacy and influence with him.

Klaus Heinrich did not see much on his educational tour which took him far afield, and was keenly followed by the *Courier*. He visited various foreign Courts, met the sovereigns, attended gala dinners with Captain von Braunbart, and on his departure received one of the country's superior Orders. He took a look at such sights as Captain von Braunbart (who also received several Orders) chose for him, and the *Courier* reported from time to time that the Prince had expressed his admiration of a picture, a museum, or a building to the director or curator who happened to be his cicerone. He travelled apart, protected and supported by the chivalrous precautions of Captain von Braunbart, who kept the purse, and whose devoted zeal was responsible for the fact that at the journey's end Klaus Heinrich would still have been unable to so much as register a trunk.

A couple of words, no more, shall be devoted to an interlude which had for scene a big city of the greater fatherland, and was brought about by Captain von Braunbart with all due circumspection. The Captain had a friend in that city, a member of the aristocracy, captain of a Cavalry regiment and a bachelor, who was on terms of intimacy with a young lady-member of the theatrical world; an accommodating and at the same time trustworthy person. In pursuance of an agreement by letter between Captain von Braunbart and his friend, Klaus Heinrich was introduced to the lady - to wit in her own suitably arranged apartment - and the acquaintance developed *à deux*. Thus an expressly foreseen item in the educational tour was conscientiously realized, without Klaus Heinrich being involved in a more than casual acquaintance. The lady received a memento for her services, and Captain von Braunbart's friend a decoration. So the incident closed.

Klaus Heinrich also visited the fair countries of the south, incognito, under the pseudonym of a romantic-sounding title. There he would sit, alone perhaps for a quarter of an hour or so, dressed in a suit of discreet elegance, among the foreign guests on the white terrace of some restaurant overlooking a dark blue lake, and it might happen that he was observed from the next table, by some òne trying to sum him up and place him socially, as is the way of travellers. Who could he be, that quiet and self-possessed young man? They tried the various spheres of middle-class professional life. Business? The army? A University student? But he didn't fit anywhere, not quite. They sensed his royal station, but nobody guessed it.

FIVE

ALBRECHT II

GRAND Duke Albrecht died of a terrible disease, which has something naked and abstract about it, and to which no other name but just that of death could be given. It seemed as if death, sure of its prey, in this case disdained any mask or gloss, and came on the scene as its very self, as dissolution by and for itself. What actually happened was a decomposition of the blood, caused by internal suppuration; and a radical operation which was conducted by the director of the University Hospital, a famous surgeon, could not arrest the corroding progress of the gangrene. The end soon came, all the sooner that Johann Albrecht made little resistance to the approach of death. He showed signs of an unutterable weariness, and often remarked to his family as well as to the surgeons who attended him that he was 'sick to death of the whole thing' – meaning presumably his princely existence, his whole exalted life in the glare of publicity. The lines on his cheeks, those two deep furrows carved by weariness and pride, deepened in the last few days into an exaggerated, truly grotesque grimace, and remained thus until death smoothed them out.

The Grand Duke's last illness occurred in wintertime. Albrecht, the Heir Apparent, recalled from his warm, dry *séjour* in the south, arrived in snowy, wet weather, which was as bad for his health as could be. His brother Klaus Heinrich interrupted his educational tour, which anyhow was nearly over, and with Captain von Braunbart-Schellendorf hastened home by long stages from the fair countries of the south. Besides the two princes, the Grand Duchess Dorothea, Princesses Katharina and Ditlinde, Prince Lambert – without his dainty wife – the surgeons in attendance and the valet Prahl waited at the bedside, while the Court officials and ministers on duty were collected in the adjoining room. If credence might be given to the assertions of the servants, the ghostly noise in the 'Owl Chamber' had been exceptionally loud in the last weeks and days. According to them it was a rattling and a shaking noise, which recurred periodically, and which could not be heard outside the room.

Johann Albrecht's last act of government was to bestow on the professor who had performed the useless operation with such skill his nomination to the Privy Council. He was dreadfully exhausted, 'sick to death of the whole thing', and his consciousness, even in his more lucid moments, was not at all clear, but he performed the act with scrupulous care and made a ceremony of it. He had himself propped up a little and, shading his eyes with his wax-coloured hands, made a few alterations in the chance disposition of those present, ordered his sons to stand on either side of the canopied bed – and while his mind began to wander and his soul was carried along unknown currents, he composed his features with mechanical skill into a gracious smile for handing the diploma to the Professor, who re-entered the room after a fitting absence.

Quite towards the end, when the dissolution had already attacked the brain, the Grand Duke made one wish clear, which, though scarcely understood, was hastily complied with, although its fulfilment could not do the slightest good to the Grand Duke. Certain words, apparently disconnected, kept recurring in the murmurings of the sick man. He named several clothing materials, silk, satin, and brocade, mentioned Prince Klaus Heinrich, used a technical expression in medicine, and said something about an Order, the Albrecht Cross of the Third Class with Crown. Between whiles one caught quite ordinary remarks, which apparently referred to the dying man's princely calling, and sounded like 'extraordinary obligation' and 'comfortable majority'; then the recital of the names of materials began again, ending with the word 'Sammet' spoken in a louder voice.* At last it was realized that the Grand Duke wanted Doctor Sammet to be called in, the doctor who had happened to be present at the Grimmburg at the time of Klaus Heinrich's birth, twenty years before, and had been practising in the capital for a long time now.

* This is a pun, *Sammet* being the archaic form of *Samt*, velvet. – Translator's note.

The doctor was really a children's doctor, but he was summoned and came: already greying at the temples, with a carelessly drooping moustache surmounted by a nose that was rather too flat at the bottom, clean-shaven otherwise and with cheeks slightly sore from shaving. With his head on one side, his hand on his watch-chain, and elbows close to his sides, he examined the situation, and began at once to busy himself in a practical, gentle way about his exalted patient, whereat the latter expressed his satisfaction in no uncertain fashion. Thus it was that it fell to Doctor Sammet to administer the last injections to the Grand Duke, with his supporting hand to ease his difficult departure, and to be, more than any of the other doctors, his mentor in death – a distinction that did indeed provoke some secret irritation among these gentlemen, but on the other hand resulted in the Doctor's appointment shortly afterwards to the vacancy in the most important post of Director and Chief Surgeon of the Dorothea Children's Hospital, in which capacity he was destined later to play a part in certain developments.

Thus died Johann Albrecht III; he breathed his last on a winter night, and the Old Castle was festively illuminated while he passed away. The stern lines of boredom were smoothed out on his face and, relieved of any exertion on his part, he was subjected to formalities which surrounded him for the last time, carried him along, and made his wax-like shell just once more the focus and object of mimetic rites. Herr von Bühl zu Bühl directed the funeral, which was attended by numerous princely guests, with his usual brisk energy. The gloomy ponderous ceremonies, the lying-in-state, the moving of the body: for eight hours at a stretch Johann Albrecht's body, surrounded by a guard of honour consisting of two colonels, two first lieutenants, two cavalry sergeants, two infantry sergeants, two corporals, and two chamberlains, was exposed to public view. At last the moment arrived when the lead coffin, which had reposed in an altar niche of the Court Church, between candelabra draped with crêpe and man-high candles, was brought into the outer hall by eight lackeys, placed in the mahogany coffin by eight chasseurs, lifted by eight Grenadiers into the mournfully draped hearse drawn by six horses, and with the tolling of bells and booming of cannons started off towards the mausoleum. Drenched by the rain the standards hung heavily from the centre of their poles. Although it was early afternoon the gaslights were burning in the streets where the funeral cortège passed. Johann Albrecht's bust was displayed amongst mourning decorations in the shop-windows, and postcards with the portrait of the deceased ruler, which were everywhere for sale, were in great demand. Behind the rows of troops, the sports clubs and veterans' associations which kept the road open, the people stood on tiptoe in the slush, and with bowed heads looked after the slowly-passing hearse preceded by lackeys carrying wreaths, by Court officials, and by the bearers of the Insignia and the Court Chaplain Dom Wislezenus; the silver embroidered pall was upheld at the four corners by the Lord Marshal von Bühl, Master of the Royal Hunt von Stieglitz, chief aide-de-camp Count Schmettern, and Minister of Home Affairs von Knobelsdorff. By the side of his brother Klaus Heinrich, immediately behind the charger which followed the hearse, and at the head of the other mourners, walked Grand Duke Albrecht II. His uniform, the tall, stiff aigrette on his fur *csáko*, the high patent leather boots visible beneath the bright, pleated hussar's coat with the crêpe band did not suit him. He advanced diffidently under the eyes of the crowd, and his shoulder-blades, slightly uneven by nature, were twisted in an awkward, nervous way as he walked along. Repugnance at having to be the chief actor in this funereal display was written on his pale face. He did not raise his eyes as he walked, and he sucked his short rounded lower lip against the upper . . .

The expression persisted during the ceremonies of succession, which were so arranged as to spare him as much as possible. The Grand Duke signed the oath in the Silver Hall of the Gala Rooms, before the assembled ministers, and, standing in the Throne-room in front of the curved armchair under the baldachin, he read his speech of accession drawn up by Herr von Knobelsdorff. The economic situation in the country was touched upon with grave delicacy, while appreciative mention was made of the perfect accord which despite all troubles existed between the rulers and the country – at which point a prominent official, probably disgruntled over a matter of promotion, was said to have whispered to his neighbour that the accord consisted of the fact that the rulers were as deeply in debt as their people – a caustic remark which circulated widely, and even found its way into the hostile press. In conclusion the President of the Diet called for a cheer for the Grand Duke, a service was held at the Court Church, and that was all. Albrecht also signed an edict by virtue of which a number of fines and prison sentences, chiefly for lesser crimes and the infringement of forest laws, were remitted. The solemn procession through the city and the acclamation in the Town Hall were omitted altogether, as the Grand Duke felt too fatigued. Having so far been a Captain, he was promoted on the occasion of his accession to the Colonelcy *à la suite* of his Hussar regiment, but he hardly ever wore the uniform, and kept his military entourage at arm's length. He made no changes whatsoever in his staff, perhaps out of respect for his father's memory, either among the Court officials or the Ministries.

The public saw him but rarely. His proud and bashful disinclination to show himself, to be on parade, to be acclaimed became evident to a degree which saddened the public. He never appeared in the royal box at the Court Theatre. He took no part in the Corso at the Municipal Gardens. When in residence at the Old Castle he had himself driven in a closed carriage to a remote and deserted part of the enclosure, where he descended to take a little exercise; and during the summer he scarcely left the grounds of Hollerbrunn.

If the people caught sight of him at the Albrecht Gate for instance, as he entered his coupé clad in a thick fur coat which his father had worn before him, his delicate head resting on its bulky collar, the glances levelled at him were timid and the cheers faint and hesitating. For the simple people felt quite clearly that with a Prince like this there could be no question of cheering him and thereby cheering themselves. They looked at him and did not recognize themselves in him; his thoroughbred nobility did not bear the stamp of their homely race. To this they were not accustomed. Was there not a commissionaire posted on the Albrechtsplatz to this day who, with his side-whiskers and high cheekbones, looked a robust and homely replica of the late Grand Duke? And did one not meet with Prince Klaus Heinrich's features in the lower classes? It was not so with his brother. The people could not see him as an idealized version of themselves, whom to cheer would make them happy. His nobility, his indubitable breeding were of a general nature, not of a local kind, and without the stamp of the race. He knew it too; and the consciousness of his royal station together with that of his lack of popular appeal probably accounted for his shyness and his haughtiness. Already at this time he began to delegate his representational duties to Prince Klaus Heinrich. He sent him to unveil the fountain of Immenstadt, and to attend the historical town festival of Butterburg. Indeed, his dislike of any exhibition of his princely person went so far that Herr von Knobelsdorff had the greatest difficulty in persuading him to receive the Presidents of both Chambers in person, and not to delegate this ceremony to his younger brother, as he had intended to do, 'for reasons of health'.

Albrecht II lived a lonely life in the Old Castle; that was un-avoidable under the circumstances. In the first place, since the death of Johann Albrecht, Klaus Heinrich held separate court. Etiquette demanded it, and so he had been allotted the Eremitage, the small Empire castle on the fringe of the northern suburbs which, silent and of a severe grace, but long uninhabited and neglected in the midst of its unkept grounds adjoining the Municipal Gardens, faced the small muddy pond.

Some time ago, when Albrecht came of age, the most urgent repairs had been effected at the Eremitage, and nominally it had been declared the residence of the Heir Apparent; but as Al-brecht had always gone straight from his warm, dry séjour in the south to Hollerbrunn, he had never yet made use of this home.

Klaus Heinrich lived there without excessive luxury, with one major-domo who presided over his household, a Baron von Schulenburg-Tressen, nephew of the Mistress of the Robes. Besides his valet Neumann he had two other footmen for his daily service; the chasseur he required for his daily outings was lent by the Grand Ducal Court. A coachman and a couple of grooms in red waistcoats looked after the carriages and the horses; one pony-cart, a brougham, a dog-cart, two hacks and two carriage horses. One gardener assisted by two youngsters kept the grounds and the garden in good order and one cook with a kitchen maid as well as two chambermaids made up the female staff of the Eremitage. It was the Court Marshal Schulenburg's business to keep his young master's establishment going on the allowance which the Diet, after Albrecht's succession, had voted for the Grand Duke's brother during a serious debate. It amounted to two thousand five hundred pounds. For the sum of four thousand pounds, which had been the original demand, had never had any prospect of recommending itself to the Landtag, and so a wise and magnanimous act of self-denial had been credited to Klaus Heinrich, which had made an excellent impression in the country. Every winter Herr von Schulenburg sold the ice from the pond. He had the hay in the park mowed twice every summer and sold. After the harvests the surface of the fields looked almost like English turf.

As for the Dowager Grand Duchess Dorothea, she no longer lived in the Old Castle, and the reasons for her retirement were both weird and dismal. For she too, the Princess whom the much-travelled Herr von Knobelsdorff had described more than once as one of the most beautiful women he had ever seen, the Princess whose radiant smiles had evoked joy, enthusiasm, and cheers whenever she had shown herself to the longing gaze of the toil-worn masses, she too had had to pay her tribute to time. Dorothea had aged; her calm perfection, the admiration and joy of every-body, had during recent years withered so fast and steadily that the woman in her had been unable to keep pace with the trans-formation. Nothing, no art, no measures, even the painful and repulsive ones, with which she tried to stave off decay, had availed to prevent the sweet brightness of her deep blue eyes from fading, rings of loose yellow skin from forming under them, the wonderful dimples in her cheeks from turning into furrows, and her proud severe lips from looking drawn and haggard. But as her heart had been as cold as her beauty, wrapped up in nothing but her beauty since her beauty had been her soul, and as she had cared for and desired nothing but the effect of her beauty on others, while it never beat faster for anything or anyone, she was now disconsolate and lost, could not accommodate herself to the change and rebelled against it. Surgeon-General Eschrich said something about mental disturbance resulting from an unusually quick climacteric, and his opinion was undoubtedly correct in a sense. The sad truth at any rate was that Dorothea during the last years of her husband's life had already shown signs of profound mental disturbance and trouble.

She began to shun the light, gave orders that during the Thursday concerts all the lights should be dimmed with red shades, and flew into a passion because she could not have the same measure extended to other functions: the Court Ball, the Private Ball, the Gala Dinner and the Grand Levee, because the sunset glow in the Marble Hall had already given rise to a good deal of malicious comment. She spent whole days before her looking-glasses, and it was noticed that she fondled with her hands those which for some reason or other reflected her image in a more favourable light. Then again she had all the looking-glasses removed from her rooms, and those fixed in the wall draped, went to bed and prayed for death.

One day Baroness von Schulenburg found her quite distracted and feverish with weeping in the Hall of the Twelve Months before the big portrait which represented her at the height of her beauty. At the same time a morbid misanthropy began to take possession of her, and the Court and people were distressed to notice how the bearing of this erstwhile goddess began to lose its assurance, her deportment became strangely awkward, and a pitiful look appeared in her eyes.

At last she shut herself up altogether, and, at the last Court Ball he attended, Johann Albrecht had escorted his sister Katharina instead of his 'indisposed' consort. From one point of view his death was a release for Dorothea as it relieved her from all her duties as a sovereign. She chose Segenhaus Castle as her dower-house, an old monastic-looking shooting lodge which lay in a melancholy park, about half an hour's drive from the capital, and had been decorated by some pious old sportsman with religious and sporting emblems curiously intermixed. There she lived, eclipsed and odd, and excursionists could often watch her from afar, walking in the park with Baroness von Schulenburg-Tressen, and bowing graciously to the trees on each side of the path.

Lastly, Princess Ditlinde had married at the age of twenty, one year after her father's death. She bestowed her hand on a prince of a formerly sovereign but now mediatized house, Prince Philipp zu Ried-Hohenried, a small man, no longer young but well preserved, an art collector and a man of advanced views, who had courted her for some considerable time and without an official go-between, and had offered the Princess his heart and hand in a straightforward, bourgeois fashion during a charity function.

It would be wrong to say that this alliance evoked wild enthusiasm in the country. It was received with indifference; it disappointed. It is true, more ambitious hopes had been secretly entertained for Johann Albrecht's daughter, and all the critics could say was that the marriage could not be called a *mésalliance* in so many words. It was a fact that Ditlinde, in giving her hand to the Prince – which she did of her own free will, and quite uninfluenced by others – had undoubtedly descended out of her sphere of Highness into a more free and human atmosphere. Her noble spouse was not only a lover and collector of paintings, but also a businessman and industrialist on a big scale.

The dynasty had ceased to exercise any sovereign right hundreds of years ago, but Philipp was the first of his house to make up his mind to exploit his private means in a natural way. After spending his youth in travelling, he had looked around for a sphere of activity which would keep him busy and contented, and at the same time (a matter of necessity) would increase his income. So he launched out into various enterprises, started farms, a brewery, a sugar factory, and several sawmills on his property, and began to exploit his extensive peat deposits in a methodical way. As he brought expert knowledge and sound business instincts to all his enterprises, they soon began to pay, and returned profits which, if their origin was not very princely, at any rate provided him with the means of leading a princely existence which he would not otherwise have had.

On the other hand the critics might have been asked what sort of a match they could expect for their Princess, if they viewed the matter soberly. Ditlinde, who brought her husband scarcely anything except an inexhaustible store of linen, including dozens of out-of-date and useless articles such as nightcaps and shawls, which however by hallowed tradition formed part of her trousseau – she by this marriage acquired a measure of riches and comfort such as she had never been accustomed to at home : and no sacrifice of her affections was necessary to pay for them. She took the step into private life with obvious contentment and determination, and retained, of the trappings of Highness, nothing but her title. She remained on friendly terms with her ladies-in-waiting, but divested her relations with them of everything which suggested service, and avoided giving her household the character of a Court.

That might evoke surprise, especially in a Grimmburg and in Ditlinde in particular, but there was no doubt that it was her own choice. The couple spent the summer on the princely estates, the winter in the capital in the stately palace in the Albrechtsstrasse which Philipp zu Ried had inherited; and it was here, not in the Old Castle, that the Grand Ducal family – Klaus Heinrich and Ditlinde, occasionally Albrecht as well – met now and again for a confidential talk.

So it happened one day that at the beginning of autumn, not quite two years after the death of Johann Albrecht, the *Courier*, well-informed as usual, published in its evening edition the news that this afternoon His Royal Highness the Grand Duke and His Grand Ducal Highness Prince Klaus Heinrich had been to tea with her Grand Ducal Highness the Princess zu Ried-Hohenried. That was all. But on that afternoon several topics of importance for the future were discussed between the brothers and sister.

Klaus Heinrich left shortly before five o'clock. As the weather was sunny he had ordered the dog-cart, and the open vehicle, varnished in brown and brightly polished though no longer smart or new, came at a trot along the wide gravel avenue leading from the stables, which, with their paved yard, lay in the right wing of the farm buildings, towards the castle. It was a quarter to five. The farm buildings, old-fashioned ochre-yellow houses, formed one long line with the plain white castle (although they lay at some distance from it). The front of the Eremitage, adorned at regular intervals with laurel trees, looked out over the muddy pond and the Municipal Gardens. For the front part of the estate, which joined the Municipal Gardens, was open to pedestrians and light traffic, and all that was fenced off was the gently rising flower garden, at the top of which stood the mansion with its unkept grounds at the back, divided by hedges and fences from the suburban plots beyond, littered with rubbish and débris. So the dog-cart came up the drive between the pond and the home farm, turned in by the tall garden gate adorned with coach lamps that had once been covered with gold leaf, passed up the drive and stopped at the small formal terrace planted with laurel trees which led to the garden-room.

Klaus Heinrich came out a few minutes before five o'clock. As usual he wore the tight-fitting uniform of a Lieutenant of the Grenadier Guards, and his sword-hilt hung on his arm. Neumann, in a lilac livery whose sleeves were too short, ran in front of him down the steps and with his red barber's hands packed his master's folded grey overcoat into the cart. Then, while the coachman, his hand to his cockaded hat, inclined a little sideways on the box, the valet arranged the light carriage rug over Klaus Heinrich's knees and stepped back with a silent bow. The horses started off.

A few pedestrians had gathered outside the garden gates. They hailed Klaus Heinrich, waved their hats with raised eyebrows and broad smiles, and Klaus Heinrich thanked them by touching the peak of his cap with his white-gloved right hand and nodding several times with animation.

The carriage skirted a piece of waste ground along a birch avenue whose leaves were already turning, and then drove through the suburb, between the houses of the poor, over unpaved streets, where ragged children left their hoops and spinning tops for a moment to stare after the carriage with puzzled eyes. A few cheered, and ran for a bit beside the carriage, their heads turned towards Klaus Heinrich. They might have taken the road by the Thermal Gardens, but that through the suburbs was shorter and time pressed. Ditlinde was particular on points of regularity and easily put out if anyone upset her household by being unpunctual.

They passed the Dorothea Children's Hospital directed by Überbein's friend, Dr Sammet. Then the carriage left the suburban neighbourhood and turned into the Gartenstrasse, a stately avenue lined with trees in which stood the houses and villas of rich citizens, whose tramline connected the Thermal Gardens with the centre. The traffic here was fairly heavy, and Klaus Heinrich was kept busy answering the greetings which met him. Civilians took off their hats and looked up at him, officers on horseback and on foot saluted, policemen stood to attention and Klaus Heinrich in the corner of his carriage raised his hand to the peak of his cap and bowed to the right and left with that practised gesture and that smile destined to confirm the people in their sympathy for his exalted person. He had a special way of sitting in the carriage; not leaning back relaxed and comfortable, but anticipating the movements of the badly sprung vehicle as one would on horseback by crossing his hands over his sword hilt and placing one leg slightly forward, as it were, absorbing the unevenness of the ground.

The dog-cart crossed Albrechtsplatz, left the Old Castle with two sentries presenting arms, to the right, followed the Albrechtsstrasse in the direction of the barracks of the Grenadier Guards and turned left, into the courtyard of the Palais Ried. It was a building of moderate proportions in the late Rococo style, with a curved architrave over the main portal, festooned bull's-eye windows in the mezzanine, tall French windows with balconies on the first floor, and a graceful *cour d'honneur* formed by the one-storeyed side wings, and divided from the street by tall, curved gates on whose pillars frolicked stone *amoretti*. But the interior of the mansion, in contrast with the eighteenth-century style of its exterior, was decorated entirely in modern and comfortable bourgeois taste.

Ditlinde received her brother in the large drawing-room on the first floor furnished with several arrangements of curved love-seats covered in pale green silk; its farther end was separated from the front part by slender pillars and filled with potted palms, plants in metal buckets, and flower-stands aglow with a riot of colour.

'Good afternoon, Klaus Heinrich,' said the Princess. She was delicate and slight, and only her ash blonde hair, which used to lie like ram's horns round her ears, was abundant, piled in thick plaits above her heart-shaped face with the Grimmburger cheek-bones. She wore a teagown of soft blue-grey material with a pointed neckline draped with a bertha of white lace, fastened at the belt with an oval pin. In places the delicate skin of her face showed blue veins and shadows, at the temples, the forehead, in the corners of her cool and gentle blue eyes. It had become apparent that she was pregnant.

'Good afternoon, Ditlinde, you and your flowers!' replied Klaus Heinrich as he clicked his heels and bent over her small white hand which was a trifle broad. 'They smell delicious! And in there are more of them, I see.'

'Yes,' she said. 'I love flowers. I have always longed to be able to live among masses of flowers, live, fragrant flowers which I could tend and care for – it was a kind of secret wish of mine, Klaus Heinrich, and I might almost say that I married for the sake of having flowers, for in the Old Castle, as you know, there were no flowers. The Old Castle and flowers! We should have had to rummage a lot to find them, I'm sure. Rat-traps and such things in plenty . . . And really, when one comes to think, the whole thing was like a disused rat-trap, so dusty and horrid . . . ugh . . .'

'But the rosebush, Ditlinde.'

'Yes, my goodness – one rosebush. And the guidebook says that one day those roses will have a lovely natural scent, like any others. But I can hardly believe it.'

'Soon you will have something better to care for than your flowers, little sister,' he said and looked at her, smiling.

'Yes,' she said and blushed rapidly and lightly, 'Yes, Klaus Heinrich, I can hardly believe it. And yet it will be so, if God wills. But come over here. Let's sit down.'

The room, on whose threshold they had been talking, was small in comparison with its height, with a grey-blue carpet and furnished with light pieces of silver-grey lacquered woodwork upholstered in pale blue silk. A chandelier of milk-white china hung from a white stucco motif in the centre of the ceiling, and the walls were adorned with luminous studies of the new school in different sizes; acquisitions of Prince Philipp depicting white goats in the sun, poultry in the sun, sunny meadows and peasants' faces mottled by the sun and shade, blinking in the light. The spindle-legged writing desk by the white-curtained window was loaded with a hundred neatly arranged objects, bibelots, writing materials, and several dainty jotters – for the Princess was accustomed to make careful comprehensive notes about all her duties and plans. In front of the inkstand a house-keeper's book, in which Ditlinde had apparently just been work-ing, lay open and by the table on the wall hung a small engage-ment calendar trimmed with silk ribbon, with, under the printed date, a pencil note: '5 o'clock, my brothers.' Between the love-seat and a semicircle of chairs, over against the white door to the reception room, stood an oval table with a damask cloth and a blue silk runner; on it the flower-patterned teaset, an *épergne* with candied fruit, oblong dishes with biscuits and canapés were neatly arranged, and on a small glass table close by steamed the silver tea-kettle over the spirit flame. Flowers were everywhere, in the vases, on the writing desk, on the tea table, on the glass table, on the china cabinet, on the table next to the white sofa, and a flower-stand filled with potted plants stood in front of the window.

This room, situated apart and at a right angle to the suite of formal reception rooms, was Ditlinde's sitting-room, her *boudoir*, the room in which she held small afternoon receptions and made tea with her own hands. Klaus Heinrich watched her as she warmed the pot with boiling water and filled it with tea, using a small silver spoon.

'And Albrecht ... is he coming?' he asked with an involun-tarily restrained voice.

'I hope so,' she said, bending attentively over the crystal tea-caddy, as if to avoid spilling any tea (and he too avoided looking at her). 'I have of course asked him, Klaus Heinrich, but you know that he cannot commit himself. It depends on his health whether he comes. I'm making our tea at once, for Albrecht will drink his milk. By the way, Jettchen may look in for a moment today. You will enjoy seeing her again. She's so lively, and has always got such a lot to tell us.'

'Jettchen' meant Fräulein von Isenschnibbe, the Princess's friend and confidante. They had been *per Du* since they were children.

'In armour, too, as usual?' said Ditlinde, placing the filled teapot on its stand and examining her brother. 'In uniform as usual, Klaus Heinrich?'

He stood with his heels together and rubbed his left hand, which suffered from the cold, against his right hand in front of his breast.

'Yes, Ditlinde, I like it. I really prefer it. It fits tightly, you know, one feels dressed. Besides, it's cheaper, for a proper civilian wardrobe costs an awful lot of money, I believe, and as it is, Schulenburg's forever grumbling about how expensive everything is. This way I manage with two or three uniform jackets, and yet can show myself in my rich relation's home.'

'Rich relations!' laughed Ditlinde. 'That's a long way off, Klaus Heinrich!'

They sat down at the tea-table, Ditlinde on a sofa, Klaus Heinrich on a chair opposite the window.

'Rich relations!' she repeated, and the subject obviously pleased her. 'No, far from it; how can we expect to be rich when the capital is small and entirely tied up in various enterprises? And these are young and still expanding, are still at a growing stage, as my dear Philipp says, and won't bear fruit till our children have succeeded us. But things are improving, that much is true, and I keep the household straight...'

'Yes, Ditlinde, you do keep it straight and no mistake!'

'I do, and note down everything and supervise the servants, and with all the expenditure one owes to one's position we are still saving quite a bit each year for our children. And my dear Philipp ... he sends his greetings, Klaus Heinrich – I forgot, he's very sorry not to be able to be here today... We've only just got back from Hohenried, and there he is on his way again, at his office, on his estates – small and delicate though he is by nature, when it's a question of his peat and his sawmills he becomes animated, and he says himself that he has become much stronger since he has had so much work to do.'

'Does he say that?' asked Klaus Heinrich, and his eyes clouded over as he looked straight across the flower-stand at the bright window. 'Yes, I can quite imagine that it must be stimulating to have a real job of work to do. In my grounds too the meadows have been mowed for the second time this year, and I like to watch how the hay is stacked round poles so that it looks like a camp of small Red Indian huts, and Schulenburg intends to sell it. But of course it cannot be compared to . . .'

'Oh, but you!' said Ditlinde, and pressed her chin against her breastbone. 'With you things are different. The next in line of succession! You are destined for other things, I should think. My goodness yes. You ought to enjoy your popularity with the people.'

They remained silent for a while.

'And you, Ditlinde,' he resumed, 'if I am not mistaken you are happy, happier than you were before. I won't say that you are radiant, like Philipp over his peat; and you have always been delicate and still are. But you look well, don't you? I've never asked you since you were married, but I believe I needn't worry about you.'

She sat relaxed, her hands folded beneath her breasts.

'Yes,' she said, 'I'm all right, Klaus Heinrich, your eyes don't deceive you, and it would be ungrateful of me not to acknowledge my good fortune. You see, I know quite well that many people in the country are disappointed by my marriage, and say that I have ruined myself, and demeaned myself, and so on. And such people are not far to seek, for brother Albrecht, as you know as well as I do, in his heart despises my dear Philipp and me into the bargain, and can't abide him, and calls him privately a merchant and a philistine. But that doesn't bother me for I meant it when I accepted Philipp's hand – seized it, I would say if it didn't sound so wild – accepted it because it was warm and honest, and offered to take me away from the Old Castle. For when I look back and think of the Old Castle and life in it as I should have gone on living if it had not been for dear Philipp, I shudder,

Klaus Heinrich, and I feel that I could not have borne it and should have become strange and queer like poor mamma. I am a bit delicate naturally, as you know, I should have simply gone to pieces amidst so much desolation and sadness, and when dear Philipp came, I thought: now's your chance. And when people say that I am a bad Princess, because I have in a way abdicated, and fled here where it is rather warmer and more friendly, and when they say that I lack dignity and consciousness of my station, or whatever they call it, they are stupid and ignorant, Klaus Heinrich, because I have too much, I have on the contrary too much of it, that's a fact, otherwise the Old Castle would not have had such an effect upon me, and Albrecht ought to see that, for he too, in his way, has too much of it – all we Grimmburgs have too much of it, and that's why it sometimes looks as if we had too little of it. And sometimes, when Philipp is away, as he is now, and I sit here among my flowers and Philipp's pictures with all their sun – it's lucky that it's painted sun, for bless me! otherwise we should have to get sun-blinds – and everything is tidy and clean, and I think of the blessing, as you call it, in store for me, then I seem to myself like the little mermaid in the fairy-tale which the Swiss governess read to us, if you remember, who married a mortal and was given legs instead of her fish's tail . . . I don't know if you understand me. . .'

'Oh yes, Ditlinde, of course, I understand you perfectly. And I am really glad that everything has turned out so well and happily for you. For it is dangerous, I may tell you in my experience, it is difficult to be happy in an appropriate manner. It's so easy to go wrong and be misunderstood, for nobody will really protect our dignity for us if we don't do it ourselves, and then everything so easily deteriorates into a scandal. But which is the right way? You have found it. The papers have recently married me off to cousin Griseldis. That was a shot in the dark, as they call it, and they seem to think that it's time for me to marry. But Griseldis is a stupid girl, half dead with anaemia, and as far as I know all she ever says is "yeah". I've never given her a thought, nor has Knobelsdorff, thank goodness. The news was at once announced to be unfounded. . . Here comes Albrecht!' he said, and stood up.

A cough sounded outside. A footman in olive-green livery threw open the swing doors with a quick, firm, and noiseless movement of both arms, and announced in a subdued voice: 'His Royal Highness the Grand Duke.' Then he stepped aside with a bow. Albrecht advanced through the room.

He had covered the hundred yards from the Old Castle in a closed brougham, with a chasseur on the box. He was in mufti, as usual, and wore a buttoned-up frock-coat with small satin lapels and patent leather boots on his narrow feet. Since his accession he had grown a pointed beard. His short fair hair receded from his delicate concave temples. His gait was an awkward and at the same time inimitably well-bred strut which made his shoulder-blades twist in an inhibited manner. He carried his head well back and stuck his short round under-lip out, sucking gently with it against the upper one.

The Princess advanced towards the door to meet him. As he shunned the gesture of hand-kissing, he simply held out his hand with a low, almost whispered greeting – his thin, cold, strangely sensitive hand, which he stretched out from his breast while keeping his arm close to his side. Then he greeted his brother Klaus Heinrich, who had been waiting in front of his chair with his heels together, in the same way – and lapsed into silence.

Ditlinde talked. 'It's very nice of you to come, Albrecht. So you're feeling well? You look splendid! Philipp wishes me to tell you how sorry he is to have to be out this afternoon. Sit down, won't you, anywhere you like – here for instance, opposite me. That chair's pretty comfortable, you sat in it last time. I've made tea for us in the meantime: you'll have your milk directly...'

'Thanks,' he said quietly. 'I must beg pardon ... I'm late. You know, the shorter road . . And then I have to lie down in the afternoon ... There's no one else coming?'

'No one else, Albrecht. At the most, Jettchen Isenschnibbe may look in for a bit, if you don't mind ...'

'Oh?'

'But I can easily give instructions to say that I'm out.'

'Oh, please don't.'

Hot milk was served. Albrecht clutched the tall, thick, buckled glass with both hands.

'Ah, a little warmth,' he said. 'How cold it is already in these parts! And I have been cold all through the summer at Hollerbrunn. Haven't you started fires yet? I have. But then again the smell of the stoves upsets me. All stoves smell. Von Bühl promises me central heating for the Old Castle every autumn. But it seems not to be feasible.'

'Poor Albrecht,' said Ditlinde, 'at this time of year you used to be already in the south, so long as father was alive. You must long for it.'

'Your sympathy does you credit, dear Ditlinde,' he replied, still in a low and slightly lisping voice. 'But we must show that I am on the spot. I must rule the country, as you know, that's what I'm here for. Today I have been graciously pleased to allow some worthy citizen – I'm sorry I cannot remember his name – to accept and wear a foreign order. Further, I have had a telegram sent to the annual meeting of the Horticultural Society, in which I assumed the honorary Presidency of the Society, and pledged my word to further its efforts in every way – without really knowing what furthering I could do beyond sending the telegram, for the members are quite well able to take care of themselves. Further, I have deigned to confirm the choice of a certain worthy fellow to be mayor of my fair city of Siebenberge – in connection with which I should like to know whether my subject will be a better mayor for my confirmation than he would have been without it . . .'

'Well, well, Albrecht, those are trifles,' said Ditlinde. 'I'm convinced that you've had more serious business to do . . .'

'Oh, of course. I've had a talk with my Minister of Finance and Agriculture. It was time I did. Doctor Krippenreuther would have been bitterly disappointed with me if I had not received him once again. He went ahead in summary and lectured me on several topics, on the harvest, on the new principles for drawing up the budget, and on the tax reform on which he is working. The harvest is alleged to have been bad. The peasants have been hit by blight and poor weather; not only they, but Krippenreuther too is much concerned about it, because the tax-paying capacity of the country has been affected again. Besides, there have unfortunately been disasters in more than one of the silver mines. The mines are at a standstill, they make no profits and it will cost a lot of money to get them going again. I listened to all this with an appropriate expression, and did all I could by voicing my regret over such a series of misfortunes. Next I listened to an argument as to whether the cost of the necessary new buildings for the Treasury and for the Woods and Customs and Inland Revenue Offices ought to be debited to the ordinary or extraordinary estimates; I learnt a lot about sliding scales, and income tax, the pedlars' tax, the removal of the burden from the ailing agriculture and the imposition of burdens on the towns; and on the whole I got the impression that Krippenreuther was well up on his subject. I, of course, know practically nothing about it – which Krippenreuther knows and approves; so I just said "yes, yes" and "of course" and "many thanks" and let him run on.'

'You do sound bitter, Albrecht.'

'No, I'll just tell you what struck me while Krippenreuther was holding forth to me today. There's a man living in this town, a man with small private means and a wart on his nose. Every child knows him and shouts "Hi" when they see him; he is called "Dotty Gottlieb", for he is not quite all there; his surname he has lost long ago. He is always on the spot when there is anything going on, although his half-wittedness keeps him from playing any serious part in anything; he wears a rose in his buttonhole, and carries his hat about on the end of his walking-stick. Twice a day, about the time when a train starts, he goes to the station, taps the wheels, examines the luggage, and fusses. Then, when the guard blows his whistle, "Dotty Gottlieb" waves to the engine-driver, and the train starts. But "Dotty Gottlieb" deludes himself into thinking that this waving sends the train off. That's like me. I wave, and the train starts off. But it would start off without me just the same, and my waving makes no difference, it's a farce. I'm sick of it.'

The three of them sat silent. Ditlinde sadly bowed her head, and Klaus Heinrich, tugging at his small, bow-shaped moustache, gazed between her and the Grand Duke at the bright window.

'I can follow you quite well, Albrecht,' he said after a moment, 'although it's hard on you and on us to be compared to "Dotty Gottlieb". You see, I too understand nothing about sliding scales and the pedlars' tax and peat cutting, and there is a lot more about which I know nothing – all one imagines when one says "the misery of the world" – hunger and want, you know, and the struggle for existence, as it is called, and war, and the horrors of the public ward and all that. I have seen and experienced none of these, save death, when papa died, and that was hardly death as it might be, rather it was edifying, and the whole Castle was illuminated. Sometimes I'm ashamed because I have never been tried by circumstances. But then I say to myself that mine is not a comfortable life either, not comfortable at all, although I move on lonely peaks above the masses of humanity as the people express it, or perhaps just because I do, and I perhaps after my fashion know more of the bleakness of existence, of life's stern countenance, if you will permit me that expression, than many a one who is an expert on sliding scales or any other single department of life. And that's what counts, Albrecht, that one's life should not be easy – that is what matters, if I may say so to you, and is one's justification. And if the people cheer when they see me they ought, after all, to know why they do it, and my life must have some sort of a meaning, as you have so admirably shown. And yours even more. You wave to order, because the people wish you to wave, and if you do not really control their wishes and aspirations, yet you express them and represent them and give them substance, and may be that's no slight matter.'

Albrecht sat upright at the table. He held his thin, strangely sensitive-looking hands crossed on the table-edge in front of the tall, half-empty glass of milk, and his eyelids dropped, and he sucked his underlip against his upper. He answered quietly: 'I'm not surprised that so popular a prince as you should be contented with this lot. I for my part decline to express and represent somebody else in my own person – I decline, I say, and you are free to think that it is a case of sour grapes. The truth is that I care for the cheers of the people just about as little as any living soul could care. When I say "I", I don't mean my body. The flesh is weak – there is something in one which expands at applause and contracts at cold silence. But my reason rises superior to all considerations of popularity or unpopularity. I know what popularity would mean if it came my way. A misconception of my personality. Knowing this, one can only shrug one's shoulders at the thought of cheers from strangers. Another – you for instance – may derive the consciousness of a lofty calling from the support of the people. You must forgive me for being too logical to indulge in any such mysterious sensation of happiness – and too keen on cleanliness also, if you will allow me to put it thus. That kind of happiness stinks, to my way of thinking. Anyhow, I'm a stranger to the people, I give them nothing – what can they give me? With you, well, that's quite different. Hundreds and thousands who look like you, are grateful for being able to recognize themselves in you. You may well laugh, if you choose to. The danger for you consists at best in getting too readily submerged in your popularity and ending up by accepting the comfort which you reject today.'

'No Albrecht, I don't think so. I don't think I run any such danger.'

'Then we shall understand each other all the better. I have no penchant for strong expressions as a rule. But popularity is a hellish bore.'

'It's funny, Albrecht. Funny that you should use that expression. The "pheasants" were always using it, my schoolfellows, the boys, you know, at the Fasanerie. I know now what you are. You are an inveterate aristocrat, that's the thing.'

'Do you think so? You're wrong. I'm no aristocrat, I'm the opposite by taste and reason. You must concede that I don't scorn the cheers of the crowd from arrogance, but from a propensity to humanity and kindness. The social exaltation of the individual is a pitiable thing, and it seems to me that mankind ought to understand that people should behave humanely and kindly towards each other, and not cause each other humiliation and shame. A man must have a thick skin to be able to carry off all the flummery of being a Royal Highness without a feeling of shame. I'm a bit sensitive by nature, I don't feel up to the absurdity of the situation. Every lackey who plants himself at the door and expects me to pass him without noticing, without heeding him more than the door post, fills me with embarrassment, that's the way I feel towards the people. . .'

'Yes, Albrecht, quite true. It's often by no means easy to keep one's countenance when one passes by a fellow like that. The lackeys! As if one didn't know what scoundrels they are! Fine stories one hears about them.'

'What stories?'

'Oh, one keeps one's ears open. . .'

'Come, come!' said Ditlinde. 'Don't let's worry about that. You are talking generalities, and I had two topics noted down which I thought we might discuss this afternoon. . . Would you be so kind, Klaus Heinrich, as to reach me that notebook there in blue leather on the writing table? Many thanks. I note down in this everything I have to remember, both household matters and other things. What a blessing it is to be able to see everything down in black and white! My head is terribly weak, it can't remember things, and if I weren't tidy and didn't jot everything down, I should be done for. First of all, Albrecht, before I forget it, I wanted to remind you that you must escort Aunt Katharina at the first Court on November 1st – you can't get out of it. I withdraw; the honour fell to me at the last Court Ball, and Aunt Katharina was terribly put out. . . Do you consent? Good, then I cross out item 1. Secondly, Klaus Heinrich, I wanted to ask you to make an *acte de prèsence* at the Orphan Children's Bazaar on the 15th in the Town Hall. I am patroness, and I take my duties seriously, as you see. You needn't buy anything – a pocket comb . . . In short, all you need to do is to show yourself for ten minutes. It's for the orphans . . . Will you come? You see, now I can cross another off. Thirdly . . .'

But the Princess was interrupted. Fräulein von Isenschnibbe, the lady-in-waiting, was announced and tripped briskly across the big drawing-room, her feather stole waving in the draught, and the brim of her huge feather hat flapping up and down. The smell of the fresh air outside seemed to cling to her clothes. She was small, ash blonde, with a pointed nose, and so short-sighted that she could not see the stars. On clear evenings she would stand on her balcony and gaze at the starry heavens through opera-glasses, and rave about them. She wore two pince-nez with strong lenses one on top of the other, and as she curtseyed she advanced her head and screwed up her eyes.

'Heavens, Grand Ducal Highness,' she said, 'I didn't know:

I'm disturbing you, I'm intruding. I most humbly beg pardon!'

The brothers had risen, and the visitor, as she curtseyed to them, was filled with confusion. As Albrecht extended his hand from his chest, keeping his forearm close to his body, her arm was stretched out almost perpendicularly, when the curtsey which she made him had reached its lowest point.

'Dear Jettchen,' said Ditlinde, 'what nonsense! You are expected and welcome, and my brothers know that we call each other by our Christian names, so none of that Grand Ducal Highness, if you please. We are not in the Old Castle. Sit down and make yourself comfortable. Will you have some tea? It's still hot, and here are some candied fruits, I know you like them.'

'Yes, a thousand thanks, Ditlinde, I adore them!' and Fräulein von Isenschnibbe took a chair on the narrow side of the tea-table opposite Klaus Heinrich with her back to the window, drew a glove off and began peering forward, to lay sweetmeats on her plate with the silver tongs. Her bosom heaved quickly and nervously with pleasurable excitement.

'I've got some news,' she said, unable to contain herself any longer. 'News ... More than my reticule will hold! That is to say it is really only one piece of news, only one – but it's so weighty that it counts for dozens, and it is quite certain. I have it on the best authority – you know that I am reliable, Ditlinde; this very evening it will be in the *Courier* and tomorrow the whole town will be talking about it.'

'Yes, Jettchen,' said the Princess, 'it must be confessed you never come with empty hands; but now we're all agog, do tell us your news.'

'Very well. Let me get my breath. Do you know, Ditlinde, does your Royal Highness know, does your Grand Ducal Highness know who's coming, who is arriving at the Thermal Station, who will stay at the Spa Hotel for six or eight weeks, to take the cure?'

'No,' said Ditlinde, 'but do you know, dear Jettchen?'

'*Spoelmann*,' said Fräulein Isenschnibbe. '*Spoelmann*,' she repeated, leant back, and made as if to drum with her fingers on the table's edge, but checked the movement of her hand just above the blue silk runner.

The brothers and sister looked doubtfully at each other.

'Spoelmann?' asked Ditlinde . . . 'Think a moment, Jettchen, the real Spoelmann?'

'The real one!' Her voice broke with suppressed triumph. 'The real one, Ditlinde! For there's only one, or rather only one whom everybody knows, and he it is whom they are expecting at the Spa Hotel – the great Spoelmann, the giant Spoelmann, the colossus Samuel N. Spoelmann from America!'

'But my dear, what's bringing him here?'

'Really, forgive me for saying so, Ditlinde, but what a question! His yacht or some big steamer is bringing him over the sea of course, he's on his holidays making a tour of Europe and has expressed his intention of drinking the spa waters.'

'But is he ill, then?'

'Of course, Ditlinde; all people of his kind are ill, that's part of the business.'

'How peculiar,' said Klaus Heinrich.

'Yes, Grand Ducal Highness, it is remarkable. His kind of existence must bring that with it. For there's no doubt it's a trying existence, and not at all a comfortable one, and must wear the body out quicker than an ordinary man's life would. Most of them have stomach trouble, but Spoelmann suffers from the stone, as everybody knows.'

'Stone, does he?'

'Of course, Ditlinde, you must have heard it and forgotten it. He has kidney stones, if you will forgive me the horrid expression – a serious, agonizing illness, and I'm sure he can't get the slightest pleasure from his frantic wealth.'

'But how on earth has he chanced upon our waters?'

'Why, Ditlinde, that's simple. The waters are good, they're excellent; especially the Ditlinde spring, with its lithium or whatever they call it, is admirable against gout and stone, and only waiting to be properly publicized and recognized throughout the world. But a man like Spoelmann, as you may imagine, a man like him is not taken in by labels and advertisements, and follows his own judgement. And so he has discovered our waters – or his physician has recommended them to him, it may be that, and bought it in the bottle, and it has done him good, and now he may think that it must do him still more good if he drinks it on the spot.'

They all kept silence.

'Goodness gracious, Albrecht,' said Ditlinde at last, 'whatever one may think of Spoelmann and his sort – and I reserve my judgement, of that you may rest assured – but don't you think that the man's visit to the Spa may be very useful?'

The Grand Duke turned his head with a formal and fastidious smile.

'Let's ask Fräulein von Isenschnibbe,' he replied. 'No doubt she has already considered the question from this point of view.'

'If your Royal Highness asks me ... enormously useful! Immeasurably, incalculably useful – that's obvious! The directors are in the seventh heaven, they're getting ready to decorate and illuminate the Spa Hotel! What a recommendation, what an attraction for strangers! Will your Royal Highness just consider – the man is a curiosity! Your Grand Ducal Highness spoke just now of "his kind" – but there are none of "his kind" – at most, only a couple. He's a Leviathan, a Croesus! People will come from miles away to see a being who has about a half a million a day to spend!'

'Gracious!' said Ditlinde, taken aback. 'And there's dear Philipp worrying about his peat beds.'

'The whole thing begins with two Americans hanging about the promenade arcades out there for the last two days. Who are they? It transpires that they are journalists, the special correspondents of two big New York papers. They have preceded Mr Leviathan, and at the moment are cabling home news of our scenery. Once he's here they will report his every move – just as the *Courier* and the *Advertiser* report about Your Royal Highness.'

Albrecht acknowledged this with a bow, his eyes lowered and his lower lip protruding.

'He has reserved the Grand Ducal Suite at the Spa Hotel, for the time being,' said Jettchen.

'For himself alone?' asked Ditlinde.

'Oh no, Ditlinde, do you suppose he'd be coming alone? There isn't any precise information about his suite and staff, but it's quite certain that his daughter and his physician-in-ordinary are coming with him.'

'You talk of a "physician-in-ordinary", Jettchen, it annoys me. And then these journalists. And the Grand Ducal Suite. He's not a king, after all.'

'A railway king, as far as I know,' remarked Albrecht gently, with downcast eyes.

'Not only a railway king, according to what I hear. In America, it appears they have those large business concerns called Trusts, as your Royal Highness knows – the Steel Trust for instance, the Sugar Trust, the Petroleum Trust, the Coal, Meat, and Tobacco Trusts, and goodness knows how many more, and Samuel N. Spoelmann has a finger in nearly all these trusts, and is chief shareholder in them, and managing director – that's what I believe they call them – so his business must be what is called over here a "Mixed Goods Concern".'

'A nice sort of business,' said Ditlinde, 'it must be a nice sort of business! For you can't persuade me, dear Jettchen, that honest work can turn a man into a Leviathan and a Croesus. I am convinced that his riches are steeped in the blood of widows and orphans. What do you think, Albrecht?'

'I hope so, Ditlinde, I hope so, for your own and your husband's comfort.'

'If that is so,' explained Jettchen, 'Spoelmann – our Samuel Spoelmann – can hardly be blamed, for he is nothing but an heir, and may easily not have had any particular taste for the business. The one who made the money was his father – I've read all about it and may say that I know the general facts. His father was a German, a nobody, an adventurer who emigrated and became a gold prospector. And he was lucky and made a small fortune with his gold-digging – quite a large fortune in fact – and began to speculate, in oil and steel and railways, and then all sorts of things, and kept becoming more and more rich, and then he died and everything was already in full swing, and his son Samuel, who inherited the Croesus' firm, really had nothing to do but collect the princely dividends and kept growing richer and richer till he beat all records. That's the way things have gone.'

'And he has a daughter, has he, Jettchen? What's she like?'

'Yes, Ditlinde, his wife is dead, but he has a daughter, Miss Spoelmann, and he's bringing her with him. She's a strange girl, from all I've read about her. He himself is a bit of a mixture, for his father married a woman from the South, a Creole, the daughter of a German father and a native mother. But Samuel in turn married a German-American who was half English, and Miss Spoelmann is their daughter.'

'Gracious, Jettchen, she's a colourful creature!'

'You may well say so, Ditlinde, and she's clever, so I've heard; she studies like a man, algebra, and highbrow subjects of the sort.'

'Hm, that doesn't especially endear her to me.'

'But now listen to this, Ditlinde; Miss Spoelmann has a chaperone, and that chaperone is a Countess, a real Countess who keeps her company.'

'Really,' said Ditlinde, 'she ought to be ashamed of herself. No, Jettchen, my mind is made up. I am not going to bother about Spoelmann. I'm going to let him drink his waters in peace and depart, he and his Countess and his algebraical daughter, and I'm not going to so much as turn my head to look at him. He and his doubtful riches don't impress me. What do you think, Klaus Heinrich?'

Klaus Heinrich looked past Jettchen's head at the bright windows.

'Impress?' he said. 'No, wealth doesn't impress me, I think, I mean wealth in the ordinary sense. But it seems to me that it depends; it depends, I believe, on one's standards. We have one or two rich people too in the town here. Soap manufacturer Unschlitt is estimated at a million. I often see him in his carriage. He's awfuly fat and common. But when a man is sick and lonely from sheer wealth ... I don't know.'

'An uncomfortable sort of man anyhow,' said Ditlinde, and the subject of the Spoelmanns gradually dropped. The conversation turned on family matters, the 'Hohenried' property, and the approaching season. Shortly before seven o'clock the Grand Duke sent for his carriage. Prince Klaus Heinrich was going too, so they all got up and said good-bye. But while the brothers were being helped into their coats in the hall, Albrecht said: 'I should be obliged, Klaus Heinrich, if you would send your coachman home and would give me the pleasure of your company for a quarter of an hour longer. I've got a matter of some importance to discuss with you – I might come with you to the Eremitage, but I can't bear the evening air.'

Klaus Heinrich clicked his heels together as he answered:

'No, Albrecht, you mustn't dream of it! I'll drive to the Castle with you if you like. Of course, I am at your disposal.'

This was the prelude to a memorable conversation between the young Princes, the result of which was published a few days later in the *Advertiser* and received with general approval.

The Prince accompanied the Grand Duke to the Castle, through the Albrecht Gate, up stone stairs with wide railings, through corridors where naked gas lamps were burning and silent ante-rooms, past the lackeys into Albrecht's private cabinet, where the aged Prahl had lit two bronze spirit lamps on the mantelpiece. Albrecht had taken over his father's study; it had always been the study of the reigning sovereign, and lay on the first floor between the aide-de-camp's room and the dining-room in daily use facing the Albrechtsplatz, which all the reigning princes had overlooked and watched from their writing table. It was an exceptionally unhomely and disharmonious room, small, with cracked murals on the ceiling, walls covered in red silk with a gilt frame, and three french windows through which the draught blew keenly, and which at the moment were hidden by claret coloured fringed curtains. It had an imitation French Empire mantelpiece, with a semicircle of small quilted modern plush chairs grouped in front of it, and a hideously ugly white stove of ornate tiles which gave out considerable heat. Two big quilted sofas stood opposite each other by the walls, and in front of one stood a square book-table with a red plush cover. Between the windows two narrow gold-framed mirrors with marble ledges reached up to the ceiling, the right hand one of which bore a rather salacious alabaster group, the left a decanter with water and some medicine bottles. The writing desk, an antique piece made of palisander wood with a rolltop and brass fittings, stood in the centre of the room, on a red carpet. From a pedestal in one corner a marble bust stared with dead eyes at the room.

'What I have to suggest to you,' said Albrecht – he was standing at the writing table, unconsciously toying with a paper knife, a silly object shaped like a cavalry sabre, 'is directly related to our conversation this afternoon. I may begin by saying that I discussed the matter thoroughly with Knobelsdorff this summer at Hollerbrunn. He agrees, and if you do too, as I don't doubt you will, I can carry out my intention at once.'

'Please let's hear it, Albrecht,' said Klaus Heinrich, who was standing to attention in a military attitude by the sofa table.

'My health,' the Grand Duke went on, 'has lately been going from bad to worse.'

'I'm very sorry, Albrecht – Hollerbrunn didn't agree with you, then?'

'Thank you. No, it didn't. I'm in a poor way, and my health is showing itself increasingly unequal to the demands made upon it. When I say "demands" I mean chiefly the duties of a ceremonial and representative nature which are inseparable from my position, and this is where our conversation with Ditlinde comes in. The performance of these duties may be a source of happiness where there is some contact with the people, some bond, a common heartbeat. To me it is torture, and the falseness of my role exhausts me to such an extent that I must think of taking precautionary measures. In this, as far as my health is concerned, I am in agreement with my doctors who entirely support my proposal, so listen to me. I'm unmarried. I have no intention, I can assure you, of ever getting married. I shall have no children. You are heir to the throne by the right of birth, you are still more so in the consciousness of the people, who love you ...'

'Oh, Albrecht, you are always talking of my popularity ... I don't believe in it at all. Perhaps at a distance, that's how it is with us. It's always at a distance that we're loved.'

'You're too modest. Listen to me. You've already been kind enough to relieve me of some of my representative duties now and then. I should like you to relieve me of all of them absolutely and for always.'

'You're not thinking of abdicating, Albrecht?' asked Klaus Heinrich, dismayed.

'I daren't think of it. Believe me, I gladly would, but I shouldn't be allowed to. What I'm thinking of is not a regency, but only a substitution – perhaps you have some recollection of the distinction in public law from your student days – a permanent and officially established substitution of all representative functions, warranted by the need of indulgence required by my state of health. What is your opinion?'

'I'm at your orders, Albrecht. But I'm not quite clear yet. How far does the substitution extend?'

'Oh, as far as possible. I should like it to extend to all occasions on which a personal appearance in public is expected of me. Knobelsdorff stipulates that I should only devolve the opening and closure of Parliament on you when I'm bedridden, only now and again. Let's grant that. But otherwise you would be my substitute on all ceremonial occasions, on journeys, visits to cities, opening of public festivities, opening of the Citizens' Ball . . .'

'That too?'

'Why not? We also have the open audiences here every week, a charming custom no doubt, but it's killing me. You would hold the audiences in my place. I needn't go on. Do you accept my proposal?'

'I am at your orders.'

'Then listen to me while I finish. For every occasion on which you act as my representative, I'll lend you my aides-de-camp. It is further necessary that your military promotion should be hastened – are you first lieutenant? You'll be made a captain or a major straight away *à la suite* of your regiment – I'll see to that; but in the third place, I wish duly to emphasize our arrangement, to make your position at my side properly clear, by lending you the title of "Royal Highness". There were some formalities to attend to. Knobelsdorff has already seen to them. I'm going to express my intentions in the form of two missives to you and to my Minister of State. Knobelsdorff has already drafted them. Do you accept?'

'What am I to say, Albrecht? You are father's eldest son,

and I've always looked up to you because I've always felt and known that you are superior to me and the more distinguished of us two, and that I am a mere plebeian compared to you. But if you think me worthy to stand at your side and to bear your title and to represent you before the people, although I don't think myself anything like so presentable (and I've this deformity here, my left hand which I'm obliged to hide all the time), then I accept with gratitude and I'm at your orders.'

'In that case may I ask you to leave me now. I need a rest.'

They advanced towards each other, the one from the writing table, the other from the book table, across the carpet into the centre of the room. The Grand Duke extended his hand to his brother; his cold, thin hand which he advanced from his chest without even removing his arm from his side. Klaus Heinrich clicked his heels together and bowed as he took the hand, and Albrecht nodded his narrow head with the fair pointed beard in token of dismissal, while with his short, rounded lower lip he sucked at the upper. Klaus Heinrich returned to the Eremitage.

A week later both the *Advertiser* and the *Courier* published the two missives containing the momentous decision, the one addressed to: 'My dear Minister of State, Baron von Knobelsdorff', and the other beginning: 'Most Serene Highness and well beloved brother', and signed 'Your Royal Highness's most devoted brother Albrecht'.

SIX

THE LOFTY CALLING

THIS is how Klaus Heinrich lived from day to day and how he exercised his calling.

He would descend from his carriage, and with his cloak flung over his shoulder, would walk across a pavement covered with a red runner, between a short phalanx of cheering people, would enter a portal wreathed with laurel over which an awning had been erected, and ascend a staircase flanked by a pair of candle-bearing footmen. After a gala dinner he would walk, his whole breast down to the waist covered with decorations, the fringed epaulettes of a major on his narrow shoulders, and followed by his suite, along the Gothic corridor of some town hall. Two servants would hurry in front of him and quickly open an old window whose panes rattled in their lead fastenings. For down below in the small market square stood the people, wedged together shoulder to shoulder, a slanting surface of upturned faces glowing darkly in the smoky torchlight. They cheered and sang, and he stood at the open window and bowed, offered himself for a moment to the general enthusiasm and waved his thanks.

There was no workaday element about his life and nothing was quite real; it consisted wholly of a succession of exceptional moments. Wherever he went it was feastday, the people glorified themselves in the person of their sovereign, the humdrum of existence became transfigured by an element of poetry. The poor wretch became a simple, honest fellow, the low dive a little hut, snotty street urchins turned into mannerly little boys and girls in Sunday suits, their hair plastered down with water, reciting verses, and the dim citizen in his frock-coat and top-hat was moved to a sudden awareness of himself. But not only he, Klaus Heinrich, saw the world in this light; it saw itself that way, as long as his presence lasted. A strange unreality and pretence prevailed in places where he exercised his calling, a symmetrical and transitory make-believe, a false and uplifting disguise of reality by papier-mâché and tinsel, by garlands, Chinese lanterns, draperies and bunting was conjured up for one fair hour, and he himself stood at the centre of attention, on a carpet which camouflaged the naked earth, between parti-coloured poles wreathed with garlands – stood with his heels together, surrounded by the odour of fresh varnish and fir branches, and smilingly hid his left hand behind his back.

He laid the foundation stone of a new town hall. By certain financial transactions the citizens had raised the necessary money, and a trained architect from the capital had been entrusted with the plans. But it fell to Klaus Heinrich to lay the foundation stone. Amid the cheers of the populace he drove up to the fine hut which had been especially erected on the building site, with a light and concise movement he stepped from his carriage onto the rolled ground sprinkled with yellow sand, and walked alone towards the gentleman in a dress-coat and white tie who awaited him at the entrance. He asked for the architect to be presented to him, and in full view of the public and under the fixed smiles of the officials who surrounded him, conversed for five minutes about the advantages of various styles of architecture, whereupon he made a certain movement which he had inwardly rehearsed during this conversation and allowed himself to be conducted across the carpet and up the wooden steps towards his chair on the edge of the centre tribune. There he sat, decorated with his star and cordon, one foot placed slightly forward, his white-gloved hands crossed lightly on his sword hilt, his helmet on the floor beside him, visible from all sides to the festive assembly, and listened with composure to the Lord Mayor's speech. After which, when the request was addressed to him, he rose, and without noticeable caution, without looking at his feet he descended the steps leading to the foundation stone, and with a small hammer gave three slow taps to the block of sandstone, at the same time repeating in the deep hush, with his rather sharp voice, a short sentence which Herr von Knobelsdorff had devised for him. School-children sang in shrill chorus, and Klaus Heinrich drove away.

On National Defence Day he reviewed the Veterans. A grey-haired corporal shouted in a voice which seemed hoarse from the smoke of gunpowder: 'Halt! Hats off! Right turn!' And they stood still, with medals and crosses on their coats, the shaggy top-hats pressed against their thighs and looked up at him with the bloodshot eyes of mastiffs, while he passed along their ranks with friendly interest, and paused here and there to inquire where a man had served, where he had been under fire. He took part in the Sports Festival, graced the games of the Regional Athletic Club with his presence, and requested that the victors be presented to him, in order to honour them with a conversation. The well-built, athletic young men stood before him, after having just performed their remarkable feats, and Klaus Heinrich dropped a few technical terms which he remembered from Herr Zotte and used with great fluency, while hiding his left hand behind his back.

He attended the Fünfhauser Fishermen's Day; seated on a tribune of honour covered in red bunting, he witnessed the Grimmburg Races and distributed the prizes. He also assumed the Honorary Presidency and Patronage of the privileged Grand Ducal Rifle Club. According to the *Courier* he 'partook cordially of the toast of welcome' by raising the silver cup briefly to his lips, and then, with his heels together, towards the marksmen. After which he fired several shots at the target of honour, concerning which nothing was said in the report as to whether they were hits or misses, and later had an identical conversation with three of the men on the advantages of rifle shooting, which in the *Courier* was described as an 'informal exchange of views', and finally took his leave with a cordial 'Good shooting' which evoked indescribable enthusiasm. This formula had been whispered to him at the last moment by Adjutant-General von Hühnemann, who had made inquiries on the subject, for of course it would have had a bad effect, would have shattered the fair illusion of technical knowledge and serious enthusiasm, if Klaus Heinrich had wished the marksmen, say, 'Fair winds', and the miners, on visiting a pit, 'Good shooting'.

As a general rule he needed in the exercise of his calling a certain amount of technical knowledge, which he acquired as he went along, with a view to applying it at the right moment

and in suitable form. It consisted chiefly of technical terms
current in the different departments of human activity and of
historical data, and before setting out on an official assignment
Klaus Heinrich used to absorb the necessary information by
studying various printed memoranda and listening to oral
instructions at the Eremitage. When he unveiled the statue of
Johann Albrecht at Knüppelsdorf in the name of the Grand
Duke, 'my most gracious brother', he delivered an address in
Festival Square, directly after the performance of the Choral
Society, which contained all the information he had noted down
on Knüppelsdorf, and which produced the delightful general
impression that he had busied himself all his life with nothing
so much as the historical vicissitudes of this centre of civiliza-
tion. In the first place, Knüppelsdorf was a city and Klaus Heinrich mentioned this three times, to the pride of the inhabitants.
He went on to say that the city of Knüppelsdorf, as her historical past witnessed, had been connected by bonds of loyalty to
the House of Grimmburg for several centuries. As long ago as
the fourteenth century, he said, Landgrave Heinrich XV, the
Rutensteiner, had signalled out Knüppelsdorf for special favour.
He, the Rutensteiner, had resided in the castle on the nearby
Rutenstein whose 'proud battlements and strong walls built for
the protection of Knüppelsdorf had been visible far and wide in
the countryside'. Then he reminded his hearers how through
inheritance and marriage Knüppelsdorf had at last come into
the branch of the family to which his brother and he himself
belonged. Heavy storms had in the course of years burst over
Knüppelsdorf. Years of war, conflagration, and pestilence had
visited it, yet it had always risen again and had always remained
loyal to the house of its hereditary princes. And this characteristic
the Knüppelsdorf of today proved that it possessed by raising
a memorial to his, Klaus Heinrich's, blessed father, and it would
be with special gratification that he would render account to his
gracious brother of the brilliant and heartfelt reception accorded
to himself, as his representative. The veil fell, the Choral Society
performed once more. And Klaus Heinrich stood smiling, with
a feeling of having fired all his guns, beneath the theatrical awning, happy in the certainty that no one dare question him further.

For he couldn't have said another word on the subject of Knüppelsdorf.

How tiring life was, how strenuous! At times it seemed to him as though he were constantly compelled to keep up something with enormous expenditure of energy which normally could not be kept up, save under the most favourable circumstances, and which taxed his elasticity to the utmost. At other times his calling seemed to him sad and barren, although normally he loved it and gladly went towards his representational duties.

He travelled across country to an Agricultural Fair, drove in his badly sprung carriage from the Eremitage to the station, where the Premier, the President of Police, and the station-master awaited him by the saloon car. He travelled for an hour and a half, the while carrying on a conversation, not without difficulty, with the Grand Ducal aides-de-camp who had been attached to him, and the Agricultural Commissioner, Assistant Secretary Heckepfeng, a stern and deferential gentleman who also accompanied him. When he reached the station of the small town which had organized the Agricultural Fair, the Mayor, with his chain of office over his shoulder, awaited him with six or seven officials. The station was decorated with a quantity of fir-branches and festoons. In the background stood the plaster busts of Albrecht and Klaus Heinrich in a frame of greenery. The public behind the barriers gave three cheers, and the bells pealed.

The Mayor read an address of welcome to Klaus Heinrich. He thanked him, he said, brandishing his top-hat in his hand, he thanked him on behalf of the city for all the favour which Klaus Heinrich's brother and he himself showed them, and heartily wished him a long and blessed reign. Then he repeated his request that the Prince crown the work which had prospered so well under his patronage and open the Agricultural Fair.

This Mayor bore the title of Agricultural Councillor, a fact of which Klaus Heinrich had been apprised, and on account of which he addressed him thus three times in his answer. He said that he was delighted that the work of the agricultural exhibition had prospered so famously under his patronage. (As a matter of fact he had forgotten that he was patron of the exhibition.) He had come to put the finishing touch that day to the great work, by opening the exhibition. He then made inquiries concerning four points: the economic situation of the town, the increase in population of recent years, the labour-market (not that he had a very clear idea what the labour-market was), and the price of food. When he heard that food prices had risen he 'received the information with deep concern', which was of course all he could do. Nobody expected more of him, and it came as a comfort that he had in fact received the information that the food prices had risen with such deep concern.

Then the Mayor presented the city dignitaries to him: the District Judge, an aristocratic landowner from the surroundings, the Rector, the two doctors, a forwarding agent, and Klaus Heinrich addressed a question to each, thinking over, while the answer came, what he should say to the next. The local veterinary surgeon and the local inspector of stockbreeding were also present. Finally they climbed into carriages, and drove, amid the cheers of the inhabitants, between rows of schoolchildren, firemen and patriotic societies, through the gaily decked city to the exhibition ground – not without being stopped once more at the gates by young girls dressed in white with wreaths on their heads, one of whom, the Mayor's daughter, handed the Prince a bouquet wrapped in white satin, and in lasting memory of the occasion received one of those pretty and inexpensive knick-knacks which Klaus Heinrich carried with him on his journeys, a bosom-pin embedded, for a reason she could not guess, in velvet – Sammet – which figured in the *Courier* as a 'precious jewel mounted in gold'.

Tents, pavilions, and stands had been erected in the fields. Gaudy pennons fluttered on long rows of poles strung together with festoons. On a wooden platform hung with bunting, between drapings, festoons, and parti-coloured flagstaffs, Klaus Heinrich read the short opening speech. And then began the tour of inspection.

There were cattle tethered to low crossbars, prize beasts of the best blood with smooth round parti-coloured bodies and numbered shields on their broad foreheads. There were horses stamping and snorting, heavy plough horses with arched Roman noses and hairy fetlocks, and restless thoroughbreds. There were naked and short-legged pigs and both prize and ordinary pigs. With their bellies touching the ground, and grunting happily, they dug up the soil with their pink snouts, while the bleating of woolly sheep filled the air with a confused chorus of bass and treble. There was the noisy poultry exhibition, cocks and hens of every sort, from the big Brahmaputra to the copper-coloured bantam; ducks and pigeons of all sorts, eggs and fodder, both fresh and artificially preserved. There were exhibits of agricultural produce, grain of all sorts, beets and clover, potatoes, peas and flax; vegetables too, both fresh and dried; fresh and bottled fruit; berries, jams and syrups.

Lastly there were exhibits of agricultural implements and machines, displayed by several technical firms, provided with everything of service to agriculture, from the hand-plough to the great black-funnelled motors, looking like elephants in their stall, from the simplest and most intelligible objects to those which consisted of a maze of wheels, chains, rods, cylinders, arms and teeth, a world, a whole disconcerting world of ingenious utility.

Klaus Heinrich looked at everything; with his sword hilt over his forearm he walked along rows of beasts, cages, barrels, jars and implements. With his white-gloved hand the gentleman on his right pointed out details, now and then venturing on an explanation, and Klaus Heinrich performed his duty. He spoke words of appreciation of all he saw, he stopped from time to time and engaged the owners of livestock in conversation, inquired graciously after their circumstances, and put questions to which these country people replied while scratching behind their ears. And as he walked along he bowed to the right and left, thanking the people lined up on both sides for their ovation.

Especially near the exit of the pleasure grounds where the carriages were waiting, the populace had assembled to watch his departure. A path was kept free for him, a straight passage to the steps of his brougham, and he crossed it briskly, with his hand to his helmet and nodding continuously, alone and formally separated from all those people who, in cheering him, cheered their own archtype, their own kind, and whose lives, work and worth he represented in a splendid manner, without having any real part in them.

With a light and easy step he mounted the carriage and sat back adroitly, at once assuming a graceful and self-possessed pose which needed no further adjustment, and drove, saluting as he went, to the Clubhouse where luncheon was awaiting him. During lunch – indeed, directly after the second course – the District Judge proposed the health of the Grand Duke and the Prince, whereupon Klaus Heinrich rose without delay to drink to the welfare of the country and the city. But after the banquet, he retired to the room put at his disposal by the Mayor in his official residence and went to bed for an hour; for the exercise of his calling exhausted him in a strange way, and that afternoon he was due not only to visit the church of that city, the school, and various factories, especially the cheese deposits, of the Behnke Brothers, and to express his glowing satisfaction with all he saw, but also to extend his journey one stage farther and visit the scene of a disaster, a burnt-out village, in order to convey to the authorities his brother's sympathy and his own, and to cheer the afflicted by his exalted presence.

Returned to the Eremitage, to his austerely-furnished Empire rooms, he read the newspaper accounts of his expeditions. Then Privy Councillor Schustermann of the Press Bureau (which was under the Ministry of Home Affairs) appeared at the Eremitage and produced the press cuttings neatly pasted on white sheets, dated and labelled with the name of the paper. And Klaus Heinrich read of the impression he had made, read of the grace and majesty of his bearing, read that he had acquitted himself nobly and taken the hearts of the young and old by storm – that he had lifted the people's minds above the rut of everyday existence, and moved them to loyalty and gladness.

And then he held open audiences at the Old Castle, as had been arranged.

The custom of free audiences had been introduced by a well-meaning ancestor of Albrecht II, and the people clung to it. Once every week Albrecht, and now Klaus Heinrich in his stead, was accessible to every citizen. Whether the petitioner was a man of rank or not, whether the subject of his petitions was of a public or personal nature – he had only to put down his name with Herr von Bühl, or even with the aide-de-camp on duty, and he was given an opportunity to lay his case before the highest authority. Indeed, an admirable and philanthropic custom. For it meant that the petitioner did not have to go round by way of a written application, with the sad prospect of his memorandum disappearing forever in the chancellery, but had the happy assurance that his request would go straight to the most exalted quarters. It must be admitted that the most exalted quarters – Klaus Heinrich in this case – were naturally not in a position to judge the case, to examine it seriously and come to a decision upon it, but that he handed it over to the chancellery where it promptly 'disappeared'. But the custom was helpful all the same, although not in the sense of actual utility. The citizen, the petitioner, came to Herr von Bühl with the request to be received, and a day and hour were fixed for him. With glad and nervous anticipation he saw the day approach, in his mind he went over the phrases he would use to present his case, he had his frock-coat and his silk hat pressed and steamed, put out his best shirt, and prepared himself in every way. But even these festive preparations were conducive to diverting the man's thoughts from the desired, strictly utilitarian end in view and to make the audience itself seem the main object of his pleasurable anticipation. The hour came, and the citizen did what he would never ordinarily have done; he took a cab, so as not to dirty his shining boots. He drove between the lions of the Albrecht Gate, and the sentries as well as the stalwart gatekeeper gave him free passage. He descended in the courtyard, in front of the colonnade and the weatherbeaten portal, and was at once admitted by a lackey in a brown coat and sand-coloured gaiters, to an ante-room to the left of the ground floor, in one corner of which stood a group of flags where a number of other applicants, talking in low whispers, waited for their reception in a state of devout expectancy. Holding a list of those with appointments the aide-de-camp went backwards and forwards, and led the one next on the list into a corner, to ply him in a low voice with instructions on how to behave. But in the next room, called the 'Open Audience Room', Klaus Heinrich, in his tunic with a silver collar and several stars, stood at a round table with three gilt legs and received. Major von Platow gave him some superficial information about the identity of each petitioner, called the man in, and came back in pauses, to prompt the Prince in a few words about the next comer. And the citizen entered; with a red face and perspiring slightly, he stood before Klaus Heinrich. It had been impressed upon him that he was not to approach His Royal Highness too closely but stand at a certain distance, that he should not speak unless spoken to, and even then should not blurt out everything at once but answer sparingly, in order to allow the Prince to formulate his questions; that eventually he should retire backwards, without showing the prince his backside. The result was that the citizen's whole attention was centred on not breaking any of these rules, but on contributing to the smooth and harmonious progress of the conversation. Klaus Heinrich questioned him as he was wont to question the veterans, the marksmen, the athletes, the country folk, the victims of the fire; smiling the while, and with his left hand pressed to the small of his back; and the citizen too smiled involuntarily – feeling that in some way his smile lifted him far above his usual troubles. This common man, whose wits were usually dull, who considered nothing beyond his small gains and interests and lacked even the most elementary good manners, and who had come here precisely with such a petty problem – this man now felt that there were greater things than his own problems, or any personal problem, and he left with a feeling of elation, purified, with unseeing eyes and with a smile on his flushed countenance.

That was the way in which Klaus Heinrich gave free audiences, that was the way in which he exercised his exalted calling. He lived at the Eremitage, in his small suite of Empire rooms furnished so simply and austerely with a cool disregard for comfort and intimacy. Faded silk covered the walls above the panelling, crystal chandeliers hung from the plain ceiling, straight sofas, mostly without tables, and what-nots with spindly legs topped by Empire clocks stood along the walls; the white doors were flanked by white chairs with oval backs upholstered in fine silk, and in the corners stood white lacquered round tables supporting candelabra shaped like vases. Such was the aspect of Klaus Heinrich's apartments, and he for his part was well content with his surroundings.

He led a life of inward quiet, taking no part in controversial public issues. As representative of his brother, he opened Parliament, but he took no personal part in its proceedings and avoided the yeas and nays of party divisions – with the impartiality and want of passionate convictions proper to one whose function it was to stand above all parties. Everybody recognized that his position imposed reserve upon him, but many felt that his lack of interest affected his bearing in a strange and paralysing way. Many who came in contact with him described him as 'cold'; and when Doctor Überbein loudly refuted this 'coldness' people wondered whether this prejudiced and disconcerting man was qualified to pass judgement in the matter. Of course it sometimes happened that Klaus Heinrich's glance crossed with those who did not recognize his calling, impertinent, sarcastic, spitefully astonished glances which expressed contempt for his entire effort and achievement. But even in the well-meaning, loyal people, who showed themselves ready to esteem and honour his work, he sometimes noticed after a time a certain irritability and exhaustion, as if they could no longer breathe in his atmosphere; and this saddened Klaus Heinrich, although he was at a loss to know how to prevent it.

He had no place in everyday life; what mattered and were of decisive importance were the greeting, the gracious address, a winning and yet dignified wave of the hand. Once he returned in his cap and greatcoat from a ride, advancing slowly at a trot on his chestnut Florian down the birch avenue which skirted the waste land and led to the park and the Eremitage, and in front of him walked a shabbily dressed young man in a fluffy cap and ridiculously long hair, with sleeves and trousers that were too short for him, and unusually large feet, which he turned inward as he walked. He might have been a science student or something of the sort, for he carried a drawing-board under his arm, on which was pinned a big drawing, a symmerical maze of lines in red and black ink, a projection or something of the sort. Klaus

Heinrich rode behind that young man for a long while, and examined the red and black projection on the drawing-board. Sometimes he thought how nice it must be to have a proper surname, to be called Doctor Fischer and to have a real profession.

He played his part at Court functions, the big and the small Court Ball, the Gala Dinner, the Concerts and the Grand Levee. In the autumn, he took part in the royal shooting party with his red-haired cousins and the gentlemen of his suite, for custom's sake and although his left hand made shooting difficult. In the evening he was often seen at the Court Theatre, seated in the royal box lined with crimson, between the two female sculptures with crossed hands and stern, unseeing eyes. For the theatre amused him, he loved watching the actors, to observe how they behaved, how they walked on and off the stage, how they acted their parts. As a rule he thought them rather poor, crude in the means they employed to please, and untrained in the fine art of feigning to be natural and artless. For the rest he was inclined to give preference to low comedy and popular plays over the exalted ceremonious ones.

A soubrette called Mizzi Meyer was engaged at the Vaudeville Theatre in the capital who in the newspapers and on the lips of the public was never called anything but 'our Mizzi Meyer', because of her boundless popularity with high and low. She was not beautiful, hardly pretty, she sang in a raucous voice, and strictly speaking, she could lay no claim to special gifts. And yet she had only to come on to the stage to evoke a storm of approbation, applause and encouragement. For this fair and sturdy person with her blue eyes, her broad high cheekbones, her healthy, jolly, and frequently a little sentimental manner was flesh of the people's flesh, and blood of their own blood. So long as she faced the crowds from the boards, dressed and made up and lit by stage lights from every angle, she was indeed the embodiment of the people – and in applauding her the people applauded themselves, and therein lay the popular appeal of Mizzi Meyer. Klaus Heinrich was very fond of visiting the Vaudeville Theatre with Herr von Braunbart-Schellendorf when Mizzi Meyer was performing, and joined heartily in the applause.

One day he had a rencontre which on one hand gave him food for thought, but on the other disappointed him. It was with Martini, Axel Martini, the author of *Evoël* and *The Hallowed Life*, two volumes of poetry which had been much acclaimed by the experts. The meeting came about in the following way.

In the capital lived a well-to-do old gentleman, a Privy Councillor who, since his retirement from the Civil Service, had devoted his life to the advancement of the fine arts, especially of poetry. He was the founder of what was known as the 'Battle of May', a poetry contest which was held annually in springtime, which the Privy Councillor encouraged the male and female poets of the country to attend by means of circulars and posters. Prizes were offered for the tenderest love-song, the most fervent religious poem, the most ardent patriotic song, for the happiest lyrical effusion in praise of music, the forest, the spring, the joy of living – and these prizes consisted of sums of money, supplemented by judicious and valuable souvenirs such as gold pens, gold pins shaped like lyres or flowers, and so on. The city authorities, too, donated a prize, and the Grand Duke gave a silver cup as a reward for the most excellent poem. The founder of the 'Battle of May', who was responsible for the initial sifting of the invariably numerous entries, shared the duties of the jury with two University Professors, and the literary editors of the *Courier* and the *People*.

The chosen and laudably recommended contributions were printed and published annually in book form at the Privy Councillor's own expense.

That year Axel Martini had taken part in the 'Battle of May', and had won the first prize. The poem he had submitted, an inspired praise of the joy of living, or rather a tempestuous effusion of the joy of living, a thrilling hymn on the beauty and terror of existence, was conceived in the style of his two volumes of poetry, and carried dissent into the Board of Jurors. The Privy Councillor himself and the Professor of Philology had wanted to dismiss it with a notice of commendation, for they considered it exaggerated in expression, crude in its passion, and in places downright obscene. But the professor of literature together with the editors had outvoted them, not only in view of the fact that Martini's contribution was the best poem on the joy of living, but also in view of his undeniable distinction, and finally the two opponents too had been unable to resist the appeal of its frothy and stunning eloquence.

So Axel Martini had been awarded three hundred marks, a gold lyre-shaped pin, and the silver cup of the Grand Duke into the bargain, and his poem had been published on the first page of the Annual, framed by an artistic drawing from the hand of Professor Lindemann. What is more, the custom was for the victor (or the victrix) to be received in audience by the Grand Duke, and as Albrecht happened to be unwell, the task fell to his brother.

Klaus Heinrich was a little afraid of Herr Martini.

'Good Lord, Doctor Überbein,' he said during a brief meeting with his tutor, 'what am I to do with him? He's sure to be a wild, impertinent fellow.'

But Doctor Überbein replied: 'Not in the least, Klaus Heinrich, have no fear! He's quite a tame little man. I know him. I see quite a few among his friends. You'll get on splendidly with him.'

So Klaus Heinrich received the author of the 'Joy of Living', received him at the Eremitage so as to give the audience an informal character. 'In the yellow room, Braunbart, if you please,' he said, 'that's the most presentable on an occasion like this.' There were three handsome chairs in this room, the only valuable pieces of furniture in the castle, heavy mahogany chairs with snail-shaped scrolls on the arms, upholstered in yellow cloth with a design of lyres embroidered in blue-green silk. On this occasion Klaus Heinrich did not take his stand as for an audience, but waited with some trepidation in the next room while Herr Martini waited for eight or ten minutes in the yellow room. He then entered the room with animation, almost hurriedly, and walked towards the poet who made a low bow.

'I'm very glad to meet you, dear sir, dear Doctor, I believe?' he said.

'No, Royal Highness,' replied Axel Martini, in an asthmatic voice, 'not Doctor, I have no degree.'

'Oh, forgive me ... I assumed ... Let us sit down, dear Herr
Martini. I am, as I have said, delighted to be able to congratu-
late you on your great success.'

Herr Martini lowered the corners of his mouth. He sat down
on the edge of one of the mahogany armchairs at the uncovered
table, round whose edge ran a gold border, and crossed his feet,
which were cased in cracked patent-leather boots. He wore a
frock-coat and discoloured kid gloves. His collar was frayed at
the edges. He had rather bulging eyes, hollow cheeks, and a dark
blond moustache which was clipped like a hedge. His hair
was already turning grey at the temples, although according to
the 'Battle of May' Annual he was not more than thirty years
old, and red blotches underneath his eyes suggested ill-health. He
answered Klaus Heinrich's congratulations by saying: 'Your
Royal Highness is very kind. It was not a difficult victory. Perhaps it was hardly tactful of me to compete.'

Klaus Heinrich did not understand this; but he said:

'I have read your poem repeatedly with great pleasure. It
seems to me a complete success, as regards both metre and
rhyme. And it entirely expresses the "Joy of Living".'

Herr Martini bowed in his chair.

'Your skill,' continued Klaus Heinrich, 'must be a source of
great pleasure to you – an ideal recreation. What is your profession, Herr Martini?'

Herr Martini indicated that he had not understood, by twisting, as it were, the upper half of his body into an interrogation
mark.

'I mean your main profession. Are you in the Civil Service?'

'No, Royal Highness, I have no profession. I dedicate myself
exclusively to poetry.'

'None at all? Oh, I understand. So unusual a gift deserves
that a man's whole powers be devoted to it.'

'I don't know about that, Royal Highness. Whether it deserves
it or not, I don't know. I must own that I had no choice. I have
always felt myself entirely unsuited to every other branch of
human activity. It seems to me that this undoubted and uncon-
ditional unsuitability for everything else is the sole proof and
touchstone of the poetical calling – indeed, that a man must not

see poetry as a calling, but solely as the expression and refuge of that unsuitability.'

It was a peculiarity with Herr Martini that when he talked tears came into his eyes just like a man who comes out of the cold into a warm room and lets the heat stream through and melt his limbs.

'That is a singular view,' said Klaus Heinrich.

'Not really, Royal Highness. I beg your pardon, no, not singular at all. This view is generally accepted. What I say is nothing new.'

'And since when have you been dedicating yourself exclusively to poetry, Herr Martini? I suppose you attended University?'

'Not regularly, Royal Highness. No, the unsuitability to which I alluded before began to show itself in me at an early age. I did not do well at school. I left it before passing my finals. I went up to the University with the full intention of taking it later, but I never did. And when my first volume of poems attracted a good deal of attention, it no longer suited my dignity to do so, if I may say so.'

'Of course not ... But did your parents then agree to your choice of career?'

'Oh no, Royal Highness! I must say to my parents' credit that they by no means agreed to it. I had a decent home background; my father was Solicitor to the Treasury. He naturally disliked my choice of a career so much that until his death he would never give me a farthing. I was on bad terms with him, although I had the greatest respect for him because of his strictness.'

'Oh, so you have seen hard times, Herr Martini, you have had to struggle hard. I can well believe that you have been tried by circumstances.'

'Not in the least, Royal Highness! No, that would have been awful, I couldn't have borne it. My health is delicate – I dare not say "unfortunately", for I am convinced that my talent is inseparably connected with my bodily infirmity. Neither my body nor my talent could have survived hunger and cold, and they did not have to bear them. My mother was weak enough to provide me with means of subsistence behind my father's back, modest but adequate means. I owe it to her that my gift has been able to develop under fairly favourable circumstances.'

'The result has shown, Herr Martini, that they were the right conditions ... Although it is difficult to say now what actually are good conditions. Permit me to suppose that if your mother had shown herself to be as strict as your father, and you had been alone in the world, and left entirely to your own resources ... don't you think that it might have been to a certain extent a good thing for you? That you might have gained an insight, if I may use the term, which as things are has eluded you?'

'People like me, Your Royal Highness, gain quite enough insight without actually learning what hunger is; and the idea is generally accepted that it is not so much physical hunger, but rather the hunger for truth ... ha, ha! ... which a talent requires for its growth.'

Herr Martini had been compelled to laugh a little at his witty pun. He now quickly raised a gloved hand to his mouth with the moustache clipped like a hedge and corrected himself by pretending to cough. Klaus Heinrich looked at him with friendly expectancy.

'If Your Royal Highness will allow me ... It is a widely held view that for people like myself the lack of actual experience is the seedbed of talent, the source of inspiration, and, indeed, our inspiring genius. To savour life is forbidden to us, strictly forbidden, we make no secret of it, and the savouring of life includes not only happiness, but care, but passion, in brief every serious contact with life. The reproduction of life in writing claims all our energies, especially when these energies are not allotted to us in abundant measure,' and Herr Martini coughed several times, hunching up his shoulders as he did so. 'Renunciation,' he added, 'is our pact with the muse, our strength depends on it, our dignity, and life for us is the forbidden fruit, our great temptation, to which we sometimes submit, but never to our own good.'

The flow of words once more brought tears to Herr Martini's eyes. He tried to get rid of them by blinking.

'Every one of us,' he added, 'knows of such aberrations and

mistakes and greedy incursions into the festive halls of life. But we return to our isolation, humiliated and sick at heart.'

Herr Martini sat in silence. But now it happened that his gaze under the raised brows became momentarily fixed, lost in a void, while his mouth assumed a sour expression and his cheeks glowing with an unhealthy colour seemed more hollow than usual. It lasted only for a second, and then he changed his position and focused his eyes.

'But your poem,' said Klaus Heinrich, not without urgency. 'Your poem laureate to the joy of living, Herr Martini... I am seriously obliged to you for your exposition. But would you mind telling me ... Your poem – I have read it carefully. It deals on the one hand with misery and horror, with the wickedness and cruelty of existence, if I remember correctly, and on the other with the pleasures of wine and beautiful women, does it not?'

Herr Martini smiled, but he rubbed the corners of his mouth with his thumb and middle finger, as if to erase the smile.

'All that,' said Klaus Heinrich, 'is written in the first person singular, is it not? And yet you say that it does not arise from personal experience? You have not experienced any of it?'

'Very little, Royal Highness. Mere samples. No, in fact it is the other way round; were I the man to have experienced all this I would certainly not have written such poems but would heartily despise my present form of existence. I have a friend, his name is Weber; a rich young man who enjoys himself. His chief amusement consists of driving his car across country at top speed, and picking up peasant wenches from the roads and fields to whom he ... but that is another story. Well, that young man laughs when he catches sight of me, he finds me and my occupation very funny. As for myself, I understand his hilarity perfectly and I envy him. I might add that I also despise him a little, but not quite sincerely; rather, I envy and admire him ...'

'You admire him?'

'Certainly, Royal Highness. I cannot help doing so. He spends, he squanders, and this he does perpetually in the most carefree and generous manner – while it is my lot to scrape and save like a miser, and that for purely hygienic reasons. My hygiene is

what I and my kind need most of all – it is our form of morality.
But nothing is more unhygienic than life. . .'

'So you will not empty the cup of the Grand Duke, will you,
Herr Martini?'

'Will I drink wine from the Cup? No, Your Royal Highness.
Although it would be a handsome gesture. But I never touch
wine. Besides, I go to bed at ten and generally take care of
myself. Otherwise I would never have won the cup.'

'It must be as you say, Herr Martini. Judging from the outside
one obviously gets the wrong idea of what a poet's life must be
like.'

'That is understandable, Your Royal Highness. But it is not
on the whole a very glorious life, I can assure you, especially as
we aren't poets all the time. In order to, from time to time,
produce a poem – who would believe how much idleness and
boredom and peevish indolence are necessary. A postcard to the
cigar merchant is often a whole day's literary output. One over-
sleeps, one hangs about with a heavy head. Well yes, it is often
a dog's life.'

Someone knocked very gently on the white painted door –
Neumann's signal that it was high time for Klaus Heinrich to
change and be prepared for his next appointment. For it was
Concert Night at the Old Castle.

Klaus Heinrich rose. 'I've talked too much,' he said; for this
was the formula he used on similar occasions. And then he dismissed Herr Martini, wished him success in his literary career
and accompanied the poet's respectful exit with a smile and
that certain genial, somewhat theatrical wave of the hand which
did not always succeed equally well, but in which he had
achieved a considerable degree of proficiency.

Such was the Prince's conversation with Axel Martini, the
author of *Evoë!* and *The Hallowed Life*. It gave him food for
thought, it continued to occupy his mind after it had ended. He
continued to think over it while Neumann renewed his parting
and helped him into his dazzling gala tunic with the stars, even
during the concert at Court, and for days afterwards he thought
of it and tried to reconcile the poet's utterances with the other experiences which life had awarded him.

This man, Herr Martini, who, with an unhealthy flush on his cheeks, kept proclaiming that life was 'beautiful and strong', and yet took care to be in bed by ten o'clock, who kept aloof from life for reasons of hygiene, and avoided all serious contact with it – this poet with his frayed collar and watery eyes, and with his envy of young Weber who made love to peasant wenches in his racing car – he roused mixed feelings, it was difficult to form a definite opinion. Klaus Heinrich expressed this when he told his sister of the encounter, saying : 'He doesn't have an easy life, one can see that, and it ought to prejudice one in his favour. But I'm not quite sure all the same whether I'm glad to have met him or not, because there's something repellent about him, Ditlinde, yes, in spite of everything he is definitely a little repulsive.'

SEVEN

IMMA

FRÄULEIN von Isenschnibbe had been well informed. On the very evening of the day on which she had brought the Princess zu Ried the great news, the *Courier* published the announcement of Samuel Spoelmann's, the world-renowned Spoelmann's, impending arrival; and ten days later, at the beginning of October (it was the October of the year in which Grand Duke Albrecht entered his thirty-second and Prince Klaus Heinrich his twenty-sixth year), thus barely giving public curiosity a chance to reach a true climax, this arrival became a fact, became a simple actuality which happened on an overcast autumn day, a perfectly ordinary weekday that was destined to impress itself on the future as a date to be remembered forever.

The Spoelmanns arrived by special train, that to begin with being the only evidence of luxury on their part; for everybody knew that the Grand Ducal Suite at the Spa Hotel was by no means dazzling or luxurious. A few idlers, guarded by a small detachment of policemen, had gathered behind the platform barriers; some representatives of the press were present. But whoever expected anything out of the ordinary was disappointed. Spoelmann would almost have passed unrecognized, he was so unimposing. At first people mistook his personal physician for Mr Spoelmann (his name, people said, was Doctor Watercloose), a tall American with a short white beard who wore his hat pushed back, and with closed eyes kept his mouth, surrounded by short white whiskers, distended in a benign smile. Only at the last moment did it become known that Spoelmann was the small, clean shaven gentleman in a dun-coloured overcoat who wore his hat pulled down over his eyes, and the spectators were agreed that there was nothing striking about his appearance. Fantastic tales about him had been circulating; some witty fellow had spread the report that Spoelmann had front teeth of solid gold and a diamond set in the middle of each. But although the truth or untruth of this report could not be tested at once – for Spoelmann did not show his teeth, he did not laugh, but rather seemed angry and irritated by his infirmity – when they saw him nobody was any longer inclined to believe it.

As for Miss Spoelmann, his daughter, she wore the collar of her fur coat turned up, and stuffed her hands in the pockets, so that there was hardly anything to be seen of her except a pair of abnormally large, dark brown eyes which searched the crowd with earnest eloquence, albeit not in a generally current idiom. By her side was a lady whom the onlookers identified as her companion, Countess Löwenjoul, a woman of thirty-five, soberly dressed and taller than either of the Spoelmanns, who carried her small head with its smooth, sparse parting pensively cocked on one side, and stared in front of her with a sort of rigid meekness. What caused most excitement was a Scottish sheepdog on a leash, led by a manservant with bland slavonic features – an uncommonly fine, but as it seemed madly excitable animal which, shivering and prancing, filled the platform with its frenzied barks.

It was rumoured that a few of Spoelmann's staff, both male and female, had already arrived at the Spa Hotel some hours earlier. At any rate it was left to the servant with the dog to look after the luggage by himself; and while he was doing so his masters drove to the Thermal Gardens in two ordinary cabs, Mr Spoelmann with Doctor Watercloose, and Miss Spoelmann with her Countess. There they descended, and there they lived for the next six weeks, far more cheaply than their ample means permitted.

They were lucky; the weather was fine, it was a blue autumn, a long succession of sunny days from October into November, and Miss Spoelmann rode out daily – that was her only luxury – with her companion on horses which she hired by the week from a riding school. Mr Spoelmann did not ride, although the *Courier*, with obvious reference to him, published a notice by its medical correspondent according to which riding, owing to the jolting movement, had a soothing effect in cases of kidney trouble, and helped to rid the patient of the stones. But through the hotel staff it became known that the famous man practised

artificial riding within the four walls of his room with the help
of a machine, a stationary velocipede to whose saddle a jolting
motion was imparted by the working of the pedals.

He drank assiduously of the healing waters of the Ditlinde
spring by which he seemed to set great store. First thing every
morning he appeared at the Pavilion accompanied by his daughter, who for her part was perfectly healthy, and only drank with
him for company's sake; and then, in his dun-coloured overcoat
and with his hat pulled down over his eyes, he walked in the
Thermal Gardens and the covered arcades, sipping the water
through a glass tube from a blue glass tumbler, watched from a
distance by the two American journalists whose job it was to
cable their paper a thousand words daily on Spoelmann's holiday, and who therefore were bound to try and get a story.

Otherwise he was rarely seen. His illness, colic of the kidneys,
so people said, with extremely painful attacks, seemed to con-
fine him frequently in his room, if not to his bed, and while Miss
Spoelmann, in the company of Countess Löwenjoul, appeared
two or three times at the Court Theatre (in a black velvet dress
with a wonderful golden-yellow stole of Indian silk round her
childlike shoulders and looking quite bewitching with her small,
pale face and large, eloquent dark eyes), her father was never
once seen inside her box. It is true that once or twice he drove
through the town with her, to do a little shopping, visit the city
and see the sights; that he walked with her in the Municipal
Gardens and visited Delphinenort twice, the second time alone,
and that on this occasion his interest was so great that he extracted an ordinary yellow yardstick from his dun-coloured overcoat and proceeded to take measurements of the walls. But he
was never seen in the dining-room of the Spa Hotel; whether
because he was on an almost wholly vegetarian diet or for some
other reason, he and his party took their meals almost exclusively
in his private suite, and the curiosity of the public on the whole
had remarkably little to feed on.

As a result Spoelmann's arrival at the Thermal Establishment
did not at first prove as beneficial as Fräulein von Isenschnibbe
and many others besides her had expected. The export of bottled
water increased, to be sure; it rose to almost double its previous

quota and maintained itself at that level. But the tourist traffic did not increase noticeably, the guests who came to catch a glimpse of so fantastic a being soon afterwards departed, satisfied or disappointed, as the case may be. Besides it was for the most part not the most desirable elements of society that were attracted by the millionaire's presence. Strange individuals appeared in the streets, unkempt and wild-eyed creatures, investors, cranks, would-be benefactors of mankind who hoped to enlist Spoelmann's sympathies for their mad ideas. But the millionaire made himself absolutely inaccessible to these people; indeed, purple with rage, he snapped at one of them who had tried to approach him in the Municipal Gardens, so loudly that the crazy fellow speedily took himself off, and it was asserted from several sides that the avalanche of begging letters which arrived daily – letters with stamps which the officials of the Grand Ducal Post Office had never seen before – went straight into a waste paper basket of unusual capacity.

Spoelmann seemed to have given orders not to forward business correspondence. He seemed determined thoroughly to enjoy his holiday, and during this trip to Europe to live exclusively for his health – or ill-health. The *Courier*, whose correspondent had lost no time in making friends with his American colleagues, was in a position to announce that a reliable person, a business manager, acted for Mr Spoelmann in the States. It went on to say that his yacht, a luxuriously fitted vessel, awaited the great man in Venice, and that, as soon as he had finished his cure, he intended to go south with his party. It also told, in answer to an urgent demand of the public, of the romantic origins of the Spoelmann millions; of the beginnings in Victoria whither his father had immigrated from some office stool back in Germany, young, poor, and armed only with a pick and shovel, and a tin plate. There he had begun as an assistant to a gold digger, a day labourer working in the sweat of his brow. And then he had struck a lucky vein. One man, the proprietor of a small mine, had fared so badly that he could no longer afford his lunch of dry bread and tomatoes, and in his extremity had been obliged to sell his claim. Spoelmann senior had bought it, had staked his all on one card, and, with his whole savings, amounting to

£5 sterling, had bought this piece of alluvial land called 'Paradise Field', not more than forty feet square. The very next day he had struck a nugget of pure gold only a foot below the surface; the tenth biggest nugget in the world, the 'paradise nugget', weighing 980 ounces and worth £5,000.

That, related the *Courier*, had been the beginning. Spoelmann's father had emigrated to South America with the proceeds of his find, to Bolivia, and as gold-washer, amalgam-mill owner, and mine-owner had continued to extract the yellow metal directly from the rivers and mountains. It was at that period and in those parts that Spoelmann Sr had married, and in this connection the *Courier* went so far as to hint that he had done so in defiance of the prejudices prevalent in that country. He had also doubled his capital by investing it most profitably.

He had moved on northwards to Philadelphia, Pa. That was in the 'fifties, the time of a great boom in railway construction, and Spoelmann had begun with one investment in the Baltimore and Ohio Railway. He had also leased a coalmine in the west of the State, the profits from which had been enormous. Finally, he had joined that group of fortunate young men which bought the famous Blockhead Farm for a few thousand pounds – the small farm which on account of its oil wells shortly increased a hundred-, then a thousandfold in value.

This enterprise had made a rich man of Spoelmann Senior, yet he had by no means rested on his oars, but unceasingly practised the art of turning money into more money, and finally into superabundant money.

He had started steel works, had floated companies for the turning of iron into steel on a large scale, and for building railway bridges. He had bought up the major part of the shares of four or five big railway companies, and had been elected in the later years of his life president, vice-president, manager or director of the companies. When the Steel Trust was formed, so the *Courier* said, he had joined it, with a holding of shares which guaranteed him an income of $12,000,000. But at the same time he had been chief shareholder and expert adviser of the Petroleum Combine, and in virtue of his holding had dominated three or four of the other Trust Companies. And at his death his fortune, reckoned in German currency, had amounted to a round thousand million marks.

Samuel, his only son, the offspring of that early marriage contracted in defiance of public opinion, had been his sole heir, and the *Courier*, with its usual delicacy, interpolated a remark to the effect that there was something almost melancholy in the idea of anyone finding himself by birth, and without any merit or fault of his own, in a similar situation. Samuel had inherited the mansion in Fifth Avenue, the various country houses, and all the shares, trust bonds and revenues of his father; he also inherited the isolated position to which the latter had risen, his world fame, and the hatred of the underprivileged masses for his amassed wealth, all that hatred to allay which he yearly made large donations to colleges, music schools, libraries, charitable institutions, and to the University founded by his father which bore his name.

Samuel Spoelmann did not deserve the hatred of the underprivileged; the *Courier* made this quite clear. He had joined the business early and already during the last years of his father's life had carried on the administration of the staggering fortune single-handed. His real passion, strange to say, had always been music, in particular organ music – and the proof of this bit of news in the *Courier* was that Mr Spoelmann actually kept a small organ in the Spa Hotel and made a hotel servant blow the bellows. From the Municipal Gardens he could be heard to practise for an hour every day. He had married, not from financial considerations according to the *Courier*, but a beautiful and penniless girl, half German and half English. She had died but left him a daughter, that strange mixture of a girl whom we now had as a guest within our walls and who was just nineteen years old. Her name was Imma, a true German name, as the *Courier* pointed out, an older form of Emma, and it was easy to observe that though their conversation was interspersed with bits of English, the Spoelmanns' household on the whole spoke mostly German. And how devoted father and daughter were to each other! By going to the Thermal Gardens at the right time one could watch Miss Spoelmann, who used to arrive at the Pavilion after her father, take his head between her hands and kiss him good morning on mouth and cheeks, while he patted her affectionately on the back. Then they went through the Pavilion arm in arm, sucking at their glass tubes.

That is how the well-informed paper gossiped, fostering public curiosity. It also reported painstakingly on the visits which Miss Imma and her chaperone made to several charitable institutions of the city. Yesterday she had made a detailed inspection of the Municipal Kitchens. Today she had made a prolonged tour of the Trinity Almshouses for Old Women, and twice recently she had attended Professor Klinghammer's lectures on the theory of numbers at the University – had sat on the bench, a student among students, and scribbled away with her fountain-pen, for everybody knew that she was a learned girl and devoted to the study of algebra. Yes, all that was absorbing reading, and furnished ample food for conversation. But the topics which made themselves talked about without any help from the *Courier* were, firstly, the dog, that noble black-and-white collie which the Spoelmanns had brought with them, and secondly, in a different way, the chaperone, Countess Löwenjoul.

Concerning the dog, who was called Perceval (pronounced the English way) and generally Percy for short, he was an animal of a nervous excitability that defied description. Inside the hotel he afforded no grounds for complaint, but lay in a dignified attitude on a small carpet outside the Spoelmanns' suite. But every time he went out he had an attack of light-headedness, which caused general interest and surprise, indeed more than once actual obstruction of traffic.

Followed at a distance by a swarm of local dogs, common mongrels who, incited by his antics, ran after him with abusive yelps and to whom he paid not the slightest attention, he raced through the streets with a foam-flecked nose and barking loudly, capered in front of tramcars, upset cab horses, and more than once knocked down the pastry stall of Frau Classen, the widow, in front of the Town Hall, and that with such violence that her cakes and buns rolled halfway across the market place. But as Mr Spoelmann and his daughter at once met these mishaps with a more than adequate compensation, and as it became clear that Percy's tantrums were not dangerous, that he was by no means rabid and aggressive, but on the contrary would not be touched by anyone and was simply very highly strung, the people became fond of him, and especially to the children his outings were a source of fun.

Countess Löwenjoul, on the other hand, supplied food for gossip in a quieter but none the less peculiar manner. At first, when her personality and position were not yet known in the city, she had attracted the gibes of the street urchins because when walking alone she had talked to herself with a gentle and pensive expression, and accompanied these soliloquies with lively, yet graceful and elegant gestures. But she had shown such meekness and kindness to the children who called after her and tugged at her dress, had spoken to them with such tenderness and dignity, that the pursuers had slunk back abashed and confused; and later, when she became known, respect for her relations with the famous guests secured her from molestation, although some cryptic anecdotes were secretly circulated about her. One man related how the Countess had handed him a golden sovereign with instructions to slap the face of a certain old woman, who allegedly had made some unseemly proposals to her. The man had pocketed the sovereign without, however, discharging his commission. Further it was stated as a fact that the Countess had accosted the sentry outside the barracks of the Fusiliers of the Guards, and had told him to arrest at once the wife of a sergeant of a certain company, on account of her moral aberrations. She had also written to the Colonel of the regiment a letter to the effect that all sorts of secret and unspeakable abominations were going on inside the barracks. Whether she was right in her facts Heaven only knew. But many people at once concluded that she was wrong in the head. At any rate there was no time to investigate the matter, for six weeks passed rapidly, and Samuel N. Spoelmann, the multi-millionaire, departed.

He left after having his portrait painted by Professor von Lindemann, and giving the expensive portrait to the hotel proprietor as a parting gift; departed with his daughter, the Countess and Doctor Watercloose, with Perceval, the chamber velocipede and his servants; left for the south by special train, to spend the winter on the Riviera, where the two correspondents from New York preceded him, and then to return across the Atlantic. It was all over. The *Courier* wished Mr Spoelmann a heartfelt farewell and expressed the hope that the cure would be found to have done him good. With that the notable interlude seemed to be closed and done with. Everyday life claimed its due, and Mr Spoelmann began to fade into oblivion. The winter passed. It was the winter in which Her Grand Ducal Highness the Princess zu Ried-Hohenried was confined with a daughter. Spring came, and His Royal Highness Grand Duke Albrecht repaired as usual to Hollerbrunn. But then a rumour cropped up amongst the people and in the press, which was received at first with a shrug by the sober-minded, but became more concrete, crystallized, assumed the form of precise details, and finally entered the news as a real and definite piece of information.

What was going on? – A castle of the Crown domain was to be sold? Nonsense. Which castle? – Delphinenort. Castle Delphinenort on the north side of the park. – Rubbish. Sold? To whom? – To Spoelmann. – Ridiculous. What would he do with it? – Restore it and live in it. – That was all very well, but perhaps our Diet ought to have had a say in this whole matter. – Had the negotiations advanced very far? Indeed they had. They had been completed. – Really, in that case, was one in a position to name the exact sum for which it had been sold? At your orders. The purchasing price was exactly two million marks. – Impossible! A Crown property! – Crown property fiddlesticks. It was not a question of the Grimmburg. Nor of the Old Castle. It was a question of a disused summer residence which was falling to pieces for lack of funds. – And did Spoelmann intend to come every year and spend a few weeks at Delphinenort? – Not at all. What he intended to do was to come and live among us for good. He was tired of the States, he wanted to turn his back on them, and his first stay here had been a reconnaissance journey. He was a sick man; he wanted to retire from business. He had always remained a German at heart. The father had emigrated, the son wanted to come back home. He wished to take part in the sedate life and to avail himself of the intellectual resources of our capital, and to spend the rest of his days in the immediate neighbourhood of the Ditlinde waters.

Surprise, confusion and endless discussions. But public opinion as a whole, with the exception of a few reactionaries, and after some initial misgivings, was strongly in favour of the plan, and, indeed, without this general approval the matter could never have gone very far. It was in fact Minister von Knobelsdorff who gave the daily press a careful hint concerning the Spoelmann offer. He had waited, and had allowed popular feeling to come to a decision. And after the initial confusion a number of good reasons in favour of the project had made themselves felt. The business world was enchanted at the idea of having such a strong consumer permanently in the city. The aesthetes showed themselves delighted at the prospect of seeing Delphinenort repaired and kept up; at seeing this noble building restored to youth and eminence in so unforeseen and indeed romantic a fashion. The economically-minded brought forward figures which, as things stood, were calculated to shake the public. If Samuel Spoelmann settled among us he was bound to become liable to tax; he was bound to pay income tax in this country. Perhaps it was worth considering what this meant. It would be left to Mr Spoelmann to declare his income, but from what one knew – and knew fairly accurately – this taxpayer was worth a million and a half per year; that is taxes alone, not to speak of rates due for the period. Worth thinking about, was it not? The question was put straight to the Minister, Doctor Krippenreuther. He would be wanting in this duty if he did not do all he could to recommend the sale in the highest quarters. For patriotism demanded that the Spoelmann offer be accepted, and patriotism was paramount above all other considerations.

So His Excellency von Knobelsdorff had had an interview with the Grand Duke. He had informed his master of public opinion; and added that the offer of two millions considerably exceeded the actual value of the castle in its present condition; had commented that such a sum was a real windfall for the Treasury, and had concluded by slipping in a hint about the central heating of the Old Castle which, if the sale was carried through, would no longer be an impossibility. In brief, the disinterested old gentleman had brought his whole influence to bear in favour of the sale, and had recommended the Grand Duke to bring the matter before a family council. Albrecht had sucked his upper lip and had summoned the family council. It met over tea and biscuits in the Hall of Knights. Only the two female members, Princess Katharina and Ditlinde, opposed the sale on the grounds of loss of dignity. 'You will be misunderstood, Albrecht,' said Ditlinde. 'You will be charged with lack of respect for your station, and that is not right, for you have, on the contrary, too much of it; you are so proud, Albrecht, that you don't give tuppence for anything. But I will say no. I do not wish to see a Croesus live in one of your castles, it isn't right, and it was bad enough that he should have a physician-in-ordinary and occupy the Grand Ducal Suite at the Spa Hotel. The *Courier* stresses all the time that he is a taxpaying subject, but in my eyes he is simply a subject and nothing more. What is your opinion, Klaus Heinrich? – But Klaus Heinrich voted for the sale. In the first place, Albrecht would get his central heating; secondly, Spoelmann was not just anybody, he was not soap manufacturer Unschlitt, he was a special case, and it was no disgrace to let him have Delphinenort. Finally, with downcast eyes Albrecht had declared the whole family council to be a farce; the people had decided long ago; the ministers were pressing him to agree to the sale; and there was really nothing left for him to do but once more 'repair to the station and wave the flag'.

The family council had taken place in the spring. From then on the negotiations for the sale carried on between Spoelmann on the one hand and the Lord Marshal von Bühl zu Bühl on the other proceeded apace, and the summer was not far advanced when Delphinenort with its adjacent buildings and the grounds became the property of Mr Spoelmann.

And now the castle and its interior became the scene of bustle and activity, and every day it attracted crowds of people to the north side of the park. Delphinenort was being restored, was being partly rebuilt on the inside, and a vast contingent of workmen was employed for the job. Speed was the order of the day, those were Spoelmann's orders, and he had given them a bare five months in which to complete everything for his arrival. A

wooden scaffold with ladders and platforms went up rapidly
around the splendid derelict building, foreign labourers swarmed
all over it, and an architect arrived from the States with full
power to supervise the work in progress. But the greater part of
the task fell to the local workmen; the stone cutters and tilers, the
joiners, gilders, upholsterers, glaziers and parquet layers from the
city, the landscape gardeners, and the plumbers and electricians
had plenty of well-paid work throughout the summer and
autumn. When His Royal Highness Prince Klaus Heinrich left
his window at the Eremitage ajar, the building noises from
Delphinenort penetrated into his Empire rooms, and several
times he drove past the castle amidst the respectful acclamations
of the public, in order to verify the progress of the restoration.
The gardener's cottage was being repaired; the stables and
coach-houses, which were to accommodate the Spoelmanns' fleet
of carriages and motor-cars, were being enlarged, and in October
quantities of furniture and rugs arrived, and cases with materials
and household utensils, while rumour went round among the
bystanders that inside the walls skilled hands were at work
fitting Spoelmann's costly electric organ which had been sent
from overseas. There was much excited speculation whether
the grounds belonging to the castle, which had been so marvellously put in order and replanted, were going to be fenced off
from the public by a wall or hedge. But nothing of the sort was
done. It was Spoelmann's wish that the property should continue to be accessible, that no restraint should be placed on the
citizens' enjoyment of the park. The Sunday promenaders should
have access right up to the castle, up to the clipped hedge which
surrounded the big square pond – and this did not fail to make
an excellent impression on the population; indeed, the *Courier*
published a special article on the subject, in which it praised Mr
Spoelmann for his philanthropy.

   And lo and behold! When the leaves began to fall once more,
exactly a year after his first appearance, Samuel Spoelmann
descended a second time at our railway station. This time the
general interest in the event was much greater than in the preceding year, and it is on record that, when Mr Spoelmann, in
his well-known dun-coloured overcoat and with his hat pulled

down over his eyes, left the saloon car, loud cheers were raised
by the crowd of spectators; a public manifestation which seemed
to annoy Spoelmann, and which Doctor Watercloose acknowledged in his stead with a benign smile and closed eyes. When
Miss Spoelmann emerged another cheer was raised, and one or
two playful onlookers even huzzaed when Percy, the collie,
alighted on the platform, trembling and prancing and quite
beside himself with excitement. In addition to the Doctor and
Countess Löwenjoul there were two strangers in attendance, clean
shaven and purposeful-looking gentlemen with exceptionally
bulky overcoats. These were Mr Spoelmann's secretaries, Messrs
Phlebs and Slippers, as the *Courier* announced in its report.

At that time Delphinenort was far from ready, and for the
time being Spoelmann and his party moved into the first floor
of the Residenz Hotel where a big haughty man with a paunch
and dressed all in black, the Spoelmanns' butler who had arrived
ahead of them, had prepared the suite and installed the chamber
velocipede with his own hands. Every day, while Miss Imma
with her Countess and Percy went for a ride or visited some
charitable institution, Mr Spoelmann stayed in his house to
supervise the work and give orders, and when the end of the
year approached shortly after the first snowfall, the project was
completed and the Spoelmanns took up their abode at Delphinenort. Two motor-cars (whose arrival had been noted a short
while ago – and fine cars they were, with high-powered engines
and moving with a gentle, metallic purr) driven by chauffeurs
in leather uniforms with footmen in snow-white fur coats and
crossed arms beside them, bore the members of the party in a few
minutes from the hotel through the Municipal Gardens. Messrs
Phlebs and Slippers sat in the second car, and as both vehicles
drove up the stately chestnut avenue leading to the front drive,
street urchins clung to the four lamp posts at the corners of the
large pond, and cheering loudly, waved their caps at them.

So now Samuel Spoelmann, his daughter and his household,
settled down among us, and his presence became a cherished
institution. His servants in white and gold liveries became a
familiar sight, as were the Grand Ducal lackeys in brown and
gold. The negro dressed in red plush who acted as doorkeeper

in front of Delphinenort soon became a public institution, and when passers-by heard the subdued rumble of Mr Spoelmann's organ from the interior of the castle they lifted a finger and said : 'Listen, he's playing. That means he's not got colic at the moment.' Miss Imma was seen daily with Countess Löwenjoul, followed by a groom with Percy capering madly at their feet, either on horseback or driving a splendid four-in-hand through the Municipal Gardens, while the footman who sat on the back seat stood up from time to time, drew a long silver horn from a leather sheath and sounded a shrill warning of their approach. By getting up early one could see father and daughter arrive every morning in a dark red brougham, or, in fine weather, walk across the park of the Eremitage from Delphinenort to the Thermal Gardens in order to drink the waters. Imma for her part, as already mentioned, resumed her visits to the charitable institutions, though she did not appear to neglect her studies for all that; for from the beginning of term she regularly attended the lectures of Professor Klinghammer at the University – sat daily, in a black dress with a white collar and cuffs, among the students in the lecture hall, and scribbled in her exercise book with her forefinger pressed high and hard against her fountain-pen – for this was her way of writing. The Spoelmanns lived in retirement, they did not mix with local society, as was natural in view of Mr Spoelmann's ill-health and his social isolation. What set could they have attached themselves to? Nobody even suggested that he should consort with soap manufacturer Unschlitt or Bank Director Holfsmilch. Yet he was soon approached with appeals to his generosity, and these appeals were not in vain. For Mr Spoelmann, who, it was well known, had made a large donation to the Board of Education of the United States before his departure, and had stated in so many words that he had no intention of withdrawing his yearly contributions to the Spoelmann University and his other educational foundations, shortly after his arrival put his name down at Delphinenort for a subscription of ten thousand marks to the Dorothea Children's Hospital for which a collection was then being made; an action the generosity of which was warmly praised by the *Courier* and the rest of the press.

In fact, although the Spoelmanns lived in seclusion in a social sense, a certain amount of publicity attached to their life among us from the earliest moments, and in the local section of the daily newspapers at least their movements were followed with as much particularity as those of the members of the Grand Ducal House. The public were informed when Miss Imma had played a game of tennis with the Countess and Messrs Phlebs and Slippers in the park of Delphinenort; it was noted when she had appeared at the Court Theatre, and when her father had accompanied her to hear one or two acts of an opera; and if Mr Spoelmann avoided publicity, if he did not leave the box during the intervals and was hardly ever seen walking in the streets, he was obviously not unaware of the representational duties imposed on him by his unusual position and made allowances for public curiosity. As had been noted the grounds of Delphinenort were not fenced off from the Municipal Gardens. No walls divided the castle from the outer world. Especially from the back one would walk straight across the lawn to the foot of the wide, covered porch which had been added, and if one was bold enough, could look straight through the big glass door into the white and gold drawing-room in which Mr Spoelmann and his party had their tea at five o'clock. And when the summer came, tea was laid on the terrace outside, and Mr and Miss Spoelmann, the Countess and Doctor Watercloose drank tea as though sitting on a stage. For at least on Sundays there was no lack of an audience to savour the spectacle from a respectful distance. People pointed out the huge electrically-heated silver kettle, an unheard-of innovation, and the astonishing liveries of the footmen who handed the tea and cakes : white coats with gold braid and swansdown trimming at the collar, cuffs and hem. They listened to snatches of English and German conversation, and with bated breath followed every move of the strange group up there on the platform. They then went round to the other side, to the main portal, and addressed a few jokes in local dialect to the blackamoor in red plush, which he acknowledged with a wide and dazzling grin.

Klaus Heinrich saw Imma Spoelmann for the first time on a bright winter's day, at noon. That does not mean that he had not frequently caught sight of her either at the theatre, in the street, or in the park. But that was not the same thing. He really saw her for the first time on that day at noon, under dramatic circumstances.

He had been holding open audience at the Old Castle until eleven-thirty, and after it was over had not returned straight to the Eremitage, but had ordered his coachman to keep the carriage waiting in one of the courts while he smoked a cigarette with the Guards officers on duty. As he wore the uniform of that regiment, to which his personal aide-de-camp also belonged, he made an effort to maintain the semblance of a certain camaraderie with the officers; he dined from time to time in their mess and occasionally gave them half an hour of his company on guard, although he had a dim suspicion that he was rather a nuisance as he kept them from their cards and smoking-room stories.

So there he stood, the convex silver star of the Noble Order of the Grimmburg Gryphon on his breast, his left hand planted well back on his hip, with Herr von Braunbart-Schellendorf, who had given due notice of the visit in the officers' mess, which was situated on the ground floor of the Castle near the Albrechts Gate – engaged in a trivial conversation with two or three officers in the middle of the room, while a further group of officers chatted at the deep-set window. Owing to the warmth of the sun outside, the window stood open and from the barracks along the Albrechtsstrasse came the strains of the drum and fife band of the approaching relief guard.

Twelve o'clock struck from the Court Chapel tower. The loud 'Fall in!' of the non-commissioned officer was heard outside, and the rattle of grenadiers standing to arms. The public collected in the square. The lieutenant on duty hastily buckled on his sword belt, clapped his heels together in a salute to Klaus Heinrich and went out. Looking out of the window the lieutenant on duty exclaimed with the rather forced show of familiarity which characterized the relations between Klaus Heinrich and the officers: 'I say! Look Your Royal Highness, there's a pretty sight . . . The Spoelmann girl with her algebra under her arm . . .' Klaus Heinrich advanced towards the window. From

the right side of the pavement Miss Imma came towards them all
by herself. Both hands thrust into the big, flat muff whose flap
was trimmed with tails she pressed her exercise book against
her side. She wore a three-quarter jacket of shining black fox
and a toque of the same dark fur on her small exotic head. She
was obviously on her way from Delphinenort to the University,
and in a hurry. She reached the guard house at the moment at
which the relief guard marched up the gutter, over against the
guard on duty which occupied the pavement standing at attention in two ranks. She was faced with having to retrace her steps,
walk round the band and the crowd of spectators, indeed, if she
wished to avoid the open square with its tram lines, to make a
fairly wide détour on the footpath which encircled it – or to
await the end of the military routine. She showed no intention
of doing either. She made as if to walk along the pavement in
front of the Castle right through the double rank of soldiers.
The sergeant with a hoarse voice stepped hastily forward. 'No
thoroughfare!' he shouted and thrust the butt of his rifle in front
of her. 'No thoroughfare! Right turn! Stand still!' At this point
Miss Spoelmann flared up. 'How dare you!' she exclaimed. 'I'm
in a hurry!' But these words were nothing in comparison to the
heartfelt expression of passionate and irresistible indignation
with which they were uttered. How small and foreign she appeared! The fair haired soldiers round her towered head and
shoulders above her. Her face was waxen pale at that moment,
her black brows met in an angry and expressive line, the nostrils
of her small and unformed nose were distended, and her eyes,
coal-black with emotion and abnormally large, spoke so expressive and compelling a language that no protest seemed possible.
'How dare you!' she exclaimed. 'I'm in a hurry!' And saying
this she brushed the stupefied sergeant with his rifle butt aside
and walked straight through the ranks, passed straight on,
turned left into University Road and was lost from sight. 'By
Jove!' cried Lieutenant von Sturmhahn. 'That's one up to Spoelmann!' The officers at the window laughed. Outside among the
pedestrians too there was much hilarity, which by the way
sounded entirely sympathetic. Klaus Heinrich joined in the
general laughter. The changing of the guard proceeded with

loud words of command and snatches of march tunes. Then Klaus Heinrich returned to the Eremitage.

He lunched alone. In the afternoon he went for a ride on his chestnut Florian, and spent the evening at a big reception given by the Minister of Finance, Dr Krippenreuther, at his home. In an animated voice he repeated the episode in front of the guardhouse to several guests who showed themselves delighted with his account although by now the story had gone round and become generally known. The following day he had to leave, to represent his brother at the inauguration of a new town hall in a neighbouring city. For some reason he went reluctantly, he disliked leaving the capital. He felt that he was leaving behind an important matter, pleasant, though somehow disquieting, which imperatively demanded his presence. But his exalted calling must not be neglected. Yet while he sat upright and festively attired on the seat of honour in the town hall, listening to the Mayor's address, Klaus Heinrich's thoughts were not concentrating on the impression he was making on the people, but were secretly busy with that new and urgent matter. And briefly he thought of a person he had met once years ago, a Fräulein Unschlitt, the daughter of the soap manufacturer, a memory connected with this urgent matter.

Imma Spoelmann angrily pushed aside the hoarse-voiced sergeant – and with her algebra under her arm walked all alone through the ranks of big, fair-haired Grenadiers. How pale was her small face, framed by her dark hair and the fur toque, and how eloquent her eyes! There was no one like her. Her father was surfeited with riches and had quite simply bought a castle belonging to the Crown. What was it that the *Courier* had said about his undeserved reputation and the 'romantic isolation of his life'? He bore the hatred of the underprivileged masses – that was more or less what the article had said. Her nostrils had been distended with indignation. There was no one like her, no one at all. She was unique. Supposing it had been her at the Citizens' Ball. He would have had a companion, he would not have lost his way and the evening would not have ended in humiliation and shame. 'Down, down, down with him!' How awful! To see her walk once more, so dark and foreign looking, among the ranks of fair-haired soldiers!

These were the thoughts that occupied Klaus Heinrich during the next few days – just these three or four mental pictures. And it was amazing how richly they fed him, leaving no room for any others. But all things considered it seemed more than desirable that he should see her pearl-white face again as soon as possible.

In the evening he drove to the Court Theatre where the *Magic Flute* was being performed. And when from the box he discovered Miss Spoelmann sitting next to Countess Löwenjoul in the front row of the circle, he trembled. During the act he could observe her in the dark through his opera glasses, for the light from the stage fell on her. She rested her head on her slender ringless hand, unselfconsciously propping her bare arm on the velvet parapet, and now she no longer looked angry. She wore a dress of shimmering sea-green silk with a light wrap embroidered in multi-coloured flowers, and on her neck and breast glistened a diamond necklace. She really was not as small as she appeared, Klaus Heinrich decided when she got up after the curtain fell. No, it was the childlike character of her head and her slender, tawny shoulders which made her appear like a little girl. Her arms were well developed and one could see that she played games and rode. But her wrists were those of a child.

When the actors arrived at the passage: 'He is a Prince, he is more than a Prince,' Klaus Heinrich felt an urge to talk to Doctor Überbein. As it was, Doctor Überbein dressed, as usual when he visited Klaus Heinrich, in his black frock-coat and white tie, called at the Eremitage quite by chance the following day. Klaus Heinrich inquired whether he had heard the story of the changing of the guard. 'Yes,' replied Doctor Überbein several times. But if Klaus Heinrich wished to relate it to him once more . . . ? 'Not if you know it already,' said Klaus Heinrich, disappointed. Then Doctor Überbein changed the subject. He began to talk of opera glasses and stressed what an excellent invention they were. They, as it were, brought within reach what was unfortunately far away, didn't they? They bridged the distance between oneself and the desired goal. What were Klaus Heinrich's thoughts on the matter? Klaus Heinrich was inclined to agree up to a point. It was rumoured that he had made generous use of them last night, added the Doctor. Klaus Heinrich failed to understand this. And then Doctor Überbein said brusquely: 'Look here, Klaus Heinrich, this won't do. You are being stared at. Little Imma is being stared at. That's quite enough. Now if you begin to stare at little Imma it is really going to be a bit much. Surely you must see that.'

'Oh dear, Doctor Überbein, I never thought of that.'

'You are not usually so forgetful.'

'I have felt so strange these last few days,' said Klaus Heinrich.

Doctor Überbein leant back, pulled at his red beard close to the neck and slowly inclined his head and thorax.

'Really, you have, have you?' he said and nodded again.

Klaus Heinrich said: 'You won't believe how reluctant I felt the other day to go to the inauguration of that town hall. Tomorrow I must attend the swearing-in of the Grenadier recruits. Then the bestowing of those family orders. I'm sick of it. I don't feel in the least like doing my stuff. I've no mind to exercise my exalted calling.'

'I am sorry to hear that!' said Doctor Überbein sharply.

'Yes, I might have imagined how this would annoy you. I'm sure you'll call it sloppiness. And I know you; you'll begin to talk of destiny and courage. But last night at the Opera I thought of you during a certain passage, and I was wondering whether you are really right in some respects . . .'

'Look here, Klaus Heinrich, if I'm not mistaken, I've had to pull Your Royal Highness up once before.'

'That was different, Doctor Überbein! Oh, if only you could see that this was something totally different. That was at the Bürgergarten long ago, and I have no desire to repeat it. But she . . . You see, you used to explain to me what you understood by the term "Highness"; that it was something touching, and that one had to approach it with tender sympathy, as you used to put it. Don't you think that the person we are talking about is touching, and that one needs to have sympathy for her?'

'Maybe,' said Doctor Überbein. 'Maybe.'

'You've often told me that one mustn't discount exceptions, that this was sloppiness and cheap sentimentality. Don't you think that the person we are talking about is an exception?'

Doctor Überbein remained silent.

And then he said suddenly in his booming voice: 'So now I'm being asked to, as it were, turn two exceptions into a rule?'

With that he took himself off. He said he had to return to his work, placing a marked emphasis on the term 'work', and begging leave to withdraw, he took his departure in a strangely ceremonious, unpaternal fashion.

Klaus Heinrich did not see him for about ten or twelve days. Once he invited him to lunch but Doctor Überbein asked to be excused, his work at the moment was too pressing. At last he came unasked. He seemed in high spirits and looked more green in the face than ever. He talked of this and that, and then began to discuss the Spoelmanns, gazing at the ceiling and squeezing his throat as he did so. One had to admit that there was a striking amount of public feeling for Samuel Spoelmann in the city. One could see everywhere how popular he was. Chiefly of course as a taxpayer, but in other ways as well. People of all classes simply doted on him, on his organ-playing hobby, his dun-coloured overcoat, and his kidney trouble. Every errand boy was proud of him, and if he were not so inaccessible and morose people would gladly make him feel his popularity. Of course the donation of ten thousand marks to the Dorothea Hospital had made an excellent impression. His friend Sammet had told Überbein that with its help far-reaching improvements had been made. By the way, now he came to think of it: Sammet had told him that Imma planned to look at these new improvements tomorrow morning. She had sent one of her swansdown flunkeys to inquire whether it would be convenient if she came in the morning. In fact, the misery of those children was none of her concern, thought Überbein, but perhaps she was out to learn. Tomorrow at eleven, if he remembered right. Then he spoke of other things. But on leaving he added: 'The Grand Duke ought to take more interest in the Children's Hospital, Klaus Heinrich; people expect it of him. It is a worthy institution. In brief, one of you ought to visit it. Give proof of interest in high quarters. Forgive my meddling . . . God bless.'

But he turned back once more, and in his greenish face a flush spread underneath his eyes which looked entirely unreal. 'If I ever catch you again with a punchbowl cover on your head, Klaus Heinrich,' he said loudly, 'I'm not going to move a finger.' And pressing his lips together he turned and quickly left the room.

The following morning shortly before eleven Klaus Heinrich and Herr von Braunbart-Schellendorf drove from the Eremitage down the snow-covered birch avenue, through badly paved suburban streets, past shabby homesteads, and stopped in front of a plain white building with 'Dorothea Children's Hospital' in broad black lettering above the portal. The medical superintendent in a dress suit and with the Albrecht Cross of the Third Class on his breast awaited him in the hall, with two junior surgeons and the female nursing staff. The Prince and his companion wore helmets and fur coats. Klaus Heinrich said: 'This is the second time that I renew an old acquaintance, my dear Doctor. You were present when I was born. Again, you were at his bedside when my father died. And you are a friend of my tutor Doctor Überbein. I am delighted to meet you.'

Doctor Sammet, gone grey during his life of active charity, bowed with his head laid on one side, with one hand clutched his watch-chain and pressed his elbow to his side. He presented the two junior doctors and the Matron to the Prince. Then he said: 'I should explain that the gracious visit of your Royal Highness coincides with another. We are expecting Miss Spoelmann. Her father has helped our institution in such a generous way that we could not very well cancel the arrangement. The Matron will show Miss Spoelmann round.'

Klaus Heinrich acknowledged the coincidence with an affable smile. He then remarked on the nurses' uniform which he declared to be most becoming, and repeated his desire to be shown round the building. They set out on their tour of inspection. The Matron and three nurses remained in the hall.

Every wall in the hospital was painted with waterproof paint. The water taps were large ones, designed to be worked with the elbow, for reasons of hygiene. Special jets had been installed to rinse the milk bottles. They passed first through a reception room, empty save for a few spare beds and the surgeons' bicycles. In the surgery next door there stood, beside the writing desk and the hanger for the surgeons' white coats, a kind of swaddling table with an oilcloth cover, an operating table, a cupboard with baby food, and curved baby scales. Klaus Heinrich stopped in front of the cupboard and inquired after the chemical formula of the baby food. Doctor Sammet thought that if this whole tour was going to be made with such attention to detail an awful lot of time would be wasted.

Suddenly there was a commotion in the street outside. A car drew up, hooting and braking in front of the hospital. Cheers could be heard distinctly from the surgery although it was only a few children calling. Klaus Heinrich paid scant attention to these noises. He was looking at a tin of glucose which, by the way, had nothing of particular interest about it. 'It seems you are having a visitor,' he said. 'Of course, you did tell me that you were expecting someone. Shall we go on?'

The party proceeded to the kitchen, the milk kitchen, the big tiled room for preparing the milk, the pantry for full milk, skimmed milk and buttermilk. The daily rations in small bottles stood lined up on clean white tables. A sour, insipid smell pervaded the room.

To this room Klaus Heinrich gave his undivided attention. He even tasted the buttermilk and declared it to be excellent. How the children must thrive on such good milk, he commented. During this inspection the door opened and Miss Spoelmann entered between the Matron and Countess Löwenjoul, followed by the three nurses.

The jacket, toque and muff she was wearing today were made of the costliest sable, and her muff was suspended on a gold chain set with coloured precious stones. Her black hair showed a tendency to fall in smooth strands across her forehead. She took in the room at a sweeping glance. Her eyes were really almost too big in proportion to her face; they dominated it like a cat's, save that they were as black as anthracite and spoke an eloquent language of their own...

Countess Löwenjoul, in a feather hat and dressed neatly and plainly but with simple elegance as usual, smiled distraitly.

'The milk kitchen,' said the Matron, 'this is where the children's milk is being prepared.'

'I guessed that much,' replied Miss Spoelmann. She said it rapidly and lightly, without an English accent, with pursed lips and a small, haughty toss of her head. Her voice consisted of one deep and one treble note, with a break in the middle.

The Matron was taken aback. 'Yes,' she said, 'it is obvious.' And a small frown of bewilderment passed over her face.

The situation was not easy. Doctor Sammet looked to Klaus Heinrich for a directive; but though Klaus Heinrich was accustomed to perform his duty within limits set by fixed convention, he was not used to dealing with unforeseen and confusing circumstances and an awkward pause ensued. Herr von Braunbart was on the point of intervening, and Miss Spoelmann for her part made as if to leave the milk kitchen when the Prince made a small courteous gesture with his right hand in the direction of the young lady. This was the sign for Doctor Sammet to advance towards Miss Spoelmann.

'May I introduce myself, Doctor Sammet. Yes.' He requested the honour of presenting Miss Spoelmann to His Royal Highness. 'Miss Spoelmann, Royal Highness, the daughter of Mr Spoelmann to whom the hospital is so deeply indebted.'

Klaus Heinrich clicked his heels together and held out his right hand in a white military gauntlet, and placing her small hand encased in a brown suède glove in it, she gave him a regular handshake, at the same time and with a boyish grace sketching a curtsey without taking her big, starry eyes off Klaus Heinrich's face. He could think of nothing better to say than: 'So you are paying a visit to the hospital, Miss Spoelmann?'

And as before she replied in a husky voice, with a pout and a proud movement of her head: 'So it would seem, would it not?'

Herr von Braunbart involuntarily raised his hand, Doctor Sammet examined his watch-chain in silence, and one of the junior surgeons emitted a short gasp which was out of place. And now it was on Klaus Heinrich's face that one could see a small frown of bewilderment. He said: 'Of course, I shall have the pleasure of visiting the hospital in the company of Miss Spoelmann. Lieutenant von Braunbart, my aide-de-camp,' he added hastily as his remark seemed to him not more fortuitous than the previous one. She countered by saying: 'Countess Löwenjoul.'

The Countess made a dignified curtsey accompanied by an enigmatic smile and an ambiguous sidelong glance which had something coolly alluring about it. But when she straightened and let her strangely evasive eyes rest once more on Klaus Heinrich, who stood before her in a disciplined and soldierly attitude, the smile faded from her face and a peevish and aggrieved expression took its place, and for a split second it was as though a flash of hatred from her slightly swollen grey eyes struck Klaus Heinrich. It was a fleeting impression. Klaus Heinrich had no time to take it in, and he forgot about it forthwith. The two young surgeons were introduced to Miss Spoelmann. And then Klaus Heinrich suggested that they resume their tour of inspection.

They mounted the stairs to the first floor; Klaus Heinrich and Imma in front of the others, escorted by Doctor Sammet. The older children up to fourteen years of age were housed on that floor. A passage with lockers for linen divided the wards for boys and girls. In their white cots, with name plates over their heads and a movable frame at the foot end which contained the charts with the temperature and weight of each child, attended by nurses in white caps, surrounded by order and cleanliness lay the small patients, and their coughs filled the room while Klaus Heinrich and Imma Spoelmann walked between the rows.

He kept courteously to the left and smiled, as he always did when he visited exhibitions, inspected veterans, sports clubs or guards of honour. But every time he turned to the right and saw Imma Spoelmann watching him, he met her dark gaze resting on his with a searching expression. This was so unfamiliar that Klaus Heinrich could not remember ever having experienced anything so strange as her way of watching him out of her big eyes, quite unselfconscious and unconcerned with his or anybody else's reaction. When Doctor Sammet stopped at a small bed to explain a case, that of a little girl for instance whose leg in plaster was tied in a vertical position, one could see that she was listening intently to what he said, yet while she did so she never looked towards him but her eyes went back and forth between Klaus Heinrich and the child which lay there, flat and motionless, gazing up at him with hands folded on its breast; they rested in turn on the Prince and on the hospital case which was being explained to them, as though checking Klaus Heinrich's reaction, or searching for the effect of Doctor Sammet's words on his face – and it was not quite clear what made her do it. Yes, this was especially noticeable in the case of the boy who had been rescued from drowning. A second sad case, as Doctor Sammet observed. 'The scissors, sister, please,' he said, and showed them the double wound in the child's upper arm where a bullet had passed in and out. 'The wound,' said the Doctor in an undertone to his guests, turning his back on the bed, 'was caused by his own father. The boy was the lucky one. The man shot his wife, three of his children and himself with a revolver. He missed this one ...' Klaus Heinrich looked at the double wound. 'What made the man do it?' he asked shyly, and Doctor Sammet replied: 'He acted in desperation, your Royal Highness; want and dishonour made him do it.' He said no more, gave no more than this general indication – same as with the small boy who had been rescued from the river, a ten-year-old child. 'He's wheezing,' said Doctor Sammet, 'he's still got water in his lungs. They fished him out of the river this morning early, yes. By the way, it is highly improbable that he should have fallen in by mistake. Several indications are against it. He ran away from home. Yes.' He stood silent. And again Klaus Heinrich felt Miss Spoelmann's gaze on him, her dark, shining, serious eyes searching for his own, imperatively challenging him to reflect jointly with her on these 'sad cases', to complete Doctor Sammet's hints in imagination, and visualize the dreadful realities summed up and embodied in these two sick children ... A small girl was crying bitterly when the steaming and hissing inhaler, together with a box full of coloured pictures, was placed on her bed. Miss Spoelmann bent down towards the child. 'It doesn't hurt,' she said, imitating the childish accent. 'Not a bit, you mustn't cry.' And as she straightened out she said with

a pout: 'I bet those pictures make her cry as much as anything.'
Everybody laughed. One of the young assistant surgeons picked
up the covers of the box, and examining them laughed more
loudly than the rest. They passed into the laboratory. On the
way Klaus Heinrich reflected on the odd brand of Miss Spoelmann's humour. She seemed to find amusement not only in
the pictures, but in the way she deftly handled her dry and
humorous phrases. And this was surely the very essence of
humour ...

The laboratory was the largest room in the building. Jars,
retorts, funnels and chemicals stood on the tables, as well as
specimens in alcohol which Doctor Sammet explained to his
guests in a few quiet and well chosen words. A child had
choked in a mysterious way; here was the larynx with a mush-
room-like growth instead of vocal chords. Yes. This here in a jar
was a case of pernicious enlargement in the kidneys of a child,
and these were cancerous bones. Klaus Heinrich and Miss Spoelmann looked at everything together; they gazed at the jars which
Doctor Sammet held up to the light and their eyes were thoughtful, while an identical expression of faint revulsion hovered
round their mouths. They took turns at the microscope, and with
one eye glued to the lens, examined a malignant secretion on a
piece of tissue stained with blue and smeared on to a glass slide
which showed up large and small spots; these latter were bacilli.
Klaus Heinrich beckoned to Miss Spoelmann to take the first
turn at the microscope but she declined, raising her brows and
pursing her lips as if to say: 'On no account, after you!' So he
took precedence for he thought it immaterial who had the first
look at such ominous and horrible things as bacilli. After that
they were taken up to the second floor, to the ward of new-born
babies.

They laughed at the chorus of concerted bawls which greeted
them on the stairs. And then they and their party passed between
the cots, side by side they bent over the bald-headed creatures
who slept with closed fists or, howling at the top of their lungs,
showed their naked gums, stopped their ears with their hands
and laughed again. In an incubator lay a prematurely born
infant. And Doctor Sammet showed his distinguished guests a

dreadful-looking corpselike baby of paupers, with large and ugly hands, the sign of lowly birth.

He lifted a squealing infant from its cot and it stopped crying at once. Expertly he supported the limp head in the hollow of his hand and held up the purple little creature, blinking and twitching, for them to see, and they stood side by side and looked down at the baby. Klaus Heinrich looked on with his heels close together while Doctor Sammet replaced the baby in its cot, and when he turned he met Imma Spoelmann's shining, searching gaze as he had expected.

Finally, they went over to one of the three windows of the ward and looked out across the squalid suburb, down into the street where, surrounded by a crowd of children, the brown Ducal brougham and Miss Spoelmann's smart dark red car stood in a row. The Spoelmanns' chauffeur in his shaggy fur coat was leaning back in his seat, with one hand on the wheel of the powerful car, watching his colleague, the footman in a white livery, trying to keep up a conversation with Klaus Heinrich's coachman.

'Our neighbours,' said Doctor Sammet lifting the white muslin curtain with one hand, 'are the parents of our charges. On Saturday night we can hear the fathers stagger past in a drunken stupor. Yes.'

They stood still and listened, but Doctor Sammet said nothing further about the fathers, and they made ready to leave as they had now seen everything.

The procession with Klaus Heinrich and Imma at the head proceeded downstairs and found the nurses assembled once more in the front hall. Leave was taken with compliments and the clicking of heels, with bows and curtseys. Klaus Heinrich, standing in a formal attitude in front of Doctor Sammet, who listened to him with his head cocked sideways and his hand on his watch-chain, expressed his satisfaction with what he had seen with the customary phrases, the while feeling Imma Spoelmann's big eyes resting on him. When the leave-taking from the doctors and nurses was over he and Herr von Braunbart-Schellendorf escorted the ladies to their car. While they crossed the pavement packed with children and women with babies in their arms, and briefly stopped by the running board of the car, Klaus Heinrich and Imma Spoelmann exchanged the following remarks:

'It has been a great pleasure to meet you,' he said.

She did not reply to this but pursed her lips and turned her head from side to side.

'It was an absorbing inspection,' he went on. 'A regular eye opener.'

She looked at him with her big black eyes, then said quickly and lightly in her broken voice: 'Yes, to a certain extent . . .'

He ventured on the question: 'I hope you are pleased with Castle Delphinenort?' to which she replied with pursed lips: 'Oh, why not? It's quite a convenient house.'

'Do you like being there better than in New York?' he asked. And she replied: 'Just as much. It's much the same. Much the same everywhere.'

That was all. Klaus Heinrich, and one pace behind him Herr von Braunbart, stood with their hands raised to their helmets while the chauffeur went into gear and the car started off with a tremor.

It may be imagined that this encounter did not remain an internal matter of the Dorothea Hospital for long but made headlines that very evening. The *Courier*, under a lyrical heading, published a detailed account of the meeting which, without being quite correct in all its details, excited the public imagination and caused such a virulent outbreak of general curiosity that the paper saw itself compelled to keep a vigilant eye on any further *rapprochement* between the Grimmburg and Spoelmann mansions. There was little enough to relate. It reported a couple of times that after the performance at the Court Theatre His Royal Highness, Prince Klaus Heinrich, when passing through the corridor of the gallery, had stopped for a moment in front of the Spoelmanns' box to pay his respects to the ladies. And in the report of the fancy-dress Charity Bazaar which took place in the middle of January at the Town Hall – an elegant function at which Miss Spoelmann, at the urgent request of the Committee, took a stall – no small space was devoted to a description of how Prince Klaus Heinrich, when the Court made a round of the Bazaar, had stopped before Miss Spoelmann's stall, how he had bought a goblet of cut glass (for Miss Spoelmann sold china and glass) and had lingered for full eight or ten minutes. It did not mention their topic of conversation. And yet it had not been without importance.

The Court (with the exception of Albrecht) had appeared in the Town Hall about noon. By the time Klaus Heinrich, with his newly acquired goblet wrapped in tissue paper on his knees, drove back to the Eremitage, he had announced his intention of visiting Delphinenort and seeing the castle in its renovated state, and on this occasion looking at Mr Spoelmann's collection of antique glass. For among the glass sold by Miss Spoelmann were three or four collector's pieces presented to the Bazaar by her father, of which Klaus Heinrich had bought one.

He saw himself again in a semicircle of people who were watching him, alone and facing Imma Spoelmann, separated from her by the counter laden with glasses and decanters, and with groups of white and painted porcelain; he saw her red fancy dress, which, cut in one piece, moulded her well-shaped and yet childlike figure, exposing her tawny shoulders and round, firm arms with the wrists of a child. He saw the gold ornament, half garland and half diadem, in her loose black hair which had a tendency to fall in strands across her forehead, her shining, questioning eyes in her pearl-white face, her soft, full mouth which she pursed with fastidious disdain when talking, and all round her in the large, vaulted hall the scent of firs, a babel of noise, music, the clash of gongs, laughter, and the cries of vendors.

He had admired the piece of glass, a rare goblet mounted on silver foliage which she had offered him for sale saying that it came from her father's collection. Did her father possess a number of these fine collector's pieces in his collection? Indeed he did. And naturally he had not parted with his most valued treasures. She did not hesitate to declare that he had much more beautiful pieces in his collection. Klaus Heinrich would very much like to see them! – Well, that might be easily arranged, Miss Spoelmann had replied in her husky voice, pursing her lips and turning her head from side to side. Her father, she thought, would certainly have no objection to displaying the fruits of his collector's zeal to an appreciative visitor. The Spoelmanns were always at home at teatime.

She had gone straight to the point, had turned the hint into an invitation, and had spoken in a casual way. And then, in reply to Klaus Heinrich's question as to which day would suit them she had replied: 'Whenever you like, Prince, as we shall be delighted to see you any day that suits you.'

'We shall be delighted,' that was how she put it, with a sharp inflexion of exaggerated irony in her voice that was almost painful, and one had had difficulty in preserving a bland countenance. How she had hurt and confused the poor matron at the hospital the other day! But with all that there was something childlike about her way of speaking, indeed, some of the sounds she made were those of a child, and not only that time when she comforted the little girl with the inhaler. And how she had opened her eyes wide when told about the drunken fathers and the sad cases.

Next day, the very following day, Klaus Heinrich called at Delphinenort for tea. Miss Spoelmann had said that he might come any day that suited him. It suited him to call the very next day, and as the matter seemed so urgent he saw no point in putting it off.

Shortly before five o'clock – it was already dark – his brougham carried him across the sodden drive of the bare, deserted Municipal Gardens, and soon he reached the Spoelmanns' grounds. Arc-lamps lit the park, the opaque surface of the big square pond shone between the trees, and behind it rose the white façade with its pillared porch, its spacious drive between two wings ascending gently towards the ground floor, its tall windows divided into small panes, and with Roman busts standing in niches, and as Klaus Heinrich drove along the avenue of ancient chestnut trees he noticed the blackamoor in wine-red plush standing at the foot of the drive and keeping watch with a staff in his hand.

Klaus Heinrich entered the brightly-lit and pleasantly-heated stone hall with a shining floor of gilt mosaic, and white marble deities all round, and made straight for the broad, red-carpeted staircase which the Spoelmanns' butler was descending with squared shoulders and hanging arms, proudly carrying his portly paunch and clean-shaven double chin. He was led to the upper hall hung with tapestries and with a marble fireplace where a couple of swansdown-trimmed footmen removed the Prince's cap and cloak, while the butler went in person to announce him to his master. Between the footmen who flung back a tapestry Klaus Heinrich descended two or three steps.

He was met by the scent of flowers and heard the soft trickle of falling water; but just as the curtain closed behind him, a dog began to bark so loudly and furiously that Klaus Heinrich, deafened for a moment, stopped dead at the foot of the stairs. Perceval, the collie, dashed at him with unequalled excitement. He slobbered, he was quite beside himself, he writhed, he beat his flanks with his tail, he tried to catch it, turning madly on his own axis and seemed ready to burst with noise. A voice – it was not Imma's – called him back, and Klaus Heinrich found himself in a winter garden, a glass conservatory with a ceiling supported by slender marble columns, and a floor inlaid with large, shining marble squares. It was filled with palm trees whose trunks and feathery tops in places reached up to the ceiling. A flowerbed consisting of countless potted plants arranged in a mosaic pattern spread beneath the strong white arc-light and scented the warm air. Silvered jets trickled from a fine carved fountain into a marble basin, and rare specimens of duck swam on the illuminated surface. The background was made of a pillared arcade with niches.

It was Countess Löwenjoul who advanced smiling towards the guest and curtseyed.

'Your Royal Highness will forgive us,' she said. 'Percy is so vehement. Besides, these days he is unaccustomed to visitors. But he does no harm. Your Royal Highness must excuse Miss Spoelmann. She will be back in a minute. She was here just now. She has been called away. Her father sent for her. Mr Spoelmann will be delighted.'

And she conducted Klaus Heinrich to an arrangement of basket chairs with embroidered linen cushions which stood in front of a group of palms. She spoke in a brisk and lively way, bending her small head with the sparse ash-blonde parting to one side and showing her white teeth in a smile. Her figure looked decidedly distinguished in a close-fitting brown dress, and as she moved towards the chairs, briskly rubbing her hands together, she had the elegant, agile movements of an officer's wife. Only in her eyes, whose lids she screwed up till they were half closed, there was something of spite and distrust, something hard to define. They sat down, facing each other across the round garden table on which lay several books. Exhausted by his outburst Perceval curled up on the narrow carpet with a mother-of-pearl sheen. His black coat was like silk, with white at the paws, the chest and muzzle. He had a white collar, golden eyes, and a parting ran along his spine. Klaus Heinrich began a conversation for conversation's sake, a formal dialogue about nothing in particular, which was all he could do.

'I hope, Countess, that I have not come at an inconvenient time. Luckily I need not feel myself an unauthorized intruder. I do not know whether Miss Spoelmann has told you . . . She was so kind as to suggest my calling. It was a question of those beautiful glasses which Mr Spoelmann had been kind enough to present to the Bazaar. Miss Spoelmann thought her father would have no objection to showing me the rest of his collection. That is why . . .'

The Countess ignored the question as to whether Imma had informed her of the arrangement. She said: 'This is tea-time, Royal Highness. How could Your Royal Highness's presence be unwelcome? Even if, as I hope will not be the case, Mr Spoelmann were too unwell to appear . . .'

'Oh, is he not well?' In reality Klaus Heinrich almost wished that Mr Spoelmann might be prevented from appearing. He anticipated their meeting with vague anxiety.

'He was feeling ill today, Your Royal Highness. Unfortunately, he had a touch of fever, cramps and a spell of fainting. Doctor Watercloose was with him all morning. He gave him an injection of morphia. The question is whether another operation will be necessary.'

'I'm sorry to hear that,' said Klaus Heinrich, with sincerity. 'An operation. How dreadful.' To this the Countess replied with an evasive look: 'Oh yes, but there are worse things in life, many much worse things than that.'

'Undoubtedly,' said Klaus Heinrich. 'I can quite believe it.' He felt his imagination stirred in a vague and general way by the Countess's allusion.

She looked at him with her head inclined to one side, and a scornful expression on her face. Then her slightly swollen eyes shifted, one knew not quite where, with that secretive smile which Klaus Heinrich already knew and which had something alluring about it.

He felt it necessary to resume the conversation.

'Have you lived long with the Spoelmanns, Countess?' he asked.

'A fairly long time,' she answered, and appeared to calculate. 'Fairly long. I have lived through so much, have had so many experiences, that I naturally cannot reckon to a day. But it was shortly after the blessing – soon after the blessing was vouch-safed to me.'

'The blessing?' asked Klaus Heinrich.

'Indeed,' she said emphatically and with some irritation. 'For the blessing happened when the number of my experiences had become too great and I was near breaking point, so to speak. You are so young,' she added, neglecting to address him by his title, 'so ignorant of all the misery and sordidness of existence, you can have no idea of what I went through. I brought an action in America which entailed the appearance in court of a large number of generals. Things came to light which were more than I could bear. I had to clean all the barracks without succeeding in ejecting all the loose women. They hid in the cupboards, some underneath the floorboards, and that is why they continue to torment me at night. I should return at once to my estates in Burgundy were it not for the rain leaking through the roof. The Spoelmanns know this, and that is why it is so kind of them to let me live with them for the time being, my only duty being to put the totally innocent Imma on guard against the world. Only of course my health suffers from having these women sit on my chest at night and force me to watch their obscene grimaces. And this is the reason why I beg to be called simply "Frau

Meier",' she added in a whisper, leaning forward and touching Klaus Heinrich's arm with her hand. 'The walls have ears, and it is absolutely imperative that I keep to my enforced incognito in order to protect myself against the persecutions of these lascivious creatures. You will do what I ask of you, won't you? Look on it as a joke . . . a game which does no harm. Why not?'

She stopped.

Klaus Heinrich sat upright and without a sign of slackness in his wicker chair opposite her and looked at her. Before leaving his rectilineal rooms he had dressed with his valet Neumann's help, with all the care which his existence in the public eye demanded. His parting ran from over his left eye, straight up to the crown of his head, without a hair sticking up, and his hair was brushed up into a crest off the right side of his forehead. There he sat in his undress uniform, whose high collar and close fit helped him to maintain a composed attitude, the pleated silver epaulettes of a major on his narrow shoulders, leaning back lightly but without indulging in the luxury of total relaxation, collected, calm, with one foot placed slightly forward, and his right hand above his left on his sword hilt. His young face was a little drawn from the unreality, the stern isolation and the difficulty of his life; yet he was looking at the Countess with calm and friendly, absolutely self-possessed composure.

She stopped. A peevish and aggrieved expression showed on her features and while something like hatred against Klaus Heinrich flashed from her sleepless grey eyes, she changed colour in the strangest way, for one half of her face blushed while the other half turned pale. Dropping her eyelids she answered: 'I have been living with the Spoelmanns for three years, Royal Highness.'

Perceval jumped up. Capering and wagging his tail he trotted towards his mistress – for Imma Spoelmann had come into the room – and with great dignity rose on his hind legs and placed his forepaws on her chest. His jaws were wide open and his bright red tongue protruded from between his splendid white teeth. Standing thus erect before her he looked like some heraldic beast.

She was exquisitely dressed; in a teagown of brick-red wild

silk, with long, open sleeves and a bodice encrusted with gold embroidery. A large, egg-shaped gem suspended from a pearl necklace lay on her bare neck the skin of which was the colour of smoked meerschaum. Her blue-black hair was parted on one side and gathered in a chignon, and showed a tendency to fall in smooth strands across her brow and temples. Holding Perceval's overbred head in her beautiful slender, ringless hands, the hands of a child, she addressed him, putting her face close to his: 'Now then . . . Well, my friend, what a welcome! We have been pining for each other, haven't we, we tasted the pains of separation. Good afternoon, my friend; and now go back and lie down nicely.' And disentangling his paws from the embroidery on her chest she stepped aside and set him down on his four feet.

'Oh, Prince,' she said, 'welcome to Delphinenort. You hate breaking your promise, I can see. Let me sit down beside you. We'll be told when tea is ready. No doubt it's against all rules that I have kept you waiting. But my father sent for me – and besides you had somebody to entertain you.' Her bright eyes going back and forth between Klaus Heinrich and the Countess were a little doubtful.

'Indeed,' he said, 'I had.' And then he inquired after Mr Spoelmann's health, and received a fairly reassuring answer. Mr Spoelmann would have the pleasure of making Klaus Heinrich's acquaintance at teatime, he begged to be excused till then . . . What a lovely pair of horses Klaus Heinrich had in his brougham! And then they talked about their horses; about Klaus Heinrich's good-tempered chestnut Florian from the Hollerbrunn stud, about Miss Spoelmann's milk-white Arabian mare Fatme presented to Mr Spoelmann by an oriental potentate, about her fast Hungarian bay horses which she drove herself four-in-hand. 'Do you know the neighbourhood?' asked Klaus Heinrich. 'Have you been to the Hofjäger? To the Fasanerie Gardens? There are some very lovely excursions.' No, Miss Spoelmann was not at all clever in discovering new roads, and the Countess, well, she was not enterprising by nature. So they ended up by always taking the same route in the Municipal Gardens. It was perhaps a little dull, but Miss Spoelmann was not on the whole spoilt by overmuch variety and adventure.

Then he proposed that they should go for a ride together, on a fine day, to the Hofjäger or the Fasanerie, to which she replied with pursed lips that they might consider it sometime. Then the butler arrived and gravely announced that tea was ready.

Led by the solemnly-strutting butler, accompanied by the capering Percy and followed by Countess Löwenjoul they passed through the hall with the tapestries and the marble fireplace.

'Has the Countess been letting her tongue run away with her?' asked Imma *en route*, without bothering to lower her voice.

Klaus Heinrich started and looked at the floor. 'But she can hear us!' he said softly.

'No, she doesn't hear us,' answered Imma. 'I can read her face. When she cocks her head like that and blinks her eyes it means her mind is wandering and she's lost in thought. Did she let her tongue run away with her just now?'

'For a bit, yes,' said Klaus Heinrich. 'I got the impression that the Countess lets herself go every now and then.'

'She has had a lot of trouble.' And Imma looked at him with the same big searching dark eyes with which she had scanned him in the Dorothea Hospital. 'I'll tell you all about it another time. It's a long story.'

'Yes,' he said. 'Some other time. Next time. Perhaps on the way.'

'On the way?'

'Yes, on our way to the Hofjäger or the Fasanerie.'

'Oh, I forgot how conscientious you are, Prince, when it comes to your appointments. All right, on the way. This way down.'

They found themselves at the rear of the castle. From a gallery hung with large paintings, carpeted steps led down to the white and gold drawing-room whose tall glass doors opened on to the terrace. Everything here – the large crystal chandeliers which hung from the centre of the high, stuccoed ceiling, the symmetrically arranged armchairs with gilt woodwork and petit point upholstery, the heavy white silk curtains, the solemn Empire clock and the vases and gilt candlesticks on the white marble mantelpiece in front of the tall looking-glass, the massive, lion-footed gilt candelabra which towered on either side of the

entrance – everything reminded Klaus Heinrich of the Old
Castle, of the Gala Rooms reserved for public functions, in which
he had played his part since his earliest childhood – with the
difference that here the candles were electric, with bright in-
candescent bulbs instead of wicks, and that at the Delphinenort
of the Spoelmanns everything was new and in excellent condition. In the corner of the room a swansdown-trimmed footman put the last touches to the tea-table; Klaus Heinrich spotted
the electric kettle about which he had read in the *Courier*.

'Has Mr Spoelmann been told?' asked the daughter of the
house... The butler bowed. 'Then there's nothing to prevent
us from sitting down and beginning without him,' she said in
her rapid and casual way. 'Come on Countess! I would advise
you, Prince, to unbuckle your sword, unless some reason that
eludes me prevents you from doing so.'

'Thank you,' said Klaus Heinrich. 'No, nothing prevents me.'
And it hurt him that he was too dumb to find a quick repartee.

The footman took his sword and carried it off, down the
gallery. With the help of the butler, who held the backs of chairs
and pushed them forward underneath them, they sat down by
the tea-table, while he retired to the top of the steps and assumed
a decorative attitude.

'You should know, Prince,' said Miss Spoelmann pouring the
water into the pot, 'that my father won't touch the tea unless I
make it myself. He hates tea which is served in cups. That is
absolutely forbidden. You will have to conform to our habits.'

'Oh, it's much nicer that way,' said Klaus Heinrich, 'much
more cosy and informal like this *en famille*.' He broke off and
wondered as he said this why Countess Löwenjoul shot a spiteful glance in his direction. 'And your studies, Miss Spoelmann?'
he asked. 'May I inquire how they are going? You go in for
mathematics, I believe. Is it not very exhausting? Is it not a very
difficult subject?'

'Not at all,' she said. 'I can imagine none better. One plays with
it sir, so to speak. Or shall we say one moves above it, in a
dust-free atmosphere. Cool as the Adirondacks.'

'The what?'

'The Adirondacks. That's geography, Prince. Wooded mountains over there and pretty lakes. We have a country house there, for the month of May. In summer we used to go to the seaside.'

'At any rate,' he said, 'I can testify to your zeal in your studies. You won't allow yourself to be prevented from arriving punctually at your lectures. I haven't asked you whether you got there on time the other day?'

'The other day?'

'Yes, a couple of weeks ago. After the incident at the guard-house.'

'Good Lord, Prince, now you too are bringing that up. The story seems to have got round from the palace to the suburbs. Had I known what excitement it would cause I would rather have walked three times round the square. I'm told that it was even in the papers. And now the whole town thinks I'm a fiend for bad temper and ferocity. But I'm really the most peaceful creature in the world, and merely object to being ordered about. Am I a fiend, Countess? I demand a truthful answer.'

'No, you are very kind,' said Countess Löwenjoul.

'Well, kind, that's saying a great deal, that's going too far to the other extreme, Countess.'

'No,' said Klaus Heinrich, 'no, not too far. I believe the Countess implicitly.'

'You honour me. But how did your Royal Highness come to hear that story? Through the papers?'

'I was an eye-witness of it,' said Klaus Heinrich.

'An eye-witness?'

'Yes. I happened to be standing at the window of the officers' mess, and saw the whole thing from beginning to end.'

Miss Spoelmann blushed. There was no doubt about it that her small pale exotic face grew a shade darker.

'Well, Prince,' she said, 'I assume that you had nothing better to do at the moment.'

'Better?' he cried. 'But it was a splendid sight. I give you my word that never in my life . . .'

Perceval, who lay with gracefully crossed forepaws at Miss Spoelmann's feet, raised his head with a look of tense expectation and beat the carpet with his tail. At the same time the butler began to move as fast as his bulk permitted; he ran down the steps and towards the tall side-door facing the tea-table, and swiftly pulled aside the silk *portière*, thrusting his double chin into the air with an expression of authority. Samuel Spoelmann, the multi-millionaire, walked into the room.

He was of slight build and had unusual features. From his clean-shaven face with the feverish cheeks protruded an exceptionally pointed nose, and his small, round eyes of a metallic blue-black colour, like those of small babies and animals, lay close together and bore a distrait and irritable expression. The upper part of his cranium was bald, but on the back of his head and round the temples Mr Spoelmann had abundant grey hair, combed in a fashion not current in our parts. He wore it neither long nor short, but brushed upwards, full, and trimmed only in the nape of his neck and round the ears. His mouth was small and well shaped. Dressed in a black house-coat and a velvet waistcoat on which rested a long, thin, old-fashioned watch-chain, and with soft moccasins on his small feet, he approached the tea-table with a sullen and preoccupied expression but his face lit up with gentleness and pleasure as he caught sight of his daughter. Imma had risen to meet him.

'Good afternoon, my admirable papa,' she said and, throwing her tawny, childlike arms in their loose, brick-red sleeves round his neck, she kissed him on the bald spot which he tendered to her, lowering his head.

'Of course you knew,' she continued, 'that Prince Klaus Heinrich is having tea with us today?'

'No, I'm delighted, delighted,' said Mr Spoelmann hastily in a rasping voice. 'Please don't move!' And as he shook hands with Klaus Heinrich who stood up by the table in a formal attitude (Mr Spoelmann's hand was thin and half-protected by a soft white cuff) he nodded vaguely once or twice in an undefined direction. This was his way of greeting Klaus Heinrich. He was a foreigner, an invalid, and his ill-health had made him eccentric. He was excused and exonerated from all formalities – Klaus Heinrich recognized the fact and took great pains to master his secret consternation. 'You're at home here anyway, in a sense,' added Mr Spoelmann, swallowing Klaus Heinrich's title, and a shadow of malice appeared round his clean-shaven lips. He gave the sign for everyone to sit down again. The butler offered him the chair between Imma and Klaus Heinrich, facing the Countess and the door to the veranda As Mr Spoelmann showed no intention of apologizing for his delay, Klaus Heinrich said: 'I'm sorry to hear that you felt unwell this morning, Mr Spoelmann, I hope you are better now.'

'Thanks, better, but not all right,' replied Mr Spoelmann in a rasping voice. 'How many spoonfuls did you put in?' he asked his daughter, referring to the tea.

She had filled his cup and handed it to him.

'Four,' she replied. 'One for each person. Nobody shall say that I stint my aged father.'

'Nonsense!' answered Mr Spoelmann. 'I'm not aged. You ought to have your tongue clipped.' And from a silver box he took a rusk which seemed to be his special diet, broke it and dipped it peevishly into the golden tea, which, like his daughter, he drank without milk or sugar.

Klaus Heinrich tried again: 'I am much looking forward to seeing your collection, Mr Spoelmann.'

'Quite right,' said Mr Spoelmann. 'So you want to see my glass. Are you an amateur? Or a collector?'

'No,' said Klaus Heinrich, 'my interest has not extended to my becoming a collector.'

'No time?' asked Mr Spoelmann. 'Are the military duties so exacting?'

Klaus Heinrich replied: 'I am no longer on the active service list, Mr Spoelmann. I am *à la suite* of my regiment. I wear the uniform, that is all.'

'I see, *pro forma*,' said Mr Spoelmann in his rasping voice. 'What do you do all day long?'

Klaus Heinrich had stopped drinking his tea, had pushed everything aside during this conversation which demanded his undivided attention. He sat upright and gave an account of himself while he felt Imma Spoelmann's big, black and searching eyes resting on him.

'I have duties at Court, during the balls and ceremonies. I have to represent the State in my military capacity, at the swearing-in of recruits and the presentation of colours. I have to hold Levees as a deputy for my brother, the Grand Duke. And there are short official journeys to the provincial cities in the country, for unveilings, openings, and other public solemnities.'

'I see,' said Mr Spoelmann, 'ceremonies, solemnities. Food for ideal spectators. Well, that sort of thing's beyond me. I'll tell you once and for all that I think nothing of your profession. That's my stand-point, sir,' he added in English.

'I understand perfectly,' said Klaus Heinrich. He sat bolt upright in his major's uniform and smiled painfully.

'Well, I suppose it takes practice, like everything else,' continued Mr Spoelmann somewhat mollified, 'practice and training, I can see. For my part, I shall never cease to be annoyed when I'm treated like a prodigy.'

'I hope,' said Klaus Heinrich, 'that our population is not lacking in consideration.'

'Thanks, they're not too bad,' replied Mr Spoelmann. 'At least the people here are friendly; they haven't got murder written in their eyes when they gape at us.'

'I hope altogether, Mr Spoelmann,' – and Klaus Heinrich felt much better now that the conversation had turned and it was up to him to interrogate his host – 'that notwithstanding the unaccustomed circumstances you continue to enjoy your stay among us.'

'Thanks,' said Mr Spoelmann, 'I'm quite comfortable, and the water is just about the only thing that gives me some relief.'

'You were not sorry to leave the States?'

Mr Spoelmann gave Klaus Heinrich a quick, suspicious glance from below which the latter could not interpret.

'No,' said Mr Spoelmann sharply in his rasping voice. And that was all he said in answer to the question whether he had been sorry to leave the States.

A pause ensued. Countess Löwenjoul kept her small smooth head cocked to one side and smiled her absent Madonna smile. Miss Spoelmann fixed Klaus Heinrich with her large, shining dark eyes, as if testing the effect of her father's blunt eccentricity on the guest – and Klaus Heinrich had the impression that she was waiting calmly and with understanding for him to

get up, take his leave and go, never to return. He met her gaze
and stayed. Mr Spoelmann for his part took out a good case and
extracted a large cigarette which, after he had lit it, diffused a
delicious aroma.

'D'you smoke?' he asked. And as Klaus Heinrich thought that
after all the foregoing it really didn't much matter either way,
he accepted and took one from the proffered box.

They talked of different things before proceeding to see the
collection – chiefly Klaus Heinrich and Miss Spoelmann, for
the Countess was lost in thought, and Mr Spoelmann merely
added a word now and then in his rasping voice – of the Court
Theatre, of the big liner which had brought the Spoelmanns to
Europe. No, they had not come in their yacht. Mr Spoelmann
used it mainly during the summer heat, when Imma and the
Countess went to Newport, and he was detained in the city by
his work, and would sail out in the evening to spend the night
on deck on the open sea. At present, the yacht lay anchored in
Venice. A gigantic liner had brought them over, a floating hotel
with concert rooms and games decks. 'She had five decks,' said
Imma Spoelmann.

'Counting from below?' asked Klaus Heinrich. And she
answered at once:

'Of course. Six counting from above.'

He became confused, didn't get the point and did not notice
that his leg was being pulled. Then he tried to explain, to justify
his simple question, to show that he had meant whether she
included everything, the hull of the ship as well, the cellar so to
speak – in fact, to prove that he was by no means a fool, and at
last joined in the general laughter that greeted his efforts. Talking of the State Theatre Company, Imma Spoelmann, pursing
her lips and turning her head from side to side, suggested that
the actress who played *ingénue* parts would be well advised to
take the waters at Marienbad and a course in dancing and deportment, while the leading actor ought to be told that a voice
like his should be used with the utmost restraint, even on the
stage . . . notwithstanding her, Miss Spoelmann's, warm admiration for the said theatre.

Klaus Heinrich laughed and, with a small pain in his heart,

admired her ready wit. How well she talked, how brilliant and incisive were her words. They went on to discuss the Opera and the plays which had been performed during the winter season, and Imma Spoelmann contradicted Klaus Heinrich's views, contradicted them on principle, as though not to contradict them would be a weakness, and in a trice beat him at the game, and her large black eyes in her pale face shone with mischievous triumph while Mr Spoelmann, leaning back with the large cigarette between his clean-shaven lips, blinked through the smoke and watched his daughter with fond satisfaction.

More than once Klaus Heinrich felt the small twinge of pain which he had seen in the face of the kind matron, and yet he was convinced that it was not Imma's intention to wound his feelings, that she did not consider him humiliated if he failed to counter her remarks, that on the contrary she let his inadequate answers pass as though she were convinced that he had no need for the weapon of wit – that only she herself was in need of it. But how was that, and why? Some of her sallies reminded him of the voluble, dexterous Überbein, whose birth had been an unfortunate accident and who had grown up under conditions which he described as good: a miserable childhood, loneliness and exclusion from the happy-go-lucky times of youth. He had not put on fat, had known no comfort and found himself thrown on his own resources, which most certainly gave him an advantage over those who had no need to work. But Imma Spoelmann reclined idly at the table in her red and gold dress, relaxed, and with the capricious look of a spoilt child, sat there in opulent ease while her tongue ran on sharply and freely, as if she were one who needed all her wits, toughness, and intelligence about her. Why was that? Klaus Heinrich tried hard to fathom the reasons while he conversed about Atlantic steamships and the theatre session. Upright, with perfect self-control, and without indulging in a relaxed attitude, he sat at the table, hiding his left hand, and from time to time caught an oblique and spiteful glance from Countess Löwenjoul.

A footman appeared and handed Mr Spoelmann a telegram on a silver salver. Mr Spoelmann opened it with irritable haste, read it with blinking eyes, with the remains of the cigarette in

the corner of his mouth, and threw it back on the salver with
the curt order: 'Mr Phlebs.' Crossly he lit a fresh cigarette, Miss
Spoelmann added: 'In spite of strict medical orders this is your
fifth cigarette this afternoon. Let me tell you that the unbridled
passion with which you abandon yourself to this vice ill becomes
your grey hair.'

One could see that Mr Spoelmann tried to laugh this off, and
also that he did not succeed, could not take her sharp, aggressive
tone which drove the blood to his head.

'Be quiet!' he snarled angrily. 'You think you can get away
with anything, but I won't have your impertinence. You talk
too much.'

Klaus Heinrich looked at Imma with shocked surprise, saw
her raise her eyes with alarm at her father's irascible face, and
then sadly lower her dark head. Certainly, she had enjoyed
using big and unusual words, had expected to raise a laugh, and
had been snubbed instead. 'But father, dear little father,' she
said entreatingly and got up to stroke his angry cheeks. 'Be off,'
he mumbled. 'You aren't big either.' But then he relented and
allowed her to kiss his bald head and calmed down. Once peace
was restored Klaus Heinrich reminded them of the glass collection, and they left the tea-table to pass, with the exception of
Countess Löwenjoul who retired with a deep reverence, into the
adjacent room which housed the collection. Mr Spoelmann gave
orders for the big electric chandeliers to be lit there.

All round the walls stood fine baroque vitrines with curved
glass doors, alternating with formal silk armchairs, containing
Spoelmann's collection of cut and blown glass. Yes, this was
obviously the most important collection of its kind in the Old
and the New World, and the goblet Klaus Heinrich had bought
was merely a modest sample. It started in one corner of the room
with the earliest luxury products of the industry, finds of painted
glass from ancient cultures, it continued with the products of the
East and West of all ages, included garlanded vases and beakers
of manifold shapes covered with arabesques from the blow-
pipes of Murano, and precious pieces from Bohemian glass huts,
bellied tankards from Germany, glass from the craftsmen's
guilds intermixed with richly figurative designs of grotesque

scenes and heraldic beasts, huge crystal goblets reminiscent of the old ballad *Das Glück von Edenhall*, in whose facets the light broke and sparkled, ruby-coloured glasses that shone like the Holy Grail, and finally choice samples of modern industry, delicate flowers balancing on precarious stems and modern decorative pieces made iridescent with atomized precious metals. Followed by Percy who looked on as well, the three of them paced slowly round the room on the thick carpet, and Mr Spoelmann commented on various pieces in his rasping voice, picking them up from their velvet shelves with his thin hands half protected by soft cuffs, and holding them up to the light.

As Klaus Heinrich was well trained in inspecting, asking questions, and expressing heartfelt approval, he was able at the same time to reflect on Imma Spoelmann's way of talking; a strange way of talking which preoccupied him painfully. The things she said with her pursed lips, the expressions she glibly used! 'Passion', 'Vice'. How did she come to use them so boldly? Had not Countess Löwenjoul, who in her confused way also referred to such matters and obviously had had terrible experiences, described her as perfectly innocent? That was no doubt the truth, for she was not an exception by birth and upbringing, like himself, reared in seclusion and purity, excluded from the commerce of ordinary life and sheltered from the things which in real life corresponded to those concepts. But she had got hold of those words and handled them casually, in a mocking voice. Yes, that was how it was: this sweet-and-bitter creature in her red-gold dress lived with words; she knew no more of life than those words, she played with serious and dreadful concepts as with coloured baubles and did not realize that she shocked by doing so! Klaus Heinrich's heart was full of sympathy while he thought of it.

It was almost seven o'clock when he begged for his carriage to be called, slightly uneasy about his long stay, in view of the Court and the public. His departure started new tantrums on the part of Perceval, the collie. Every change or interruption of the accustomed round seemed to throw this thorough-bred animal off his balance. Quivering and barking madly, deaf to all attempts to call him to order, he raced through the rooms and down the hall and stairs, drowning the words of leavetaking in his noise. The butler escorted Klaus Heinrich downstairs, as far as the entrance hall with the marble deities. Mr Spoelmann did not accompany him. Miss Spoelmann just managed to make herself heard above the hububb: 'I trust, dear Prince, that the séjour in the bosom of our family has filled you with delight.' And it was doubtful whether her mocking tone referred to the expression 'in the bosom of our family,' or to the actual situation. In any case Klaus Heinrich hardly knew what to say. Leaning back in the corner of his brougham, a little sore and battered from his unaccustomed treatment but at the same time refreshed, he returned across the dark Municipal Gardens to the Eremitage, to his sober Empire rooms, to dine with Herr von Braunbart-Schellendorf. The following day he read the notice in the *Courier*. It said simply that His Royal Highness, Prince Klaus Heinrich had been to tea at Delphinenort and had viewed the famous glass collection of Mr Spoelmann.

And Klaus Heinrich continued to lead his unreal existence and to exercise his lofty calling. He made gracious speeches, performed routine gestures, represented his brother at Court and at the dance given by the President of the Council, granted open audiences, lunched at the mess of the Grenadier Guards, put in an occasional appearance at the Court Theatre, and honoured this or that provincial locality with his princely presence. Smiling and with his heels together he carried out all due formalities and performed his irksome duty with complete self-command, although just then he had much to think of, the irascible Mr Spoelmann, the dotty Countess Löwenjoul, the frantic Percy, and especially Imma, the daughter of the house. As yet he had no answer to many questions raised by his first visit to Delphinenort, and these were furnished only gradually, in the course of his further social intercourse with the Spoelmanns, which he sustained in full view of the tense, and eventually feverish, public interest, and which advanced a step further when one morning early, to his own surprise and that of both masters and servants, and so to speak against his will and driven by fate, the Prince appeared at Delphinenort, to interrupt the mathematical studies of the daughter of the house and take her out riding.

The grip of winter had relaxed early in that memorable year. After a mild January, an early spring set in at the middle of February, with singing birds, sunshine like spun gold and soft breezes, and when, on the first of these hopeful days, Klaus Heinrich woke up early at the Eremitage, in his huge mahogany double bed, with a spherical crown missing from one of the posts, he felt compelled by a strange hand to rise and undertake fresh deeds.

He pulled the bell for Neumann (there were no electric bells at the Eremitage), and ordered Florian to be ready and saddled in an hour's time. Should a horse be got ready for the groom as well? No, it was not necessary. Klaus Heinrich declared that he wished to ride alone. He then gave himself to Neumann's skilful hands for his morning toilette, breakfasted impatiently in the garden-room, and mounted his horse at the foot of the small terarace. With his spurred top-boots in the stirrup, the yellow reins in his brown-gloved right hand, and the left planted on his hip under his open cloak he rode at a slow trot through the delicate morning, scanning the bare branches over his head for the birds that twittered there; the road across that part of the grounds which was open to the public, through the Municipal Gardens and the park of Delphinenort. He reached it at half-past nine. Great was the general surprise.

At the main gate he handed Florian to an English groom. The butler, about to cross the mosaic hall on one of his errands, stopped dead and gaped at the sight of Klaus Heinrich. To the inquiry after the ladies made by the Prince in a clear and almost ringing voice, he made no reply, but turned helplessly towards the marble staircase and gazed from Klaus Heinrich to the topmost stair, for Mr Spoelmann was standing there.

It appeared that he had breakfasted a short while ago and was in a pleasant mood. He kept his hands deep in his trouser pockets, pushing his coat back from his waistcoat, and the blue smoke from the cigarette between his lips made him blink. 'Well, young Prince?' he said and looked down at him.

Saluting, Klaus Heinrich ran up the red-carpeted stairs. It seemed to him that this incredible situation could only be saved by acting quickly and, as it were, taking it by storm.

'You will be surprised Mr Spoelmann,' said he, 'at this early hour.'

He was out of breath, and it frightened him; so unused was he to such a thing.

Mr Spoelmann replied with a movement of the shoulders and an expression as if to say that he was unconcerned but awaited an explanation.

'I came because of our appointment,' said Klaus Heinrich. He stood two steps below the multi-millionaire and addressed him from there. 'Miss Imma and I agreed to go out riding together. I promised her to show the ladies the Fasanerie or the Hofjäger. Miss Imma knows almost nothing of the surrounding country, so she told me. We arranged to go out riding on the first fine day. Now this is a lovely day. Provided of course that you give your permission.'

Mr Spoelmann raised his shoulders and pursed his lips as if to say: 'What d'you mean – permission?'

'My daughter is grown up,' he said. 'I'm not in the habit of interfering. If she wants to go riding, she rides. But I believe she hasn't time. You'll have to ask her yourself. She's in there.' And stepping aside Mr Spoelmann pointed with his chin towards the tapestry door through which Klaus Heinrich had passed the other day.

'Thank you!' said Klaus Heinrich. 'Yes, I'll go and see for myself.' And he mounted the rest of the stairs and with a determined gesture flung back the portière towards the sunlit flower-scented winter-garden.

In front of the trickling fountain and the basin with the exotic duck sat Imma Spoelmann bent over a small worktable, almost entirely turning her back to the door. Her hair hung loosely over her shoulders. Blue-black and shining it flowed from her parting, covering her back and showing nothing but a blunt and child-like three-quarter profile, pale as ivory against her dark hair. Draped thus she sat over her studies, working at the figures in the notebook in front of her, her lips resting on the slender back of her left hand, and with the raised forefinger of her right hand pressed against the pen.

The Countess too was present, writing busily. She sat at some distance under the group of palm trees where Klaus Heinrich had conversed with her before, and with her head cocked to one side, wrote in an upright hand on loose leaves of notepaper, a pile of which lay beside her. The clatter of Klaus Heinrich's spurs made her raise her head. With her long spindle-shaped pen poised in mid-air she looked at him for two seconds with narrowed eyes. Then she rose to make a deep curtsey and said: 'Imma, His Royal Highness Prince Klaus Heinrich is here.'

Miss Spoelmann spun rapidly round in her wicker chair, flung back her hair and for a moment looked at him in puzzled silence with large, startled eyes, until Klaus Heinrich bid the ladies good morning with a military salute. Then she said in her husky voice: 'Good morning to you, Prince. But you are too late for breakfast. We've finished it long ago.'

Klaus Heinrich laughed.

'Well, it's lucky,' he said, 'that both parties have had breakfast for now we can start at once for a ride.'

'A ride?'

'Yes, as we agreed.'

'We agreed?'

'Now, don't say that you have forgotten!' he said pleadingly. 'Didn't I promise to show you the countryside? Weren't we going for a ride together when it was a fine day? Well, this is a glorious day. Just look out ...'

'Not a bad day,' she said, 'but I find you impetuous, Prince. I recall that we spoke of a ride, but not in the immediate future. Might I have not expected a small note, some sort of notification if Your Highness will excuse my saying so. You must agree that I can't very well go out riding as I am.'

And she stood up to show her morning dress, a loose frock of shot silk and a small open bolero of green velvet.

'No,' he said, 'unfortunately you can't. But I will wait here while the ladies change. It is still early ...'

'Unusually early. And secondly, I was just about to indulge in my harmless pastime, as you see. I have a lecture at eleven o'clock.'

'No,' he exclaimed, 'today you can't be allowed to study algebra, Miss Spoelmann, or play in a dustfree stratosphere, as you say! Look at the sun! ... May I ...' And he went towards the table and picked up her exercise book.

What he saw was puzzling enough. Greek and Latin letters grouped with figures at various heights, interspersed with crosses and lines, placed above and below fractional lines, topped by other lines, equated by double lines, drawn together into massed formulae by large brackets. Single letters totally unintelligible to the layman circumvented both letters and numbers, while square root symbols preceded them, and numbers of letters hovered above and below them. Peculiar syllables, abbreviations of mysterious words were scattered everywhere, and among the necromantic columns were sentences and notes in ordinary language whose meaning was nonetheless far above the head of the average person, so that one could read them with no more understanding than if listening to an incantation.

Klaus Heinrich looked at the slight figure by his side, standing there in her loose, shimmering dress, draped in her long hair, and in whose small exotic head all this made sense. He said: 'And so you want to waste a lovely morning over this unholy practice?'

Puzzled, she looked at him for a moment with her big dark eyes. Then she replied with pursed lips: 'It would seem that His Highness chooses to retaliate for the lack of understanding for his profession shown recently in this house.'

'No,' he said, 'no, don't say that. I give you my word of honour that I have the highest respect for your studies. They frighten me, I admit, I have never understood a thing about mathematics. And I'll also admit that today I particularly dislike them as they might hinder us from going out riding...'

'Oh, it's not only myself whom you have stopped from working, Prince. There is the Countess. She was writing. She's writing her memoirs, not for publication but for home consumption, and I can assure you, Prince, that it will be a document from which both you and I shall be able to learn a lot.'

'I'm quite sure of it. But what I'm equally convinced of is that the Countess will be unable to refuse a request coming from you.'

'And my father? We have arrived at objection number four. You know my father's temper. Is he going to approve?'

'He has approved. If she wants to go out riding, she rides. Those were his words.'

'You have made sure beforehand? I am beginning to admire your tact and foresight, Prince. You have acted like a Field Marshal, although you aren't a real soldier, only a make-believe one, as you told us the other day. But there is a fifth objection to our ride, and that one is decisive. It's going to rain.'

'No, that excuse is no good. The sky is clear.'

'It's going to rain. The air is much too soft. I saw that when I went to the Thermal Gardens before breakfast. Come and look at the barometer if you don't believe me. It's in the hall.'

They went out into the hall with the tapestries where a big barometer was suspended next to the marble fireplace. The Countess followed them. Klaus Heinrich said: 'It's gone up.'

'Your Highness is pleased to deceive,' answered Miss Spoelmann, 'the refraction misleads you.'

'That's beyond me.'

'The refraction misleads you.'

'I don't know what that is, Miss Spoelmann. It's the same as with these Adirondacks. I've not had much schooling, that's a necessary result of my kind of existence. You must make allowances for me.'

'Oh, I humbly beg your pardon. I ought to have remembered that one must use ordinary words when talking to Your Highness. You're standing at the wrong angle to the hand and that makes it look as if it had risen. If you would bring yourself to stand straight in front of the glass, you would see that the black has not risen above the gold hand, but has actually dropped a little below it.'

'I really believe you are right,' said Klaus Heinrich sadly, 'the atmospheric pressure there is higher than I thought!'

'It is lower than you thought!'

'But how about the falling quicksilver?'

'The quicksilver falls at low pressure, not at high, Royal Highness.'

'Now I am completely lost.'

'I believe, Prince, that you are exaggerating your ignorance by way of making a joke in order to conceal its extent. But as the atmospheric pressure is so high that the quicksilver drops, thus showing an absolute disregard for the laws of nature, let's go for a ride, Countess – shall we? I cannot assume the responsibility of sending the Prince home again, now that he has come. He might care to wait in there till we're ready . . .'

When Imma and the Countess returned to the winter garden they wore riding clothes, Imma a close-fitting black wool habit with breast pockets and a felt tricorne, the Countess a black-cloth habit with a starched shirt and a top-hat, and stepped out into the garden where two grooms waited with the horses between the columns of the portal and the pond. But they had not yet mounted when Perceval, the collie, shot out of the house, and slobbering and barking loudly, began to cavort madly round the horses who nervously tossed their heads.

'Now we've had it,' said Imma, in the midst of the noise, and patted the shying Fatme on the neck. 'There was no hiding it from him. He found out at the last moment. Now he wants to come and make a great ado about it. Shall we drop the whole thing, Prince?'

But although Klaus Heinrich understood that he might just as well have allowed the groom to ride in front with a silver trumpet, so far as calling the public attention to the expedition was concerned, yet he said cheerfully that Perceval must come too; he was a member of the family and must learn to know the neighbourhood too.

'Well, where shall we go?' asked Imma as they rode at a walk down Chestnut Avenue. She rode between Klaus Heinrich and the Countess. Perceval barked in the van. The English groom, in cockaded hat and yellow boot tops, rode at a respectful distance behind.

'The Hofjäger is very nice,' replied Klaus Heinrich, 'but it takes a bit longer to get to the Fasanerie and we have time until lunch. I should like to show you the castle. I spent three years there as a boy. It was a seminary, you know, with tutors and other boys of my age. That's where I got to know my friend Überbein, Doctor Überbein, my favourite tutor.'

'You have a friend?' asked Miss Spoelmann, with some surprise, and gazed at him. 'You must tell me about him sometime;

and you were brought up at the Fasanerie, were you? Then we must see it as you are obviously set on showing us. Trot!' she said and they turned into a loose riding-path. 'There lies your hermitage, Prince. There are plenty of ducks to eat in your pond. Let's give a wide berth to the Spa gardens, if that does not take us far out of our way.'

Klaus Heinrich agreed so they left the park and trotted across the country to reach the high road which led to their goal in the north-west. In the town gardens they were greeted with surprise by a few promenaders, whose greetings Klaus Heinrich acknowledged by raising his hand to his cap, Imma Spoelmann with a grave and rather embarrassed inclination of her dark head in the three-cornered hat. By now they had reached the open country and were no longer likely to meet people. Now and then a peasant's cart rolled along the road, or a crouching bicyclist plodded ahead, but they kept to the turf beside the road which provided better going for their horses. Perceval danced backwards in front of them, restless and with feverish expectation, spinning, capering and wagging his tail – his breath came fast, his tongue protruded from the slobbering jaw, and from time to time his senseless nervous tension found vent in pent-up yelps. Later he dashed off into the distance with cocked ears, pursued some animal close to the ground or ran after a rabbit, while his voice resounded far and wide under the open sky.

They discussed Fatme whom Klaus Heinrich had not yet seen at close quarters and whom he much admired. Fatme had a long muscular neck and a small, proud head with fiery, rolling eyes; she had the slender fetlocks of the Arab and a white wavy tail. White as a moonbeam, she was saddled, girthed and bridled with white leather. Florian, a somewhat sleepy chestnut with a short back, a cropped mane and yellow fetlock bandages, seemed as homely as a donkey next to the distinguished foreigner, although he was most carefully groomed. Countess Löwenjoul rode a big, dun-coloured mare named Isabeau. With her tall, erect figure she had an excellent seat; but she held her small head with the top-hat cocked to one side, narrowing her lids. Riding behind Miss Spoelmann and turning in his saddle Klaus Heinrich addressed some remarks to her but she made no reply, but continued to gaze in front of her with half closed eyes and a Madonna-like expression, and Imma said: 'Don't let's bother about the Countess, Prince, her mind is wandering.'

'I hope,' he said, 'that the Countess was not annoyed at having to come out with us.' And he was sincerely dismayed when Imma Spoelmann answered casually, 'To tell you the honest truth, she very likely was.'

'Because of her memoirs?' he asked.

'Oh, her memoirs, they aren't so urgent and are merely a pastime, although I expect a good deal of useful information from them. But I don't mind telling you, Prince, that the Countess is not too well disposed towards you. She has told me so. She said you were harsh and stern and had a chilling effect on her.'

Klaus Heinrich had blushed.

'I know quite well,' he said softly, looking down at his reins, 'that I am not encouraging, Miss Imma, or perhaps only at a distance ... That too is connected with the kind of life I lead, as I have said before. But I am not conscious of having been harsh and stern with the Countess.'

'Probably not in so many words,' she replied. 'But you haven't allowed her to let herself go, you haven't done her the kindness of allowing her to let her tongue run a little – that's why she is annoyed with you – I know quite well how you set about it, how you made things difficult for her and chilled her – quite well,' she repeated and turned her head away.

Klaus Heinrich said nothing. He kept his left hand hidden behind his back and his eyes were weary.

'You know it well?' he said after a moment. 'In that case I have a chilling effect on you too, Miss Imma?'

'I warn you,' she replied without hesitation in her husky voice, turning her head from side to side and with pursed lips, 'I warn you on no account to overrate the effect you have on me, Prince.' And suddenly she put Fatme into a gallop and flew at such a pace across the fields towards the dark mass of the distant pine-woods that neither the Countess nor Klaus Heinrich could keep pace with her. Not till she reached the edge of the woods where the highway ran did she stop and turn round to await them with a mocking look on her face.

Countess Löwenjoul on her mare was the first to catch up with the runaway. Then came Florian, foaming and bewildered over the unaccustomed treatment. They laughed and their breaths came fast as they entered the echoing forest. The Countess had woken up and talked with animation, moving briskly and with elegance, and showing her white teeth. She joked with Perceval at her feet, whose excitement had been roused by the gallop and who spun on his own axis between the trees, in front of the horses.

'Royal Highness,' she said, 'you ought to see him jump and turn somersaults. He can take a ditch or a brook six yards wide, and he does it so lightly and gracefully that it is a joy to see. But only of his own accord mind you, of his own free will, for I believe that he'd rather let himself be whipped to death than submit to any training or teaching of tricks. He is, one might say, his own trainer by nature, and sometimes unruly, but he is never rough. He is a gentleman – an aristocrat, full of character and oh, so proud. He may seem mad but he's quite able to control himself. Nobody has ever heard him yelp from pain when he is hurt or punished. He will eat only when he's hungry, and at any other time won't even look at the most tempting morsels. In the morning he has cream . . . he must be fed. He wears himself out, he's quite thin really under his glossy coat, you can feel all his ribs and I'm afraid he won't grow old but will die early of consumption. The common mongrels pursue him, they go for him at every corner, but he gets away without being involved, and bites only when he's attacked, and they won't forget it either when he does. One cannot but be fond of such a combination of chivalry and virtue.'

Imma agreed in words which were the most serious and grave which Klaus Heinrich had ever heard from her mouth.

'Yes,' she said, 'you're a good friend to me, Percy, and I shall always love you. Someone, an expert declared you to be mentally deficient and told us that this often happens with thoroughbred dogs like you, advising us to have you put down as you were impossible and would drive us mad. But they shan't take my Percy from me. He is impossible, I know, and sometimes difficult to bear, but with all that he's touching and a good dog, and I love him dearly.'

The Countess continued to talk of the collie's character, but soon her remarks became disconnected and confused and she lapsed into a monologue accompanied by lively and elegant gestures. At last, after an acid look at Klaus Heinrich, her thoughts began to wander again.

Klaus Heinrich felt happy and cheered, whether as the result of the canter – for which he had had to pull himself together, for although he had a good seat and looked well on horseback he was not, on account of his hand, a very good horseman – or for some other possible reason. After leaving the pinewood they rode on slowly, along the quiet highway, between meadows and ploughed fields, with here and there a cottage or some farm buildings. As they drew near the next wood he asked in a low voice: 'Would you fulfil your promise and tell me about the Countess, Miss Imma? How did she come to be your companion?'

'She is my friend,' she replied, 'and in a certain sense also my teacher, although she only came to us after I was grown up. That was three years ago, in New York, and the Countess was then in a desperate situation. She was on the brink of starvation,' said Miss Spoelmann, and as she said this she turned her big dark eyes on Klaus Heinrich with a terrified and searching expression.

'Was she really?' he asked and returned her gaze ... 'Do please go on.'

'Yes, I said the same thing when she came to us, and although of course I was aware that her mind was affected, she made such an impression on me that I persuaded my father to let her be my companion.'

'How did she get to America? Is she a Countess in her own right?' asked Klaus Heinrich...

'No, not a Countess, but of noble birth and brought up in gentle and well-to-do surroundings, sheltered and protected from all unpleasantness, she told me, because she had been delicate and of a sensitive disposition since early childhood. But then she married Count Löwenjoul, an officer, captain in the

cavalry – and judging from her accounts he was a strange specimen of the aristocracy – not quite up to the mark, to put it
mildly.'

'What could he have been like. . . ?' Klaus Heinrich asked.

'That I can't tell you exactly, Prince. You must remember
that the Countess has a somewhat muddled way of talking. But
judging from her allusions, he must have been one of those
shameless characters difficult even to imagine, a dissolute individual, you know . . .'

'Yes, I do know,' said Klaus Heinrich; 'what's called a libertine, a rake or a cad.'

'Right. Let's call him a libertine – but in the widest, most
reckless sense, for to judge by the Countess's accounts there are
no limits to such vice . . .'

'No, that's what I gathered,' said Klaus Heinrich. 'I've met
several people of the sort – regular devils, so to speak. I heard of
one who used to make passes at girls in his car, driving at full
speed.'

'Did your friend Überbein tell you this?'

'No, somebody else. Überbein would not think it proper to
mention anything of that sort to me.'

'Then he must be a useless sort of friend, Prince.'

'You'll think better of him when I tell you more about him,
Miss Imma. But please go on !'

'Well, I don't know whether Löwenjoul acted like your libertine. In any case he behaved disgracefully.'

'I expect he gambled and drank.'

'Certainly, one may assume that. And in addition he had
affairs, he was unfaithful to the Countess with loose women, of
which there are a great many everywhere – at first behind her
back and then quite openly, without regard for her grief.'

'But tell me, why did she marry him in the first place?'

'She married him against her parents' wish because, so she
told me, she fell in love with him. For firstly, he was good-
looking when they first met – later he went to pieces even
physically – and secondly he had the reputation of being a libertine, and that, according to her words, must have been an irresistible attraction because although she was sheltered and protected,

nothing could shake her resolve to share his life. If one thinks of it one can quite understand it.'

'Yes,' he said, 'I can understand it. She wanted to see life, and she saw it with a vengeance.'

'One might put it like that. Although your way of expressing it seems a little mild for her experience. Her husband ill-treated her.'

'Do you mean that he beat her?'

'Yes, he ill-treated her physically. But now I'll tell you something Prince, which even you will not have heard of. She made me understand that he ill-treated her not only in anger, not only when they had a fight, but without any such reason, simply for his own pleasure, that is to say in such a way that his cruel acts became abominable caresses.'

Klaus Heinrich was silent. Both looked very grave. At last he asked: 'Did the Countess have any children?'

'Yes, two. They died quite young, both only a few weeks old, and that's the greatest sorrow the Countess had to bear. It would seem from her hints that it was the fault of the loose women for whom her husband betrayed her that the children died directly after birth.'

Both remained silent and their eyes were thoughtful.

'Add to that,' continued Imma Spoelmann, 'that he dissipated his wife's considerable dowry, at cards and with loose women, and after her parents' death, her entire fortune. Her relations helped him out once, when he very nearly had to quit the service on account of his debts. But then there was a scandal, some utterly sordid affair in which he got himself involved and which finished him off completely.'

'What can it have been?' asked Klaus Heinrich.

'I can't tell you for certain, Prince. But judging by the hints the Countess has dropped to me, it was a scandal of the grossest kind – we agreed just now that there are generally no limits to that sort of thing.'

'Was that why he went to America?'

'As you say, Prince. I can't help admiring your astuteness.'

'Please go on, Miss Spoelmann! I've never heard anything like the Countess's story.'

'Neither had I; so you may imagine what an impression it made on me when she first came to us. Well then, Count Löwenjoul, with the police at his heels, escaped to America, leaving considerable debts, needless to say, and the Countess went with him.'

'She went with him? Why?'

'Because she loved him in spite of everything – she loves him still – and because she was determined to share his life whatever happened. He took her with him though, because he had a better chance of getting help from her relations so long as she was with him. The relations sent in one further instalment of money from home and then stopped – they finally buttoned up their pockets; and when Count Löwenjoul saw that his wife was no more use to him, he just left her, left her in absolute destitution and cleared out.'

'I knew it,' said Klaus Heinrich, 'I expected as much. That's how things are.' And Imma Spoelmann went on: 'So there she was, destitute and helpless, and since she had never learnt to earn her living, she was left to face hunger and want. Add to this that life in the States is supposed to be much harder, more tough than in your country, and on the other hand that the Countess had always been delicate and easily hurt, and how cruelly she had been treated for many years. In brief, she was not at all fit to cope with a life such as hers. And it was then she received the blessing.'

'Really! What blessing? She mentioned it to me too. What sort of a blessing was it, Miss Imma?'

'The blessing came in the form of a mental breakdown. In her extreme misery something *snapped* inside her – that is how she put it to me – so that she was no longer forced to face life with a clear and sober mind but, so to speak, received permission to let herself go, to allow herself a little licence, and to let her tongue run from time to time. In brief, the blessing was the fact that she became slightly dopy.'

'I certainly had the impression that the Countess let herself go when she talked,' said Klaus Heinrich.

'That is how it is, Prince. She knows quite well when she talks like that, and maybe smiles, and lets her hearer understand that she means no harm in doing so. Her oddity is a pleasant sort of release which she can control to a certain extent, and which she occasionally allows herself to indulge in. It is, if you like, a lack of ...'

'Of self-control,' said Klaus Heinrich and looked down at his reins.

'Right, of self-control,' she repeated and turned her gaze on him. 'It seems you don't approve of that, Prince.'

'It is true,' he said in a low voice, 'that I am of the opinion that it is not permissible to let oneself go and to be too comfortable, but that it is necessary to practise self-control whatever the circumstances.'

'Your Highness,' she replied, 'is giving proof of a praiseworthy morality.' Pursing her lips and turning her dark head in the tricorne felt from side to side she added in her husky voice: 'Now I am going to say something to Your Highness, and I beg you to take note of it: If Your Excellency is not inclined to exercise a little charity and loving kindness I shall have to renounce the pleasure of your illustrious company once and for all.'

He bowed his head and they rode on in silence.

'Won't you go on to tell me how the Countess came to live with you?'

'No, I will not,' she said, and looked straight in front of her. But as he pleaded with her she finished her account and said: 'Well, it was simple enough. When she heard that we were looking for a German chaperone, the Countess applied, and came to our house on Fifth Avenue. And although there were fifty other aspirants my choice, for it was I who had to choose, fell at once on her – I was so much taken with her after our first interview. She was odd, I could see that; but she was odd merely from too much experience of misery and wickedness, that much was clear from every word she said; and as for me, I had always been a little lonely and isolated and absolutely ignorant of life, except for my studies at the University.'

'Of course, you were always a little lonely and isolated!' repeated Klaus Heinrich and joy rang in his voice.

'As I told you. In some respects it was a dull and stupid life I led, and am still leading because nothing much has changed and it is much the same wherever we go. There were parties with games and dances, and sometimes we drove to the Opera in our closed car, where I used to sit in a small, shallow box above the stalls, so as to be visible to everyone, "for show", as they say in the States. That was part of my position.'

'For show?'

'Yes, for show, it was an obligation to be seen, not to erect a barrier between ourselves and the people, but to be seen in the park, across the lawn and on the terrace where one sits and has tea. My father, Mr Spoelmann, detested it intensely. But it was part of our position.'

'And how did you live otherwise, Miss Spoelmann?'

'Well, in the spring we went to our castle in the Adirondacks and in summer to our castle in Newport, at the seaside. There were garden-parties of course and battles of flowers and tennis tournaments, and we rode and drove four-in-hand or went out by car, and the people stopped and gaped, because I was Samuel Spoelmann's daughter. And some of them cursed behind my back.'

'They cursed?'

'Yes, they probably had their reasons. At any rate it was a somewhat conspicuous existence that we led, and one which invited comment.'

'And in between,' he said, 'you played with air, didn't you, or above the air, in a dustfree atmosphere.'

'I did. Your Highness is very observant. But in view of all this you may imagine how extraordinarily welcome the Countess was to me when she presented herself on Fifth Avenue. She does not express herself very clearly, but rather in a cryptic sort of way, and the point where she begins to let her tongue run away is not always very clear. But that seems to me quite right and most instructive, because it gives one a good idea of the limitless misery and wickedness in the world. You envy me the Countess, don't you?'

'Do I envy you the Countess? You seem to think, Miss Imma, that I've never had my eyes opened.'

'Have you?'

'Once or twice, maybe. For instance, things have come to my ears about our lackeys which you would scarcely dream of.'

'Are the lackeys so bad?'

'Bad? Good-for-nothing, that's what they are. For one thing they play into each other's hands and scheme, and take bribes from the tradesmen.'

'But Prince, they are comparatively harmless.'

'Yes, true, it's nothing to compare with the way the Countess has had her eyes opened.'

They broke into a trot and near the road-sign left the gently rising and falling main road which they had followed through the pinewoods, and turned into a hollow sandy short-cut bordered by brambles which led to the lush meadows of the Fasanerie. Klaus Heinrich was at home in these parts; with his arm – the right one – he pointed out every detail to his companions although there was not much to show. The castle stood there, closed down and silent, with its shingle roof and lightning conductors, at the edge of the woods. On one side was the game enclosure which gave the place its name, and on the other Stavenüter's beer-garden, where he had sat from time to time with Raoul Überbein. The spring sun shone mildly over the damp meadow land and shed a soft haze over distant woods.

They reined in their horses outside the beer-garden, and Imma Spoelmann took stock of the austere country house which bore the proud name of Fasanerie Castle.

'Your childhood does not seem to have been surrounded by excessive luxury,' she said with pursed lips.

'No,' he laughed, 'there's nothing to see in the castle. It's the same inside as out. No comparison with Delphinenort, even before you had it restored.'

'Let's go in and have a drink,' she said. 'Don't you think, Countess, on an excursion one must stop and have a drink. Shall we dismount, Prince? I'm thirsty and want to see what your friend Stavenüter has to offer us.'

Herr Stavenüter stood there in his green baize apron and with his trousers tucked into his greased boots, bowed, and with both hands pressed his embroidered cap against his breast, laughing with pleasure and showing his naked gums.

'Royal Highness!' he said and his voice trembled with joy, 'does your Royal Highness mean to honour me once again? And the young lady,' he added in a deferential tone; for he recognized Samuel Spoelmann's daughter, and had been as assiduous a reader as any of the press notices which linked Klaus Heinrich's name with Imma's. He helped the Countess dismount, while Klaus Heinrich, who was the first to jump off his horse, devoted himself to Miss Spoelmann, and he called a stable hand who, together with the Spoelmanns' groom, took charge of the horses. But after that Klaus Heinrich went through the motions of reception and welcome as he was accustomed. Assuming a formal attitude he addressed a few befitting questions to Herr Stavenüter who bowed as he replied, inquired in a winning manner after his health and the business, and acknowledged the replies with a lively nod of assumed interest. Twisting her riding crop back and forth Imma Spoelmann watched this chilly arti- ficial scene with serious, searching eyes. 'May I venture to remind you that I'm thirsty,' she said at last with sharp annoyance, and they entered the beer-garden and discussed whether to sit there or in the coffee-room. Klaus Heinrich urged that it was still too damp under the trees, but Imma insisted on sitting outside, and herself chose one of the long narrow tables with benches on each side, which Herr Stavenüter hastened to cover with a white cloth.

'Lemonade!' he said. 'That's the best thing for the thirst and pure fruit juice. No substitute, Royal Highness, and you, my ladies, but sweetened natural juice, and good for you, there's nothing better!'

The ball-shaped glass stopper had to be pushed down into the bottle; and while his distinguished guests tasted the drink, Herr Stavenüter hung about the table, to supply them with a little more gossip. He had long been a widower, and his three chil- dren, who in days gone by had recited the song of common humanity under those trees, using their fingers instead of hand- kerchiefs, had all left home. The son was in the army in the capital, one of the daughters was married to a neighbouring farmer, while the other, with a mind for higher things, had gone into domestic service in town. So Herr Stavenüter was in soli- tary control of this remote spot, in a threefold capacity as

tenant of the Crown farm, caretaker, and gamekeeper, and well
contented with his lot he was. Soon, if the weather continued to
be fine, the season for bicyclists and excursionists on foot who
filled the beer-garden on Sundays would begin again. Then his
business flourished. Would His Highness and the ladies like to
take a look at the pheasantry?

Yes, they would love to, later on; Herr Stavenüter withdrew
for the present, after placing a saucer with milk for Perceval by
the table.

The collie had got into a bog or puddle on the way and looked
like nothing on earth. His legs were wet and thin, and the white
bits of his fur were ragged and dirty. His gaping muzzle, with
which he had dug up the ground in search of field mice, was
black down to the larynx, and his slobbering tongue, like that of
a gryphon, protruded as a red and black triangle. He hastily
lapped up the milk, and with heaving flanks flopped down
sideways by his mistress, throwing back his head in complete
exhaustion.

Klaus Heinrich declared that it was irresponsible of Imma to
expose herself to the deceptive spring air after her ride. 'Take
my cloak!' he said. 'I really don't need it, I'm quite warm, and
my tunic is padded across the chest!' She would not hear of it;
but he insisted and at last she gave way and let him wrap her in
his grey military greatcoat with the major's epaulettes. Then she
propped her dark head with the tricorne felt in the hollow of her
hand, and watched him as, with outstretched hand, he pointed at
the castle and described the life he had once led there.

The dining-room had been level with the ground where one
could see the tall windows, and there was the schoolroom, and
up there Klaus Heinrich's study with the plaster torso and the
tiled stove. And he told her of Professor Kürtchen's tactful system of interrogation during lessons, of the Mayoress Amelung,
the aristocratic 'pheasants' who dubbed everything a 'hellish
bore', and especially of his friend Raoul Überbein, to talk of
whom Imma Spoelmann repeatedly encouraged him.

He told her of the Doctor's obscure origin and of the child
lost in the bog or swamp and the life-saving medal; of Überbein's
brave and ambitious career, pursued under difficult and exact-

ing circumstances which he himself used to call favourable circumstances, and of his friendship with Doctor Sammet whom Imma had met. He painted his unprepossessing exterior and explained the attraction his tutor had exercised on him from the beginning by describing the latter's attitude towards himself – that hearty and paternal blustering camaraderie which had set him apart so sharply from everybody else – and to the best of his ability gave Imma an insight into Überbein's views of life, and finally he expressed his concern that the Doctor seemed to enjoy no real popularity among his fellow-citizens.

'I'm not surprised,' said Imma.

Taken aback, he asked her why not.

'Because I'm convinced,' she replied, turning her head from side to side, 'that your Doctor Überbein for all his high-falutin talk is an unhappy sort of fellow. He may well throw his weight about; but he has no backbone, Prince, and for that reason will come to a bad end.'

Klaus Heinrich remained dismayed and pensive over her words. Then he turned to the Countess, who woke up from her reveries with a smile, and paid her a compliment about her horsemanship, for which she thanked him with brisk and courteous phrases. One could tell, he said, that she had learnt to ride as a child, and she admitted that riding lessons had formed an important part of her education. She spoke clearly and gaily; but gradually, almost imperceptibly, her mind began to wander and she told a strange story about a bold sortie she had made as a lieutenant in the last campaign, and altogether unexpectedly began to talk of the unspeakably immoral wife of a sergeant in the Grenadier Guards, who had come into her room the previous night and had scratched her breasts in a merciless fashion, using language which she could not bring herself to repeat. Klaus Heinrich asked gently whether the doors and windows had been shut. 'Of course, but anyone could remove the panes!' she answered hastily, and as, while saying this, she blushed on one side of her face and turned pale on the other, Klaus Heinrich agreed with a nod and a few gentle words. Lowering his eyes he even offered to call her 'Frau Meier' for the time being, a proposal which she accepted with haste and alacrity, not without a confidential smile and an ambiguous sidelong glance which had something strangely alluring about it.

They rose to visit the pheasantry, after Klaus Heinrich had taken back his cloak; and as they left the garden Imma Spoelmann said: 'Well done, Prince, you're progressing,' praise which made him blush, which indeed gave him far more pleasure than the most fulsome newspaper report on the uplifting effect of his princely person at some ceremony, submitted to him by prim Councillor Schustermann.

Herr Stavenüter escorted his guests into the fenced-off enclosure in which six or seven pheasant families led a safe bourgeois existence in the meadows and undergrowth, and they watched the behaviour of the colourful birds with the red eyes and stiff tails, inspected the breeding-place, and saw Herr Stavenüter feed them for their benefit under a fine, solitary fir tree, whereupon Klaus Heinrich expressed his full approval of all that they had seen. During this formality Imma Spoelmann watched him with her dark, searching eyes. Then they mounted their horses outside the beer-garden and started for home, while Perceval barked wildly and spun on his own axis in front of the horses.

Now on their way home Klaus Heinrich was to receive an important indication of Imma Spoelmann's real nature and her character; a direct commentary on certain sides of her personality which gave him much food for thought.

For soon after they had left the lane with the bramble hedges and rode along the softly undulating highway, Klaus Heinrich reverted to a subject which had been touched on during his first visit to Delphinenort during the conversation at tea, and which had not ceased to preoccupy him vaguely ever since.

'May I,' he said, 'ask you one question, Miss Spoelmann? You need not answer it if you don't want to.'

'We shall see,' she replied.

'Four weeks ago,' he began, 'when I first had the pleasure of a talk with your father Mr Spoelmann, I asked him a question which he answered so curtly and abruptly that I could not help feeling that my question had been a tactless blunder.'

'What did you ask him?'

'I asked him whether he had not been sorry to leave the States.'

'Now you see, Prince, this is another one of your typical questions, a real Prince's question. If you had learnt to think logically you would have silently drawn the conclusion that if my father had not been glad to leave America, he would not have left it at all.'

'That may be so, Miss Imma, forgive me, I don't think very clearly. If my question was merely based on poor reasoning I shall be well content. Can you reassure me that this is so?'

'No, Prince, I'm afraid I can't,' she said, and suddenly she looked him squarely in the face with her big, dark, shining eyes.

'You see, you see! What is the matter, Miss Imma? Do tell me the reason why. You owe this to our friendship.'

'Are we friends?'

'I thought we were,' he said pleadingly.

'Well, well, be patient. I didn't know we were. But I'm quite ready to learn. But to go back to my father, he really was annoyed at your question – he's easily annoyed, he has a quick temper, and has had plenty of opportunity of losing it. The truth is that public opinion and sentiment were not too friendly towards us in America. Intrigues were rife. I should add that I'm not well informed on details, but there is a strong political movement towards setting the general public, you know, the masses who have not made a success of things, against us. The result was legislation and restrictions which made my father's life in the States a burden. You know of course, Prince, that it was not him who made us what we are, but my horrid grandfather with his paradise nugget and Blockhead Farm. It was not my father's fault, he inherited his fortune and has not found it an easy burden, because he is rather retiring and sensitive by nature, and would have much preferred to play his organ and collect glass. I really believe that the hatred which surrounded us as a result of all these intrigues, and which made people curse behind my back when we passed by car – that this hatred has brought on his kidney trouble, it's quite possible.'

'I am cordially attached to your father,' said Klaus Heinrich with emphasis.

'I should have made that a condition of our friendship, Prince.

But there was another point which aggravated things and made our position over there more difficult still, and that was our origin.'

'Your origin?'

'Yes, Prince; we're not aristocratic pheasants, unfortunately we're not descended either from Washington or from the Pilgrim Fathers.'

'No, for you are Germans.'

'Oh yes, but nonetheless there's something wrong with us. I beg you to take a good look at me. Doesn't it strike you that there is nothing to be proud of in having blue-black, wispy hair that is forever falling where it shouldn't?'

'God knows you have wonderful hair, Miss Imma,' said Klaus Heinrich. 'I know that you are of southern extraction because I read somewhere that your grandfather married in Bolivia or thereabouts.'

'So he did. That is precisely where the trouble lies. I am a quintroon.'

'A what?'

'A quintroon.'

'That belongs to the category of the Adirondacks and refraction, Miss Imma, I don't know what it means. I told you already that I'm not very well educated.'

'Well, it's like this. My grandfather, who didn't give a rap about anything, married a lady with Indian blood.'

'Indian!'

'As you say. The lady in question was of Indian stock, at the third remove, daughter of a white and a half-caste, and therefore a terceroon as it is called. Oh, they say she was a ravishing beauty! – and she became my grandmother. The grandchildren of a terceroon are called quintroons. That's how things are.'

'Yes, it's a strange story. But didn't you say that it affected people's attitude towards you?'

'My dear Prince, you don't understand. You should know that in the States, Indian blood is considered a grave blemish – a blemish which, whenever such a descent on either side comes to light, causes friendships and love affairs to be ignominiously broken. True enough, it isn't quite so bad with us as with quadroons – why, of course the taint is nothing like so great, and a quintroon is considered almost untainted. But in our own case, exposed to gossip as we were, it was a different matter still, and more than once when people cursed behind my back as I passed I heard them call me coloured. In short, our origin was a handicap and made things difficult for us, it even separated us from the few families who held a social position similar to our own – it remained something which had either to be hidden or carried off with bravado. My grandfather had been the man to carry it off, and he knew what he was doing; besides, he was of pure white stock and only his beautiful wife bore the blemish. But my father was her son, and irascible and quick-tempered as he was, he resented being gaped at, hated and despised, to be, in his own words, half prodigy and half monster, and he became thoroughly fed up with the United States. That is the story, Prince', said Imma Spoelmann, 'and now you know why my father resented your discerning question.'

Klaus Heinrich thanked her for her explanation; indeed, he repeated his thanks for what she had told him when, with his hand to his cap, he saluted the ladies at the portal of Delphinenort – for by now it was lunch-time – and rode home slowly, pondering on what he had heard.

Imma Spoelmann sat at the table in her red and gold dress, relaxed and with an air of a spoilt child, sat there in ease and opulence while her tongue ran sharply, as if she were someone who needed all her wits, toughness and intelligence about her. Why was that? Now Klaus Heinrich realized why, and with each passing day he understood it better. She had been gaped at, hated and despised, half prodigy and half monster, and it lent bitterness to her speech, a sharpness and sarcasm which seemed aggressive but was merely a form of self-defence, and which brought a small frown of pain to the faces of those who had never needed the weapon of sharp wit. She had demanded mercy and loving kindness from him for the poor Countess in her lack of self-control, but it was she herself who was in need of love and release from a solitude which was hard to bear – like his own. At the same time he was reminded of a painful scene which had the buffet room at the Bürgergarten for background, and had

ended with the cover of a punchbowl. 'Little sister,' he said
inwardly and hastily turned away from the memory, 'Little
sister!' But what he thought of most was how to arrange
another meeting with Imma Spoelmann at the earliest possible
moment.

It happened soon, and then repeatedly, under varying circumstances. February drew to its close, March with its hint of spring
arrived, then April and its fickle showers and the tender month
of May. And during all this time Klaus Heinrich came and went
at Delphinenort, perhaps once a week, in the morning or the
afternoon, and always in the same irresponsible frame of mind
in which he had appeared at the Spoelmanns that February
morning, as it were devoid of a will of his own and driven by
fate. The proximity of the two castles favoured his coming and
going, the short distance between the Eremitage and Delphinenort could be covered on horseback or by dog-cart without
attracting too much attention. And if, with the advancing season,
more and more people came to the park and it became increasingly difficult for them to ride without being seen, the Prince's
state of mind at that period could be defined as a total indifference and blind disregard for the world at large, the Court, the
city and the country. Only later did the sympathy of the public
begin to play an important, and even a gratifying, part in his
thoughts and plans.

He had not taken leave of the ladies without suggesting
another excursion, to which Imma Spoelmann, pursing her lips
and turning her head from side to side, raised no objections. So
he came again, and they rode to the Hofjäger, a farm and inn on
the wooded northern side of the Municipal Gardens; and then
he came again, and they chose a third goal for their expedition
which could also be reached without crossing the town. Later,
when spring drew the townspeople out of doors and the beer-
garden filled up again, they favoured a solitary path which was
really not a proper fairway but a dyke, the sloping edge of flower-
ing meadows which stretched towards the north beside a swift-
running tributary stream. The quickest way of reaching it was
by passing along the back of the Eremitage and through the park,
across the meadows bordering the northern part of the Municipal

Gardens, as far as the Hofjäger, not crossing the river by the wooden bridge at the weir, but keeping to this side. The inn was left behind on the right and young plantations stretched all the way. To the left lay meadows flecked with white and the colours of hemlock and dandelion, buttercups and bluebells, clover, daisies and forget-me-nots; the belfry of a village church rose above tilled fields, and they rode on, sheltered from the distant main road with its traffic. Farther on willows and hazel bushes grew thickly on the slope and screened the view, and they rode on in complete seclusion, generally side by side, and followed by the Countess, for the path was narrow; rode talking casually or in silence, while Perceval jumped back and forth across the stream or plunged in for a swim, and lapping hastily, quenched his thirst. Then they retraced their steps and rode back the way they had come.

When, owing to low atmospheric pressure, the barometer fell and it rained, and Klaus Heinrich nonetheless thought a meeting with Imma Spoelmann indispensable, he drove to Delphinenort in his dog-cart and they stayed indoors. Two or three times Mr Spoelmann joined them for tea. His health was worse just then, and sometimes he was forced to stay in bed with warm compresses. When he did come down he would say: 'Well, young Prince,' and with his thin hand half protected by a soft cuff would dip his health biscuit in his tea, throw in a word here and there in his rasping voice, and end by offering his guest a cigarette from his gold case, after which he would leave the room with Doctor Watercloose who had sat silently smiling at the tea-table. Even in fine weather they sometimes chose to stay within the park and play a game of tennis on the smooth court beneath the terrace. On one occasion they even went for a drive beyond the Fasanerie in one of Mr Spoelmann's fast cars.

One day Klaus Heinrich inquired: 'Is what I have read true, Miss Spoelmann, that your father daily receives a fantastic number of letters and requests?'

Then she described to him the appeals to her father's generosity and the subscription lists which poured ceaselessly into Delphinenort, and there received careful attention; the stacks of begging letters arriving with every mail from all over Europe and America, to be dealt with by Messrs Phlebs and Slippers who sifted and submitted them to Mr Spoelmann. Sometimes, she said, she would amuse herself by running through the mail and reading the addresses, for these were often quite fantastic. The needy or calculating senders vied with each other in the deferences of servility of their address; and every conceivable rank or title could be found on those letters. One correspondent had recently beaten the lot by heading his letter: 'To His Royal Highness, Mr Samuel Spoelmann.' He, by the way, had received no more than the rest...

On another occasion the Prince fell to talking in a hushed voice of the Owl Chamber in the Old Castle, and confided to her that lately noises had again been heard coming from it, pointing to impending events in his, Klaus Heinrich's, family. At this, Imma Spoelmann laughed, and pursing her lips and turning her head from side to side, gave him a scientific explanation of the noises, as she had done in connection with the barometer. It was nonsense, she said; it must be that part of the lumber-room was ellipsoidal, and a second ellipsoidal surface with the same curvature and with a sound-source at the focus existed somewhere outside, which resulted in noises in the haunted room which were not heard in the immediate neighbourhood. Klaus Heinrich was rather crestfallen over this explanation and loath to give up the common belief in the connection between the lumber-room and the fortunes of his house.

They talked, and the Countess took part in their conversation, now sensibly and now confused; Klaus Heinrich took great pains not to hurt her feelings by his manner, but called her 'Frau Meier' whenever he felt that she required it as a precaution against the persecutions of lascivious women. He told the ladies of his unreal existence, of the drinking sessions with the students, the dinners at the mess, and of his educational tour. He told them about his family, his mother who had been so beautiful, whom he visited from time to time at Segenhaus Castle, where she held mournful court, and of Albrecht and Ditlinde. Imma Spoelmann countered by telling him more details of her strange and pampered childhood, and the Countess dropped hints about the horrors and riddles of existence, to which both of them listened with grave attention.

They shared some sort of private game; they liked to guess who people were, approximately to place their fellow-men in the various divisions of bourgeois existence – a distant and inquisitive observation of passers-by, from horseback or from the Spoelmanns' terrace. Who could these young people be? What were their occupations? Where did they belong? They were hardly apprentices, perhaps technical students or budding foresters, to judge by certain signs, or students of the Agricultural College, a little raw, but able youngsters who would make their way in life. But that small and untidy girl who strolled past looked like a factory hand or a dressmaker's assistant. Such girls usually had a lover of their own class who took them to an open-air café on Sunday. Thus they told each other what they knew of people's lives, they spoke of them with appreciation and felt more stimulated than by any amount of lawn-tennis.

As for their drive, Imma Spoelmann explained to Klaus Heinrich on the way that she had asked him solely in order to show him the chauffeur, a young American in a brown leather uniform whom she declared to resemble the Prince. Klaus Heinrich objected laughingly that he was unable to judge from the chauffeur's back, and asked the Countess for her opinion. After having denied it at first with courtly indignation, she assented at length, pressed by Imma, and with an embarrassed glance at Klaus Heinrich. Then Imma Spoelmann related that the grave and sober young man had originally been Mr Spoelmann's personal chauffeur who used to take him daily from Fifth Avenue to Broadway and other places. Mr Spoelmann, however, had insisted on exceptional speed, like that of an express train, and the intense strain put upon the chauffeur in the crowded streets of New York had at last proved too much for the young man. As a matter of fact there had never been an accident, he had stuck to his job and performed his exacting duty with amazing care. But in the end he had repeatedly felt faint and had to be helped from his seat at the end of a long day, proof of the inordinate strain to which he had been subjected. In order to avoid having to dismiss him Mr Spoelmann had made him his daughter's personal chauffeur, and he had continued in this capacity in their new home. Imma had noticed the likeness between him and Klaus Heinrich the first time she saw the prince. It was of course a similarity not of features but of expression. The Countess had admitted it. Klaus Heinrich said that he had no objection to it, as the heroic young man had all his sympathy. They went on talking of the difficult and exacting life of a chauffeur, and Countess Löwenjoul took no further part in the conversation. She did not let her tongue run during the drive, but later on made some sensible and clear comments, accompanied by lively gestures.

For the rest, his daughter seemed partly to share Mr Spoelmann's craze for speed, for she repeated the mad gallop of their first outing on several occasions. And as Klaus Heinrich, spurred on by her sarcastic manner, and in order to hold his own, had made the utmost demands on the disconcerted and reluctant Florian, these reckless gallops assumed the character of a race, provoked by Imma Spoelmann in an unexpected and capricious manner. Several of these races began on the isolated path beside the stream, and one especially was long and embittered. It followed upon a brief conversation about Klaus Heinrich's popularity which was broken off by Imma Spoelmann as abruptly as it had begun: 'Is what I hear about you true, Prince? They say you are immensely popular with the people, that you have won every heart,' she asked.

He replied: 'So they say. Some characteristics which may not even be good qualities may account for it. What's more, I don't even know whether to believe it or be glad of it. I doubt whether it's a good sign. My brother, the Grand Duke, declares outright that popularity is despicable.'

'Yes, the Grand Duke must be a proud man; I have the greatest respect for him. And so you are surrounded by an atmosphere of adulation, everybody loves you ... Get on,' she exclaimed suddenly and gave Fatme a sharp lash with her white leather crop. The mare started and the race began.

It lasted for quite a time. Never before had they followed the stream so far. The view on the left had become shut in. Lumps of earth and grass flew from their horses' hooves. The Countess soon dropped behind. When at last they reined in their horses

Florian was trembling with exhaustion, and they were pale and breathed with difficulty. They rode back in silence...

On the afternoon before his birthday Klaus Heinrich received a visit from Doctor Überbein at the Eremitage. The Doctor came to wish him many happy returns of the day as if he expected to be prevented by his work from doing so the following morning. They strolled up and down the gravel path at the back of the park, the tutor in his frock-coat and white tie, Klaus Heinrich in his military tunic. Under the slanting rays of the afternoon sun the grass stood ready for cutting and the lime trees were in bloom. In a corner, close to the hedge which divided the grounds from the unattractive suburban grass plots, stood a small, decaying wooden summerhouse.

As this topic was nearest to his heart Klaus Heinrich began to talk of his visits to Delphinenort; he spoke with animation, without telling the Doctor anything he didn't know already, for the latter seemed to be perfectly *au courant*. Who had told him? Oh, he had had it from various sources. Überbein knew no more than most people. So the matter was being talked about in the capital? – 'No of course not, Klaus Heinrich. No one is the least bit interested, either in the rides, or the visits at tea-time, or the drives. Of course these things concern no one.' 'But we are being so careful!' 'How splendid the "we", Klaus Heinrich, and your caution too. By the way, His Excellency von Knobelsdorff keeps himself accurately informed of your movements.'

'Knobelsdorff?'

'Knobelsdorff.'

Klaus Heinrich was silent. Then he asked: 'And what is Baron von Knobelsdorff's attitude to these reports?'

'Well, the old gentleman has not yet seen fit to take a hand in the events.'

'But what of public opinion?'

'The people? The people of course hold their breath.'

'And you yourself, dear Doctor Überbein!'

'I am waiting for the punchbowl cover,' replied the Doctor.

'No!' exclaimed Klaus Heinrich in a ringing voice. 'No, there will be no punchbowl cover, Doctor Überbein, for I am happy, happy whatever is in store for us – do you understand that?

You have taught me that happiness is not for the likes of me, and have brought me back to my senses when I tried to find it, and I am unspeakably thankful to you, for it was awful, awful, and I shall never forget it. But this now is no excursion into the ball-room of the Bürgergarten from which one returns humiliated and sick at heart. It is no aberration or degradation. Don't you see that the person we are talking about belongs neither to the Bürgergarten nor among the aristocratic "pheasants" nor any-where else in the world, but to me – that she is a *Princess*, Doc-tor Überbein, and my own kind, and that in consequence there can be no question of a punchbowl cover! You taught me that it is loose thinking to maintain that all men are equal, and that for me it would be hopeless to pretend they are, a kind of for-bidden happiness which could only end in shame. But this is not a shameful and forbidden happiness; for the first time it is a legitimate and hopeful, blissful happiness, Doctor Überbein, to which I may yield without misgivings and whatever the future may hold for us.'

'Good-bye, Prince Klaus Heinrich,' said Doctor Überbein, without making a move to go. On the contrary, he continued to walk on Klaus Heinrich's left side, hands clasped behind his back and with his red beard pressed against his breast.

'No,' said Klaus Heinrich, 'no, not good-bye, Doctor Über-bein – that is the point. I mean to retain your friendship, you who have had such a hard life and have shown such high stan-dards of courage and endurance, and who have honoured me by treating me as an equal. Now that I have found happiness I don't intend to become slack, but to remain true to you, and to myself and my exalted calling.'

'It cannot be,' said Doctor Überbein in Latin, and shook his ugly head with the protruding, pointed ears.

'It can, Doctor Überbein, I am quite sure that it is possible to have both. And you, you oughtn't to walk by my side and show yourself so cold and distant when I am so happy, and on the eve of my birthday, too. Tell me ... You've had so much experience and have been tried by circumstances – have you never felt as I do now? You know what I mean. Have you never been shaken as I am now?'

'Hm,' said Doctor Überbein and tightened his lips so that his red beard shot up and the muscles on his cheeks stood out. 'I might have been, once.'

'You see! I knew it! Tell me about it now, Doctor Überbein! You must tell me about it today!'

So in this grave and quiet hour filled with the scent of lime blossom, Raoul Überbein gave an account of an incident in his career which he had never mentioned before, but which none-theless had been an incisive influence on his whole life. It had taken place in those early days when Überbein had taught the lower forms, had studied in his free time, tightened his belt and given private lessons to the podgy sons of wealthy businessmen in order to buy the books he needed. With his hands clasped behind his back, and pressing his beard against his breastbone, the Doc-tor told his story in curt, abrupt sentences punctuated at intervals by a tightening of the lips.

In those days fate had tied him closely to a fair and beautiful woman, the wife of a decent, honourable man and mother of three children. He first came to their house as tutor to the chil-dren, and later on became a friend and frequent guest, and a genuine sympathy developed between himself and the husband. What grew between the young preceptor and the lady of the house remained unsaid and unconscious for a long time; but it became even stronger through the mutual silence, and one even-ing, when the husband was away on business, during one burn-ing, sweet and dangerous hour it flared up and almost robbed them of their senses. Their craving for each other cried out for fulfilment – but now and then in this world, remarked Doctor Überbein, people would still be found to behave honourably. They had been too proud to choose the way of mean and degrad-ing deceit, and to go and confront the unsuspecting husband and destroy his home by asking for the freedom to pursue their passion had not appealed to them either. In short, for the sake of the children and the kind and decent husband whom he esteemed so highly, they had renounced each other. Yes, such things did happen, but of course it needed a good deal of strength and resolution. Überbein continued to visit the house of his fair friend from time to time. He dined there when he could and

played a game of cards, kissed his hostess's hand, and said Good
Night! But when he had told the Prince that much he added
something in an even more brusque and abrupt manner, while
the muscles knotted round the corners of his mouth. When he
renounced his fair friend, Überbein had said good-bye for good
and all to happiness, to 'dallying with the idea of happiness' as
he put it. Because he could and would not win her he had sworn
to honour her and the bond which united them by achieving
something and rising in his profession, had based his whole life
on ambition and on nothing else, and had become the man he
was. That was the secret, at least in part, of Doctor Überbein's
pomposity, his arrogance and professional climbing. As he took
leave with a deep bow and said: 'Give my regards to little
Imma, Klaus Heinrich,' the Prince noticed with concern the
unusually greenish colour of the Doctor's skin.

The following morning Klaus Heinrich received the con-
gratulations of his staff in the yellow room, and later those of
Herr von Braunbart-Schellendorf and Herr von Schulenburg-
Tressen. In the course of the morning the members of the Grand
Ducal house appeared at the Eremitage, and at once Klaus
Heinrich drove in his chaise to attend a family luncheon at the
Prince and Princess Ried's, and on the way was cheered with
more warmth than usual by the public. At the elegant *Palais* in
the Albrechtsstrasse the Grimmburgs were present in full force.
The Grand Duke too appeared in a morning-coat and nodded
to everyone with his narrow head, lightly sucked at his upper
lip, and during lunch drank a mixture of milk and mineral
water. Almost immediately afterwards he retired. Prince Lambert had come without his lady. The aged balletomane was made-
up and cadaverous-looking; he moved like a puppet and spoke
in a sepulchral voice. His relatives ignored him discreetly.

At the table, the conversation revolved round Court matters,
then round little Princess Philippine's progress, and later almost
exclusively round Prince Philipp's industrial schemes. The small
and delicate host held forth on his breweries, factories and mills,
and especially on his peat-cutting enterprise. He described various improvements in equipment, quoted figures of capital invested and returns and his cheeks began to glow, while his

wife's relatives listened with looks of curiosity, condescension or derision.

When coffee was being served in the large drawing-room with the flowers, the princess, balancing a gilded cup, went up to her brother and said: 'You have quite deserted us lately, Klaus Heinrich.'

Ditlinde's heart-shaped face with the Grimmburg cheekbones was not quite as ethereal as it used to be; it had gained a little colour since the birth of her daughter, and her head was less weighed down by the burden of her fair hair.

'Have I deserted you?' he said. 'Forgive me, Ditlinde, perhaps I have. But there have been so many calls on my time, and I knew that there were on yours too; for you have no longer only your flowers.'

'Yes, the flowers have had to make way; they don't get much attention from me these days. A more precious life and growth keeps me busy, and I believe gave me those red cheeks, like the peat to my dear Philipp (he ought not to have talked about it all through lunch though, but what can you do, it's his hobby). And since I'm so busy I haven't been cross with you for not coming to see us, and for going your own way, even though that way has surprised me a little.'

'Are you familiar with my ways, Ditlinde?'

'Yes, though unfortunately not through you. But Jettchen Isenschnibbe has kept me informed – you know what a gossip she is – and to begin with I was horrified, I won't deny it. But after all they live at Delphinenort and have a private physician, and Philipp thinks that in their way they are as good as ourselves. I believe I once spoke disparagingly about them, Klaus Heinrich, and talked nonsense about a "Croesus" and a tax-paying subject. But if you consider these people worthy of your friendship I was wrong, and of course withdraw everything I said, and will try to think differently of them in the future, that I promise. You have always been fond of rummaging,' she continued and he kissed her hand with a smile, 'and I had to follow you, and my dress (the red velvet, do you remember?) suffered for it. Now you are rummaging on your own, and I hope to God that you aren't in for some unpleasant experience, Klaus Heinrich.'

'My dear Ditlinde, I'm inclined to believe that every experience is to be welcomed, whether it be a good or bad one, but mine, I feel sure, is a good one.'

At half-past five, the Prince left the Eremitage once more by dog-cart which he drove himself, back to back with his groom. It was warm, and the Prince was wearing white trousers and a double breasted jacket. Bowing to the right and left he drove back to town, to be precise, to the Old Castle; leaving the Albrecht Gate on the right and entering the maze of buildings by a side gate he passed two courtyards, and drew up inside the one with the rosebush.

A stony silence greeted him there; from the turrets with their oblique windows, from wrought iron balustrades with fine sculptures rising at the corners; light and shade played upon the various architectural details which were partly grey and weathered, partly of more recent date, with gables and balconies, open loggias, and views disclosed by wide gothic windows, of vaulted halls and low colonnaded arcades. But in the centre, in its fenced-in bed, stood the rosebush covered with blossoms, for it had been a good year for roses.

Klaus Heinrich threw the reins to his groom and went to look at the dark crimson blossoms. They were exceptionally fine specimens, full and of a velvety texture, exquisitely shaded, a real masterpiece of nature. A few were already in full bloom.

'Will you call Hesekiel, please,' said Klaus Heinrich to a doorkeeper with a twirling moustache who came towards him with his hand raised to his tricorne.

Hesekiel the custodian of the rosebush appeared. He was an old man of seventy, with watery eyes and a bent back, and he wore a gardener's apron.

'Have you secateurs, Hesekiel?' inquired Klaus Heinrich distinctly. 'I would like a rose.' And Hesekiel produced the garden shears from his apron pocket.

'This one,' said Klaus Heinrich, 'is the most beautiful.' And the old man severed the thorny stem with trembling fingers.

'I will sprinkle it with water, Royal Highness,' he said and shuffled towards a water tap in a corner of the courtyard. When he returned glittering drops clung to the petals, as to the feathers of aquatic birds.

'Thank you, Hesekiel,' said Klaus Heinrich and took the rose. 'Are you keeping well? There!' And he pressed a coin into the old man's hand, climbed into the dog-cart and, with the rose beside him on the seat, drove across the courtyard, and all those who saw him thought that he was on his way from the Old Castle, where he had had an interview with the Grand Duke, to the Eremitage.

He, on the contrary, drove through the Municipal Gardens, to Delphinenort. The sky had darkened, heavy drops splattered on the leaves, and thunder sounded in the distance.

The ladies were having tea when Klaus Heinrich, led by the corpulent butler, appeared in the gallery and descended the steps into the garden-room. As usual these days, Mr Spoelmann was absent. He was in bed with his compresses. Perceval, who lay curled up like a snail close to Imma's chair, beat the carpet with his tail by way of greeting. The gilt woodwork of the furniture shone dully, and through the glass panes of the door one could see the trees darken before the storm.

Klaus Heinrich shook hands with the daughter of the house and kissed the Countess's hand, at the same time raising her gently from her curtseying position. 'Summer has come,' he said to Imma Spoelmann and offered her the rose. It was the first time he had ever brought her flowers.

'How kind of you!' she said. 'Thank you, Prince, what a beauty!' she continued with sincere admiration (as a rule she never praised anything) and shielded the glorious calyx with the scrolled leaves in her slender cupped hands. 'Do these lovely roses grow here? Where does it come from?' And she bent her dark head over the flower with a thirsty gesture.

When she raised it again her eyes were troubled. 'It has no scent?' she said while an expression of disgust formed round her mouth. 'Wait, I know, it smells of decay!' she said. 'What have you brought me, Prince?' And her abnormally large black eyes in her pale face shone with dismay.

'Yes,' he said. 'Forgive me, those are our roses. They come from a bush in one of the courtyards of the Old Castle, have you never heard of them? A special tale is attached to them. The people say that one day they will have a delicious scent.'

She seemed not to listen. 'It is as though this rose had no soul,' she said and looked at it. 'But it is perfectly beautiful all the same. Well, it's a strange freak of nature, Prince. And thank you all the same for the kind thought, Prince. As it comes from your ancestral home one must treat it with reverence.'

She placed the rose in a glass vase by her plate. A footman with a livery trimmed with swansdown brought a cup and saucer for the Prince. And over tea they talked of the enchanted rose, and then of their usual subjects, the Court Theatre, the horses, and all sorts of controversial questions of the day, and Imma Spoelmann contradicted him on principle, with polished phrases, mocking and defeating him with her witty sallies, which she pronounced rapidly in her husky voice, turning her head from side to side. Later a heavy parcel wrapped in white paper from the bookbinder was brought in for Miss Spoelmann, containing a number of volumes freshly bound in handsome, durable bindings. She undid it, and the three of them checked whether the bookbinders had done a good job.

Nearly all were learned books whose contents were either cryptic symbols like those in Imma Spoelmann's exercise books, or dealing with deep psychology, the penetrating analysis of inner processes; all were luxury editions, bound in parchment or pressed leather, with gold lettering, choice paper and silken bookmarks. Imma Spoelmann was only mildly satisfied with the consignment, but Klaus Heinrich, who had never seen such expensive volumes, was full of praise.

'Are you going to arrange them in your bookcase?' he asked, 'together with the others you have upstairs? Have you many books? And are they all as handsome as these? Do let me see how you arrange them! I can't go home yet, the thunderstorm is still over us and threatens my white trousers. I don't know at all how you live at Delphinenort. I've never been inside your study. Will you show me your books?'

'That depends on the Countess,' she said, and busied herself with the new volumes. 'Countess, the Prince wishes to see my books. May I ask you to give your opinion.'

Countess Löwenjoul seemed absentminded. With her small head cocked to one side she gave Klaus Heinrich a sharp, even malicious glance, and then her eyes went to Imma Spoelmann, while her face changed and a tender, almost worried expression appeared instead. Smiling, she came out of her reverie and pulled a small watch from her close-fitting brown dress.

'Mr Spoelmann is expecting you to read to him at seven o'clock, Imma,' she said briskly. 'You have half an hour to comply with His Royal Highness's request.'

'Well, then, come along, Prince, and look at my study!' said Imma. 'And if your royalty permits you might even help carry some of these books. I'll take half of them.'

But Klaus Heinrich picked up the lot. He clasped them with both arms, although the left was not much use, and the pile reached up to his chin. Then, bending over backwards and careful not to drop any he followed Imma to the wing facing the main drive whose first storey contained the suites of Imma and Countess Löwenjoul.

In the large comfortable room which they entered through a massive door he deposited his burden on a hexagonal ebony table, standing in front of a sofa upholstered in gold brocade. Imma Spoelmann's study was not furnished in the style proper to the castle, but in modern taste, simply, but with elegant and serviceable luxury. It was panelled throughout in precious wood and adorned with antique pottery that shone with reflected light on shelves just below the ceiling, with oriental rugs, a chimneypiece of black marble carrying fine vases and a gilt clock, comfortable velvet armchairs and curtains of the same material as the sofa. A large desk stood facing the bow window which gave onto the fountain in front of the castle. One wall was entirely covered with books, but the main library was housed in the adjacent smaller room. It was visible through an open sliding door, carpeted, and with bookshelves covering the entire walls.

'Well, Prince, this is my "eremitage",' said Imma Spoelmann. 'I hope you like it.'

'Why, it's magnificent,' he said, but he was not looking round him; instead he looked at her leaning against the sofa by the hexagonal table. She wore one of her beautiful tea-gowns, a summer dress of white pleated material, with open sleeves and a bodice embroidered in yellow. The tawny skin of her arms and neck seemed like smoked meerschaum in contrast to the white gown, and her big shining eyes in the strange child's face spoke an eloquent and irresistible language. A smooth strand of blue-black hair fell sideways across her forehead. In her hand she held Klaus Heinrich's rose.

'It's lovely!' said he, standing in front of her, and he knew not what he meant. His blue eyes above the high cheekbones were troubled as though he were in pain. 'You have as many books as my sister Ditlinde has flowers,' he added.

'Has the Princess so many flowers?'

'Yes, but of late she has not set so much store by them.'

'Let's clear these away,' she said and took up some books.

'No, wait,' he said anxiously, 'I have so much to say to you, and our time together is so short. You must know that this is my birthday – that's why I came and brought you the rose.'

'Oh,' she said, 'that *is* an event! Your birthday? Well, I'm sure you have received all the congratulations with your usual dignity. Accept mine too, please! It was sweet of you to bring me that rose today, although it's a strange flower.' And she tried the mouldy scent once more with a timorous expression. 'How old are you today, Prince?'

'Twenty-seven,' he replied. 'I was born twenty-seven years ago in the Grimmburg. I have led a stern and lonely life ever since.'

She remained silent. And suddenly he saw her sorrowful gaze search for his left side. Yes, although he confronted her standing a little sideways, as was his custom, he could not prevent her eyes from searching for his left hand with a quiet, thoughtful expression.

'Were you born that way?' she asked softly.

He grew pale. Then with a cry which sounded like a cry of liberation he fell on his knees before her and threw both his arms round her slender form. There he knelt in his white trousers and his blue and red tunic with the Major's epaulettes on the narrow shoulders.

'Little sister,' he said, 'little sister.'

She answered with pursed lips: 'What about self-control, Prince? I am of the opinion that it is inadmissible to let oneself go, that one should control oneself under any circumstances.'

But he, oblivious and with unseeing eyes raised towards her face, merely repeated: 'Imma, little Imma.'

Then she took hold of his hand, the crippled left, the impediment to his exalted calling, which he had learnt to hide with skill since his earliest youth – took it in her own and kissed it.

EIGHT

THE FULFILMENT

GRAVE reports concerning the health of the Minister of Finance, Doctor Krippenreuther, were circulating in the country. People spoke of a nervous breakdown, a progressive stomach ailment indicated by Doctor Krippenreuther's flabby, sallow complexion. What is greatness? Neither the day labourer nor the itinerant tramp envied this sorely tried dignitary his title, his portfolio and his important office which he had obtained through an arduous career, only to be worn out by it. His retirement had been announced repeatedly, and the people held that it was due solely to the Grand Duke's aversion to new faces, and to the fact that at this point nothing could be gained by a change of personnel, that his resignation had not become a fact. Doctor Krippenreuther had spent his summer leave in a health resort in the hills. Perhaps he might have recovered up there but after his return his freshly accumulated energy was soon exhausted, for immediately after the opening of parliament there was a dissension between the ministers and the Budget Commission – a serious dissension which was certainly not due to any lack of flexibility on his part, but to the general state of affairs and the disastrous situation.

In the middle of September Albrecht II opened the Diet in the Old Castle with the traditional ceremonies. They were inaugurated by a service in the Court Church held by the Court Chaplain, Dom Wislezenus. Accompanied by Prince Klaus Heinrich the Grand Duke led a solemn procession to the Throne-room. Here the members of both Chambers, the ministers, the Court officials and numerous gentlemen in uniform or civilian dress hailed the princely brothers with three cheers started by the President of the Upper Chamber, Count Prenzlau.

Albrecht had earnestly desired to transfer his role during this ceremony to this brother, and it was due only to the urgent remonstrances of Herr von Knobelsdorff that he walked in the procession, behind the cadets dressed as pages. He was so ashamed of his braided hussar's tunic, of his skintight trousers and of the entire hocus-pocus, that scorn and embarrassment were written unmistakably all over his features. His shoulder-blades were twisted as he mounted the steps to the throne. Then he took his stand in front of the theatrical-looking chair under the worn canopy and sucked at his upper lip. His narrow un-military head, with the pointed beard and the lonely blue eyes that saw no one, rested on a white collar showing inside the silver-embroidered hussar's collar. The jingle of the aide-de-camp's spurs rang out in the silent hall as he handed the Grand Duke the opening address. And in a low voice, with a slight lisp, and clearing his throat several times the Grand Duke read out what had been prepared for him by his brother.

It was the most tactful speech that had ever been heard, weigh-ing each negative external factor against a virtue innate in the people. It began by praising the inborn industriousness of the race, and admitted that in spite of this no progress had been made in the various branches of economic life, and that in con-sequence the national income did not show the desired increase. It acknowledged with satisfaction that public spirit and a sense of sacrifice for the common good were on the increase among the population, and then declared bluntly that 'notwithstanding a most commendable increase in taxation returns, as the result of the arrival of wealthy foreigners' – (meaning Mr Spoelmann) – 'relaxation of the afore-mentioned spirit of self-sacrifice was not to be thought of.' Even without this, he continued, it had been impossible to budget for all the objects of the financial policy, and should it prove that sufficient reduction in the public debt had not been successfully provided for, the Government con-sidered that the continuation of a policy of moderate loans would prove the best way out of the financial complications. In any event it – the Government – felt itself supported in these most unfavourable circumstances by the confidence of the nation, that faith in the future which was so fair a heritage of our stock ... And the Speech from the Throne left the sinister topic of public economy as soon as possible, to apply itself to less disruptive subjects, such as ecclesiastical, educational and legal matters. Minister von Knobelsdorff declared the Diet to be open in the sovereign's name. And the cheers which accompanied Albrecht as he left the hall sounded somewhat defiant and desperate.

As the weather was still fine, he returned at once to Hollerbrunn from whence he had come reluctantly. He had done his bit, the rest was the concern of Herr Krippenreuther and the Diet. As has been said before, dissent broke out immediately on several points: the property tax, the meat tax, and the Civil Service estimates.

For, when the deputies proved adamant against attempts to persuade them to sanction fresh taxes, Doctor Krippenreuther's speculative mind had hit on the idea of converting the income tax which had been usual hitherto into a property tax, which on the basis of thirteen and a half per cent would produce an increment of about a million. How direly needed, indeed how inadequate such an increment was, was clear from the main budget for the new financial year, which, leaving out of account the new burdens imposed on the Treasury, concluded with an adverse balance calculated to damp the courage of any economic expert. But when it was realized that practically only the towns would be hit by the property tax, the combined indignation of the urban deputies turned against the assessment of thirteen and a half per cent, and they demanded as compensation at least the abolition of the meat tax, which they called undemocratic and antediluvian. Add to this that the Commission adhered resolutely to the long-promised and always postponed improvement of civil servants' pay – for it could not be denied that the salaries of the Government officials, clergy, and teachers of the Grand Duchy were miserable.

But Doctor Krippenreuther could not make gold – he said so in so many words – and he also found himself unable to abolish the meat tax and to ameliorate the conditions in the Civil Service. His only resource was to anchor himself to his thirteen and a half per cent, although no one knew better than he that its sanction would not really bring things any nearer their solution. For the position was serious, and despondent spirits painted it in gloomy colours.

The journal of the Grand Ducal Bureau of Statistics contained alarming returns of the harvest for the last year. Agriculture had a succession of bad years to show; storms, hail, droughts, and inordinate rain had been the lot of the peasants; an exceptionally inclement but snowless winter resulted in the destruction of the seed crops, and the critics maintained, though with little proof to show for it, that the timber-cutting had already influenced the climate. At any rate figures proved that the total yield of corn had decreased in a most disquieting degree. The straw, besides being deficient in quantity, according to the official report, left much to be desired from the point of view of quality.

The figures of the potato harvest fell far below the average of the preceding decade, not to mention that no less than ten per cent of the potato crop was diseased. As for artificial feeding-stuffs, these showed for the last two years results both in quality and quantity which, for clover and manure, were as bad as the worst of the years under review, and things were no better with the rape seed harvest or with the first and second hay crops. The decline in agriculture was baldly shown in the increase of forced sales, whose figures in the year under review had advanced in a striking way. But the failure of crops entailed a falling off in the produce of taxation which would have been regrettable in any country, but in ours could not help having a fatal effect.

Speaking of the forests; no income had been derived from them. One disaster followed another; parasites and the caterpillars of moths had attacked the woods repeatedly. And it will be remembered that owing to excessive felling the forests as a whole had lost in capital value.

The silver mines? They had been unproductive for ages. Natural catastrophes had brought them to a standstill, and since the repairs would have swallowed more than their proceeds warranted, it had been found expedient to suspend their workings provisionally, though this threw a number of miners out of work and caused distress in whole areas.

Enough has been said to explain how matters stood with the ordinary State revenues in this time of trial. The slowly advancing crisis, the deficit carried forward from one year to another, had become a burning problem owing to hostility of the elements and lack of national income derived from taxes, and in casting about for a remedy, or simply for a palliative, even the most pur-blind could not fail to perceive the inadequacy of our financial policy. There could be no thought of voting for new expenditure, the country was naturally incapable of bearing much taxation. It was now exhausted, its tax-paying powers adversely affected, and the critics declared that the sight of insufficiently nourished human beings was becoming more and more common in the country. They attributed this firstly to the shocking taxes on food-stuffs, and secondly to the direct taxation, which was known to oblige owners of livestock to convert all their full milk into cash. As to the other, less respectable though temptingly easy remedy for a shortage of ready money of which the financial authorities were aware, namely the raising of a loan, the time had come when an improper and ill-considered use of this means must begin to entail its own punishment.

After the liquidation of the national debt had been pursued for a long time in a clumsy and obnoxious manner it had stopped altogether under Albrecht II. The yawning rifts in the budget had received an emergency stuffing of new loans and paper issues, and the Government saw itself confronted by a floating consolidated debt redeemable at an early date, whose total was scandalously large for the number of the population.

Dr Krippenreuther had not shrunk from the practical steps open to the State in such a predicament. He had steered clear of big capital obligations, had demanded compulsory redemption of bonds, and, while reducing the rate of interest, had convertd short-dated debts over the heads of the creditors into perpetual rent-charges. But these rent-charges had to be paid; and while this incumbrance was an unbearable burden on the national economy, the lowness of the rate of exchange caused every fresh issue of bonds to bring in less capital proceeds to the Treasury. Still more: the economic crisis in the Grand Duchy had the effect of making foreign creditors demand payments at an excep-tionally early date. This again lowered the rate of exchange and resulted in an increased flow of gold out of the country, and bankruptcies were daily occurrences in the business world.

In brief: our credit was shaken, our stocks and shares were listed far below their nominal value; and though the Diet might perhaps have preferred to vote a new loan to voting new taxes, the conditions which would have been imposed upon the country were such that the negotiation seemed difficult, if not impossible. For on the top of everything else came this unpleasant factor, that the people were at that moment suffering from the burden of that general economic disorder, that appreciation in the price of gold, which is still vivid in everybody's memory.

What was to be done to recreate a firm basis? Whither turn to appease the hunger for cash which was devouring us? The disposal of the then unproductive silver mines and the application of the proceeds to the payment of the debts at high interest was discussed at length. Yet, as matters stood, the sale could not help turning out disadvantageously. Further, not only would the State lose altogether the capital sunk in the mines, but would relinquish its prospects of a return, which might perhaps sooner or later materialize. Finally, buyers were not easy to come by. For the moment – it was a moment of depressive gloom – the sale of the national forests was considered. But it must be conceded here that there was still enough sense in the country to prevent our woods being surrendered to private industry.

And let us not gloss over facts: still further rumours of sales were afloat, rumours which suggested that the financial straits penetrated even to quarters which the loyal populace had always hoped were safe from the hardships of the present. The *Courier*, which was never one to sacrifice a piece of news to the delicacy of its feelings, was the first to print the information that two of the Grand Ducal castles, 'Pastime' and 'Favorita', both situated in the open country, were up for sale. Considering that neither property was of any further use as a residence for the royal family, and that both demanded yearly-increasing outlay, the administrators of the Crown trust property had given notice in the proper quarter for steps to be taken to sell them: what did that imply?

It was obviously quite a different case from that of the sale of Delphinenort, which had been the result of a quite exceptional and favourable offer, as well as a smart stroke of business on behalf of the State. People who were brutal enough to give a name to things which finer feelings shrink from specifying, declared right out that the Treasury had been mercilessly set on by disquieted creditors, and that their consent to such sales showed that they were exposed to relentless pressure.

How far had matters gone? Into whose hands would the castles fall? The more benevolent who asked this question were inclined to find comfort in, and believe, a further rumour which was spread by busybodies; namely, that on this occasion too the buyer was no one else but Samuel Spoelmann – an entirely groundless and fantastic report, which, however, proves what a role in the world of popular imagination was played by the lonely, suffering little man who had settled down in such princely style in their midst. There he lived with his physician, his electric organ, and his glass collection; behind the pillars, the bow windows, and the stone garlanded façade of the country seat which he had saved from ruin with a single stroke of the pen. One hardly ever saw him; he lay in bed with his compresses. But one did see his daughter, this exotic, pampered-looking creature who lived in splendid isolation, with a Countess for chaperone, studied algebra and passed unhindered and scornful through the ranks of the Palace guard – people saw her, and sometimes they saw Prince Klaus Heinrich at her side.

Raoul Überbein had used a strong expression when he declared that the public 'held their breath' at the sight. But he really was right, and it can be truly said that the population of our town as a whole had never followed a social or public proceeding with such passionate, such surpassing eagerness as Klaus Heinrich's visits to Delphinenort. Up to a certain point – namely up to a conversation with His Excellency, the Minister of State von Knobelsdorff – the Prince himself had acted blindly, without regard for the outside world and in obedience only to an inner impulse. But his tutor was justified in deriding him in his paternal way for his belief that his behaviour could be kept a secret from the world, for whether it was that the servants on both sides did not hold their tongues, or that the public had opportunity for direct observation, Klaus Heinrich had not met Miss Spoelmann once since their first encounter in the Dorothea Hospital without it being noticed and discussed. Noticed is putting it mildly. No, spied on, stared at, greedily talked about.

Discussed? Smothered in cataracts of gossip would be a more apt description. Their friendship was the topic of conversation in Court circles, in the drawing-rooms, the sitting-rooms and bed-rooms, the barbers' shops, the inns, workshops and servants' halls, of cabmen at their stands and servant girls at the front doors, it occupied the minds of men no less than women, of course from the different angles inherent in the ways of looking at things which characterize the sexes. The unfailing common interest had a uniting, levelling effect: it bridged social differ-ences, and one might hear a tram conductor ask a smartly-dressed passenger on the platform whether he knew that yesterday after-noon the Prince had again spent an hour at Delphinenort.

But what was at once remarkable in itself and at the same time decisive for the future was that throughout there never seemed for one moment to be any feeling of scandal in the air, nor did all the tongue-wagging seem merely the vulgar pleasure in scabrous events in high quarters. From the very beginning, before any *arrière pensée* had had time to form, the thousand-voiced discussion of the subject, however animated, was always pitched in a key of approval and agreement. Indeed, the Prince, if it had occurred to him at an earlier stage to adapt his conduct to public opinion, would have realized at once to his delight how entirely popular that conduct was. For when he called Miss Spoelmann a 'princess' to his tutor, he had, as was befitting, accurately expressed the people's minds – the people who will always surround the uncommon and romantic with a halo of poetry. Yes, to the people that pale and dark-haired exotic crea-ture with her outlandish loveliness and mixed heredity, who had arrived from the antipodes to lead an isolated and unprecedented existence among them – to the people she was a child of kings or fairies from the land of fable, a princess in the rarest sense of the term. But all she did, her own behaviour as well as the attitude of the world towards her, contributed to make her a princess in the ordinary sense too. Did she not inhabit a castle with a Countess for chaperone, as was right and proper? Did she not, for the general edification and her own instruction, visit charit-able institutions, the Homes for the Blind, the Orphans and

Deaconesses, the Municipal Kitchens, and the Milk Kitchens, like any princess of the blood might do?

Had she not subscribed to support the victims of flood and fire out of her 'privy purse', as the *Courier* took pains to put it with precision, subscriptions which nearly equalled those of the Grand Duke (did not exceed them, as was noticed with general satisfaction)? Did not the newspapers publish almost daily, immediately under the Court news, reports of Mr Spoelmann's varying health – whether the colic kept him in bed or whether he had resumed his morning visits to the spa-garden? Were not the white liveries of his servants as much part of the urban scene as the brown ones of the Grand Ducal lackeys? Did not foreigners with guide-books ask to be taken to Delphinenort to view Mr Spoelmann's residence even before having seen the Old Castle? To what social set belonged the creature born as Mr Spoelmann's daughter, who lived cut off from all forms of communal existence? With whom should she make friends and to whom attach herself? Nothing could be less surprising, more obvious and natural than to see Klaus Heinrich at her side. And even those who had never seen them together rejoiced in the thought and embroidered upon it: the trim, princely and yet familiar figure beside the daughter and heiress of the prodigious little foreigner who, crossly and afflicted by ill-health, carried the burden of his fortune amounting to double the entire national debt!

Then it came about that a memory, a strange phrase was revived in the consciousness of the people: no one could say who first pointed it out, perhaps a woman, or a child with trusting eyes to whom it had been told as a bedside story – Heaven only knew. But a ghostly form assumed shape in the public imagination: the shade of an old gypsy woman, bent and with matted grey hair, with inward-turned eyes tracing signs in the sand with her stick and whose mumblings had been recorded and handed down from generation to generation. The 'greatest good fortune' ... it would befall the country through a Prince 'with one hand'. He would give the country more with one hand, so the prophecy ran, than any other monarch with both. With one hand? But was all as it should be with Klaus Heinrich's trim, princely appearance? Was there not, come to think of it, a weakness, a defect about his person, which one ignored when addressing him, partly out of respect, and partly because he made it easy to do so by his gracious manner? One saw him in his carriage, covering his left hand on the sword hilt with his right. One saw him representing the Grand Duke under a baldachin, take up his stand on a tribune hung with banners, turn slightly to the left, and place his left hand well back on his hip. His left arm was too short, the hand was stunted; everybody knew it, and knew of various explanations of the origin of this defect, although respect and distance had not allowed a clear view of it, or even a clear admission of its existence. But now it was remembered. It will never be known who first reminded us of it in whispers and connected it with the prophecy – a child, a servant girl, or an old man on the threshold of the grave. But what is certain is that it was the people who started the rumour, the people who imposed certain hopes and ideas, including their own conception of Miss Spoelmann's personality, on the educated classes, right up to the highest quarters, and who exercised a powerful pressure on them from below: that the impartial, unprejudiced belief of the people afforded a broad and firm foundation for all that came later. 'With one hand?' the people asked, and 'the greatest good fortune?' They pictured Klaus Heinrich next to Imma Spoelmann hiding his left hand and, unable to carry their thoughts to a logical conclusion, they trembled at their own unformulated hopes.

At that time everything was still uncertain, and nobody carried their thoughts to a conclusion – not even those immediately concerned, for things between Klaus Heinrich and Imma Spoelmann were at a strange stage, and neither her thoughts nor his own could reach out for a definite goal. As a matter of fact, that brief conversation on the afternoon of the Prince's birthday (when Miss Spoelmann showed him her books) had changed little, if anything, in their relations, and if Klaus Heinrich had returned to the Eremitage in that state of seething and heated enthusiasm proper to young men on such occasions, thinking that something decisive had happened, he was soon given to understand that his wooing for that which he had recognized as his sole happiness was only now about to begin. But, as has been said, this wooing could not aim at a practical result, a bourgeois engagement – such a thing for the time being was inconceivable, and moreover they both lived in too great seclusion from everyday life to envisage such a thing. What Klaus Heinrich henceforth pleaded for with words and looks was not so much that Imma Spoelmann should reciprocate the feelings he entertained for her, but that she should feel impelled to *believe* in the sincerity of those feelings. For that she did not do.

He let two weeks pass before he called again at Delphinenort, and during that time lived on the memory of what had happened. It did not seem imperative to let that happening be replaced by fresh impressions; besides, his time was occupied by several representative functions, including the festival of the Home Range Rifle Club whose patron he was, and in whose anniversary he took part every year. He arrived dressed in a green shooting outfit, looking as if his sole interest in life were rifle shooting, was given an enthusiastic welcome by the assembled members of the Association, and after partaking of a fork luncheon which he did not want with the beaming members of the committee, with expert grace fired several shots in the direction of various targets. When he reappeared for tea at Delphinenort – it was the middle of June – Imma Spoelmann's mood was more ironical than ever and her manner of speech unusually stilted and literary. Mr Spoelmann too was present this time, and although his presence robbed Klaus Heinrich of the *tête-à tête* with the daughter of the house he so much desired, yet it helped him in an unexpected way over the pain caused by Imma's sharpness; for Samuel Spoelmann was kind and almost affectionate towards him.

Tea was served on the terrace, and they sat in modern cane chairs fanned by the scented breezes from the flower garden. The master of the house lay on a couch beside the table, under a fur-lined cover of green silk embroidered with parrots. He had left his bed because of the mild air but his cheeks today were not hot; they were waxen, and his small eyes looked tired. His chin was sharp, and his straight, pointed nose seemed more prominent than ever; he was not cross as usual but melancholy

– a bad sign. The tall and benignly smiling Doctor Watercloose sat by his side.

'Well, young Prince,' said Mr Spoelmann in a faint voice, and to an inquiry after his health replied with a feeble grunt. Imma, in a high-waisted shimmering dress with a green velvet bolero, poured water from the electric kettle into the teapot. She congratulated the Prince with pursed lips on his personal prowess at the rifle festival. She had, she said turning her head from side to side, 'read an account of it in the papers with deep gratification and had recited the description of his appearance as a marksman to the Countess'. The latter, in her close-fitting brown dress, sat bolt upright at the table and fingered her spoon with elegant gestures, without letting herself go in any way. This time it was Mr Spoelmann who kept the conversation going. He did this, as has been said, in a gentle, even melancholy manner which was the result of his pain.

He recounted an incident, an experience he had had years ago, which obviously still rankled, and especially on the days when he felt most unwell – recounted the brief and simple story twice, and the second time felt more grieved than the first. In those days he had planned to make a donation – not a very big one, but quite considerable all the same – he had informed a big charity institution in the United States in writing that he wished to devote a million dollars in railway bonds to the furtherance of their good works, sound shares of the South Pacific Railway, said Mr Spoelmann, and slapped the palm of his hand as if to illustrate his point. But what had the charity institution done? It had refused the gift, rejected it – adding in so many words that it preferred to go on without the support of questionable and ill-gotten plunder. They had actually done that. Mr Spoelmann's lips quivered as he recounted it, the first time less than the second, and longing for comfort and an expression of disapproval, he looked round the table with his small, close-set eyes of metallic colour.

'That was not charitable of the charity institution,' said Klaus Heinrich, 'now was it?' and the shake of his head was so emphatic, his disgust and sympathy so obvious, that Mr Spoelmann cheered up a little and commented on the mild day and the sweet smell of flowers coming from the garden. Indeed, he took the first opportunity of showing his young guest his appreciation and satisfaction in an unmistakable manner. For Klaus Heinrich had caught a chill due to the summer's sudden changes from warm weather to hailstorm and showers; his throat was sore, and swallowing caused him pain, and since his exalted calling and the excess of care for his person destined for public exhibition had made him rather delicate he did not refrain from mentioning his health and complaining of his throat. 'You ought to apply moist compresses,' said Mr Spoelmann. 'Have you any gutta-percha paper?' Klaus Heinrich had not. Then Mr Spoelmann threw off his parrot-embroidered cover and went indoors. He would not answer any questions nor be detained, and went off by himself. When he had gone the others wondered what he intended to do, and Doctor Watercloose, fearing lest an attack had seized his patient, hurried after him. But when Mr Spoelmann returned he carried a piece of gutta-percha whose whereabouts in some drawer he had remembered; a crumpled piece which he handed over to the Prince with precise instructions how to use it to the best advantage. Klaus Heinrich thanked him delightedly and Mr Spoelmann went back to his couch with obvious satisfaction. This time he stayed till tea was over, when he proposed a stroll in the park, walking between Imma and Klaus Heinrich in his soft moccasins, while Countess Löwenjoul and Doctor Watercloose followed at a distance. When the Prince took his leave Imma Spoelmann made some caustic remark about his sore throat and the compresses, entreating him with hidden sarcasm to nurse himself and take the utmost care of his sacred person. But although Klaus Heinrich did not know what to reply – and she hardly expected him to – yet he was fairly cheerful as he climbed into his dog-cart; for the piece of crumpled gutta-percha in the back pocket of his uniform tunic seemed to him, although he did not analyse why, to be the pledge of a happy future.

Be this as it may, his struggle was only just beginning. It was a struggle for Imma Spoelmann's faith, the struggle to make her trust him sufficiently to leave the chilly and rarified atmosphere, the realm of algebra and wit where she usually moved, and to venture with him into the untrodden zone, warmer, hazy and more fertile, which he had shown her. For her reluctance to take this step was formidable.

The next time he was alone with her, or as good as alone, Countess Löwenjoul being the third in the party, it was a cool, overcast morning after a break in the weather the previous night. They rode along the sloping meadow; Klaus Heinrich in top-boots, with the crook of his riding crop stuck between the buttons of his grey cloak. The sluices at the wooden bridge up-stream were shut, the stony bed of the tributary stream was empty. Perceval, whose first outburst had died down, jumped hither and thither or trotted sideways, dog-fashion, in front of the horses. The Countess, mounted on Isabeau, smiled and kept her small head cocked to one side. Klaus Heinrich said: 'I am thinking of something day and night, it must have been a dream. I lie awake at night and hear Florian snort in his pad-dock, it is so still and silent. And then I think it can't have been a dream. But when I see you as I did the other day at tea, I can hardly believe it to have been anything else.'

She replied: 'That needs elaborating, sir.'

'Did you show me your books nineteen days ago, Miss Spoel-mann – yes or no?'

'Nineteen days? Let me think. No, it was eighteen days and a half, if I'm not mistaken.'

'You did show me your books, then?'

'That is correct, Prince. And I may delude myself in thinking that you liked them.'

'Oh, Imma, you shouldn't talk like that, not now and not to me! My heart is so full, and I have so much to say to you which I didn't get a chance of saying nineteen days ago, when you showed me your books. All those books. I would like to carry on from where we broke off and forget all that lies between.'

'For heaven's sake, Prince. Much better forget it! Why do you talk about it? Why remind ourselves! I should think you had good reason to observe the strictest silence on this matter. Fancy letting yourself go to that extent! Losing your self-control to such a degree!'

'If only you knew what an unutterable blessing it was for me to lose my self-control!'

'Thank you very much! This is an insult, you know. I insist that you approach me with the same restraint that you show to the rest of the world. I'm not here to provide a relaxation from your princely existence.'

'How you misunderstand me, Imma! But I am well aware that you do it deliberately and not in earnest, and it shows me that you don't believe me and won't take seriously what I say to you.'

'No, Prince, you are asking too much of me! Did you not tell me all about your life? You went to school for show, attended University for show, you did your military service for show, and for show you are still wearing a uniform; for show you grant audiences and play at being a marksman and God knows at what else; you were born for show, and now I am supposed to suddenly believe that you are serious about me.'

Tears came to his eyes while she said these things; her words hurt him so much. He answered in a low voice: 'You are quite right, Imma, much of my life is utterly spurious. But you should know that I neither chose it nor made it that way, and have only done my duty as it was laid down for me for the edification of the people, and it is not enough that it has been difficult, full of restrictions and self-denial, it now takes its revenge by causing you not to believe in me.'

'You are proud of your calling and your way of life, Prince,' she said, 'I know this, and even I can't wish you to be untrue to yourself.'

'Oh,' he exclaimed, 'leave that to me, about being true to myself, forget about it! I've had my experiences. I've been untrue to myself and have tried to disregard the rules, and it ended in disgrace. But since I've known you, I know, and know for the first time that I may let myself go like any ordinary mortal, without remorse, and without disgracing what is called my exalted calling, although Doctor Überbein has said, and in Latin too, that such a thing is not possible.'

'You see what your friend has told you!'

'Didn't you yourself call him an unfortunate creature who

would come to a bad end? He is a noble character, I have great respect for him and owe him much insight into my own situation and life in general. But lately I have thought about him quite a lot, and when you spoke of him as you did I thought about it for several hours, and I came to the conclusion that you were right. And I'll tell you, Imma, what is the matter with Doctor Überbein. He is averse to happiness, that's what it is.'

'That seems to be a proper attitude,' said Imma Spoelmann.

'Proper,' he replied, 'but ill-fated, as you yourself have remarked, and sinful into the bargain – for it is a sin against something which is more splendid than his severe propriety, I know that much now, and he has tried to train me for this sin, as I now see. But I've outgrown his training on this point. I am independent now and know better, and even if I haven't convinced Überbein – I'll convince you, Imma, sooner or later.'

'Yes, Prince, I'll grant you that. You are very convincing, your ardour sweeps one off one's feet. Nineteen days, did you say? I maintain it was eighteen and a half, but it comes to the same thing. During all that time you deigned to appear at Delphinenort precisely once, four days ago.'

He looked at her in dismay.

'But Imma, you must be patient with me, and indulgent. Consider that I'm not used to – I'm on strange ground. I don't know why I didn't come. I think I meant to give us time. And I had many obligations.'

'Of course. You had to do some target shooting, for show. I read all about it. As usual you were a great success. You stood there in your fancy dress and let yourself be admired by a crowd of people.'

'Stop, Imma, please don't gallop! It's impossible to talk that way. You speak of love, but what sort of love is this? A superficial approximation of love, a love at a distance which means nothing – a gala love without any intimacy! No, you shouldn't be cross with me for accepting it for it isn't me who enjoys it; it is the people who feel elated by it, and that is what they want and crave to be. But I have my own longings, Imma, and it is to you that I bring them.'

'What could I do for you, Prince?'

'Oh, you know very well! I need your confidence, Imma –
can't you give me a little confidence?'

She looked at him; never before had her huge, dark eyes
probed him so deeply. But for all the intensity of his dumb
pleading she turned away from him and said with a reserved expression on her face: 'No, Prince Klaus Heinrich, that I cannot
do.'

He uttered a short cry of pain, and his voice trembled as he
asked: 'And why can't you confide in me?'

She replied: 'Because you prevent me from doing so.'

'But how do I prevent you? Please tell me!'

With the same reserved expression still on her face, with eyes
averted to her white reins and rocking gently in the saddle she
replied: 'By your whole behaviour, your manner, your illustrious presence. Do you remember how you prevented the poor
Countess from unbending and forced her to be clear and coherent although, precisely because of her dreadful experiences,
she has been granted the gift of eccentricity and forgetfulness,
and how I told you then that I was well aware of how you had
contrived to chill her. Yes, I am aware of it, for you hinder me
too from letting myself go, you affect me in the same way, you
do it all the time, with all you do and say, with your manner
of speaking, your way of looking at people, of sitting and standing, and it is quite impossible to be natural with you. I've had
the opportunity of watching you with other people, but whether
it be with Doctor Sammet at the Dorothea Hospital, or Herr
Stavenüter at the Fasanerie, it is always the same, and it chills
and frightens me. You carry yourself well and ask the appropriate questions, but your heart is not in it, you don't think of
the meaning of your questions, no, not in the least, and you
don't care. I've seen it happen often – you talk, you express an
opinion, but you might just as well express the contrary, for in
reality you have neither an opinion nor do you hold beliefs, and
you don't care for anything save your princely dignity. You
sometimes tell me that your profession is not an easy one, but
since you have provoked me to do so I will say that you would
find it a lot easier if you had an opinion of your own and some
convictions, Prince – that is *my* opinion and my conviction. How

could one possibly confide in you? No, you don't inspire confidence, you chill and embarrass people, and even were I to try and come closer to you, this awkward and embarrassed feeling would prevent me – so, now I have answered.'

He had listened to her with painful tension, and while she spoke had more than once searched her pale face, and then lowered his eyes to his reins, like herself.

'Thank you, Imma,' he replied at last. 'Thank you for speaking so sincerely – for you know very well that you don't always do so, but generally speak in jest, and in your own way take things no more seriously than I do.'

'How else could one speak to you, Prince?'

'And sometimes you are harsh and cruel, as for instance with the matron of the Dorothea Hospital, whom you embarrassed so much.'

'Oh, I'm quite aware that I too have my faults and would need someone to pull me up and help correct them.'

'Let me be the one, Imma, let's help each other.'

'I don't think we could help each other, Prince.'

'Yes we can. Have you not just now spoken to me quite candidly and without mockery? But as for me, you are quite wrong when you say that I care for no one and have nothing at heart, for I care for you, Imma, and have you at heart, and since I am so serious about this I surely cannot fail to win your confidence in the end. If only you knew what it meant to me to hear you say those things about trying to come closer to me! Yes, do try, and do not be put off by that awkward feeling or something, which you say you experience with me! Oh, I know, I know very well how much I am at fault! But you should laugh at yourself and at me when I make you feel that way, and you ought to stand by me! Promise that you will try?'

But Imma Spoelmann would promise nothing and insisted on her gallop, and so this conversation remained without issue, as indeed did many subsequent ones.

Sometimes, after Klaus Heinrich had called for tea at Delphinenort, they went for a walk in the park: the Prince, Miss Spoelmann, the Countess, and Perceval. The collie kept decorously close to Imma's side, and the Countess walked two or three paces behind the young couple; for soon after they set out she stopped for a moment to examine some shrub with her bent and spread-out fingers, and after that never made up for the lost distance. Klaus Heinrich and Imma walked in front of her and argued. After having gone a certain distance they retraced their steps, and now the Countess was two or three paces ahead of them. At that point Klaus Heinrich reinforced his pleadings by, gently and without looking at her, taking hold of Imma's slender, ringless hand and clasping it with both his – the left as well, for he was oblivious of it and had no inhibitions about it as he did when facing the public – and he asked her whether she was trying, and had made any progress in acquiring confidence in him. He wasn't pleased to hear that she had been working at her algebra, had moved in the cool realm of abstractions since their last meeting, and he begged her to forget about her books for the time being, as these would merely distract her from the one subject to which all her thoughts ought to be directed. He spoke of himself, of the constraint and embarrassment which she said he inspired, and tried to explain, and refute her argument. He spoke of the loveless, stern and empty life he had led up till now, described how people had always surrounded him merely in order to be in his presence and to see him, while it had been his function to be seen and accessible, which was much the more difficult part to play, and he did his best to make her understand that the remedy for that which caused him to prevent the poor Countess from letting herself go, and which also put Imma off, to his own great chagrin – that this remedy was in her hands, and in hers alone. She raised her eyes to him, and they were full of questions; one could see that she, too, was struggling with herself. But then she shook her head, or put an end to the conversation with a joke, incapable of giving him the one reply he longed for, to make the undefined and, as matters stood, more absolutely non-committal surrender.

She did not prevent him from calling once or twice a week; did not stop him from speaking, pleading and protesting, and from time to time holding her hand in his own. But she merely tolerated it, she remained unmoved, and her fear of a decision, of leaving the domain of cool sarcasm and openly declaring herself for him seemed insurmountable, and it would sometimes happen that she exclaimed, disheartened and exhausted: 'Oh, Prince, it would have been better if we'd never met, so much better! You would have continued unperturbed in your exalted calling, I would have peace of mind, and neither need torment the other!' It was difficult to make her recant and admit that she did not altogether regret having met him. In this way time passed; summer came to an end, an early frost killed the green leaves on the trees, the hooves of Fatme, Florian and Isabeau stirred the red-gold foliage as they rode, autumn arrived with mists and acrid smells, and in this strange and unresolved affair no end or decisive change was in sight.

The credit for having given events a firm basis of reality, for having directed them towards a happy solution, must forever go to the high-placed personality who until then had observed a certain reserve, and who at the right moment intervened gently but with a firm hand. That person was His Excellency Herr von Knobelsdorff, Minister of Home Affairs, of Foreign Affairs and of the Grand Ducal Household.

Doctor Überbein had been correct in his assertion that the President of the Council kept himself well informed of Klaus Heinrich's private life and his love affair. What is more, assisted by his intelligent and sagacious underlings, he had kept himself briefed on public opinion, concerning the part played by Mr Spoelmann and his daughter in the public imagination, the quasi-royal rank with which it invested them, the intense, superstitious tension with which the public watched the comings and goings between Eremitage and Delphinenort, the popularity of these movements, in brief, how obvious that popularity was, not only inside the capital but throughout the whole country, to anyone eager to listen to gossip and rumour. One characteristic incident was enough to confirm Herr von Knobelsdorff in his view.

At the beginning of October, when the Diet had been sitting for a fortnight, and the dispute between the Budget Commission and the deputies was at its height, Imma Spoelmann fell ill, it was said at first, very gravely ill. It transpired that the foolhardy young lady, God knows in what frame of mind or mood, had insisted during one of her outings with the Countess on over half-an-hour's canter against a strong north-east wind, and so had contracted a congestion of the lungs which very nearly asphyxiated her. Within a few hours the news became public. It was rumoured that the young girl was in mortal danger, which luckily soon proved a gross exaggeration. But the general consternation and sympathy could not have been greater if it had been a member of the house of Grimmburg or the Grand Duke in person. The illness was the sole topic of conversation. In the humbler parts of the town, round the Dorothea Children's Hospital for instance, housewives stood in their doorways in the evenings, pressing the flat palms of their hands against their chests and panting to illustrate what it was like to choke. The evening papers published detailed health bulletins describing Miss Spoelmann's condition, and these were passed from hand to hand, read over the family table or the evening beer, and discussed in tram-cars. A correspondent of the *Courier* had been seen hastening to Delphinenort by cab, where he was dealt with by the butler in the hall with the mosaic floor, and even spoke to him in English, though with some difficulty. The press, let it be said, could not be exonerated from the reproach of having inflated the news and fostered unnecessary alarm. There was absolutely no question of a serious danger. Six days in bed under the care of Mr Spoelmann's personal physician sufficed to relieve the congestion and restore Miss Spoelmann's lungs. But these six days showed the eminence which the Spoelmanns, and especially the person of Miss Imma, had acquired in the public consciousness. Every morning found the various newspaper correspondents as delegates of public curiosity gathered in the mosaic hall at Delphinenort, in order to receive a brief communiqué from the butler, which they then published in the lengthy form demanded by the reading public. People read of fragrant greetings and good wishes sent to Delphinenort by various charitable institutions which Imma Spoelmann had visited and to which she had richly subscribed (and the wits remarked that the Grand Ducal Treasury might have taken the opportunity of offering their homage in a similar fashion). They also read of a 'magnificent' floral token sent by

Klaus Heinrich with his card – and dropped their papers to exchange significant glances – (the truth being that Prince Klaus Heinrich, so long as Miss Spoelmann kept to her bed, sent flowers not once but every day, a fact which was not divulged by those in the know, so as not to cause too great a sensation). The public learnt further that the popular young patient had left her bed for the first time, and soon the news was passed that her first outing was imminent. This drive, which took place on a sunny autumn morning, eight days after the patient had been taken ill, was to give rise to such an outburst of popular feeling that the more reserved elements deplored it as exaggerated. A large crowd gathered round the Spoelmanns' huge olive-green motor with brick-red leather seats waiting outside the front door of Delphinenort, with the pale young driver who looked like an Englishman at the wheel. And when Miss Spoelmann and Countess Löwenjoul emerged, followed by a footman with a rug, cheers broke out, hats and handkerchiefs were waved, until the car, hooting loudly, had forced its way through the crowd and left the demonstrators in a cloud of petrol fumes. Admittedly, they consisted of the rather doubtful elements that usually gather on such occasions, some half-grown lads, women with shopping baskets, schoolchildren, idlers, loafers, and out-of-works of various descriptions. But then what is the public and what should its composite parts be to make it representative of the people? One further assertion, which was later disseminated by the cynics, must not be passed over in silence. It was to the effect that among the crowd round the car was an agent in Herr von Knobelsdorff's pay, a member of the secret police who had started the demonstration and vigorously kept it going. We can leave that in doubt and need not grudge the belittlers of important news their pleasure. At the worst, that is if the assertions of these people hold good, it had been a case of the mechanical release of feeling already existing or they could not be released at all. At any rate this scene, on which of course the daily press dwelt at length, did not fail to impress everyone, and persons with a flair for things did not doubt that a further bit of news which occupied people's minds a few days later was closely connected with these symptoms and events.

It was to the effect that His Royal Highness, Prince Klaus Heinrich, had received His Excellency, the Minister of State Herr von Knobelsdorff, in private audience at the Eremitage, and that it had lasted without a break from three o'clock in the afternoon until seven o'clock at night. Four whole hours! What had they talked about? Surely not the next Court Ball. As a matter of fact, the Court Ball had been one among several topics of conversation.

Herr von Knobelsdorff had advanced his request for a confidential talk with the Prince during a royal shooting party which took place on the tenth of October at Jägerpreis castle in the western woods, and where Klaus Heinrich, like his red-haired cousins, had appeared in a green uniform with an up-turned felt hat, top-boots, and fitted with a hunting knife, a cartridge-belt, field-glasses and a gun-case. Herr von Braunbart-Schellendorf had been consulted, and the audience was booked for three o'clock on October 12th. Klaus Heinrich had offered to visit the old gentleman at his official residence, but Herr von Knobelsdorff had preferred to come to the Eremitage. He had arrived on time, and was received with all the warmth and affection which Klaus Heinrich thought proper to display to the aged counsellor of his father and his brother. The sober little room with the three fine mahogany armchairs embroidered with blue-green lyres on a yellow ground was the scene of their interview.

Though close on seventy, His Excellency von Knobelsdorff was vigorous in body and mind. His frock-coat was uncreased, filled by the compact and comfortable form of a man of happy disposition. His thick hair was pure white, like his short moustache, and parted smoothly in the middle, and his chin had a cleft which might pass for a dimple. The fan-shaped wrinkles at the corners of his eyes played as of old, indeed, they had gained small ramifications and additional lines, and this intricate and mobile network lent to his blue eyes an expression of good-natured cunning. Klaus Heinrich liked Herr von Knobelsdorff, though no confidential relationship existed between them. Certainly, the Minister of State had supervised and organized the Prince's life, had chosen Schulrat Dröge as his first teacher, had founded the Fasanerie Seminary for his convenience, later had sent him to the University with Doctor Überbein as tutor, had arranged his fictitious military service, and finally made the Eremitage available as his residence – but all this he had done from a distance and had but rarely dealt with Klaus Heinrich in person; indeed, when Herr von Knobelsdorff and Klaus Heinrich met during his years of study, he had inquired most respectfully after the prince's plans and resolutions as though he knew nothing of them at all, and perhaps it was just this fiction firmly adhered to on both sides which had kept their relations permanently within formal bounds.

Herr von Knobelsdorff, who had begun the conversation in an easy though respectful tone, while Klaus Heinrich tried to discover the object of his visit, chatted at first of the shooting party of two days ago, discussed the bag in leisurely fashion, and then made casual mention of his esteemed colleague, the Minister of Finance Doctor Krippenreuther, who had been among the guests and whose unwholesome appearance he lamented. Herr Krippenreuther had missed every shot. 'Yes, worry makes the hand unsteady,' remarked Herr von Knobelsdorff, giving Klaus Heinrich his cue for an inquiry after the reasons of the said worry. He spoke of the 'by no means trifling' shortage in the estimates, of the Minister's dispute with the Budget Commission, the new income tax, the bank rate of three and a half per cent, and the bitter opposition of the urban deputies, the antediluvan meat tax, and the cries of the hungry civil servants. Klaus Heinrich, surprised at first by so many technicalities, listened and nodded with earnest and eager attention.

The two gentlemen, one young and the other old, sat facing each other on a dainty, somewhat uncomfortable settee with wreath-shaped brass mountings, covered in yellow cloth, which was standing behind a round table, facing the narrow glass door leading to the terrace, with leafless trees and the duckpond veiled by autumn mists visible in the distance. A low stove of white tiles with a crackling fire warmed the severe and sparsely-furnished room, and Klaus Heinrich, though not entirely up to the political explanations, yet proud and happy to be so seriously spoken to by the experienced dignitary, drifted into a grateful, confidential mood. Herr von Knobelsdorff spoke pleasantly about the most unpleasant subjects, his voice was comforting, his speech adroit and insinuating – and suddenly Klaus Heinrich became aware that he had dropped the subject of finance and passed from Doctor Krippenreuther's worries to his, Klaus Heinrich's, own condition. Was Herr von Knobelsdorff mistaken in thinking that His Royal Highness was not feeling as well, as fresh and gay as usual? His eyesight was not what it used to be, but he thought he detected signs of weariness and grief. Herr von Knobelsdorff feared to seem importunate; he could but hope that no serious illness or depression caused these symptoms.

Klaus Heinrich looked out at the misty landscape. As yet his gaze gave away nothing; but although he sat on the settee in his usual collected and attentive attitude, with crossed feet, the right hand laid over the left and his shoulders turned towards Herr von Knobelsdorff, yet his inner tension relaxed during this conversation and, worn out as he was by his strangely delicate, inconclusive wrangles, it did not take much more to make his eyes fill with tears. He was so lonely and devoid of counsellors. Doctor Überbein had lately kept away from the Eremitage. Klaus Heinrich said feebly: 'Dear Excellency, that would take us too far.'

But Herr von Knobelsdorff replied: 'Too far? No, Your Royal Highness need not be afraid of being too explicit. I will admit that I am better informed of Your Royal Highness's moves than I allowed myself to appear just now. Your Royal Highness will scarcely tell me anything I don't know, apart from the finer points and details which rumour can never detect. But if it be a comfort to Your Royal Highness to open your heart to an old servant who has carried you in his arms – perhaps I might not be entirely inept in assisting your Royal Highness in word and deed.'

And then it happened that something gave way in Klaus Heinrich and poured out in a stream of confidences: he told Herr von Knobelsdorff the whole story. He told it as one speaks when the heart is full and everything comes tumbling out at once: not very coherent, not in the right order, and with undue emphasis on inessentials, but urgently, and with the vivid powers of description that are the outcome of passionate observation. He began in the middle, jumped unexpectedly to the beginning, hastened to the (nonexistent) end, stumbled over his own words, and more than once got hopelessly involved. But Herr von Knobelsdorff's previous knowledge eased his task, and by suggestive questions he set him afloat again, and at last the picture of Klaus Heinrich's experiences with all its characters and situations, with Samuel Spoelmann, the dotty Countess Löwenjoul, even the collie Perceval, and especially Imma Spoelmann in all her complexity lay there complete and ready for discussion. Even the piece of gutta-percha was mentioned in full detail, for Herr von Knobelsdorff seemed to attach importance to it, and nothing was omitted from the impressive incident at the changing of the guard to the latest fervent and tormenting struggles on foot and on horseback. Klaus Heinrich was flushed and wrought up when he finished and his steel-blue eyes above the high cheekbones brimmed with tears. He had left the settee, thereby forcing Herr von Knobelsdorff to get up too, and positively insisted on opening the glass door to the small terrace on account of the heat, but was prevented by Herr von Knobelsdorff who pointed out the danger of catching a cold. He implored the Prince to sit down again, as His Royal Highness could not fail to see the need for a dispassionate discussion of the situation. So both sat down once more on their sparsely-cushioned seats.

Herr von Knobelsdorff reflected for a while, and his face was as grave as the dimple and the play of wrinkles allowed it to be. Breaking the silence he thanked the Prince warmly for the honour of his confidence, and immediately following upon this declaration, emphasizing each word, Herr von Knobelsdorff made the following declaration: whatever attitude the Prince expected of him, he, Herr von Knobelsdorff, was certainly not the man to oppose the Prince's hopes and wishes, but was prepared to smooth His Royal Highness's path towards the desired goal to the best of his abilities.

A long silence ensued. Nonplussed, Klaus Heinrich looked into Herr von Knobelsdorff's eyes with the fan-shaped wrinkles. So he was permitted to have hopes and desires? So there was a goal? He was not sure he had heard aright. He said: 'Your Excellency is so kind.'

Then Herr von Knobelsdorff added something about a condition and said that he, as the first official of the State, could dare to make his modest influence felt under one condition only.

'Under one condition?'

'Under the condition that Your Royal Highness does not consider merely your own happiness in a petty and selfish manner, but mindful of your lofty calling, regards your personal destiny from the viewpoint of the whole.'

Klaus Heinrich was silent and his eyes were heavy with thought.

'Permit me, Royal Highness,' continued Herr von Knobelsdorff after a pause, 'to leave this delicate, and as yet so largely incalculable subject for a while and turn to more general matters. This is the moment for mutual confidence and understanding; may I beg humbly to be allowed to take advantage of it? Your exalted calling places Your Royal Highness apart from the harsh actualities of existence, and careful arrangements shield you from them. I shall not forget that these actualities are not, or are only indirectly, a concern of Your Royal Highness. And yet the moment seems opportune to bring at least a certain portion of this harsh reality to the immediate notice of Your Royal Highness. I plead beforehand for forgiveness lest I manage to upset Your Royal Highness by my disclosures.'

'Please begin, your Excellency!' said Klaus Heinrich, not without alarm. Involuntarily he assumed the position of someone in a dentist's chair bracing himself against a painful operation.

'I must ask for your undivided attention,' said Herr von Knobelsdorff almost severely. And then, as a corollary to the dispute of the Budget Commission, followed a lecture, a clear, exhaustive, unembellished lesson with figures and commentaries on basic facts, and with technical expressions which demonstrated the economic position of the State and brought home to the Prince the whole miserable plight of our country. Of course these things were not altogether new and strange; indeed, ever since he had shouldered his representational duties

they had served as a point of departure and the subject of those
formal questions addressed by him to the city mayors, agri-
culturists and high-ranking civil servants, and to which he received replies which were given for the sake of talking and not
of the subject itself, and often were accompanied by a smile
which he knew from his childhood meaning 'you lilywhite boy'.
But never before had all this forced itself upon him in its total,
factual objectivity, to claim his undivided attention and powers
of reasoning. Herr von Knobelsdorff was by no means content
with Klaus Heinrich's customary mannerism of nodding his
head encouragingly; he pressed the matter home, he cross-
examined the young man and made him memorize whole sentences, kept him relentlessly to the point, and reminded the
Prince of a dry and wrinkled index finger which had lingered at
each word and syllable and would not budge until one had
given proof of having understood.

Herr von Knobelsdorff began at the beginning and spoke of
the country and its underdeveloped industry and commerce;
he spoke of the people, Klaus Heinrich's people, that thoughtful, homely, wholesome and backward race; of the deficiency
in the national reserves, the poor dividends paid by the railways,
the insufficient coal supplies. He touched on the administration
of the forests, game preserves and pastures; he talked about the
woods, about excessive fellings, the immoderate raking away
of litter, the untended young growth and diminishing forestry
revenues. Then he went into the question of our gold reserves,
discussed the inability of the people to pay the heavy taxes, and
the reckless financial policy of the past. This led him to the
total amount of the national debt which Herr von Knobelsdorff
made the Prince repeat several times. It amounted to six hundred
million marks. The lesson extended to the debentures, to conditions of interest and repayments; it came back to Doctor Krippenreuther's present plight and described the inauspicious nature
of the present moment. With the *Journal of the Bureau of
Statistics*, which he suddenly extracted from his pocket, in his
hand, Herr von Knobelsdorff acquainted his pupil with the
harvest returns of the previous years, summed up the reasons for
their decline, described the deficit in tax returns caused by them,

and mentioned the underfed country population. He then turned to the condition of the gold market and discussed inflation and the general economic discontent. And Klaus Heinrich learnt of the low exchange, the restlessness of the creditors, the leakage of gold, the many bankruptcies; he saw our credit shaken, our stocks and shares devalued, and he understood that it would be almost impossible to raise a new loan.

Night fell, and it was long past five o'clock when Herr von Knobelsdorff ended his lesson in national economics. Klaus Heinrich usually had his tea about this time, but now gave it only a fleeting thought, and no one from outside dared interrupt a conversation whose importance was indicated by its length. Klaus Heinrich listened intently. He scarcely realized how shaken he was. But how was it that he was told of these things? Not once during the whole lecture had he been addressed as Royal Highness; he had been forced out of his role, his sheltered position had been ignored. And yet it was good and heartwarming to be told these things and for their sake to come to grips with them. He quite forgot to have the lights brought in; he was so utterly absorbed.

'It was these circumstances,' concluded Herr von Knobelsdorff, 'which I had in mind when I begged Your Royal Highness to consider your personal wishes and desires in the light of the general interest. I have no doubt that Your Royal Highness will profit by this talk and by the facts I have been privileged enough to lay before you. And with this in mind I beg Your Royal Highness to allow me to revert once more to your own personal problem.'

Herr von Knobelsdorff waited until Klaus Heinrich signalled his consent and then went on: 'If this affair is to have a future it is imperative that it should reach a further stage of development. It is now stagnating, it remains as formless and obscure as the mists outside. That is not tolerable. We must give it a form and clarify it, outline it before the eyes of the world.'

'Quite so, quite so! Give it a form, clarify it. That's it! It's absolutely necessary,' agreed Klaus Heinrich agitatedly, and he left the settee once more to pace up and down the room. 'But how? For heaven's sake, Your Excellency, tell me how.'

'The next formal step,' said Herr von Knobelsdorff – and remained seated, so unusual was the occasion – 'must be that the Spoelmanns be seen at Court.'

Klaus Heinrich stopped.

'No,' he said 'never as I know him will Mr Spoelmann be persuaded to appear at Court.'

'Which doesn't prevent his daughter from giving us this pleasure,' replied Herr von Knobelsdorff. 'The Court Ball is not too far off, it is up to Your Royal Highness to persuade Miss Spoelmann to attend. Her chaperone is a Countess – said to be very eccentric, but still, she is a Countess – which makes things easier. If I assure you, Royal Highness, that the Court will not be lacking in cordiality, I am speaking in full agreement with the Chief Master of Ceremonies, Herr von Bühl zu Bühl.'

For the next three quarters of an hour the conversation turned on questions of precedence and the ceremonial with which the presentation must be carried out. It would be necessary to leave cards on the Mistress of the Robes of Princess Katharine, a widowed Countess Trümmerhauff, who held sway over the ladies-in-waiting at the Old Castle. Concerning the act of presentation, Herr von Knobelsdorff had obtained concessions of a deliberate, in fact a defiant nature. There was no American chargé d'affaires in the city – no reason, explained Herr von Knobelsdorff, for letting the ladies be presented by the next best chamberlain; no, the Master of Ceremonies himself requested the honour of presenting them to the Grand Duke. When? At what point of the prescribed procession? Why, without doubt unusual circumstances demanded an exception from the rule. In the first place, then, in front of all the debutantes of various ranks. Klaus Heinrich might assure Miss Spoelmann of this exceptional measure. It would give rise to talk and cause a sensation at Court and in the town. But never mind, so much the better. Sensation was by no means undesirable, sensation was useful, even necessary.

Herr von Knobelsdorff departed. By the time he left it had become so dark that he and the Prince could hardly see each other. Klaus Heinrich, who only now became aware of it, excused himself in some confusion, but Herr von Knobelsdorff declared it to be unimportant in what sort of light a conversation like theirs was carried out. He took the hand which Klaus Heinrich offered him and clasped it in both his own. 'Never,' he said warmly – and these were his last words before he went – 'never was the happiness of a Prince more inseparable from that of his people. No, whatever Your Royal Highness thinks and does, please bear in mind that by the grace of providence the happiness of Your Royal Highness has become a condition of the general good, but that Your Royal Highness in turn must recognize in the welfare of the country its indispensable condition and justification.'

Klaus Heinrich remained behind in the austere Empire room, deeply moved and as yet unable to collect the thoughts which assailed him from all sides.

He spent a restless night and on the following morning, in spite of wet and foggy weather, went for a long and solitary ride. Herr von Knobelsdorff had spoken clearly and exhaustively, had supplied facts and had listened to them, but he had provided him with no more than the merest indications for the merging and digesting of the raw material, and Klaus Heinrich did some hard thinking while he lay sleepless, and later, while riding Florian.

Returned to the Eremitage, he did a strange thing; he wrote out a list in pencil on a slip of paper, he made out a certain order and sent his valet Neumann to town with it, to the Academic bookshop in University Street. What Neumann, staggering under the load, brought back was a parcel of books which Klaus Heinrich made him unpack in the big room, and which he tackled then and there.

They were works of a sober and school-bookish appearance, with glazed paper backs, ugly leather sides, and coarse paper, and the contents were divided up minutely into sections, main divisions, subdivisions, and paragraphs. Their titles were not stimulating. They were manuals and hand-books of economy, abstracts and outlines of State finance, systematic treatises on political economy. The prince shut himself up in his study with these books, and gave instructions that he wished on no account to be disturbed.

The autumn was damp, and Klaus Heinrich did not feel tempted to leave the Eremitage. On Saturday he drove to the Old Castle in order to grant free audiences; for the rest of the week his time was his own, and he knew how best to employ it. Dressed in his military tunic he sat close to the warm tiled stove, at his small, old-fashioned and unused desk, and with his fore-head resting in his hands he read his books on economics. He read of national expenditure and what it consisted in, of revenues and where they came from, in the best of cases; he plodded through the subject of taxation in all its ramifications; he buried himself in the doctrine of the budget, of the balance, the sur-plus, and especially the deficit; he lingered longest over and went most deeply into the question of the national debt, its separate items, the loan, the relation between capital interest and repay-ment; and from time to time he raised his head from the page and smiled, dreaming of what he had read as though it were sheer poetry.

He did not find it hard to grasp the facts once he had set his mind to it. No, this sober reality in which he now took a part, this simple and crude web of material interests, this edifice of pedestrian needs and necessities which countless young men of ordinary birth had absorbed with nimble minds in order to pass their exams, they were by no means as difficult to master as he had thought in his lofty isolation. His representational duties were far more difficult, he thought, and much, much more difficult were his exacting struggles with Imma Spoelmann on foot and on horseback. But they made him feel warm and glad, these studies of his, and he felt his cheeks grow hot with zeal, like his brother-in-law zu Ried-Hohenried's over his peat.

After he had thus given the facts supplied by Herr von Knobelsdorff a general academic basis, and accomplished a feat of hard thinking by weighing possibilities and making inward connections, he presented himself once more for tea at Del-phinenort. The electric lights in the lion-footed candelabra and the big crystal chandelier in the drawing-room were lit. The ladies were alone.

After the intitial questions and answers concerning Mr Spoelmann's health and Imma's past indisposition – Klaus Heinrich reprimanded her severely for her unaccountable impetuosity, to which she retorted with pursed lips that, as far as she knew, she was her own mistress, free to do what she chose with her health – they fell to talking of the autumn, the damp weather which precluded riding, of the late season and the oncoming winter, and Klaus Heinrich mentioned the Court Ball in passing, and inquired casually whether the ladies – since Mr Spoelmann would no doubt be prevented by his health – would care to take part in it. But when Imma replied : No, truly, she had no desire to be rude but had not the slightest inclination to go, he did not press her but dropped the subject for the time being.

What had he been doing these last few days? Oh, he had been very busy, one might say he had been up to the ears in work. Work? No doubt he meant the royal shooting party at Jägerpreis. Well, the shooting party – no, he had been engaged in serious studies and as a matter of fact was still deeply immersed in the subject. And Klaus Heinrich began to tell of his unwieldy books, his studies in Finance and Economics, and he spoke with such animation and respect for his new activity that Imma Spoelmann's large eyes rested on him full of surprise. But when she asked him – almost timidly – for the cause and reason of his studies he replied that vital, and indeed burning questions of the day had driven him to it; circumstances and conditions which unfortunately were not suited to be talked of gaily over a cup of tea. This remark obviously offended Imma Spoelmann. Turning her head from side to side she asked sharply what made him think that she was exclusively, or even preferably accessible by way of gay conversation. And she commanded rather than begged him to be kind enough to explain what he meant by burning questions of the day.

Then it transpired what Klaus Heinrich had learnt from Herr von Knobelsdorff, and he spoke of the country and its plight. He was well informed on every point on which the wrinkled index finger had lingered; he talked of the country's misfortunes, those due to natural causes and those caused by its own follies, the general and the particular, the long-standing ones and those of more recent date which aggravated them; he particularly emphasized the national debt and the burden it imposed on the economy – six hundred million marks – and he even remembered to mention the underfed population in the rural districts.

He did not speak connectedly; Imma Spoelmann interrupted him with questions and helped him on with questions, she was very thorough and asked for explanations of what she did not understand. Dressed in her loose-sleeved brick-red tea-gown of Chinese silk with the rich embroidery on the bodice, with an old Spanish necklace round her childlike neck, she sat leaning over the table sparkling with a profusion of silver, crystal, and rare china, with one elbow propped up against it and her chin buried in a slender, ringless hand, and listened intently, with her eyes resting on his face. But while he talked and replied to the questions in Imma's eyes and on her lips, while he struggled and was carried away by his subject, Countess Löwenjoul no longer felt compelled by his presence to be sober and coherent, but let herself go and indulged in the luxury of divagating. All the misery, she explained with elegant gestures and oblique glances, even the bad harvest, the burden of the national debt and the rise in the price of gold were due to shameless women who swarmed everywhere, and unfortunately had discovered a way through the floor, as last night the wife of a sergeant from the Grenadier Guards' barracks had scratched her breasts and tormented her with abominable gestures. Then she alluded to her castles in Burgundy, invaded by the rain coming through the ceiling, and went so far as to relate how she had taken part as a lieutenant in a campaign against the Turks, and had been the only one 'not to lose her head'. From time to time Imma Spoelmann and Klaus Heinrich addressed a kind word to her, readily promised to call her 'Frau Meier', and for the rest took no notice of her.

Their cheeks were burning when Klaus Heinrich had told all he knew – even on Imma's usually pale and pearly complexion there was a faint glow. They remained without speaking and the Countess too fell silent, with her small head cocked on one side and gazing vacantly into space. On the spotlessly white tablecloth Klaus Heinrich played with the stem of an orchid which had stood by his plate in a fluted vase, but as soon as he lifted his head he met Imma Spoelmann's eyes across the table, abnormally large, smouldering and steadfast, speaking an eloquent language.

'It has been nice today,' she said in her husky voice when he took his leave, and he felt her small, fine-boned hand clasp his in a firm embrace. 'Next time Your Highness honours our un-worthy abode, do bring me one or two of the books you have secured.' She could not entirely abstain from teasing him, but she did ask him for the books on economics and he brought them to her.

He brought two which he considered most instructive and synoptic, brought them a few days later in his dog-cart, driving across the rain-sodden Municipal Gardens, and she thanked him for doing so. As soon as tea was over they retired to a corner of the room, and there, while the Countess absently continued sitting at the tea-table, they began their common studies, seated on throne-like chairs at a small gilt table, bending over the first page of a textbook called *The Science of Economics*. They even read the headings of the sections, each one in turn reciting a sentence in a low voice; for Imma Spoelmann insisted on setting to work methodically and starting at the beginning.

Klaus Heinrich, well briefed as he was, acted as guide through the paragraphs, and no one could have followed more nimbly and intelligently than Imma.

'It's really quite easy,' she said and looked up with a laugh. 'I'm surprised it's so easy. Algebra is far more difficult, Prince.'

But since they were so thorough they did not get very far that first afternoon, and marked the page for the next time.

It arrived in due course, and henceforth Klaus Heinrich's visits to Delphinenort were given to factual studies. Whenever Mr Spoelmann did not turn up for tea, or left with Doctor Watercloose directly after having finished his health biscuits, Imma and Klaus Heinrich settled down at the gilt-topped table and stuck their heads into the *Science of Economics*. As they progressed they compared theory with fact, applied what they had read to the conditions of the country such as Klaus Heinrich had described them, and made their studies profitable, though it happened frequently that they were interrupted by considerations of a personal nature.

'It seems then,' said Imma, 'that the issue may be effected either directly or indirectly – yes, that's obvious. Either the State turns directly to the capitalists and opens a subscription list ... Your hand is twice as broad as mine,' she said: 'look, Prince,' and they looked down at their hands with a happy smile; his right and her left lying side by side on the gilt-topped table. 'Or else,' Imma went on, 'a loan is procured by negotiation, and it is some big bank, or a syndicate to which the State ...'

'Stop, Imma!' he said softly. 'Stop, and answer me one question. Aren't you forgetting the main issue? Are you making progress? Are you trying? Do I still chill and embarrass you, little Imma? Have you a little confidence in me now?' He asked her with his lips close to her hair which exhaled some rare fragrance and she kept her small head bent over the page, even though she would not reply directly.

'Must it be a banking house or a syndicate?' she mused, 'The book doesn't say, but it seems to me that in practice it may not be necessary.'

Now she spoke gravely and without affectation, for she too had to grapple with the problems which Klaus Heinrich had solved successfully after his conversation with Herr von Knobelsdorff. And when some weeks later he repeated his question as to whether she would care to attend the Court Ball, and told her of the ceremonial arrangements conceded for the occasion, she countered by saying that she would accept with pleasure, and would drive on the following morning with Countess Löwenjoul to leave cards on the widowed Countess Trümmerhauff.

This year the Court Ball was scheduled for an earlier date than usual, for the end of November – an arrangement said to be due to the wishes of the Grand Ducal family. Herr von Bühl zu Bühl bitterly deplored this hurry which forced him and his subordinates to speed up preparations for this most important Court function, especially the much-needed repairs of the Gala Rooms in the Old Castle. But the wish of one particular member of the ruling house had the support of Herr von Knobelsdorff, and the Court Marshal had to give way. Thus it came about that the people's minds scarcely had time to prepare themselves for what was to be the event of the evening, compared to which the unusual date was as nothing. Indeed, when the *Courier* published the headlines of the leaving of the cards and the invitation, not without expressing its satisfaction in glowing terms and welcoming the daughter of Mr Spoelmann at Court, the momentous evening was already close at hand, and before the tongues could start wagging the whole thing had become a fact.

Never had more envy been attached to the five hundred favoured persons whose names figured on the guest list for the ball, never had the citizens devoured the news in the *Courier* more avidly – the glittering social column written each year by a dipsomaniac nobleman, and which read like an account of fairyland, while as a matter of fact the ball at the Old Castle was usually uneventful to a degree. But the report covered events only up to supper, including the French menu, and all that came later, and especially the finer shades and imponderabilia of the great event, was necessarily left to be passed on by word of mouth.

The ladies arrived fairly punctually in the huge olive-green motor-car which pulled up in front of the Old Castle, though not so punctually that Herr von Bühl zu Bühl had not had time to feel anxious. From a quarter past seven onwards he had waited in full uniform plastered with decorations, with a shiny toupee, and a gold pince-nez on his nose, shifting his weight from one leg to another in the centre of the armour-hung Hall of Knights, where the Grand Ducal family and the Court assembled, and several times he despatched a chamberlain to the ballroom, to find out whether Miss Spoelmann had as yet arrived. He thought of all sorts of unheard-of possibilities. If this Queen of Sheba were to arrive late – and what might one not expect from the girl who had walked straight through the guard on duty! – the entry of the Grand Ducal cortège would have to be delayed, the Court would have to wait for her as she was supposed to be presented first, and it was out of the question that she should enter the ballroom after the Grand Duke. But thank heaven one minute before half past seven she arrived with her Countess (and it caused quite a commotion when the ushers on duty who received them allotted them a place next to the Diplomatic Corps, to wit, in front of the nobility, the ladies-in-waiting, the Ministers, Generals, the Presidents of the Chamber, and everybody else). Now the aide-de-camp von Platow fetched the Grand Duke from his apartment, and in the Hall of Knights Albrecht, clad in his hussar's uniform and with downcast eyes, welcomed the members of his family, and offered his arm to Aunt Katharina; and then, after Herr von Bühl zu Bühl had tapped the floor thrice with his staff, the entry of the Court into the ballroom was effected.

Eye-witnesses declared later that during the *défilé* of the Grand Ducal family general inattention had verged on the scandalous. It is true that as they advanced, round Albrecht and his stately aunt a ripple of bowings and curtseys formed hastily, but apart from that every face was turned to one point only, all eyes were fastened with burning curiosity on this point. She who stood there had many enemies in the room, especially among the women, the female Trümmerhauffs, the Prenzlaus, the Wehrzahns and Platows who fluttered their fans and scrutinized her with sharp, cold female glances. But whether her position was already too secure for criticism to venture to assail her, or whether her personality had conquered the secret oppositions, the unanimous verdict was that Imma Spoelmann had been as lovely as the daughter of the Mountain King. By next morning the whole capital, from the clerk in the Ministry to the messenger in the street, knew what she had worn: a ballgown of pale green *crêpe de chine* embroidered in silver and with a bodice of fabulous silver lace, a diamond head-dress shaped like a small crown had sparkled in her blue-black hair which showed a tendency to fall in smooth strands across her forehead, and a long diamond necklace was coiled two and three times round her tawny neck. Small and childlike, but with a sweetly grave and intelligent expression she stood in her place of honour next to Countess Löwenjoul who was dressed in brown as usual, this time in satin. When the *défilé* reached Imma she gave the merest indication of a curtsey, bowing with boyish grace, but as Klaus Heinrich, with the lemon-yellow *cordon* and the flat chain of the Order of the House 'for Constancy' over his shoulder and the silver star of the Grimmburg Gryphon on his breast, escorting his anaemic cousin whose sole conversation consisted in 'Yeah', passed her immediately behind the Grand Duke, she smiled at him with closed lips and nodded like a comrade – while something like an electric shock passed through the assembled company.

Then, after the diplomats had been received by the Grand Ducal Party, the presentations had begun – begun with Imma Spoelmann, although there had been two Countesses Hundskell and one Baroness von Schulenburg-Tressen among the debutantes. Strutting and with an ingratiating smile which showed his false teeth Herr von Bühl had presented Mr Spoelmann's daughter to his master. And, sucking at his upper lip, Albrecht had looked down on the suggestion of a *plongeon*, from which she rose to scrutinize the ailing colonel of the hussars in his solitary pride with her dark, searching eyes. The Grand Duke had addressed several questions to her whereas in general he never asked more than one, had inquired after her father's health, after the effects of the Ditlinde spring, and how she liked living in this country, to which she had replied in her husky voice, turning her head from side to side. Then, after a pause perhaps indicative of an inner struggle, Albrecht had expressed his pleasure in seeing her at Court, and it had been the turn of Countess Löwenjoul to curtsey with an oblique glance.

This scene, of Imma Spoelmann in the presence of Albrecht, long remained a favourite topic of conversation, and although it had passed, as it was bound to pass, without any unusual incident, yet its charm and importance must not be ignored. It was by no means the climax of the evening. That, in the eyes of many, was the *quadrille d'honneur*; in the eyes of others, the supper; but in reality it remained a private dialogue between the two chief actors of the play, a brief conversation overheard by no one, whose content and actual results the public could only guess – the conclusion of certain tender wrangles on foot and on horseback.

As to the *quadrille d'honneur*, there were people who declared next day that Imma Spoelmann had danced it with Klaus Heinrich as a partner. Only the first part of this assertion was true. Miss Spoelmann had taken part in the festive round dance, but led by the British chargé d'affaires and opposite Prince Klaus Heinrich. Of course this was unprecedented in itself, but more unprecedented was the fact that the majority of the guests did not consider it in the least unprecedented, but on the contrary as almost a matter of course. Yes, Imma Spoelmann's position was established; the popular conception of her person – as the public learned next day – had prevailed in the Court ballroom, and, what is more, Herr von Knobelsdorff had taken care that this conception should be expressed with all the publicity he thought advisable. Not with special consideration and with distinction : no, Imma Spoelmann had been treated *ceremoniously*, with systematic, intentional emphasis. The two Masters of Ceremony on duty, chamberlains in rank, had introduced specially selected partners to her; and when she left her place close to the low red-carpeted platform where the Grand Ducal family sat on damask armchairs, to dance with her partner, the ushers had busied themselves to clear a space beneath the central chandelier for her and protect her from collisions, as they did for princesses of the blood – an easy task in any case, for a protective circle of the curious had formed round her as she danced.

It was reported that when Prince Klaus Heinrich asked her to dance for the first time a sigh had passed through the ballroom, almost like an excited hiss from a valve, and that the leaders of the dance had been hard put to it to keep the ball going and prevent the guests from standing round the couple in avid curiosity. Especially the ladies had followed the isolated pair, with exalted rapture, which, had Imma Spoelmann's position been a trifle weaker, would undoubtedly have assumed an angry and malicious form. But the pressure of public opinion, that powerful urge below, had been felt too strongly by every one of the five hundred guests for them to be able to witness this spectacle through eyes other than those of the people. The Prince did not appear to have been advised to restrain himself. His name – shortened to 'K.H.' – appeared twice on Miss Spoelmann's programme, and he sat out several dances with her. They danced together, Klaus Heinrich and Spoelmann's daughter. Her tawny arm rested on the *cordon* of lemon yellow silk slung across his shoulder, and his right arm encircled her lithe and strangely childlike form, while as usual when he danced, he placed his left hand on his hip and steered his partner with one hand only. With one hand!

When supper-time arrived a further article in the ceremonial arrangement contrived by Herr von Knobelsdorff for Imma Spoelmann's attendance of the Court Ball came into staggering force. It concerned the seating order at the table. For while the majority of the guests supped at long tables in the picture gallery and the Hall of Twelve Months, supper for the Grand Ducal family, the diplomats and leading Court officials was laid in the Silver Hall. Punctually at eleven o'clock Albrecht and his party proceeded to the supper in solemn procession, in the same order as when they had entered the ballroom. Past the lackeys who guarded the doors to ward off the uninvited, Imma Spoelmann entered the Silver Hall on the arm of the British chargé d'affaires to take part in the Grand Ducal banquet.

That was unheard of – and at the same time, after all that had gone before, of such compelling logic that any show of surprise or disapproval would have been misplaced. It was simply a question of being prepared for signs and indications. But after supper, when the Grand Duke had withdrawn and Princess Griseldis opened the *cotillion* with a chamberlain, expectation rose once more to a high pitch, for the general query was whether the Prince would be allowed to present Miss Spoelmann with a bouquet? His instructions were obviously not to offer her the first one. He had first given one each to his aunt Katharina and his red-haired cousin, but then he advanced towards Imma Spoelmann with a posy of lilac from the Grand Ducal gardens. About to raise the lovely token to her face, she for some reason hesitated timidly, and it was not until after he encouraged her with a nod and a smile that she decided to test its fragrance. Then they danced together for a long time, and talked quietly.

Nevertheless, it was during this dance that they engaged in a private dialogue, a certain conversation of tangible bourgeois content, which had practical results. It ran like this:

'Are you satisfied with the flowers I brought you this time, Imma?'

'Yes, Prince, your lilac is beautiful and smells as it should. I like it very much.'

'Really, Imma? But I'm sorry for the poor rosebush down in the courtyard, because its roses displease you with their mouldy scent.'

'I won't say they displease me, Prince.'

'But they disenchant and chill you, don't they?'

'Yes, perhaps they do.'

'But did I ever tell you of the popular belief that the rosebush will one day be redeemed, that is to say, on a day of general rejoicing, and will bear roses which will not only be beautiful but have a lovely natural fragrance?'

'Yes, Prince, that remains to be seen.'

'No, Imma, we must help and act! We must decide and lay aside all doubt, little Imma! Tell me, tell me tonight; do you have confidence in me now?'

'Yes, Prince, lately I have gained confidence in you.'

'You see! Thank God for that! Didn't I tell you that I would succeed in the end? And so now you believe that I am in earnest about you, truly in earnest about you and ourselves?'

'Yes, Prince, lately I have thought that I may believe you.'

'At last, at last, dear irresolute Imma! I thank you from the bottom of my heart! It means you're not afraid and will affirm before the world that you belong to me?'

'Declare that you belong to me, Royal Highness, if you please.'

'That I will do, Imma, most decidedly. But under one condition only; that we don't think of our happiness in a selfish, frivolous way, but regard it all from the standpoint of the general good of the whole. For the general good and our happiness, you see, are interdependent.'

'Well said, Prince. Since without our studies for the public welfare I would hardly have gained confidence in you.'

'And without you, Imma, to warm my heart, it is unlikely that I would have tackled such serious studies.'

'Right; let us see what we can do, each in his own home, Prince. You with your family and I – with my father.'

'Little sister,' he answered quietly and pressed her a little closer. 'Little bride.'

It had indeed been an unusual sort of engagement.

Of course nothing was as yet definitely settled, and looking back one must admit that, had one single factor in the whole situation been altered or handled differently, the whole thing might yet have come to nothing. What a blessing that there was a man at the head of affairs who faced the moment firmly and undaunted, even with a sense of humour, and did not consider a thing to be impossible because it had no precedent!

The conversation between His Excellency von Knobelsdorff and his master, Grand Duke Albrecht II, held in the Old Castle about a week after the memorable Court Ball forms part of contemporary history. The previous day the President of the Council had held a meeting of the Cabinet about which the *Courier* was in a position to report that questions of finance and internal matters of the Grand Ducal House had been discussed, and further – added the paper in spaced type – that complete unanimity of opinion had been achieved among the members. Therefore, during the said audience, Herr von Knobelsdorff found himself in a strong position *vis-à-vis* his young sovereign, being backed not only by the seething mass of the people, but by the unanimous vote of the government.

The audience in Albrecht's draughty study was no shorter than that in the small yellow drawing-room at the Eremitage. A pause was made once, while the Grand Duke had a lemonade and Herr von Knobelsdorff was offered a glass of port and some biscuits. The length of the conversation was due only to the importance of the subject and not to the monarch's reservations, for he made none. In his buttoned-up frock-coat, with his thin, sensitive hands crossed in his lap, his proud, delicate head with the pointed beard erect, and with downcast eyes he sucked lightly at his upper lip, nodded from time to time at Herr von Knobelsdorff's exposition, and with precise movements indicated either agreement or disapproval; and uninvolved, formal agreement given with the still, cold reserve of his unassailable personal dignity.

Herr von Knobelsdorff went straight to the point and spoke of Klaus Heinrich's visits to Delphinenort. Albrecht was informed of them. Subdued echoes of events which kept the capital and the whole country spellbound had penetrated even his isolation; he well knew his brother Klaus Heinrich who had rummaged and talked to the lackeys and when he knocked his forehead against the nursery table, had cried for sympathy with his forehead, and in effect he required no explanations. Lisping and with a slight blush he indicated this to Herr von Knobelsdorff and added that, since the latter had not intervened, but had even presented the millionaire's daughter at Court, he took it that Herr von Knobelsdorff approved the Prince's behaviour, although he, the Grand Duke, did not see where all this could lead. The government would act contrary to the will of the people, replied Herr von Knobelsdorff, if it were to thwart the Prince's intentions. 'Has my brother, then, definite intentions?' For a long time, retorted Herr von Knobelsdorff he acted without a plan and merely as his heart dictated; but since he found himself on the firm ground of reality with his people his wishes had taken a concrete form. 'All of which means that the people approve the steps taken by the Prince?' – 'That it acclaims them, Royal Highness, that it attaches its fondest hopes to them.'

And now Herr von Knobelsdorff once more painted the country's plight, its poverty and serious difficulties, in sombre colours. Where was a remedy to be found? It was there, in the Municipal Gardens, in the second residential centre, at the home of the ailing millionaire, our guest and citizen, whose person the people's fancy invested with glamour, and for whom it would be a small matter to put an end to all our difficulties. If he could be induced to take our economy in hand its recovery would be assured. Could he be induced? Fate had decreed a mutual sympathy between the only daughter of the multi-millionaire and Prince Klaus Heinrich. Was this wise and gracious ordinance to be flaunted? Ought one for the sake of rigid and outdated tradition to prevent the union which offered such incalculable blessings to the country and the people? That it would do so was the necessary presupposition and the basis of its justification and validity. If this condition were fulfilled, if Samuel Spoelmann, to speak bluntly, were prepared to finance the State, the marriage – now the word had fallen – was not only admissible; it was a necessity, it meant salvation, the welfare of the State demanded it, and people prayed for it far beyond the national boundaries, wherever interest was felt in the restoration of our economy and the avoidance of financial disaster.

At this point the Grand Duke interpolated a question, quietly, without looking up and with an ironical smile.

'And what about the succession to the throne?'

'The law,' replied Herr von Knobelsdorff imperturbably, 'leaves it to Your Royal Highness to eliminate dynastic scruples.' With us too the bestowing of titles and the granting of royal status remain prerogatives of the monarch, and when could history show a worthier motive for the exercise of these privileges? This union bore the stamp of authenticity, it had long been prepared in the hearts of the people, and its official recognition by the State and its ruler would merely confirm their innermost intimations.

This led Herr von Knobelsdorff to speak of Imma Spoelmann's popularity, of the significant demonstrations in connection with her recovery from a slight indisposition, of the position of equal birth which this exceptional person assumed in popular fancy – and the wrinkles played round his eyes as he reminded Albrecht of the old prophecy current among the people, which told of a prince who would give the country more with one hand than others had given it with two, and eloquently demonstrated how the union between Klaus Heinrich and Spoelmann's daughter must seem to the people the fulfilment of the oracle, and thus God's will, and right and proper.

Herr von Knobelsdorff said a great deal more that was wise, outspoken and true. He mentioned Imma Spoelmann's mixed descent – for besides the German, Portuguese and English ancestry she was said to have a streak of ancient noble Indian blood – and he emphasized that he expected a great deal for the dynasty from this racial mixture added to the ancestral stock. But then the candid old gentleman scored a trick by raising the subject of the colossal beneficial changes involved for our debt-ridden and hard-pressed Court by the bold match of the Heir Apparent. It was at this point that Albrecht sucked at his upper lip in his most disdainful and haughty manner. The value of gold was falling, expenditure was mounting in obedience to an economic law governing the finances of the Grand Ducal House no less than those of any private household, and an increase in revenue was out of the question. But it was wrong that the monarch's private means should be inferior to those of many among his subjects; from the point of view of the monarchy it was intolerable that soap manufacturer Unschlitt should have installed central heating in his house long ago, while the Old Castle had to go without. A remedy was needed in more ways than one, and lucky was the princely dynasty to which such a munificent remedy was being offered! It was noticeable these days that the oldtime discretion in handling the finance of ducal Courts was on the decrease. The self-abnegation with which the public was prevented from having disillusioning glimpses of their private finances was no longer to be found, and lawsuits, interdictions, and questionable deals were the order of the day. But was not an alliance with sovereign wealth preferable to this sort of petty and bourgeois adaptation to the times – a union which would place the monarch once and for all high above all economic straits and enable him to appear before the people with all the outward signs of majesty for which he longed.

Herr von Knobelsdorff asked these questions, and he himself replied to them with an unqualified affirmation. In short, his discourse was so sedate and irrefutable that he did not leave the Old Castle without a proudly lisped consent and an authorization far reaching enough to warrant an unprecedented agreement, provided Miss Spoelmann had done her share.

And so things ran their memorable course to a happy ending. Even before the end of December names were mentioned, of people who had actually seen (instead of talking from hearsay) the Lord Marshal Bühl zu Bühl in his fur coat, a top hat on his brown toupee and his gold pince-nez on his nose, alight from a Court brougham at eleven o'clock on a dark, snowy morning, and disappear inside Delphinenort with his strutting gait. At the beginning of January certain individuals in the city swore that the gentleman who, also in a fur coat and top-hat and in the hours before midday, had left Delphinenort, dashing past the blackamoor doorkeeper in his plush uniform, and with feverish haste had flung himself into a waiting cab, was without doubt our Minister of Finance, Doctor Krippenreuther.

And at the same time there appeared in the semi-official *Courier* the preparatory notices of rumours touching an impending betrothal in the Grand Ducal House – tentative notifications which, becoming carefully more and more explicit, at last exhibited the two names, Klaus Heinrich and Imma Spoelmann, in clear print next to each other. .. It was no new collocation, but to see it in black and white had the same effect as strong wine.

It was fascinating to observe the attitude of our enlightened and free-thinking press towards the popular side of the affair, namely the prophecy which had won too great a political significance to be ignored by the educated and the intelligentsia. In so far as individual destiny was concerned, explained the *Courier*, fortune-telling, chiromancy and similar magic were to be relegated to the dark domain of superstition; they belonged to the grey Middle Ages, and no ridicule was too severe for those deluded persons who were swindled out of their money by cunning tricksters, in order to hear their insignificant future told from the palm, from cards or coffee-cups, or who asked to be cured by prayer or homeopathy, or have the evil spirits cast out from their sick cattle – for had not the Apostle said : 'Doth God take care for oxen?' But surveyed as a whole and concerning the decisive turning points in the destiny of whole nations and dynasties, the proposition did not necessarily repel a well-trained scientific mind that, since time was merely an illusion and in reality all happenings were co-existent in eternity, such revolutions, while still in the lap of the future, might move the human mind to premonitions and reveal themselves to it in visions. And as proof of this the zealous newspaper published a long essay kindly put at its disposal by one of our high-school professors, which gave a summary of all cases recorded in history where oracles and horoscopes, somnambulism and sleep-walking, clairvoyance, dreams, second sight and inspiration had played a part – a meritorious memorandum which did not fail to impress the educated classes.

So the press, the government, the Court and the public closed their ranks in complete agreement, and assuredly the *Courier* would have held its tongue had its philosophical contribution been premature or politically dangerous at the moment – if, to put it briefly, negotiations at Delphinenort had not already advanced far in a favourable direction. It is pretty accurately known by now how these negotiations developed, and what a difficult, indeed painful, task fell to our councils; the councillors who, acting as proxy for the Court, had the delicate mission of preparing the way for Klaus Heinrich's proposal, as well as the chief guardian of our financial interests who, notwithstanding his poor health, would not be deterred from pleading the country's cause with Samuel Spoelmann. Here Mr Spoelmann's irascible and irritable temper must be remembered, and also that the fabulous little man was far less interested in a favourable outcome of this business than we were ourselves. Apart from his love for his daughter, who had opened her heart to him and told him of her noble wish to be useful to her beloved, our spokesmen had not one trump in their hands, and it was not a case of Doctor Krippenreuther dictating conditions in view of what Herr von Bühl had to offer. Of Prince Klaus Heinrich Mr Spoelmann spoke repeatedly as 'that young man', and showed so little pleasure at the prospect of marrying his daughter to a Royal Highness that Doctor Krippenreuther as well as Herr von Bühl was plunged more than once in deadly embarrassment. 'If only he'd learnt something and had a respectable profession!' he said peevishly in his rasping voice, 'but a young man who knows nothing except how to be cheered!' He became really angry when the question of a morganatic marriage was raised. His daughter, he declared, was no concubine and left-hand consort. Whoever married her, married her. But at this point the interests of the dynasty and the country coincided with his own; the birth of an heir entitled to the succession was a necessity, and Herr von Bühl was equipped with all the powers extracted by Herr von Knobelsdorff from the Grand Duke. As for Doctor Krippenreuther's mission, it did not owe its success to the eloquence of its envoy, rather, to the complaisance of an ailing, weary father whose abnormal existence had made him an eccentric, to his paternal love for his only daughter and heir, who would be free to pick the State securities in which she chose to invest her fortune.

And thus resulted the agreement which was at first shrouded in deep secrecy and became known only step by step, as events developed, though they can be summarized here in a few plain words.

The betrothal of Klaus Heinrich and Imma Spoelmann was approved and recognized by Samuel Spoelmann and the House of Grimmburg. Simultaneously with the publication of the engagement in the *Official Gazette* the elevation of the bride to the rank of Countess was announced – under a romantic-sounding name, like that which Klaus Heinrich had borne during his voyage of instruction in the fair countries of the south; and on her wedding day the consort of the Heir Apparent would be invested with the title of a Princess. These two rises in rank, which ordinarily would have cost four thousand eight hundred marks, were to be conceded free of stamp duty. The marriage was to be a morganatic one only for a time and until the world got used to it; for on the day on which it became apparent that she was blessed with an offspring, Albrecht II, in view of the unparalleled circumstances, would declare his brother's morganatic wife to be of equal birth, and invest her with the rank of a Princess of the Grand Ducal House, with the title of Royal Highness. The new member of the ruling house was to waive all claim to an apanage. As for the Court ceremony, only a small Court was summoned for the celebration of the morganatic wedding, but for the declaration of equal birth, that highest and completest form of showing allegiance, the large Court *défilé* was ordained. Samuel Spoelmann for his part granted the State a loan of three hundred and fifty million marks – on such paternal terms that this loan bore all the signs of a donation.

It was Grand Duke Albrecht who informed the Heir Presumptive of these conclusions. Once more Klaus Heinrich stood in the large, draughty study, beneath the cracked murals of the ceiling, facing his brother as of old, when Albrecht had delegated his representational duties to him, and standing in a correct official attitude he received the momentous news. He wore the uniform of a major of the Fusiliers of the Guards for his audience, while the Grand Duke had lately added a pair of dark red wool mittens to his black frock-coat, knitted for him by his aunt Katharina to protect him from the draught blowing from the tall windows of the Old Castle. When Albrecht had finished Klaus Heinrich stepped sideways and clicked his heels in a fresh salute, saying: 'I beg, dear Albrecht, to offer my heartfelt and most respectful thanks, both in my own name and in that of the whole country. For in the end it is you who made all these blessings possible, and the redoubled love of the people will reward you for your magnanimous resolution.'

He clasped his brother's thin, sensitive hand which the latter kept close to his chest, extending it without loosening his arm. The Grand Duke thrust his short and rounded lower lip forward and kept his eyes lowered to the ground. He answered softly with a lisp. 'I'm the less inclined to entertain illusions about the people's love because, as you know, I'm quite prepared to dispense with this questionable love. Whether I deserve it hardly matters. When it's time to start I go to the station and wave the signal – it's silly rather than deserving, but it's my duty. Your case of course is different. You are a Sunday child. Everything turns out well for you. I wish you luck,' he added, raising his blue eyes with the remote expression. And at this moment one could see that he loved Klaus Heinrich. 'I wish you luck, but not too much, lest you rest too comfortably in the love of the people. I have already said that everything turns out well for you. The lady of your choice is most exotic, not a bit homely, totally unlike our own people. She's a fourfold mixture, I've been told that she even has Indian blood. Perhaps it's just as well. With such a companion you are less likely to become too comfortable.'

'Neither my happiness,' said Klaus Heinrich, 'nor the people's love will ever make me forget that I am your brother.'

He retired; a difficult interview awaited him, a *tête-à-tête* with Mr Spoelmann and his personal proposal for Imma's hand. He found that he had to swallow what his negotiators had swallowed, for Samuel Spoelmann showed not the slightest pleasure, and in his rasping voice told him many a home truth. But then it was over at last, and the day came when the engagement

filled the front page of the *Official Gazette*. The long tension
ended in boundless rejoicing. Staid citizens waved their handkerchiefs at each other and embraced in the streets, banners
were raised on the flagstaffs.

But the same day the news reached the Eremitage that Raoul
Überbein had committed suicide.

It was a pitiable, even a silly story, and would not have been
worth relating but for its tragic end.

No blame shall be apportioned here. Two parties formed at
the Doctor's grave; the one, shaken by his desperate deed,
affirmed that he had been driven to commit suicide. The other
declared with a shrug that his behaviour had been impossible
and crazy and that he had met with a just punishment. Be that as
it may, in any case nothing justified so tragic an end. Indeed,
it was an unworthy death for a man with the gifts of Raoul
Überbein. Here is the story.

At Eastertime of the previous year the form-master of the
second top class of the local Grammar School, who suffered
from a weak heart, had been given temporary leave, and Doctor
Überbein, notwithstanding his comparative youth, and solely
in view of his professional zeal and his unquestionably remarkable results with the middle forms, had been entrusted with the
vacant teaching post. A good choice, as events soon proved, for
the class had never done so well as this year. The professor on
leave, who, by the way, was very popular with his colleagues,
had been a good-humoured, but also careless and indolent gentleman, no doubt partly because of his ill-health, which in turn was
due to his endearing, but, in its excess, obnoxious addiction to
beer. He had shut his eyes to details and every year passed an
extremely badly-prepared batch of boys for the Selecta. It surprised no one when a new spirit entered the class with the temporary professor. His uncanny professional zeal and his one-
sided and restless ambition were well known: it was to be
foreseen that he would not waste an opportunity to show his
mettle, as he, no doubt, attached to it high hopes of advancement.
Idleness and boredom in the second class came to a sudden end.
Doctor Überbein had set high standards and his skill in stimulating even the most recalcitrant was irresistible. The pupils

adored him. His superior paternal and blustering manner held them spellbound; it kept them on their toes and made them feel it was a point of honour to follow their master through thick and thin. He won their affection by making excursions with them on Sunday, when he allowed them to smoke while he appealed to their imagination with his free-and-easy, jovial rodomontades on the greatness and sternness of an unshackled existence. And on Monday they found themselves reunited to yesterday's unconventional comrade in an eager and passionate common effort.

Three-quarters of the term had passed in this way when it was announced before Christmas that the professor on leave had sufficiently recovered to resume his duties after the holidays, and would once more take over the second class. And now it became evident what sort of a man Doctor Überbein really was; what hid behind his greenish face and his breezy and superior manner. He had objected and raised a protest : had lodged a loud and bitter, not altogether correctly worded complaint against the fact that his class, which had spent three-quarters of the school year in his care, with which he had shared work and play, and which he had brought within sight of the goal, should now be removed from his care for the last term and returned to that of a teacher who had spent three-quarters of the year on leave. It was understandable, comprehensible, and one could sympathize with his point of view. No doubt he had hoped to present a model class to the headmaster, a form whose advanced standards and excellent preparation would show up his ability to best advantage and further his career, and the thought that another man would reap the fruits of his efforts was bound to be painful. But although his irritation was excusable, his folly was not, and unfortunately it is a fact that when the headmaster turned a deaf ear to his remonstrances, he went mad. He lost his head, he completely lost his balance, he moved heaven and earth to prevent this idler, this wine-bibber and useless tramp, as he did not hesitate to call the professor on leave, from taking his class from him, and when he found no support among his colleagues in the Teachers' Union, as was only natural in the case of so unsociable a man, the wretched man forgot himself so far as to incite his pupils to insubordination. From his rostrum he had addressed them with the question: Whom did they want for a teacher during the last term, him or that other fellow? And roused to fanaticism by his own quivering excitement they had shouted that they wanted him. In that case, he had told them, they ought to take matters in their own hands, show their colours and act in unison – and goodness knows what he had imagined in his overwrought state of mind. So, when the suspended professor re-entered the classroom at the beginning of term, the boys yelled Doctor Überbein's name at him for several minutes – and there was a fine scandal.

It was kept as quiet as possible. The mutineers were let off lightly, as at the inquiry which was made at once Doctor Überbein admitted his appeal to them. But even where he, the Doctor, was concerned, the authorities seemed inclined to shut one eye to what had happened. His zeal, his ability were appreciated; certain learned works, the fruits of his nocturnal activities, had given him a name; he was esteemed in high quarters – quarters, mind you, with whom he had no personal contact and who therefore had not been irritated by his patronizing manner – and his record as Klaus Heinrich's tutor counted in his favour. In brief, he was not, as might have been expected, simply dismissed from his post. The President of the Grand Ducal Council of Education, to whom the matter was submitted, administered a severe reprimand, and Doctor Überbein, who had stopped teaching directly after the incident, was provisionally retired. But people in the know declared later that nothing was intended beyond the professor's transfer to another grammar school; that those in high quarters wished for nothing better than to let bygones be bygones, forget the whole matter, and in fact the way to a distinguished future had been kept open for the professor. Everything would have turned out all right.

But the milder the authorities showed themselves towards the Doctor, the more hostile was the attitude of his colleagues towards him. The Teachers' Union at once established a Court of Honour intended to rehabilitate their esteemed member, the form-master with the heart condition due to too much beer, whom his pupils had rejected. The written statement sent to the retired Doctor Überbein in his furnished lodgings was to the effect that: 'By refusing to hand over the second class to his colleague whom he had temporarily replaced, furthermore, by actively intriguing against him and inciting the pupils to insubordination against him, Doctor Überbein had rendered himself guilty of disloyal and dishonourable conduct towards his colleagues, and that not only in a professional but in a general sense.' That was the verdict. The expected result was that Doctor Überbein, who anyway had been a member of the Teachers' Union in name only, withdrew his membership – and there, so many thought, the matter might have rested.

But whether it was that the Doctor in his seclusion had no knowledge of the goodwill he inspired in higher quarters, or that he considered his position to be more hopeless than it was; that he could not bear the inactivity nor reconcile himself to the premature loss of his beloved class; that the talk of his 'dishonourable behaviour' poisoned his feelings, or that he was not up to the shocks of that incident; but five weeks after the New Year his landlord found him lying on the threadbare carpet of his room, no greener than usual but with a bullet through his heart.

Thus ended Raoul Überbein; this is how he slipped; such was the incident that caused his downfall; such the reason of his undoing. 'I told you so,' was the refrain of all discussions of his pitiful end. The quarrelsome and uncongenial man who had been unable to relax over his evening beer, who haughtily disdained all intimacy and based his life solely and exclusively on his achievement, thinking that this gave him a right to treat the whole world in patronizing fashion – now he was dead; the first obstacle, the first setback in his profession had finished him off. Few pitied him, nobody mourned for him – with one exception, the Chief Surgeon of the Dorothea Children's Hospital, Überbein's only congenial friend, and perhaps a fair lady with whom he had played a game of cards once in a while. But Klaus Heinrich always honoured the memory of his unfortunate tutor.

NINE

THE ROSEBUSH

AND Spoelmann financed the State. The outlines of his transaction were bold and essentially simple. A child could have understood them – and in fact beaming fathers explained them to their children as they dangled them on their knees.

Samuel Spoelmann beckoned, and Messrs Phlebs and Slippers set to work, and his all-powerful instructions flashed under the waves of the Atlantic to the mainland of the western hemisphere. He withdrew a third of his shares from the Sugar Trust, a quarter from the Oil Trust, and half from the Steel Trust. He ordered his floating capital to be paid into several banks over here; and at one stroke bought three hundred and fifty million marks worth of State bonds at a rate of three and a half per cent from Doctor Krippenreuther. That is what Spoelmann did.

Anyone familiar with the influence of psychological states on the human organs will believe that Doctor Krippenreuther revived and within a short time became quite unrecognizable. He carried himself well and upright, his sallow complexion cleared and gave way to a healthy bloom, his eyes flashed, and within a few months his stomach recovered so completely that he was rumoured by his friends to be indulging without ill effects in blue cabbage and cucumber salad. This was a laudable, though purely personal consequence of Spoelmann's intervention in our finances, of slight account compared to the effects of this intervention on our public and economic life.

A part of the loan was diverted to the sinking-fund, and the agonizing national debt was paid off. But this was scarcely needed to procure us breathing space and credit on all sides; for no sooner was it known – in spite of all the secrecy with which the matter was treated officially – that Samuel Spoelmann, in fact, if not in name, had become our State banker, than the skies cleared and all our troubles were changed into joy and rapture. An end was put to the forced sales of active debts, the current rate of interest dropped, our bonds were eagerly sought after by investors, and within twenty-four hours the rate of exchange of our high interest loan shot from a deplorably low figure to above par. The pressure, the nightmare which had weighed on our national economy for the past decades was removed. In the Diet Doctor Krippenreuther spoke with emotion of a general tax reduction, this was unanimously accepted, and amidst the cheers of all socially progressive elements the antediluvian meat tax was buried at last. A distinct improvement in the pay of civil servants, and in the salaries of teachers, parsons and all State functionaries was readily conceded. Means to reopen the silver mines were made available; several hundred miners were employed, and unexpectedly productive layers were struck. Money, ready money was forthcoming. The standards of morality in business life rose, the forests were replanted, the leaf-mould was left alone, the owners of livestock were no longer compelled to sell their full milk but consumed it on their farms, and critics would have searched in vain for undernourished peasants in the rural districts. The nation showed itself grateful to its rulers who had brought such illimitable blessings to the land and the people. Herr von Knobelsdorff had no difficulty in inducing Parliament to increase the Crown subsidies; the order to put up Zeitvertreib and Favorita for sale was withdrawn. Skilled workmen invaded the Old Castle to instal central heating throughout. The Grand Cross of the Order of Albrecht set in diamonds was bestowed by our intermediary with Spoelmann, and in addition the Minister of Finance, Herr von Krippenreuther, received a title while Herr von Knobelsdorff was honoured with a life-size portrait of the illustrious couple – painted by the aged Professor Lindemann and set in a costly frame.

Concerning the dowry which Imma Spoelmann was to receive from her father, people indulged in wild fantasies. In their state of euphoria they felt the need to juggle with truly astronomical figures. But the dowry did not exceed an earthly figure though it was considerable. It amounted to a hundred million marks.

'Good gracious!' cried Ditlinde zu Ried-Hohenried when she first heard of it. 'And my dear Philipp with his peat...' Many another had the same thought; but the nervous irritation arising in simple minds in the face of such monstrous wealth was soon allayed by Spoelmann's daughter who did not forget to do good and share her good fortune, but on the day of the official engagement made a donation of five hundred thousand marks, the yearly interest of which was to be divided among the four County Councils for charitable purposes and others beneficial to the communities.

In one of Samuel Spoelmann's olive-green motor-cars with brick-red leather seats Klaus Heinrich and Imma Spoelmann called on the members of the House of Grimmburg. A young chauffeur drove the splendid vehicle – the one Imma thought resembled Klaus Heinrich – but these outings made no demands on his nerves, for it was necessary to drive slowly and control the powerful motor, so closely were they surrounded by admiring crowds. Indeed, since the more indirect originators of our happiness, the Grand Duke and Mr Spoelmann, each in his own way, concealed themselves from the masses, they heaped all their love and gratitude on to the exalted young pair who, through the polished windows of their car, could see boys throw their caps into the air, and hear the loud, tumultuous cheers of men and women, and Klaus Heinrich with his hand raised to his cap said admonishingly: 'You must return their greetings, Imma, on your side, for otherwise they will think you cold.' Impatiently ignoring her shy resistance and unfamiliarity with the warmer spheres of loving intimacy he had called her *Du* since their conversation at the Court Ball, and how easily this pronoun came now, whereas before it had always seemed false and impossible.

They drove to see Princess Katharina and were received with dignity. The late Grand Duke, Johann Albrecht, her brother, said the aunt to the nephew, would never have permitted it. But times were changing, and she prayed to God that his fiancée would accustom herself to life at Court. They proceeded to Princess zu Ried-Hohenried's and here were received with love. Ditlinde's Grimmburger pride found comfort in the certitude that the Leviathan's daughter might well become Princess of the Grand Ducal House and a Royal Highness, but never a Grand Ducal Princess, like herself. For the rest she was delighted that Klaus Heinrich had found someone so exquisite and lovely, and as the wife of Philipp with his peat she knew how to appreciate the advantages of this match and cordially offered her new sister-in-law her friendship. They drove to the villa of Prince Lambert, and while the new Countess struggled to maintain a conversation with the dainty but quite uneducated Baroness von Rohrdorf the old petticoat hunter congratulated his nephew in a sepulchral voice on his unprejudiced choice, and on so boldly snapping his fingers at the Court and the standards of a Royal Highness. 'I am not snapping my fingers at my standards as Royal Highness, uncle; nor have I thought only of my own happiness, but have considered everything from the point of view of the general good,' said Klaus Heinrich rather non-committally, and they took their leave and drove to Segenhaus Castle where Dorothea, the poor Dowager Grand Duchess, held her mournful Court. She cried as she kissed the young bride on the forehead, and did not herself quite know why.

Meanwhile Samuel Spoelmann sat at Delphinenort surrounded by plans and sketches of furniture, patterns of silk hangings and designs of gold plate. He neglected his organ, forgot his kidney stones and almost warmed to his activities, for although he did not think much of the 'young man' or hold out any hopes of ever being seen at Court, it was to be his darling daughter's wedding, and he would have it as splendid as his means permitted. The plans concerned the Eremitage, for Klaus Heinrich's bachelor quarters were to be razed to the ground and a new castle was to be built on the site, spacious and light, and according to Klaus Heinrich's wishes, decorated in a mixture of Empire and modern, of cool severity and lived-in comfort. Mr Spoelmann in his dun-coloured overcoat arrived in person at the Eremitage in order to see whether any of the existing furniture would do for the new mansion. 'Let's see, young Prince, what you've got here,' he said in his rasping voice, and Klaus Heinrich showed him round his austere rooms; showed him the sparsely cushioned settees, the stiff-legged tables, the white corner tables. 'That's rubbish,' said Mr Spoelmann disparagingly, 'you can't do anything with that stuff.' Three armchairs only from the small yellow drawing-room, of massive mahogany, with snail-shaped scrolls, and upholstered in yellow satin with a blue-green motif of lyres, found favour in his eyes. 'We might use these in an ante-room,' he said, and Klaus Heinrich was eager to see three armchairs from the Grimmburg side contribute to the furnishing of the new home; for it could of course have been a little awkward if Mr Spoelmann had been obliged to provide everything.

The neglected park and flower parterres of the Eremitage too were to be cleared and replanted, and especially the flower garden was to be embellished by a special ornament which Klaus Heinrich solicited as a wedding gift from his brother, the Grand Duke, to wit, the rosebush from the Old Castle was to be transplanted to the large centre bed facing the front drive, and there, no longer surrounded by mouldy walls, but given plenty of air and sunshine, and rich manure, it remained to be seen what sort of roses it would produce, and whether it would belie popular tradition, if it was arrogant and stubborn enough to do so.

After March and April came the month of May, and with it the great event of Klaus Heinrich's and Imma's wedding. The day dawned gloriously, with golden clouds in an azure sky, and choral music sounding from the belfry of the Town Hall greeted its arrival. The countryfolk streamed into the town by train, on foot and by carriage; a fair and stocky, wholesome and backward race with blue, thoughtful eyes and high cheekbones, dressed in their handsome national garb; the men in red jackets and topboots and black wide-brimmed velvet hats, the women in brightly embroidered bodices, short, ample skirts, and headdresses of huge black bows. They joined the throng of townsfolk in the streets between the Thermal Gardens and the Old Castle which had been transformed into a processional route with garlands and wreathed stands, and white-washed wooden obelisks draped with flowers. Early in the morning the banners of Artisans' Guilds and of the Rifle Corps and Sports Associations began to be carried through the streets. The fire brigade turned out with gleaming helmets. One could see the office bearers of the Student Corps in full state and with their banner flying drive in open landaus. One could see groups of maids-of-honour dressed in white carrying rose-twined wands. The offices and workshops were deserted. Schools were closed. Special services were held in the churches. And the early editions of the *Courier* and the *Gazette* contained, in addition to enthusiastic leading articles, the announcement of a general amnesty by favour of the Grand Duke whereby many condemned prisoners were granted a partial or entire remission of their sentences. Even the murderer Gudehus, who had been condemned, first to death, later commuted to a life sentence of penal servitude, was released on probation. But shortly after he had to be confined again.

At two o'clock a gala luncheon with an orchestra and tele-grams of congratulation was given by the City Council in the main hall of the Museum. But outside the gates the people pic-nicked with fried foods and spiced loaves; with a fair, lucky draws and pigeon-shooting, sack-races and a climbing competi-tion for the boys with treacle buns for prizes. Then it was time for Imma to drive in state from Delphinenort to the Old Castle. She set out followed by a solemn cortège.

The banners fluttered in the spring breeze, thick garlands of red roses were festooned between the poles, on stands, rooftops and on the pavement seethed a black mass of people, and be-tween a cordon of police and firemen, of guild associations, students and schoolchildren and amid tumultuous cheers the bridal train advanced slowly along the sand-strewn festive avenue. Two outriders with braided hats and shoulder knots, preceded by an equerry with a walrus moustache and tricorne, were followed by a coach drawn by four horses, with an official of the Home Ministry, the Grand Ducal Commissary with a chamberlain, who had been dispatched to fetch the bride. Then came another four-horse carriage in which one could detect Countess Löwenjoul looking askance at two maids-of-honour whose morals she obviously distrusted. Ten postilions on horse-back in yellow breeches and blue dress-coats played: 'We wind for thee the maiden's wreath', from *Der Freischütz*. Then came twelve young girls who scattered rosebuds and twigs of *arbor vitae* on the road, and lastly fifty strapping mounted masters of their guilds preceding the delicate, transparent bridal coach drawn by six horses. A red-faced coachman in a braided hat proudly braced his gaitered legs against the front of the tall box covered with white velvet, and clutched the reins with extended arms; grooms in top-boots, two by two, led the white mares by the bridle, and two lackeys in gala uniform stood upright on the back of the tinkling coach, and no one could have guessed from their impenetrable glances that bribery and underhand dealings were not alien to their everyday lives. Behind the glass-and-gilded window frames sat Imma Spoelmann in her veil and wreath, with an aged lady-in-waiting on duty at her side. Her dress of shimmering silk shone bright as snow in the sunlight, and in her lap she held a white bouquet sent by Klaus Heinrich an hour earlier. Her exotic, childlike face had the pale glow of a pearl, and from her veil escaped a smooth strand of blue-black hair across her forehead, while her eyes, coal black and abnormally large, surveyed the packed crowd with silent eloquence. But who was the creature close beside the carriage, making a demented noise and barking wildly? It was Perceval, the collie, more beside himself than ever. The crowds and the coach ride excited him beyond all measure and rent him with emotion to the point of madness. He raved, he pranced, he suffered, he swung round on his own axis in a paroxysm of nerves, and on the stands on both sides of the road, in the street, and on the rooftops the acclamations of the people as they recognized him knew no bounds.

Thus Imma Spoelmann entered the Old Castle, and the peal of bells mingled with the cheers and with Perceval's demented barking. The procession slowly crossed the Albrechtsplatz and entered the Albrecht Gate; inside the courtyard of the Castle the mounted corps of the guilds swung to one side and took up its parade position as a guard of honour, and under the arcades, in front of the weathered portal, Grand Duke Albrecht in his uniform of a colonel of the Hussars, accompanied by his brother and the other princes, welcomed the bride, offered her his arm, and led her up the grey stone steps towards the State Rooms at whose doors the guards of honour were posted, and where the entire Court had already assembled. The Princesses of the House waited in the Hall of Knights, and it was there that Herr von Knobelsdorff, surrounded by the Grand Ducal family, performed the civil marriage ceremony. Never before, so it was said later, had the wrinkles at the corners of his eyes played so vividly as when he joined Klaus Heinrich and Imma Spoelmann in civil wedlock. Once the ceremony was over Albrecht II gave orders for the church wedding to begin.

Herr von Bühl zu Bühl had done his best to produce an impressive cortège – the bridal train proceeded by the staircase of Heinrich the Luxurious under the covered arcades to the Court Church. Bent by the burden of his years, but still in his brown toupee and strutting in youthful fashion, he advanced ahead of the chamberlains, covered with decorations down to the loins, and placing his long staff in front of him, and they followed behind, wearing silk stockings and clutching plumed hats under their arms, their keys affixed to the back of their jackets. Now the young pair entered; the exotic bride in dazzling white, and Klaus Heinrich, the Heir Apparent, in his uniform of the Grenadier Guards, with the lemon-yellow cordon across his breast and back. Four bridesmaids of the landed aristocracy with flummoxed expressions on their faces bore Imma Spoelmann's train, followed by Countess Löwenjoul who cast suspicious sidelong glances. Behind the bridegroom walked Herr von Schulenburg-Tressen and Herr von Braunbart-Schellendorf. Oberhofjägermeister von Stieglitz * and his limping Excellency, the Director of the Court Theatre, preceded the young monarch who sucked quietly at his upper lip, walking beside his aunt Katharina, and followed by the Minister of Home Affairs von Knobelsdorff, by his aide-de-camp, by Prince and Princess zu Ried-Hohenried and other members of the House. More chamberlains brought the cortège to an end.

The guests awaited the procession in the Court Church, decorated with plants and tapestries. They were the diplomats and their ladies, Court nobles and the landed aristocracy, officers of the regiment garrisoned in the capital, ministers, among them

* A Court charge; 'Jäger' is a huntsman, somewhat more important than a gamekeeper. – Translator's note.

the beaming Doctor Krippenreuther, the Knights of the Grand Order of the Grimmburg Gryphon, the Presidents of the Diet, and all manner of dignitaries. And as the Lord Marshal had ordered invitations to be sent to every class of society, the pews were filled also with proudly elated merchants, country people, and simple workmen. But in front, round the altar, the relations of the bridegroom sat in crimson velvet armchairs. The voices of the choir rang pure and sweet under the vaulted dome, and then the congregation intoned a thanksgiving hymn to the accompaniment of the organ. When it died away the melodious voice of the President of the Church Council, Dom Wislezenus, sounded alone while he, with silvery white hair and a concave star on his silk robe, stood in front of the exalted couple and preached a masterly sermon. He built it on a theme and so to speak treated it as a score of music. The theme he chose was a passage from the Psalms: 'He shall live and unto Him shall be given of the gold of Arabia.' The congregation was moved to tears.

Then Dom Wislezenus performed the marriage ceremony, and as the bridal pair exchanged their rings a fanfare of trumpets sounded and a salvo of three times twelve guns, fired by the soldiers from the bastions of the citadel, began to reverberate across the city and the countryside. Directly afterwards the fire brigade let off the town guns by way of salute; but long pauses ensued between each detonation, giving rise to unending mirth among the population.

After the blessing had been pronounced the procession formed again and returned to the Hall of Knights, where the House of Grimmburg congratulated the bride and groom. Then came the Court reception, and Klaus Heinrich and Imma passed arm in arm through the Gala Rooms where the Court had already assembled, and addressed the ladies and gentlemen, smiling at them across a distance of shining parquet floor, and Imma pursed her lips and turned her head from side to side when speaking to a person who made a deep curtsey and replied soberly and briefly. After the Court reception there was a state banquet in the Marble Hall, and a Marshal's banquet in the Hall of the Twelve Months, and everything was of the best because of the standards of Klaus Heinrich's young bride. Even Perceval, who had calmed down, was present at the banquet and was fed with roast beef. After supper the students and the populace staged an ovation for the young couple, including a serenade and a torchlight procession on the Albrechtsplatz. It was a blaze of light and resounded with unending clamour.

The lackeys drew the curtains of a french window in the Silver Hall and flung back the window, and Klaus Heinrich and Imma took their stand in the embrasure as they were, for it was a mild evening. And beside them, assuming a dignified attitude and a knowing air, sat Perceval, the collie, and looked down at the crowd, like his masters.

All the municipal bands were playing at once in the brightly lit square packed with people, and the upturned faces of the crowd glowed in the smoky light of torches carried by the students as they marched past the Castle. Cheers broke out anew as the newly married couple appeared at the window. They bowed and acknowledged the greetings and remained standing for a little while, watching the crowd and at the same time offering themselves to the general curiosity. The people from below could see their lips move. They said: 'Listen Imma, how thankful they are that we have not forgotten their needs and miseries. So many people! All standing there and calling to us. Many of them are no doubt scoundrels who cheat each other and are badly in need of being lifted above the humdrum of existence and its material interests. But they are truly grateful when one shows that one is aware of their needs and miseries.'

'But we are so ignorant and alone, Prince, on the lonely peaks above the masses of humanity as Doctor Überbein used to say, and we know nothing whatsoever about life.'

'Nothing whatsoever, little Imma? What was it then which finally gave you confidence in me, and which led me to serious studies for the sake of the general good? Can he who knows love really be called ignorant of life? That shall from now on be our task – a twofold one: To do our royal duty and to love: an austere happiness.'

POSTSCRIPT

THOMAS Mann was born on 6 June 1875, in the North German town of Lübeck. His father was a member of the local hanseatic bourgeoisie, a merchant by profession and a senator on the City Council. From his mother, born and brought up in Brazil, he inherited Portuguese-Creole blood. His early childhood and school years were spent in Lübeck, and at the age of nineteen young Mann was sent to Munich to join an insurance company. For the next year or so his free time was occupied with the study of literature, until he finally obtained permission to attend university. He moved to Italy, and three years later took over the editorship of the Munich *Simplicissimus*, then the foremost satirical weekly in Germany. His first great novel, *The Budden-brooks*, appeared in 1900. It is a family chronicle set against the patrician Lübeck background, and showing a decadent society, with the main emphasis on the pressure of rising materialism and the need to preserve fundamental and creative values. It was followed in 1903 by *Tristan*, a collection of short stories including the powerful *Tonio Kröger*.

In 1909 Thomas Mann finished *Königliche Hoheit* ('Royal Highness'), a social study in the form of a light romantic comedy. The tragic and austerely written *Tod in Venedig* ('Death in Venice') brought him worldwide fame; it was the first candid literary account of homosexual love. As soon as it was published Mann engaged in what some regard as his major work, *Der Zauberberg* ('The Magic Mountain'), in which his mature, subtle and ambiguous mind leads the reader into the labyrinth of German intellectual decadence. In the trilogy *Josef und seine Brüder* ('Joseph and his Brothers') Mann turned his back on the German scene and chose a historico-biblical setting, but his preoccupation with the forces of disruption, with sacrifice, integrity and renewal through a kind of death, persist, treated with increasing force and complexity. *Doctor Faustus* brought the author back to the haunting problem of the German psyche. Thomas Mann described the gestation and birth of this book, written 1943-7, in a recently translated work, *The Genesis of a Novel*. Of its principal hero, the musician Adrian Leverkühn, he wrote, drawing a parallel with the entire German nation : 'The best in him turned to evil through *hubris* and satanic spirit.' (Incidentally, this sort of character is sketchily outlined in *Royal Highness* in the person of the unfortunate Doctor Überbein, the princely tutor.) As soon as Hitler rose to power in 1933 Thomas Mann left his native country. In 1936 the great man of German letters was deprived of his citizenship. In his reply to an address of the Dean of the Faculty of Philosophy at Bonn University, Thomas Mann stated his point of view in no uncertain terms:

The meaning and purpose of the National Socialist State is this alone and can be only this: to put the German people in readiness for the 'coming war' by ruthless repression, elimination, extirpation of every stirring of opposition, to make them an instrument of war, infinitely compliant, without a single critical thought, driven by a blind and fanatical ignorance.

In 1944 Thomas Mann and his family moved to the States and he adopted U.S. citizenship. But in spite of his partial Latin-Indian heredity the pull of Europe proved too strong. He returned to Switzerland after World War II and died in Zurich in 1955. The last novel he published – a work that had occupied him off and on for many years – was the deceptively easy *Felix Krull*, which renewed his international fame in a somewhat superficial way.

In order to understand Thomas Mann's position in German and international letters it is necessary to have some idea of the intellectual and social climate into which he was born, of the cataclysmic changes he had witnessed from an early age, and of the far-reaching antecedents of the National Socialist movement. As a young man he saw the social revolution after 1848-9 gather momentum and enter its decisive stages, and witnessed the disintegration of an imperialist, feudal Germany in the pre- and post-war years. Over a period of several decades various socialist movements had developed in many autonomous cities and principalities. Local revolutions, strikes and negotiations led to concessions, like a wider franchise, free education, the removal of feudal tithes and burdens from the peasantry, the merging of princely incomes with state revenues, taxation proportionate to earnings, and general employment. Industry and the railways changed the aspect of the countryside and the fabric of society. A rich bourgeoisie with liberal leanings emerged. The best among German intellectuals, politicians and officials were advanced liberals or supporters of the left. But the government, headed by the Kaiser, Wilhelm II, and the leaders of the big Prussian block in North Germany, rigidly defended the traditional rights and privileges. In the southern principalities with their rich humanist tradition and a much more humane relationship between feudal masters and rural population the conflicts were, on the whole, much milder. Such a principality is the setting of *Royal Highness*. Had the whole of Germany been as civilized, the solution offered in the novel might have been viable. Although his position was never extreme, Thomas Mann belonged to a group of writers holding advanced liberal, sometimes leftist views, openly critical of the chauvinism and militarism which was the besetting Prussian sin, and of a rigid, ossified social order. This group included Gerhart Hauptmann, Nietzsche, Sudermann, and up to a point Stefan George and Rilke. Heinrich Heine, better known as a romantic poet, can be considered as its precursor. These writers gained international recognition in the western hemisphere and Europe. In his maturity Thomas Mann became a formidable factor in the world of letters, politics, sociology and psychology and his impact, not only as a novelist, but as a lecturer, broadcaster, and correspondent is incalculable.

The abiding worth of Thomas Mann as an artist is probably due in no small degree to his amazing powers of analysis of the human being. It is his sympathy and insatiable curiosity which bring his social and political reflections to life and lend them lasting value as human documents of an epoch. All his life Mann derived stimulation from the study of the new science of deep psychology, and his correspondence with Freud and Kerenyi, his investigations of myth and fairy tale which, as it were, form the rich soil of Mediterranean and German culture, never ceased to fascinate him. Indeed, had he not been a born writer he might well have become a leading psychologist.

It must of course be true that in the understanding of human nature self-knowledge and the knowledge of others are bound to go hand in hand. Most novels contain an autobiographical element that gives the reader a clue to the author's personality and his psyche. It usually enters the novel in two ways: firstly, the author reveals himself through characters that are different sides or voices of himself; secondly, he introduces incidents and situations from his life, and transposes them, more or less altered, into fiction. Both devices occur constantly in Mann's works, and can be traced in *Royal Highness* which describes the period of his courtship and marriage to Katja Pringsheim. The similarity between the young author, isolated by the quality of his mind and the consciousness of an exacting calling, and Prince Klaus Heinrich, set apart by rank and office, is self-evident. In Imma the author has united several characteristics of his highbrow fiancée and his exotic mother, but does she not also embody his own foreign 'outsider' aspect, freed from the taboos and artificial restrictions of his paternal milieu? The atmosphere of painful tension in a young man very much in love, hemmed in by his uncertainty, by a shyness and tender consideration, comes out in the letters Thomas Mann wrote to his future wife, referring to situations and feelings reproduced almost unchanged in the novel. Compare Klaus Heinrich's visit in the early summer at Delphinenort with what follows, written by Thomas Mann at the beginning of April 1904:

My headache the other day, when I had supper with your parents after the theatre, was not worth talking about; it was merely an added symptom of the sore throat I happened to have, and which I cured completely with your father's help. Of course you won't understand this because you don't know how much your father cares for my health. I let it out that I had a sore throat, that it was quite swollen. Your mother said: 'In that case you should apply a moist compress.' 'So I suppose I should,' I said in my obliging manner. 'Have you any guttapercha?' asked your father ... 'No,' I replied in my prompt manner. Then your father got up – he got up, I tell you, although he was lying on the sofa on account of his stomach, went to his dressing-room and fetched a piece of guttapercha, his last and only piece of guttapercha, which was already a trifle brittle, handed it to me and instructed me in detail how to apply it to derive the most benefit from it. What do you say to that? What follows? At least that he does not desire my death. But *more* follows from it. You will say again that your father has great self control. But say what you will, this is more than mere self control. You always make a pretext out of your father's tigerish temper because you don't really care for me.

Something of Imma's attitude to the prince is indicated by his brilliant self-portrait, sent in reply to I don't know what objection by his future wife: 'To rouse mixed feelings, "perplexity", that, if you will forgive me, is a sign of personality. A man who never causes doubt or consternation, or *sit venia verbo*, a little dread, who is simply loved and nothing else, is an idiot, a luminous apparition, an ironical figure. I have no ambition in that direction.' (*Briefe Thomas Manns*. Edited by Erika Mann, S. Fischer Verlag, Frankfurt.)

Royal Highness can be read and enjoyed by a child. I remember doing so at the age of nine and still recall the then familiar aroma of a south-eastern semi-feudal capital and social background, and even more poignantly my sense of pity mingled with breathless curiosity about the young prince. Which does not exclude that to an adult the story will mean something, not so much different, as heightened and deepened. Thomas Mann is a symbolist writer *par excellence*: his plots and characters allow for several levels of interpretation. To go into this here would lead us too far, but one might say briefly that Mann's haunting and persistent theme is ripeness and death as a necessary condition of rebirth. In *Royal Highness* the theme is the decay of an old stratified society and the renewal of the land through forces set in motion at the beginning of the twentieth century.

The overbred Grand Duke and his decrepit entourage, the fruitless, arid self-sacrifice demanded of the young heir presumptive for the sake of a monarchy that had become an empty husk and nothing more, the only just off-key rantings of his mentor Überbein, the pseudo-*Herrenmensch* of Nazi philosophy, and a sick and backward economy are symptoms of an imminent death. The love of Klaus Heinrich and Imma, their common work and liberal ideals typify the new life. Their marriage is symbolic of a political credo to which Thomas Mann remained faithful to the end; that of the need for a firm alliance between Germany and the West. Mann was probably conscious that death and rebirth were the theme of ancient German village customs in the South, possibly the fertility rites of a pagan past, rooted in the instinctive wisdom of the race. The mummers' plays, or masked carnival processions, during which an elder disguised as the Old Year, the scapegoat of past ills and wrong, was driven out to make room for the New, the coming spring, may have been in the background of his mind when he chose the theme of *Royal Highness*. Mann studied and absorbed the most varied types of information, but what he wrote came, I believe, largely from a deep stratum of his mind and consciousness. He was once heard to say in private conversation : 'People are always finding meanings in the things I write of which I am quite unaware. But then, when I look at them again, by Jove, the meanings are there, they are there!'

CONSTANCE McNAB

MORE ABOUT PENGUINS
AND PELICANS

Penguinews, which appears every month, contains details of all the new books issued by Penguins as they are published. From time to time it is supplemented by *Penguins in Print*, which is a complete list of all available books published by Penguins. (There are well over four thousand of these.)

A specimen copy of *Penguinews* will be sent to you free on request. For a year's issues (including the complete lists) please send 30p if you live in the United Kingdom, or 60p if you live elsewhere. Just write to Dept EP, Penguin Books Ltd, Harmondsworth, Middlesex, enclosing a cheque or postal order, and your name will be added to the mailing list.

Note : *Penguinews* and *Penguins in Print* are not available in the U.S.A. or Canada

HERMANN HESSE

Hermann Hesse (1877–1962), novelist and poet, won many literary awards including the Nobel prize (1946). He was interested in both psychology and Indian mysticism and his novels explore different attempts to find a 'total reality' in life.

STEPPENWOLF

This Faust-like, poetical and magical story of the humanization of a middle-aged misanthrope was described in the *New York Times* as 'a savage indictment of bourgeois society'. But, as the author notes in this edition, *Steppenwolf* is a book which has been violently misunderstood. This self-portrait of a man who felt himself to be half-human and half-wolf can also be seen as a plea for rigorous self-examination and an indictment of intellectual hypocrisy.

NARZISS AND GOLDMUND

Narziss is a teacher at Mariabronn, a monastery in medieval Germany. Brilliant and severe, he feels that Goldmund, his favourite pupil, will never be a scholar or a monk.

So Narziss helps Goldmund realize that they must each fulfil themselves in different ways: Narziss retiring from the world into a patterned order of prayer and philosophy while Goldmund quits the cloisters to plunge into a sea of blood and lust; cutting a picaresque swathe through plague, storm and murder; always chasing a fugitive vision of artistic perfection, its form 'the mother of all things'.

In a sense, both Narziss and Goldmund – the ascetic and the Dionysian – are what Hesse himself might have been. This element of conjectural autobiography gives to this masterpiece a ripe wisdom, an insight into universal dilemmas and man's role on earth, unique in the fiction of our time.

Also available

THE GLASS BEAD GAME

NOT FOR SALE IN THE U.S.A.

ANDRÉ GIDE

André Gide (1869–1951) was compelled by an inner necessity to speak the truth. His outspoken writings and the unpopular stand he took on various issues delayed widespread recognition of the greatness of his work until the end of his life. Although some of his ideas have already gained acceptance he will be remembered, not for being the first to express them, but for expressing them better than anyone else.

STRAIT IS THE GATE

This description of young love blighted and turned to tragedy by the sense of religious dedication in the beloved is often regarded as the most perfect piece of writing Gide achieved.

THE COUNTERFEITERS

In sharp and brilliant prose a seedy, cynical and gratuitously alarming narrative is developed, involving a wide range of middle-to-upper-class Parisians.

THE IMMORALIST

The story of a man's rebellion against social and sexual conformity. The problems posed here are those which confronted Gide himself.

THE VATICAN CELLARS

Through this strange drama involving the alleged abduction of the Pope, a 'miraculous' conversion, swindling, adultery, bastardy and murder, Gide works out the idea of the unmotivated crime.

LA SYMPHONIE PASTORALE / ISABELLE

La Symphonie Pastorale explores the conflict between profane love and Christian charity. *Isabelle* evokes the atmosphere of a legendary romance, set in a Norman château.

Also available

FRUITS OF THE EARTH

JOURNALS 1889–1949

NOT FOR SALE IN THE U.S.A.

FRANZ KAFKA

THE TRIAL

Kafka elucidates some fundamental dilemmas of human life in this account of the perplexing experience of a man arrested on a charge which is never specified. The story reads like the transcript of a protracted, implacable dream in which reality is entangled with imagination.

METAMORPHOSIS AND OTHER STORIES

This volume includes Kafka's best short stories. *Metamorphosis* is one of the most terrifying stories ever written. A man wakes up one morning to find himself transformed into a giant insect. His family is at first horrified, then kind, contemptuous and finally negligent.

THE CASTLE

Here the world of Kafka is further illumined; the individual struggles against ubiquitous, elusive and anonymous powers determining and yet simultaneously opposing his every step.

AMERICA

America is the lightest and most realistic of Kafka's novels. Yet beneath the surface comedy of young Karl Rossman's discovery of America, the author hints at much more than he seems to be saying.

THE DIARIES OF FRANZ KAFKA

Kafka's diaries, edited by Max Brod, his life-long friend, cover the period from 1910 to 1923 and reveal to us the extraordinary inner world in which he lived, his fear, isolation, frustration, feelings of guilt and his sense of being an outcast.

NOT FOR SALE IN THE U.S.A. OR CANADA

THOMAS MANN

CONFESSIONS OF FELIX KRULL

'Here is that unheard of, that supposedly impossible thing, a good German comic novel – a marvellously good one. There was nothing about Mann's other later novels to suggest that anything like *Felix Krull* was in store; and nothing else in modern German literature has prepared the way for it' – Edwin Muir in the *Listener*

DEATH IN VENICE

Apart from the title story, this volume contains two others of the author's widely known short works: *Tristan* and *Tonio Kröger*. *Death in Venice* tells of the tragic homosexual passion of a writer for a young Venetian boy.

THE MAGIC MOUNTAIN

A cosmopolitan collection of people are confined in a sanatorium high in the Swiss Alps. In spite of their isolation, love, war and emotions all affect and influence their conversation, and they stand as a microcosm of the sick European society which lies below them.

DOCTOR FAUSTUS

Doctor Faustus, the life of the German composer, Adrian Leverkühn, is one of the most convincing accounts of genius ever written. Thomas Mann charts Leverkühn's extraordinary career from his precocious childhood to his tragic death – when Leverkühn reveals the horrifying price he had to pay for his achievement.

LOTTE IN WEIMAR

The little provincial court of Weimar – a post-Waterloo Athens, agog with gossip and cerebral activity – is brilliantly recreated. But *Lotte in Weimar* is memorable, above all, for Mann's masterly portrayal of a creative genius, polymath and politician, and his influence on his contemporaries.

Also available

LITTLE HERR FRIEDMANN AND OTHER STORIES

BUDDENBROOKS   THE HOLY SINNER

NOT FOR SALE IN THE U.S.A. OR CANADA